A Geometric Progression - Book 1

STARTING SPHERE

Matthew Finlayson

Copyright © 2025 Matthew Finlayson

All rights reserved.

This book or any portion thereof may not be reproduced or used in any manner whatsoever without the express written permission of the publisher except for the use of brief quotations in a book review.

This is a work of fiction. Names, characters, businesses, places, events, locales, and incidents are either the products of the author's imagination or used in a fictitious manner. Any resemblance to actual persons, living or dead, or actual events is purely coincidental.

Matthew Finlayson
Visit my website at www.matthewfinlayson.com

Cover Art by J.N. Ignacio (www.coversbyjnignacio.com)

First printing: August 2025

ISBN: 978-1-918126-01-3

Prologue

"Here they come," said the young man standing at the edge of the cavern. His voice faltered slightly as he spoke, betraying his nervousness, but he stood his ground as a tide of scuttling creatures approached over the rough-hewn rock floor, spreading out as they came as if to surround him.

The cavern was vast, a couple of hundred yards across and forty or fifty feet high in the centre. The end nearest the combatants was illuminated by a pair of floating globes, which glowed with some sort of inner light.

As they approached, the wave of attacking creatures resolved into a tumbling mass of spiders. Many of them had bodies the size of a human skull, with angular spiky legs, although many smaller examples crisscrossed backwards and forwards between the legs of their larger brethren. A cacophony of clicking, made by their legs on the floor and walls and the snapping of their mandibles, threatened to drown out all other noises.

The four figures at the end of the cavern looked a token force, in the face of many hundreds or thousands of attackers. Then they acted and everything changed.

The youth who had spoken first, a teenager, had

unlimbered a black staff as tall as he was and was holding it in a guard position, apparently ready to intercept any spider who got too close. He wore armour made from some sort of animal hide, perhaps reptilian, over a plain tunic, and his hand was adorned with a blue crystal ring. His appearance was unremarkable enough, aside from recent burn marks across his face.

Some way behind him, a pretty girl of a similar age rested an arrow on a short bow, clearly designed for combat in confined spaces rather than for any great range or power. Her blonde hair was tied out of the way in a ponytail, and she looked determined.

On either side of the man wielding the staff were two more youths. One was a tall, handsome man, wielding a glowing sword with flames licking here and there across its surface. His features were set in a confident expression and he moved the sword casually in a guard pattern with practised unconcern.

The last figure was another woman, stronger and stockier looking than the first, with tightly curled black hair. She was holding a war-hammer with a vicious-looking spike for a peen, and her armour was covered in jingling chains which sparked with lightning as she shifted, ready to meet the onslaught.

In front of the staff wielder, a growing patch of spiders burst into fire, the flames quickly spreading from one to the next. The growing conflagration followed an ominous red sphere the size of a clenched fist, which moved as if guided towards particularly enormous spiders.

The bow twanged in a steady rhythm. The arrows were aimed back into the middle of the horde, and they too burst into flames one after another in mid-air, a few feet after each had left the bow. More fire could quickly be seen spreading back from their impact points into the depths of the cavern.

The swordsman had stepped sideways a little further away from the others, and his sword was whipping backwards and forwards to intercept attackers who were clearly loath to meet his glowing sword. He quickly built his own bonfire around him.

The hammer-wielder had also advanced, and lightning crackled from her hammer as she laid into her opponents.

"Scordo, watch out from above," called the blonde.

The young man with the staff had stepped forward into the host, apparently careless of their attacks. Each spider that jumped towards him was unerringly caught by his staff, however, and propelled back to crash into the others.

Arachnids dropped around him from the ceiling, and he continued to target them accurately, at one point twisting the staff one-handed behind his own back to hit a falling spider, apparently without even looking at it. There was no trace now of his earlier concern.

His companions were harder pressed. The swordsman's bare arms were covered in tiny scratches where the arachnids had pressed him too closely. The hammer wielder had stepped back, clearly feeling over-whelmed by her attackers, who weren't as vulnerable to lightning as to fire.

"Scordo, can you reach the boulder? A little more

damage will probably break them," shouted the blonde. She was still firing her bow, but the spiders were approaching her position, and she paused, seemingly unsure whether to grab for the dagger strapped to her leg.

"No problem," said the young man. He paused to get his bearings and then bent his knees and jumped straight into the air, nearly reaching the ceiling in a single bound. His crystal ring glowed with an inner blue light as he moved. As he passed the apex of his jump, he floated down into position on a boulder deep into the cavern. He then closed his eyes in a moment of concentration, and three more red spheres materialised around him and spun outwards in a spiral pattern, cutting through the carpet of spiders. A circle of fire roared up all around him, and the arachnids faltered and then gave way en masse. Their onslaught turned into a rout as they turned on their long, jagged legs and streamed away, though passages and cracks at the far end of the cave.

Within a minute or two, the battered teenagers were left all alone, standing in a suddenly deserted cavern.

"Now for the nest," growled the swordsman.

CHAPTER ONE

Journey to the Temple

Five months earlier...

I stood within a circle drawn in the ground. Packed in around me were a group of other people. Outside the perimeter of the circle, the wide open fields stretched into the distance, warmed by the light of the sun.

There were about a dozen others standing close to me. Most of them were children a few years younger than me, maybe twelve or thirteen years old. There were also a couple of older kids and two adults supervising us. The latter were officials from the royal court of Sahraya. Some way off, outside the circle, were the mage and some other representatives of the embassy of Zaronia. Well, less of an embassy, more of a trading post.

I stood a head or so taller than most of the people clustered around me, so I could look around and take in my surroundings for the last time. The unfamiliar grasslands and agricultural fields spread out in every direction around me. The very flatness of the terrain meant that there was too much sky round me, not only up above, but in all directions. Breezes drew moving patterns in the grasses and I tried to focus on them rather than the all-encompassing sky. Single story wooden buildings of the Sahrayan capital looked as if they were clinging tightly to the ground off to the east and worsened the illusion of space. My legs wobbled. I felt exposed and agoraphobic despite the press of people all around me.

I wasn't used to the famed 'big skies' that dominated most of Sahraya. I was from the relatively remote province of Arbran, located a couple of hundred miles away to the southeast. My home had been mostly lush forest, hemmed in further south by the inhospitable highlands that gradually became more mountainous as they stretched on. The unfamiliar surroundings around me caused a sudden wave of homesickness.

It had taken nearly a month for me to make my way to the capital. I had hitched a ride with a lumber caravan bringing wood to be used as building materials both locally and abroad. The free ride was probably the last favour I could expect from my late father's family.

The Zaronian mage finished inspecting the circle he had etched into the ground around my companions and me. He stepped back about ten feet and began to concentrate. I noticed the mark on his forehead again. Despite having spent some hours with him a few days earlier during my testing process, I still wasn't sure what the mark actually signified. It appeared to be a tattoo, or maybe a brand. Farmers commonly used branding for livestock, but surely no-one would use it on a human forehead?

The outside of the mark was the shape of a circle, with another couple of symbols superimposed on each other within it. Except that it didn't look quite like a flat image. It gave the impression that it wasn't on the surface of his skin, but lurking just below it, and from some angles it gave off an illusion of depth.

The children around me continued to jostle each other, some straying perilously close to the edge of the circle. The officials tried to settle them down while complaints flew back and forth. They were typically rich, pampered children of the agricultural aristocracy that dominated the Sahrayan court. They were ostensibly being sent to Zaronia in the hope of a few months of tuition in magic. I doubted that many of them were particularly suited for the assignment. Even if the Guild accepted them for tuition, it seemed unlikely that they'd have either the time or the inclination to develop any useful skills.

We were each carrying a bag containing our belongings for the trip. Mine contained little, just a couple of spare sets of clothes and, in a hidden pocket, a banker's draft representing all I'd been able to make by liquidating my inheritance. There were also a couple of books, including a dictionary of the language of Zaronia, and some personal keepsakes.

The surrounding circle suddenly glowed blue.

I saw sweat beading on the mage's forehead and his eyes focused on a point a few feet in front of him. His hands clenched, with his fingers twisting against the air. Several children screamed as we were transported into a cold, black void, which pressed in from every direction at once.

***

After that brief moment of nothingness, my senses

began to clear, and I noticed a difference in the taste of the air. The winds of the Sahrayan plains had felt warm and tasted complex: pollen from the grasses and crops and a trace of animal dung from the cattle pens ranged around the nearby markets. When I'd arrived, I'd found it strikingly different from the cool, moist, vegetal flavor I associated with the woods of Arbran. Suddenly, though, the air felt scorching, arid, and grainy. I guessed it must contain blowing sand.

I was baking hot, under an intense sunlight that felt more like the heat from a roaring fireplace. Everything I could see was tinted with reds and purples. The press around me lessened as children staggered apart seeking respite from the blinding red sun. Unfortunately, no immediate shade was available.

We were standing on a more or less circular stone platform about twenty feet across, set in the ground. On all sides, red sand and broken rocks surrounded the platform. There appeared to be carvings around the edge of the platform, but the blowing sand partially covered them, so I couldn't make out further details. My eyes watered as I tried to discern landmarks further away.

I knew I must have been here when I was much younger, before I met my father, but nothing felt familiar. I guess I'd only been about a year old when I left Zaronia, so maybe I shouldn't have expected too much, but I'd hoped for something. I felt under my robes to caress the necklace which I always wore around my neck, the only memento I had left of my life before.

One of our escorts, I'd caught his name as Lavos,

tried to take charge.

"Gentlemen, Ladies, please settle down. We need to make our way to the Temple, where our hosts will meet us. Follow me, please. Davras, please take the rear." He directed that last instruction to his younger colleague. From comments Davras had made earlier, I suspected it was his first visit to Zaronia.

Lavos walked towards the sun and I noticed he was following a rough pathway starting from the edge of the stone platform. Small heaps of the broken rocks which seemed everywhere in the desert lined the path. It led us away around a dune and, as we walked, the home of the Mage Guild of Zaronia gradually came into sight.

It was a vast stone building, sprawling across the desert. The section of wall facing us stretched into the distance in both directions and looked as if the residents had extended it on many occasions. Patches of brightly coloured fabric were dotted across the building, covering windows and doorways. Further details of the architecture were difficult to make out since my vision rippled in the intense heat. Glancing around more broadly, I saw many other circular stone platforms similar to the one on which we'd arrived. A series of paths connected them with doors set at intervals in the Temple walls.

Lavos maintained a reasonable pace to the Temple, and I followed closely behind him. I could hear Davras farther back, trying to corral and guide stragglers. As we approached the building, I saw our path led to an oak doorway with a symbol carved into it. The symbol was a circle with a triangle set into it. Inside that, in turn, was a square and finally a pentagon. Below the carving, someone had painted the number '34'.

There was a flexible pipe protruding from the wall by the doorway with some sort of wooden cone attached to the end. Lavos unhooked the cone from the wall and blew into it. He paused for a few moments and then he spoke slowly and loudly into it.

"Hello?", he said. "This is the delegation from Sahraya. We've arrived at door 34." He then moved the cone to his ear and listened. After a pause, he then spoke into it again. "Thank you." He hooked the cone back onto the wall.

"We always arrive at a transport platform, but they can't predict which one. They're on their way." I initially thought that Lavos was talking to himself, but possibly he had aimed this remark at Davras, who had finally arrived with the last of our group.

There was an uneasy silence for a few minutes while we waited. I expected more complaints from the others, but perhaps they'd been subdued by the shock of the journey and the sudden transition from one place to another. Then the door opened and a couple of figures ushered us into the cool and dark of the Temple.

***

The Guild members sent to meet us were young - a similar age to the children I'd travelled with. However, there were notable differences. These two were far more plainly dressed in a simple uniform and were much better disciplined. They each had another of the forehead tattoos that I'd noticed on the Zaronian mage, but this time the mark was of a circle with no other shapes. Or was it a ball? Again, there was an impression of depth to the image.

While the two Guild members spoke quietly with Lavos and Davras, I looked around at the large lobby they had ushered us into. The construction was of more stone, with the walls lit by occasional glowing globes. The lobby was vast, with a single interior doorway covered by a sheet of decorated fabric. I could make out more details of the workmanship now that I was out of the blazing sunlight. The walls had been constructed from enormous red stone blocks fitted closely together. Each block varied slightly in size, but most were larger than I could conceive being moved by hand. If the entire building was like this, it must have taken an immense effort to build over many years.

I looked at the light globes more carefully. They were emitting a steady, white, flicker-free radiance. Surely they couldn't be magical? Back home, the cost of even a single magical globe was impractical, but here they were regularly dotted along the walls.

"Gentlemen, Ladies." Lavos had turned to address the group. "The apprentices will now take you to your assigned rooms. Each of you will share with another one of the group."

Several of the students made various noises of mutiny and discontent at this.

"I realise that this probably isn't what most of you are used to," continued Lavos, "but I'm afraid that you'll have to get used to making some… accommodations to the expectations of your hosts if you're going to study here. I assure you that you're being treated perfectly normally. Indeed, in all my visits here, I've never heard of any exceptions being made, despite many candidates making strenuous or persuasive arguments to support their desire for special treatment."

The muttered comments from other students calmed down a bit at this, although some still looked mutinous. During this speech, I'd carefully studied the faces of the two Guild apprentices. Both had tried to maintain fixed expressions, as if they hadn't noticed the reaction of the students, but I got a distinct impression that one was amused, and the other simply resigned to the silliness.

"You'll be brought food in your rooms and then left to rest overnight," Lavos continued. "If you need to speak to me or Davras, then inform the guards stationed in the corridor outside your rooms, and they'll conduct you to us. The guards will be there to... protect you from straying into any more dangerous areas of the Temple."

More muttering followed this statement, but there were no further outright noises of discontent and Lavos clearly took that as agreement. The two apprentices then led us through the curtain. A group of armoured guards were standing there waiting and two of these detached themselves from the rest of the group to escort our party. All the guards wore leather armour strengthened by polished metal plates, and carried spears. The two that accompanied us appeared to be in their early twenties - slightly younger that some of their colleagues. None of the guards had forehead tattoos, I noticed.

We walked for a long time, down a series of corridors and stairways that were surprisingly featureless and unadorned. They differed both from the buildings in the Sahrayan capital, which had walls covered in ornate paintings, and from the carved wooden panels of my former Arbran home. We passed no-one as we walked and there was little conversation among the group. Eventually, we reached a corridor with a series of doorways covered by fabric curtains. At the start of the hall was a lobby containing a group of half a dozen guards, and at the far end it ended in a solid stone wall. The guards had a clear viewpoint of all the doorways and would have little trouble in 'protecting' us from wandering off.

One apprentice took Lavos and Davras away elsewhere to their own sets of rooms, while the other sorted us into ours. He had a piece of paper with our names and assignments - presumably provided by Lavos earlier while they talked. I found myself in a room with one of the largest of the other boys.

The room itself was surprisingly spacious, with two beds and an assortment of seating and tables. A small bathroom was visible in a further alcove. The window was covered with a coarse material, probably selected to allow some light to enter but keeping out the sand. My roommate quickly placed his bag on the bed closest to the window.

"Hello. I'm Scordo Orchan", I offered. I hadn't had a chance to interact much with the others in the group before, nor was I usually the most sociable person. I'd spent most of my childhood by myself. I'd never found it easy to make friends, and although I sometimes enjoyed conversations with groups of others, I found them tiring and usually cut them short. However, I couldn't face sharing a room with someone else in silence.

"Jemi, fifth child of the Baron of Salai," he responded more formally. I immediately placed his barony as one of the largest and most prestigious meat dynasties in the Sahrayan court. Seriously powerful and influential with vast land and stock holdings.

"Orchan? Your family would be Arbran wood... merchants, then?" he continued. I managed to hide my wince. Within Sahrayan society, the dominantly agricultural aristocracy had little time for other professions or types of land-holdings. The Orchan family probably controlled woodland whose acreage exceeded that of the farms of the Salai barony. However, despite the importance of the timber we supplied within Sahraya and exported to other countries, we were treated with little respect than the construction workers and carpenters who used our wares. At least he'd avoided using the pejorative "wood peddler" - which was commonly heard in the Sahrayan court.

Not that I, myself, could claim much honour from the Orchan line. I was the adopted son of an otherwise childless branch of the family. My father had had some level of authority within the family, as a renowned trade envoy who had travelled and negotiated on their behalf for decades, but little of that honour transferred to me. He hadn't even been allowed to leave me the bulk of his estate, since it was all entailed away to a distant blood relative. I'd had to make do with his few personal assets.

"That's right," I answered. "How long are you hoping to study here?"

I hoped that this would change the subject, although I doubted he was truly interested in being at the Temple. Most of the children of the Sahrayan aristocracy saw this as a chance for an exotic break from home, with little real desire or ability to study magic. I suspected that many of my companions would end up being rejected and sent home within a few days. However, Jemi surprised me.

"I was actually hoping to be allowed to stay for a few months - maybe as long as six? I want to learn some skills here," he said. "As the fifth child, I'm expected to find ways to assist my elder siblings in their governance of the house, and magic would be one route to help me stand out from the others. How about yourself? You look a bit old to be here," he finished bluntly.

This time, I didn't even try to conceal my wince.

"I'm actually hoping to complete a twelve month elementary course," I said. "My father didn't approve of me coming here when I was younger, but he passed away recently, and the Zaronian embassy suggested it might still be a possibility."

In return for a potential fee that was likely to swallow my entire inheritance, I didn't add.

"Indeed? Twelve months? Do you know whether you are likely to be accepted?" He was clearly surprised and intrigued despite his prejudices.

"I completed some initial tests back in the Zaronian embassy," I said. "They thought my results were promising enough that they offered to cover the cost of my travel here."

And my results should have been good enough, I

added in under my breath. For years, I'd spent hours every day trying to hone my ability to summon and control mana, the essence of magic. All I'd had to guide me was the advice in the few books, essays really, that I'd managed to find on the subject.

"I'm impressed," said Jemi. "They must have seen quite a lot of promise. I've heard mutterings that they usually charge a fortune for every transport - even for potential candidates who get rejected. The word is that it's a nice source of earning for them."

I'd heard similar rumours - all tied in with complaints about the monopoly that the Guild wielded over magical knowledge. To me, it didn't seem wildly different from the practices of many of the Sahrayan aristocracy, who were ruthless in their control over the various aspects of the Sahrayan trade in food.

Our conversation continued for a little while, but soon petered out. It was clear that, despite his apparent interest in magic, we had little else in common.

A servant brought in our food shortly afterwards. It was plain fare, which Jemi ate without commenting or complaining, and then we each went to bed. Both of us had reasons to want to be fresh and ready for the testing scheduled for the next day. Little did I know what a different turn my future was about to take.

CHAPTER TWO
Testing

The next morning, both Jemi and I rose early, as soon as it was light outside. He started some exercises while I paced around the room, looking for something to distract me. I noticed curiously that there was a series of vents covered by thick grills set in the walls, some close to floor level and some close to the ceiling. On further inspection, the floor level vents admitted a gradual flow of cool air into the room, while I couldn't detect anything coming in through the upper vents. This must be part of the explanation of why the air of the Temple was so cool. A ventilation system was supplying fresh air.

The arrival of breakfast interrupted my inspection. Again, it was plain rations, comprising cheese, dried meat and fruit, with a jug of water. Jemi ate hungrily while I toyed with the food. I was too on edge from anticipation to feel particularly hungry.

After about another hour, Davras entered and told us that it was time for us to make our way to the testing rooms. We left the room to find the other Sahrayans assembling under the gaze of the apprentices from the night before. A fresh set of guards awaited us at the end of the corridor.

***

This time, our route led much farther into the Temple than before. As we gradually took passageways and staircases leading downwards, the walls transitioned from cut stone to a mixture of carved stone and natural cave passages. The guards were more active this time, and the Guild had assigned a full squad of six to us. They checked ahead and behind us as we walked. Some of them even seemed to be periodically scanning the ceiling, as if they thought that someone might attack from above.

By the time we arrived at the testing rooms, we must have been several levels below ground. Clearly, the Temple was even bigger than I'd thought.

We emerged into a large bare space, possibly a cave, with a series of stone doors leading off in all directions. A dozen Guild members, talking in the Zaronian language, sprawled around on stone benches when we entered, but they got to their feet as they saw us approach. My quick scan of their foreheads was becoming automatic. Yes, they all had tattoos. Most of them were in their earlier twenties and had a circle with a single symbol within it, perhaps a sort of triangle or pyramid? One was clearly older, maybe in his late thirties, with prematurely greying hair and deep lines in his face. He also had a more elaborate tattoo design. As our escorts introduced to the testers, I was surprised to find I was assigned to the more senior.

He ushered me into what I assumed was a testing room, although you could just as well describe it as a windowless cell. A curved stone desk wrapped around a basic stone stool took up the middle of the room. A few more comfortable chairs were set around the outside of the desk. The setup seemed designed to allow several testers to focus on a single candidate and I wasn't surprised when the Guild member gestured me towards the stool.

He greeted me in a slightly accented Sahrayan and asked me to sit down. As I did so, he stepped around the desk, took a seat, and picked up a cardboard file. The outside of the file had my name written on it under a series of other names, all crossed out. In the top corner of the file was printed the same symbol that I'd seen carved on the Temple door the previous day. He extracted a small sheaf of papers from the file and began to read through them. They looked like the application form I'd filled out a few days earlier in the Zaronian embassy.

I was about to grunt in acknowledgement of his greeting and then thought twice. I wanted, no, needed to make a good impression on this man and I was only going to do that if I made an effort. Instead then, I looked at him, ready to make eye contact, and greeted him carefully in Zaronian. He glanced up and his frown of concentration relaxed into more of a smile.

"You speak Zaronian already? That's unusual for a Sahrayan. It should make this discussion a little easier if you're able to keep up," he said slowly in Zaronian, concentrating on making his enunciation clear.

"Thank you," I replied similarly. "I spent a long time studying it at home with the help of a tutor. And my father helped as well."

"Ah yes, your father." He put down the first sheaf of papers and extracted another from the file. These looked older, more creased and discoloured. "The incident with the Sahrayan delegation about fifteen years ago. I believe your father was considered something of a hero."

"I don't know the full details," I admitted. "I gathered that, while my father and his delegation were being taken on a tour of the city, there was some kind of attack on a group of Zaronian officials, and that my father helped defend them."

"Something like that," he grimaced. "In any case, the protesters and several of the onlookers were killed by the guards when they finally responded. All except a baby. And in gratitude for his actions, the envoy, your father, was allowed to adopt you and to take you back with him when he returned to Sahraya."

This was more detail than I'd heard previously and I wanted to ask more questions. Had my birth parents been protesters or innocent bystanders? I wondered about my necklace, which bore the design of a gold circle with a dull gray metallic star or sunburst set within it. And what were the protesters complaining about? I fought off a sudden urge to seize the report he was holding and read it myself. I told myself that was all in the past and didn't matter now.

"Let's return to your application for education from the Guild. First, I am Senior Artisan Dorrall and I welcome you to the Guild headquarters. You must have impressed my colleague at the embassy in Sahraya. We rarely consider applications for twelve month placements. I believe you're sixteen years old, correct?"

"Yes, I am. Your colleague explained that it was rare for you to educate non-Guild members for more than a few months, but that he thought that, given the time I had already spent studying on my own, you might make an exception in my case. He made it clear that it was subject to confirmation when I arrived here."

And subject to the massive tuition fee he had named, of course. I thought again about whether this was actually a worthwhile plan. Although my father hadn't been able to convey the bulk of his estate to me, he had left me enough money and other holdings to represent a small fortune, sufficient to keep me living in luxury for a number of years. Was it worth surrendering all of that for an 'elementary' course in magic? The Guild tester had been clear that I was unlikely to learn more than a handful of spells.

On the other hand, given the tight controls that the Guild imposed to limit the spread of magic beyond the Guild, I would be in a sound position to earn a comfortable way of life once I'd mastered even those basic skills. Even expertise in a truth detection spell alone was sought after in all walks of life. I suspected that was what Jemi was after to help his family's future negotiations. Besides, the idea of magic had always seized my imagination, and it had long been a goal, despite my father's unexplained refusal to let me visit Zaronia when I was younger.

"Very well", said Dorrall. "Let's start your test then." He returned the older sheaf of papers to the file and picked up my application form and the results of my preliminary testing. "Let's start with a simple crystal test."

He leaned over to the right-hand side of the desk and slid aside a lid which had concealed a well, sunk into the desk. A tray rose to desk level, carrying a series of complex looking devices, some of which I recognised and some of which were new to me. Dorrall carefully picked up a crystal globe standing on a complicated-looking stand, set with a number of crystals or gemstones in a regular pattern. He placed it in the center of the desk in front of me. From a drawer behind the desk, he extracted a pad of paper and a pencil.

"Please fill the crystal sphere with mana in a smooth motion. Don't force it, but let it out consistently. Stop when the row of blue crystals along the bottom are all lit," he said, indicating a row of ten blue crystals in the base. He took out what appeared to be a timepiece constructed of gold out of his pocket and poised ready to start the seconds hand.

I nodded tersely and took a deep breath. In my mind's eye, I visualised my mana pool, my store of magical energy, and directed it to flow gradually into the central globe. It took around thirty seconds for me to fill the globe, with the blue crystals along the base lighting up one after the other.

"Very good," said Dorrall. "Please hold it there for a moment." He inspected the other crystals, some of which had lit up and some remained dark. He made some notes and seemed to calculate something. "You clearly have conscious control over your mana pool and, given the flow rate you exhibited, I'd estimate that you've got about a hundred units available to you. That's consistent with the results from your earlier testing at the embassy and is unexpected given your lack of formal training. Yes, very good."

I let out my breath and released the mana from

the globe, feeling a little better. I'd spent many hours developing my awareness for mana, either sitting in our library at home or out under the trees of the countryside around. Curiously, my father had had a mechanism which resembled this crystal sphere, although without all the other gemstones, which seemed to display further information. It had simply glowed blue once I'd poured enough mana into it. He'd never explained where he'd got it and I'd never pried too deeply. I didn't think I'd mention that to Dorrall. Just as the Guild tried to keep a monopoly on magical knowledge, they also took a fairly proprietorial attitude towards magical Devices.

"No need to do a full formal capacity test right now - the results from your earlier testing look perfectly consistent and plausible," he said.

I breathed another sigh of relief - the capacity test had required me to pour all of my mana out into a continuous stream until there was none remaining in my reserves. When being tested in the Zaronian embassy in Sahraya, I was utterly exhausted after this exercise and could not do any further magic for the rest of the day while my reserves had replenished.

"Let's try something a little more ambitious, shall we? When I ask you to proceed, please form a sphere of mana in the air between us. Take your time about filling it - focus on producing something as regular and sustainable as you can."

Having said this, Dorrall took a pair of eye-glasses from his pocket and put them on. They had strange lenses made from a series of incredibly thin crystal sheets and a thick gold frame with various loops across the top of the frame. He flicked some of the loops backwards and forwards, which made some changes to the selection of sheets. "Please proceed."

I took another breath. This was much harder and something I'd only been able to achieve consistently within the last year or so. OK, slow and steady it was. I concentrated on the air about two feet in front of my face and began to direct mana to trace in the shell of a sphere about two inches in diameter. As I did so, I encouraged the mana to thicken slightly in order to actually form a persistent shell. It felt a bit like applying paint to thin air and having it stay where it was put.

Once the frame was complete, I shifted my focus and poured unthickened mana into the sphere until I started to feel feedback indicating that it was full. I then held it there with my mind supporting it in midair as if I was cupping my hands underneath it. In all, I'd estimate this took about three minutes to complete. I tried to breathe regularly, although I was sweating from the strain of concentration.

"Very good indeed", said Dorrall from somewhere ahead of me.

I didn't dare change my focus to look at him, in fear of letting go of the mana bubble.

"Hold it there, please." In my peripheral vision I could see him, moving around the desk peering the bubble from different angles. This was a first for me - I hadn't been aware that one person could see a mana bubble formed by another. I suspected that the eyeglasses were in some way involved.

"All right, I believe you're able to cast some form of light spell, correct? In your own time, please demonstrate."

Show-time, I thought to myself. This was definitely the peak of my current proficiency. Trying to keep my touch as light as possible, I reached into the bubble and started to trace out a pattern, setting up a current in the mana. Starting in the centre, I traced a loop up to the top of the bubble and then back to the centre, then to the left, to the bottom, and finally to the right. I then repeated myself, sketching the shape - it looked a bit like a flat four-leafed clover - in the mana. Gradually, some of the mana began to move in the current I was tracing and the loop started glowing.

"Splendid," said Dorrall, from somewhere outside the focus of my perception. "Basic two dimensional light working, minimum diffusion from the mana shell, but undeniably light for all that. I'm extremely surprised you could master this without assistance."

I allowed my focus to draw back and my view of the mana shell to fade. All that remained was the glowing image of the clover leaf current pattern in the air, with the light shining faintly out into the room. Most of the rays were being emitted in a disc in the plane of the cloverleaf shape. Nevertheless, this was the best result I'd ever achieved. And then with an inaudible pop, I lost control of the mana and it dissipated - the light gradually fading.

"That's really very promising," said Dorrall. "Completely consistent with the preliminary results and exactly what I was looking for. Now, please take the opportunity to rest for a couple of minutes, while I make some notes and then I'll have a few more questions…"

Dorrall took off his eyeglasses and carefully folded and stowed them away about his person. He'd reached for his notes again when suddenly there was a sharp peremptory knock on the stone door.

CHAPTER THREE
Further testing indicated

"Come in", called out Dorrall.

The door opened and another Guild member entered. He had a tattoo similar to Dorrall's, but looked a little older with smarter clothes and a somewhat harried looking expression on his face. He was holding a piece of paper covered in numbers and symbols.

"Ah, Dorrall, good," said the newcomer. "We've just taken the latest measurements and there's been a definite change. I'd like you to take a look immediately, please."

"Of course, Delisan. Let me look at the raw data for a moment." He raised his eyebrows at me in a grimace, possibly meant as an apology, and stood up and came around the desk to the newcomer's (Delisan, presumably) side. He took the piece of paper and scanned through it, deep in thought. "That looks a little out of kilter from what we were expecting", he said after a few moments. "Let's grind through the numbers and see if we can calculate some likely timescales and quantities."

Dorrall returned to the desk to retrieve some more blank paper and his pencil. He also placed all the papers he'd been working on back into the paper file and placed it in a drawer, which he then clicked shut. Finally, he flipped open a second panel on the top of the desk, this time on the right-hand side. As the new tray rose to desk level, he fished out a couple of reference books and a complicated-looking ruler, possibly some sort of slide-rule. The two Guild members then retreated to the stone benches in the chamber outside, leaving the door ajar, so I could continue to hear fragments of their conversation.

"It definitely looks like the emergence will take place somewhere in the next twenty-four to forty-eight hours," I heard Dorrall say. "But I can't make the number of entities come out sensibly. There's something strange about the emergence rate as well. It looks unusually hurried."

"What are you assuming about the energy concentration of the entities? We've seen a great deal of variance in the past," replied Delisan.

Their conversation then became a lot more technical. Given that I had no real idea what they were talking about, I couldn't make much sense of it and I looked around for something to distract me.

In the new tray which had risen into position on the right-hand side of the desk, I saw that there were a number of books with dry sounding titles. Given that my written Zaronian was rudimentary, I didn't fancy attempting to puzzle out the subjects. There were also a what looked like other Devices, vastly more complicated than the ones on the left-hand tray. My eye was caught by a stand made of polished and inlaid mahogany surmounted by a sizeable cube of a crystalline material which balanced on its corner. The cube was nearly the size of my head.

"All right, so if we assume that one entity has an unusually advanced energy concentration, how does that change the calculations?" came a voice from outside.

There was something strange about the interior of the cube, though. Gazing into the cloudy centre of the crystal, it looked as if there was another cube suspended in the middle, with some other cubes around it. Some trick of perspective strangely distorted the surrounding ones, and I moved my head, trying to work out what I was seeing. As my head moved, some shapes flexed and shifted strangely, in a non-intuitive way.

"We're getting somewhere now," I heard Dorrall say.

Or was it non-intuitive? I was picking up some patterns in the movement that felt familiar. In a strange way, it reminded me slightly of the strange visual effects that I'd noticed with the tattoos, where they almost looked as if they had depth to them, despite clearly being flat. If I really focused my eyes in on the central cube, and then let my vision broaden to cover the whole interior, would that make it clearer?"

"Yes, if we assume two, with one substantially more mature than the other, that would work. It would tighten the predicted emergence time of between twenty-four and twenty-six hours."

"Could it be three less developed entities?"

"No, because then the rate of change we're observing wouldn't make sense..."

I stopped paying attention to the conversation

entirely as my concentration on the cube focused. What happened next was almost an accident, which I don't think would have happened if I hadn't recently been handling mana. I reached out with mind and instinctively touched the central cube with mana. It began to glow green. While holding my mana there, I touched each of the surrounding cubes, six in total, and they glowed as well. I found I could rotate the entire structure in my vision, although whether or not this was an illusion, I couldn't tell. The cubes distorted and flexed as they moved.

"What on earth are you doing?" Dorrall's voice was loud in my ears and I jumped. He'd clearly come back in the room while I was manipulating my visualisation of the cubes. I lost my focus, and the vision faded. I saw the actual crystal cube was still sitting just as it had been on its stand, although I noted the remnants of glowing green light fading as they dissipated. I found I had a slight headache.

Dorrall was standing back on the other side of the desk, looking forbidding. I glanced behind me and saw that the door was again closed with no sign of Delisan.

"That's not a tool we use with our lay candidates," Dorrall said, sitting down. "Indeed, I really shouldn't have left it out where you could see it," he continued ruefully. "I'm surprised you could even make use of it, let alone illuminate all the facets."

His mood seemed to have shifted to one of intrigued surmise, so I took a chance.

"I've never seen anything like it. What was I looking at? It flipped between looking like a number of faceted flaws within the crystal to some sort of image of a cube surrounded by other cubes. While still remaining a cube, if that makes sense?"

"It is a tesseract visualisation model," he said, shedding no actual light as far as I was concerned. His expression sharpened as he narrowed his eyes. "I think I'd like to run a few more tests if you've got no objections. Technically, this might be a breach of the rules, but given your likely parentage, perhaps we can stretch a point a little."

The next hour or so passed quickly. He ran me through a series of what appeared to be tests familiar to him, using the various Devices from the right-hand tray. Sometimes he asked me to describe what I could see, at others he had me use mana to touch various elements, which usually lit up in unexpected ways. His focus seemed to be on determining how well I could visualise a variety of geometric shapes and patterns. He also worked through a list of shapes from a book, asking me to draw them in the air with my finger, starting with the four-leaf clover from my light spell, but rapidly getting more and more complex. Initially, he was quite talkative, usually expressing surprise or pleasure at my responses, but gradually he grew quieter.

When we'd worked through a long list, he pulled out my papers and wrote for a long time. I'd seen him making various notes as we went, but this time he produced an extensive writeup. He then sat and thought for a while, staring at the wall with a troubled expression.

"Right," he finally said. "The next step is to confirm my results. Please wait here." He walked out of the room.

I wasn't sure what was going on. Had I done well,

or badly? Was this likely to endanger my chances of being accepted for the elementary course? I hadn't really meant to break the rules and play with the cube Device.

***

When Dorrall returned, about fifteen minutes later, a young woman accompanied him. I thought she was one of the other testers I'd seen earlier, with a circle and triangle tattoo. She seemed nervous and confused.

"Symona, this is Scordo Orchan," said Dorrall. "I'd like you please to administer a complete practical aptitude test for an apprentice candidate. Omit only the full capacity test. He may have to undergo more testing later today."

Symona acknowledged the introduction briefly and then turned back to Dorrall, looking more confused than ever. "But sir, this is one of the Sahrayan candidates, isn't it? The rules state…"

Dorrall interrupted. "That's my responsibility. Please don't worry about it. I've already done most of the tests, but I need a second opinion. Please work through the full standard test, but don't ask me for assistance. Feel free to use whatever references you need to guide you. We're testing him, not you. The room is fully stocked with everything you should need. Once you're complete, I'd like you to write out your recommendations and sign them. Then we'll talk further."

Symona was clearly still confused, but seemed to be happier that she knew what she was supposed to be doing. She sat down opposite me and checked through the various books and devices in the desk and trays, returning some that Dorrall had disturbed. I noticed Dorrall hadn't given her any of my papers to read: instead she started with a blank notepad.

After about five minutes, a servant arrived carrying a tray with a jug of water and several glasses. We helped ourselves. The air was dry, and I'd been talking for a while.

The next couple of hours passed, much as my first ones had done. Symona was clearly not as familiar with the tests and calculations as Dorrall had been, but seemed competent enough. She frequently referred to the various texts in the desk.

Symona asked me more questions than Dorrall had, determining my current level of experience and using that to guide what she asked me to demonstrate. She got more confident as she progressed, but her air of confusion only deepened, particularly when she started working me through the various testing Devices from the right-hand tray. She frequently darted questioning glances in Dorrall's direction, but he remained impassive.

Dorrall didn't stay observing for the whole of the test. He was called away fairly frequently, but always returned quickly and stood at the side of the room, a silent observer.

Finally, she got to the end of her checklist and she put all the various devices and books in their places. She then wrote in silence for about twenty minutes, finishing up with a large flowing signature. She then looked up at Dorrall and raised her eyebrows.

"Yes, seal it, please," he said, apparently in reply to her query.

She then extracted a small Device from the desk. I recognised it as a blood pricker for sealing formal documents. Her eyes went distant as she concentrated and the pin glowed briefly and quickly faded. She then pricked her thumb and pressed it below her signature. Another glow and she was finished.

"Scordo, thank you for your patience. It was nice to meet you. Uh, good luck," she said.

"Thank you. Likewise", I replied. I then winced as I realised I'd accidentally wished her good luck. She smiled quickly, gathered up her papers and took them out of the room.

"Please wait here," said Dorrall. He quickly retrieved his own papers and my file, locked the various desk containers, and followed her out.

***

So, I waited. What else was I to do? I'd completely lost track of what was happening by this point. Were they planning on accepting me for the course, or had I broken some rule of the Guild in some way which meant that I was going to be sent home in ignominy? Well, actually, ignominy would imply that anyone would actually care. Now that my father had died, I wasn't sure that anyone would actually notice. At the very least though, it would mean the end of all of my plans. What else could I do?

In this cheerful way, obsessively dissecting the plans for my future, I whiled away what I estimated was the next couple of hours. Given the lack of windows and sound, it was difficult to tell how long I'd actually been there. The globe fixed to the wall continued to glow unchanged without hinting at the progress of time. At one point, a servant came in with a tray of food and drink, but other than explaining he'd been instructed to bring it to me, couldn't say how long I was going to be there. At least they didn't want me to starve.

Finally, Dorrall returned, accompanied by someone else. This Guild member was a tall man who looked slightly younger than Dorrall, but his tattoo was even more complicated. There were so many crossing lines that it almost looked black from some angles. His clothes were untidy and his general demeanour was preoccupied and somewhat frustrated to be there. I summed him up as grumpy, somehow.

"Scordo, this is Master Logross," said Dorrall. "Master Logross, this is Scordo Orchan who we've been discussing..." He trailed off awkwardly.

"Mmm hmm", grunted Logross. Definitely grumpy, I thought. I introduced myself in my best Zaronian, which didn't improve his mood as he sat down in the seat opposite me while seeming to have his attention elsewhere.

"Master Logross would like to ask some questions... And possibly repeat some of the tests...?" Again, Dorrall trailed off, and I suddenly realised that he was nervous. He didn't take one of the other chairs but shuffled round to standing at attention against the wall in a corner of the room. When Symona had been testing me earlier, Dorrall had been trying not to get involved, but clearly considered himself in charge of the process, if only silently. This time, he was pretending that he wasn't really there. Nervous, or even a little afraid?

"Form a mana sphere", Logross barked. No time for pleasantries, then I thought. Well, I could appreciate a need for efficiency. I formed a sphere in front of me gradually and smoothly. Logross was focused on the right general volume of space, but wasn't using the eye-glasses that I'd seen Dorrall and Symona using. Could he even see what I was doing?

"Release. Now, again."

I obeyed. Terse barked orders with no expression or feedback set the pattern for the next hour or so, as he took me through the hardest of the practical exercises and tests that I'd already performed, as well as several additions. He worked entirely without reference books and took no notes. Frequently, I wasn't even sure that he was paying attention to what I was doing. Periodically, he asked for something I couldn't do. Sometimes I simply couldn't even understand the request, but being told this elicited as little feedback as when I was able to comply.

Finally, he ended with a full capacity test, and I had to pour all of my available mana into a crystal measuring Device, until I was completely dry. He grunted again when I finished.

I assumed that this would be the end of the testing, but I was wrong. He then continued to bark questions at me on a series of more academic topics. Logross started with my mathematical knowledge, with a particular emphasis on geometry and number theory. He demanded that I prove that there were only five different convex regular solids and then justify why the sphere wasn't part of the group. Fortunately, I was on safe ground here. I'd always been interested in mathematics and I'd had some like-minded tutors.

He then moved over to my knowledge of the Zaronian language and then the history and culture of Zaronia itself. I was just about keeping up with our actual conversation, but the limits of my grasp of the language and my almost complete lack of knowledge of Zaronia and the Guild soon became clear. His questioning continued to be adversarial and designed to expose the gaps and inconsistencies in my knowledge. I struggled to respond calmly and with as much detail as I could, but it was hard. Not only was I exhausted after the repeated tests and the capacity demonstration, but I was feeling dizzy from all the attention and interaction I'd had to endure.

Finally, he quizzed me in detail about how I'd developed my skills in mana manipulation and the texts I'd used. He repeatedly asked about whether I'd had tuition from anyone. I explained that I'd had practically no contact with those few Sahrayan nobles who actually knew anything about magic, and that as far as I knew, there were no Guild mages in Sahraya other than the one in the Zaronian embassy.

My explanations trailed off into inaudibility, and Logross didn't ask me any more questions. His gaze focused on the corner of the desk and he remained like that, presumably thinking for about five minutes. I concentrated on bringing my breathing back under control, enjoying the respite and with no desire to break the silence.

Then suddenly Logross's gaze swung round to lock eyes with me for a few moments. He paused again, but I didn't speak. He then turned to look at

Dorrall and gave one unmistakable nod.

"Brief him," he said and swept out of the room saying nothing further.

CHAPTER FOUR
Apprenticeship

There was a brief pause after Master Logross's sudden exit and then Dorrall's posture slumped and he almost collapsed into the chair recently vacated by the master. I could almost see the tension flowing out of him. He too seemed to be trying to control his breathing.

"Well done," he said. "Master Logross can be somewhat... intense at times." I realised that my earlier guess was correct. Dorrall was almost afraid of Logross.

"So, where to start?", he asked rhetorically. I raised my eyebrows quizzically but made no other response. I felt that I'd done enough talking for the time being.

"Let's start by recapping the difference between lay members and full members of the Guild," he continued. "You and the other Sahrayan candidates came here to apply for tuition as lay members. In your case, you were applying for the full elementary course which covers basic control of mana sphere manipulation and up to around half a dozen different basic workings and a few variants. By 'working', I'm referring to mana current patterns such as the one you demonstrated in your light 'spell'".

I nodded. This all matched my understanding, although I hadn't heard it stated so succinctly previously.

"In practical terms," he continued, "that's usually the most tuition available to a student who is not native to Zaronia. In theory, there is further training allowed beyond the elementary course, but the cost is prohibitive and in any case, it would simply cover more fluency in controlling a mana sphere and further variants to the basic initial workings."

"When you say 'a student who is not native to Zaronia', are you also implying someone who isn't a full Guild member?" I asked.

"Yes, in practice I am," he confirmed. "The Guild strictly limits what can be taught to non-members, and that limitation includes lay members. In fact, there is no difference in Guild rules between lay members and everyone else. If you're not a member of the Guild, then there is a strict limit to what you're allowed to know of the mysteries. A lay member is simply someone who has been educated by the Guild within those limitations. Furthermore, both by Guild practice and Zaronian law, the Guild does not admit non-Zaronians."

The Zaronian embassy in Sahraya had explained to me that I was not eligible to join the Guild, but without spelling it out in this sort of detail. I'd periodically heard my fellow Sahrayans complaining about the near monopoly that the Zaronian Guild had on magic, but I'd not known how clearly this was set out by policy. I had never understood how they could enforce control on knowledge, but I couldn't argue that it seemed to work. After many years of searching and questioning, I had only found a few texts on the subject, and all of those matched to the sort of lay curriculum Dorrall was detailing.

"So, what's the precise relevance of this to me?" I prompted, since Dorrall appeared distracted by his inner thoughts.

"Right, of course. So, when you came today, I tested you on the criteria for the lay curriculum. This tells me whether it would be worth our time to educate you on that subset of knowledge. In contrast, when we test a Zaronian candidate for a full apprenticeship, effectively a full member of the Guild, we have a much broader set of tests that we employ. In that case, we're not purely looking to determine whether they could master the simple curriculum, but whether they'll thrive with the broader mysteries."

The word 'mysteries' kept tripping me up, and I didn't understand what Dorrall meant by this. Perhaps it was my limited command of Zaronian. He continued speaking, however.

"We're simply not interested in taking on apprentices that get stuck part way through their training. Although that happens on some occasions for various reasons. And stuck isn't necessarily the right word..."

Dorrall clearly realised that he was drifting off on a tangent again and refocused.

"Most of those tests simply aren't relevant to a lay candidate and arguably some of them are sufficiently connected to the mysteries to prohibit us from sharing that they're best... avoided. Usually, that is."

"Usually?" I prompted.

"Indeed, usually. When you started experimenting with the tesseract visualisation tool... the crystal cube Device that I inadvertently left in view... you were exposed to a... more advanced apprenticeship assessment tool and, in essence, to one of the mysteries. However, given how successful you were with the tool, and given how few apprentice candidates can activate it at all, I was intrigued."

"So you then continued to administer the rest of the full apprentice test? And then had Symona do the same?" I was beginning to understand what had happened now, but I didn't see the point. Hadn't this been a waste of my time and effort? "But where does that leave us, as a non-Zaronian citizen? I'm not eligible to be a candidate for a full guild member, am I? They made that clear to me back at the embassy."

"Well, that's actually an interesting question," said Dorrall. "What actually is a Zaronian citizen?"

"Well, presumably someone born in Zaronia," I responded with a certain amount of heat. I then stopped talking suddenly, playing back what I'd just said, and my expression changed.

"Exactly," said Dorrall. "Someone born within the borders of Zaronia or, more broadly, to Zaronian parents. And, as far as our... enquiry services were able to determine at the time, that includes you. And as far as I'm aware, you never renounced your Zaronian citizenship when your father adopted you and took you back to Sahraya. I doubt it since you were only about a year old at the time, unless you were a truly precocious youth.". He smiled faintly at his own joke.

"So, does that mean that I am eligible to join the Guild?" I asked. I was starting to feel excited at the prospect, but I tried to temper my expectations.

"Well, obviously, it's a somewhat confusing position," he replied. "You've been living as a de facto citizen of Sahraya for nearly all of your life, and that country may have their own expectations of you." He raised an eyebrow in enquiry.

"I doubt anyone will even notice that I'm not there," I said, somewhat bitterly.

"Well, that's as may be," he replied. "Normally, this situation is a can of worms that we'd simply avoid opening. That seems to have been the attitude of the embassy, even if they knew anything of your full background. And you're quite old to be committing to an apprenticeship contract. Plus, we don't really know as much as we would have liked about your birth parents and their... attitudes, which is another reason to be... cautious. Although, you appear to have demonstrated to Master Logross your lack of sympathy for..." He seemed to realise he was drifting off topic again and paused.

"Anyway, certain... aspects of your testing suggest that you might have some particular potential in the fullness of time. Nothing that is likely to help you that much in your initial studies, but... in the future, if you get that far. Given that, I talked with my... superiors. Talked with them quite a lot, in fact. Given two independent recommendations from Symona and from me, they decided to... assess your potential in more detail. And Master Logross's decision is... definitive. You qualify to be an apprentice."

This was a confusing speech. Dorrall was clearly choosing his words now with extraordinary care and trying to avoid certain topics. I decided to push a little.

"Well, that's very gratifying. It's obviously a big decision, though, given the length of the required commitment. Is there anything you can share about the potential you think you're seeing in me?"

"Err, no. Mysteries, you see." He seemed a little apologetic. "And there's no guarantee that you'd progress that far in any case. But, based on the report from the embassy, full membership of the Guild was something you were initially enquiring about, wasn't it? I should add that the cost of signing up to an apprenticeship is substantially lower than that of the elementary course that you were hoping for. Obviously, with more significant... future commitments, however."

I got the impression that Dorrall was suddenly nervous again. Maybe he'd stuck his neck out to push for this option and he was worried about the Guild reaction if I turned it down. I decided to reassure him.

"No, no, I'm excited about the opportunity. What's involved in signing up as an apprentice?"

"Excellent, that's excellent. You can leave most of the arrangements to me. Today is getting on a bit, but we should be able to have your indenture and the rest of the paperwork drawn up by early tomorrow morning. Best done quickly, there are... reasons why it would be good to have the... formalities completed as early as possible so that you can be a candidate for... err, reasons, as I say. We'll take care of... talking with the Sahrayans on your behalf as well. It'll be much better left to our legal officials. Could I ask you to just stay here for a few more minutes while I set things in motion?"

"Of course, yes. Err, thank you for everything you've done," I said, frankly shell-shocked at how fast things were moving now after an entire day of tests.

"Not at all. No need," he assured me and rushed out of the room.

About half an hour later, an apprentice entered and explained that he'd been tasked with showing me to my room. Apparently, I also rated a couple of guards who accompanied us. I was surprised to find that the apprentice wasn't taking me back the way I came. Instead, we proceeded along a couple of corridors and then down another flight of steps to a new sleeping room. The guards seemed to be unusually vigilant in watching for potential dangers. Perhaps they weren't just there to supervise tourists?

My room had only a single bed and no windows (we were well below ground level at this point) but seemed slightly plusher and better appointed than the one I had shared with Jemi the previous night. Shortly after I arrived, so did the rest of my possessions, conveyed by another of the ubiquitous guards, quickly followed by more food and drink.

I then collapsed into bed. Not only had the testing process been long and arduous, but I was still suffering the ill effects of the capacity test that Master Logross had insisted upon.

Mid-way through the night, however, I found

myself awakened by a faint scratching noise. I lay there half asleep for a while, trying to work out where the noise was coming from. Eventually, I decided to investigate. In a half-daze, I staggered across the room in the darkness, heading towards where I thought the origin of the sound might be.

My outstretched hands fumbled against a wall. The repetitive sound seemed to be below me and I felt down along the wall in the pitch black, seeking for the source. My fingers began to traverse a series of holes and then I felt a sudden and overwhelming pain across my arm.

I flung myself backwards onto my bottom. Something had just cut across my forearm. I could feel the wet warmth of blood welling out. I shuffled backwards away on my bottom, half-sitting on the floor, trying to get as much distance from the unknown assailant as I could manage. What could have attacked me here, safe in my room?

With a trembling arm, I reached behind me wildly and managed to make contact with the glow lobe next to my bed. I touched the glow globe next to my bed (trial and error the previous night had shown that this would activate it).

I stood back up in the sudden glare and stared around the room. Nothing. I looked back down at my arm. The forearm was now marked with a scratch across my skin. As I'd thought, it was bleeding slightly, but didn't appear deep enough to cause immediate concern. Whatever had done it, could do worse, however.

I slowly walked uncertainly back across the room, scanning for the source of the danger.

In the light, triangulation quickly allowed me to track the noise to the source. It was emerging from one of the grills covering a ventilation shaft set near the floor. There was no sign of anything sharp. Perhaps, I had felt down across the grill in my befuddlement, and something sharp must have emerged and scratched me?

I couldn't see any further signs of movement, but it still sounded as if something was behind it, scratching to get out. I didn't think this was much of an idea and banged loudly on the wall next to the grill. There was a sudden silence followed by a quickly receding clicking noise, and then silence once more.

I waited for a little while, fearful that whatever it was might return, but the silence continued unbroken, so eventually I extinguished the light and eventually fell back to a troubled sleep.

***

The next morning, I was awakened by the arrival of my breakfast, along with a message asking me to be ready shortly. I breakfasted and prepared myself quickly and then packed my belongings just in case. Shortly afterwards, the guards escorted me to another meeting room on a level even lower below the ground. This room was large with a stone table and chairs at one end, and a number of more casual seats at the other. It contained two people, Dorrall and a woman who he introduced as Islina, one of the Guild lawyers.

Islina was tall and was in her early thirties. Her hair was red and tied up in a tight bun. Her robes were immaculate and more elaborate than my experience to date of Guild members. In short, she came over as rather intimidating, as though she was ready to take charge of a high-level royal court meeting or negotiation. Her tattoo was unusual as well. It was the first time I'd seen a circle set in another circle.

"Candidate Orchan, good to meet with you," she said, although her smile didn't reach her eyes. "My team were asked to prepare an apprentice indenture contract for you to sign."

She removed a long scroll of parchment from a leather satchel sitting on the chair next to hers and placed it on the table. Then she followed up with a shorter looking sheaf of cut papers.

"In the circumstances, we will also need to execute these. Please look through them all. I trust you will find them in order. They're all more or less standard documents."

I definitely got the impression that she considered my acceptance of the documents something of a formality, so I decided to take my time. I pulled over the sheaf of papers first and scanned through them. These were fairly easy to understand because they were worded in both the Zaronian and Sarayan languages, although the document was careful to stress that Zaronian would be the prevailing language in the case of contradictions.

First, there was a statement of the apprenticeship fee (comfortably lower than the amount I'd put aside for the essentials course), along with a note explaining that any overpayment would be credited to my account at the Guild bank.

The longer document was a statement confirming my Zaronian citizenship and reinstating all associated rights and responsibilities. I saw, to my surprise, that a senior official from the Zaronian court already signed the document. The Guild's lawyers must have moved fast indeed to have this approved already.

As part of the documents, I also explicitly renounced and revoked any rights, responsibilities and allegiances to the royal court of Sahraya and asserted my own rights to do this, quoting several legal precedents that I'd never previously encountered. I questioned Islina on this point, and she carefully assured me that her 'team' had fully researched the references. I felt she resented the implication that they might have made a mistake.

I let this go as it wasn't as if I felt any particular attachment or warmth towards Sahraya itself. My loyalties had always been to my father's province of Arbran itself. In fact, I was slightly surprised that the document didn't mention Arbran at all. Although Arbran was often treated as being part of the Sahraya, technically, it was an independent principality which happened to be ruled by the same royal family. However, I decided given the offended response to my previous query, now wasn't the time to raise that sort of pedantry and moved on to the indenture.

The indenture was much harder to follow. Partly, this was a physical problem. It was written on a long vertical piece of parchment with a roller affixed to each end. This was old technology as far as I was concerned, and I'd never developed the knack of letting out one end gradually while rolling up the other. This meant I frequently slipped and lost my place.

The bigger problem was the language. My written Zaronian was not particularly fluent at the best of times, and the document was written in a combination of archaic wording and detailed legal jargon. However, over the next hour or so, I managed to puzzle out what I considered to be the key elements. I was signing up to a seven-year term of servitude to the Guild in return for education and board throughout that period. Although it was an apprentice indenture, my term (and my responsibilities) did not terminate if I graduated from being an apprentice during the period. Furthermore, although it was a seven-year agreement, I was agreeing in perpetuity to consider myself bound by the "varyed rules, lyabylitys and strycturs of the Guyld" as "myte be communicated to me by a duly appoynted representatyf" and that I would agree to follow, obey and accept the appropriate "mechanysms and byndings".

Islina continued to be extremely polite and helpful throughout this process, hiding any frustration she felt. Dorrall was less good at masking his impatience and cast repeated glances at his pocket timepiece. Islina explained individual words and phrases where necessary, although she was elaborately careful to clarify that her interpretation should not be considered part of the agreement and that the text itself was the ultimate arbiter. Indeed, I found a clause in the document where I "warranteth" that I wasn't relying on any independent discussions, explanations, assurances, etc.

I couldn't say that I was particularly enamoured of the indenture, but fundamentally this all appeared to be in line with normal practice of the Guild as explained by Dorrall on the previous day. Essentially, they wanted me to promise to follow their rules on the dissemination of magical knowledge. Or the "mysteries" as Dorrall had colourfully put it!

At the end of the indenture, there was the space for three signatures and seals. One for me ("The apprentice"), one for a "Duly appointed Master of the Guild" and one for the witness from the Guild legal group.)

"OK. Let's get this signed," I said. Islina nodded and begin to extract writing pens and blood prickers from her bag. Dorrall had clearly been thinking of something else, because he turned his head to look at me momentarily with a blank stare before surging into life, promising to fetch a Master.

I signed and sealed the sheaf of other documents first, since I was the only person who had to execute them (as the royal court had already signed). Then I signed my name to the agreement and added a bloody thumbprint. Dorrall came in accompanied by another senior Guild member, not Logross I was pleased to see, who he introduced as Master Parmonia. She explicitly asked Islina whether the agreement was as it should be and had the approval of the legal group and Islina confirmed. This done, first Master Parmonia and then Islina countersigned indenture and applied their seals in turn. I then passed over my counter-signed bank draft. The documents were all slipped back into Islina's satchel and she excused herself.

"Is it all done? Am I an apprentice now?", I asked.

Dorrall was the first to respond. "Legally, yes,

Scordo. However, by Guild practice, Master Parmonia needs to carry out the formal binding ceremony next. That should only take another thirty minutes or so."

At this point, inevitably, there was a pounding on the door.

CHAPTER FIVE
Entities

I suddenly had a feeling of déjà vu as Delisan, Dorrall's colleague from the previous day's interruption, bustled in.

"Dorrall, the emergence has begun. Is your candidate ready? You've only got a few minutes. Master Logross was very... umm... emphatic that he ought to attend," Delisan said.

"Err, yes, he was," said Dorrall. He fiddled nervously with his robes. "Master Parmonia, given that he has signed the indenture, can Scordo attend an emergence before the sealing ceremony?"

Master Parmonia was clearly a bit taken aback by the question. "Well, obviously normal Guild protocols are clear in this area and the ceremony would normally take place immediately. I'm not sure whether there are any practical reasons we can't vary that, however, as long as we ensure... err, Master Logross, you say? Emphatic?"

Dorrall nodded.

"Right, I see. Obviously, we don't want to risk... What is the candidate to entity ratio?" she said.

"With Scordo, Apprentice Scordo, that is, it will be twelve candidates to two entities," Dorrall said.

"So, not a high chance in any case? Very well. I need both of you to swear on your seals that you will return the apprentice to me immediately after the emergence and choosing has completed, understand?"

"I understand and confirm, Master Parmonia", said Dorrall. Delisan echoed his statement.

With that, I found myself rushed out of the room, down a corridor and around a bend to where a group of apprentices were waiting by an elaborately carved pair of stone doors, flanked by a group of guards and a few more senior Guild officials. Dorrall and Delisan immediately went over to the latter and began a hushed conversation.

The apprentices looked almost scared. There were about ten of them, split more or less evenly between genders. I noticed that all of them bore a circular tattoo, and wondered how and when I would receive mine, and whether it would hurt.

"Apprentices, please pay attention," said Delisan to our group. "In a few moments, we will open the door to the cave. You will all enter and the door will be closed behind you. Once the entities have made their choices, we will detect this. We will then reopen the door and you will leave again. Please do not have concerns about other dangers in the cave. It has been extensively checked before the emergence."

I expected questions at this point from the apprentices, but there was only a hushed sense of expectation. I was tiring of not knowing what was going on, but I didn't want to interrupt in front of all these onlookers, so I held my peace.

Delisan locked eyes with a couple of his colleagues

who were consulting various arcane-looking crystal devices. They both nodded and Delisan gave a signal to the guards. Two of them approached the stone doors and pulled them open.

The other apprentices and I were all ushered through the doorway and the doors were closed behind us with a muffled thud and click.

***

We found ourselves in a dark space. The glow-globes common elsewhere weren't present here. As I stood and waited, however, my eyes began to adjust and I could make out more and more details.

The cave was faintly lit with a blue glow which emanated from the rocks themselves. It was low but vast, stretching into the distance ahead of us. The floor, the ceiling and what we could see of the walls were rough, covered by facets of some sort of crystalline material. Blue light was coming out of the crystals, causing the illusion of strange depth to them. The only noise came from dripping water and a smell of damp filled the cavern.

I took a few steps forward, not wanting to stand too close to the others, but also reluctant to move too far from the doors. Some others did the same, although I saw several of them glancing back at the stone doors as if for reassurance.

As best I could guess, the cave was natural. Aside from the doorway, there were no signs of tools or other man-made workings. Facets of crystal entirely covered the floor and ceiling without gaps in between. Some of the largest of the crystals were as long as my arm. I remembered a geode owned by one of my adopted cousins, and I realised that this cave was a giant version of those.

I took a few more steps and the other apprentices continued to spread out as well. Soon, we were spread out in a rough semicircle across the mouth of the cave. In the distance, I could still see no end to the cavern, but I guessed it was about forty feet wide.

I began to hear a faint buzzing sound. It slowly grew in intensity and the tone of the noise varied over time. Gradually, it developed into more of a warbling, throbbing sound and my mind noticed apparent patterns in the changes. The blue glow of the crystals was much brighter now, although I couldn't tell whether it was an actual change or simply my eyes continuing to adapt.

Maybe I was hearing two distinct tones, with distinct patterns and frequencies? Occasionally they would fall into synchronisation and the noise level would grow to overwhelming levels before the two melodies fell out into different rhythms again. Before long, I could no longer discern any of the sound of dripping water and the noises of the shuffling apprentices, since the throbbing tones drowned them out. It was now so loud that I struggled to think sensibly with the echoes rebounding back and forth from the crystals all around us.

I realised that the light had definitely changed. The blue glow was still there, but there was also a gray light. No, two gray lights hanging in the ceiling. They were far off in the distance, much further away than I knew the ceiling to be. Some sort of illusion, generated some distance into the translucent crystal, perhaps?

Starting Sphere

Two gray balls, both moving towards us. One was closer than the other, but it was hard to make out how far away either actually was without a clear sense of scale.

Then suddenly, one ball broke free into the cave. It was the smaller, less bright of the two. It hovered there momentarily, and I got a sudden impression that it was looking at us somehow. In the light it was casting, I could see that all apprentice eyes were fixed upon it. I got a vague impression from it of wordless communication that I couldn't make out. As if someone were talking in an adjacent room. Except that it wasn't words, it felt more like emotions.

Then suddenly, the ball moved again and swooped straight at one of the other apprentices, a girl maybe around the same age as me. I could see her features and blonde hair illuminated in the instant before the ball hit her and then it disappeared into her head. In the sudden darkness I felt, rather than saw, that she had collapsed to the floor.

Before I or anyone else could react, the other gray glowing ball broke free of the ceiling and everyone's attention shifted to track it. The new ball was to be about three or four times brighter than the first. This time, I got a much clearer impression of the communication coming from it, a sense of enquiry, of entreaty, of welcome and greeting, all mixed with a strange subtext of geometrical patterns. It felt almost like it was communicating directly with me, and I instinctively responded with a sense of greeting.

Then I realised it was, in truth, actually trying to talk to me. The ball suddenly grew dangerously large, completely blinding me, and I felt a second presence emerging into my consciousness, sharing its thoughts with mine.

<{Greetings/welcome} {My name/identity/being} {"Pinca"} {Tired}>

Everything went black. I didn't feel myself fall to the cave floor, nor see the doors reopen.

***

"Master Logross knew what he was talking about then. As usual."

"So it appears. He suggested they would regard him as an attractive candidate and, in any case, he was reluctant to take on an unbound apprentice."

"I believe his exact words were that they'd be drawn to his mind like 'spikkans to a chicken carcass'".

"Yes, well, I don't think any of us would expect to finish a conversation with Logross without being disturbed in some way."

"How much longer will it be before…"

"Hush, I think he's coming round at last."

I realised that I was hearing the voices of other people nearby. My head hurt and I was lying on something hard and flat. I felt cold and forced my eyes open.

I thought at first that I was stretched out on a stone slab before I realised it must be a stone table, possibly the one in the earlier meeting room. The light was blinding and my head throbbed with pain. I blearily glanced around. There were several moving shapes somewhere in the distance.

I blinked several times and got a better view: I was back in the meeting room I'd been in earlier, and sitting in the casual seats at the other end of the room were a number of people. I vaguely recognised Dorrall, Delisan and Master Parmonia, but there seemed to be something wrong with their heads that was preventing me from focusing properly.

I closed my eyes for a few seconds and tried again. Yes, it was who I thought, but for some reason their heads were glowing slightly. They were also drinking tea out of glasses with metal handles. I had a nagging feeling that there was also something different about the appearance of their tattoos, but I couldn't make it out from this distance.

"What happened?" I tried.

"Nothing to worry about," Dorrall said. "The bonding process usually leaves an apprentice unconscious for a few minutes. It is the shock of the two consciousnesses colliding, I suspect. The same thing happened to Apprentice Anyana, and she'll be perfectly alright by tomorrow morning. We would have usually returned you to a room to sleep it off, but we have some further business to attend to: the sealing ceremony."

"Bonding? What was it that happened? I thought I heard something said that its name was 'Pinca'," I said.

Dorrall raised an eyebrow. "Really? Very interesting. Uncommonly mature, I wonder what that'll mean for its future development? However, I'm afraid I can't explain it right now. We've bent too many customs and protocols already, and that's something for your new master to explain. Delisan, would you help me clear a space for the ceremony?"

Delisan and Dorrall quickly cleared a wide space by pushing the furniture to the edges of the room and then helped me down from the table. I still felt a little unsteady and dizzy after whatever had happened to me. My head continued to hurt: it somehow felt as if it was too tight for me.

In the meantime, Master Parmonia extracted some sort of writing implement and sketched a circle on the floor in the middle of the space easily wide enough for me to stand inside. The circle glittered slightly and, as she helped me into the circle, I thought she must have drawn it in some sort of wax, with crystal fragments embedded in it. Indeed, Master Parmonia's implement was a wax crayon of some sort.

"Please stand here", said Dorrall, indicating the center of the sketched circle and I complied groggily.

"Now Apprentice, Scordo wasn't it?" said Master Parmonia. "I'd like you to stay there in the spell's focus. This will take less than half an hour to complete. Will you be up to that, or would you like a chair?"

I indicated that I'd be able to stay standing. Indeed, other than the strange visual effects, I was rapidly recovering from my ordeal. I gazed at the Master's tattoo. I could now make out a lot more detail. The outer shape wasn't a circle, but some sort of representation of a sphere. Or perhaps it was an actual illusion of a sphere hanging behind her forehead. By changing my focus in a way I couldn't explain, I realised that there was a triangular pyramid nested inside the sphere, and then a cube inside of that. A final shape lay in the centre, but I was unable to make out the precise details. Something with triangular faces.

"Let's begin. Dorrall, Delisan, take places around the circle please, in case I need more mana. I'm not entirely sure whether the binding will influence the energy requirements and I'll need to make a strong gateway to the Construct. Apprentice, please continue to focus on me. There will be a brief moment of discomfort when the ceremony is completed."

I sensed Dorrall and Delisan taking up positions approximately equidistant around the circle while I continued to watch Parmonia. She was standing six feet away from me and she remained there apparently focusing on a spot in between us.

Silence fell for a few minutes as Parmonia continued to gaze at empty space and then I saw her tense. At the same time, a series of blue glowing shapes formed in between us. A number of faint spheres came first, each forming smoothly and quickly, taking perhaps twenty or thirty seconds each to appear. Then a circle of pyramids formed, floating in a vertical circle in front of me with their points directed at each other. The circle gradually spun in midair. Finally, and taking much longer to form, I saw a shape with triangular sides come into existence behind the circle of pyramids, probably a twenty-sided icosahedron. I remembered answering Master Logross's questions on this subject the previous day.

This must be a magic working, but far more complicated than I'd imagined possible. For a start, I'd no idea that mana bubbles could take any shapes other than a sphere. I knew that whenever I'd failed to make a perfect sphere, a mana bubble would quickly burst and the mana dissipate.

The icosahedron was spinning too, but ominously, one of its vertexes pointed unflinchingly at me. There was something unusual about the point, the mana shell there looked different from the rest of the shape.

Presumably, Master Parmonia was establishing the necessary current flows inside her bubbles, but I couldn't perceive anything changing for a few minutes. Then, suddenly, the ring of pyramids burst into the light with a grid of light forming between many of the vertexes. It was some sort of spinning circular pattern. A haze formed in the space in the centre of the rotating ring of pyramids.

Then, through the haze, I saw a pulsing beam of light extend out of the icosahedron and gradually move towards my face, passing through the central axis of the pyramid ring. It grew slowly, almost like some sort of plant, rather than a beam of light. As it passed through the haze, it grew brighter, gaining power somehow from elsewhere. I instinctively tried to duck away from the approaching brightness and suddenly realised that I was held fast, perhaps by some other aspect of the working?

As the beam reached me, my normal vision failed, overwhelmed by the brightness. I felt as my thoughts, my consciousness, were hanging in dark space with all my other senses turned off or blocked in some way. The brightness that I somehow knew was the beam branched out to form a wireframe sphere around my consciousness in all directions and then the wireframe contracted until I could feel pressure building all around me.

Not just around me, I realised. There was a second

presence in here which I recognised must be the glowing entity that I'd encountered before. It seemed to dislike the enclosing sphere and was pushing back against it.

"Help me stabilise the link, please." Parmonia's voice sounded echoey and far off.

The sphere continued to close but irregularly now, in pulses as it pushed against the glowing entity. I got the feeling of effortless power pushing against us. Constricting us. My headache returned worse than before.

The glowing entity was now trying to hold its own, refusing to be constricted further, but the force behind the sphere didn't yet seem satisfied. There was a moment of extreme tension as the two forces fought against each other and I felt as if something must break.

At that moment, several things happened almost at once. The glowing entity bulged out into a direction that I couldn't identify that didn't seem constrained by the sphere, allowing some of my consciousness to follow it. My headache cleared. The sphere clicked down into place and the force behind it vanished. And I blacked out again.

Interlude 1

"I tell you, Davras, I can't wait to get back home. Between having to babysit a load of spoiled brats and trying to put up with the supercilious attitudes of our hosts, I've had about all I can take," said Lavos.

"Calm down, Lavos. Surely the change of scene makes a welcome break from the court?" Davras replied.

The two sat opposite each other at a long wooden table, in a drafty room on the upper floor of the Temple. Both were sweating from the heat and they'd already finished the jug of lukewarm water that had been placed on the table before the Sahrayan officials had been escorted in.

"Precious little, to be honest," said Lavos. "I'll be grateful to hand this responsibility over to you in the future."

"Along those lines, what's the form for the rest of the visit?"

"They'll keep us waiting here for a while longer, and will eventually send some junior official to announce their decision on which candidates have and have not been accepted," said Lavos. "We'll then sign some forms relating to the acceptances and agreeing to payments due. They will escort everyone not accepted for training, including ourselves, back to one of those wretched stone platforms. We'll be sent back home, and it'll then be our job to soothe the ruffled feathers of the parents whose snotty-nosed children have been rejected."

"Not all the children are that bad, surely? For example, the Salai kid seems well behaved enough, and I barely heard a word out of Orchan," said Davras.

"Yes, there are a few exceptions. Although, I'm not sure what's happened with Orchan. Jemi says that he never returned yesterday, which is ominous and somewhat unprecedented. Maybe he managed to upset our hosts in some way?" said Lavos.

Davras was about to reply, but then fell silent as the door at the end of the room opened. Lavos swung round to regard the newcomer and, after a moment of hesitation, relaxed and remained seated after he had recognised him.

"Ah, Lamman, thank you for joining us. Are you ready to discuss the results of the testing then?" said Lavos.

Then another figure entered, following Lamman into the room, and Lavos's eyes widened. He sprung to his feet and made a deep bow. Taken off guard, Davras followed his example clumsily.

"Senior Counsel Islina. We are deeply honoured by your presence," said Lavos.

Islina walked to the table, still looking as pristine as she had when she'd met with Orchan earlier in the day and nodded.

"Gentlemen, please resume your seats. I made the decision to attend this meeting since there is an item on which Lamman requires... assistance. Please, continue as usual until we get to that point," said Islina. She then took a seat a little way up the table, while Lamman took a seat next to Davras, nearly across from Lavos.

Several servants entered, with new jugs of chilled water, fresh glasses, and a selection of chilled desert delicacies. Lamman waited for them to leave before talking.

"So, Lavos, Davras, let us recap where we are. You brought twelve candidates with you this time. Eleven of them represented standard requests for mentorship. Of those..." Lamman consulted a piece of paper concealed in a file and continued, "We can accept three candidates: Silliva of the house of Dorsa; Gon of the estate of Ledfull; and Jemi of the barony of Salai. The first two are accepted for one month stays, the third will also be allowed to stay for one month, but with the option to extend to up to six months at the Guild's discretion after the probationary period. Here is a tabulation of the results along with standard agreements for accepted students for you to approve, including a commitment to cover the associated fees."

"Some of the rejected candidates represent powerful families," said Lavos. "Can I request whether there might be any grounds for reconsidering your judgement on any of them?" It was clear that Lavos didn't particularly expect them to take this request seriously, but wanted to be able to tell their parents that he had done his best.

"I'm afraid not. Our decision is definitive and final," said Lamman.

Lavos carefully read through the sheets of paper

and then laboriously signed and sealed the three acceptance papers and returned them to Lamman. He then looked up enquiringly.

"Thank you for the update on those eleven candidates," he said. "Can I ask what the decision is on Scordo Orchan and his request to enroll for an elementary course?"

"Yes, well, err Orchan has..." begun Lamman and glanced sideways at Islina.

"I am probably best placed to talk to Scordo Orchan's position," she cut in smoothly. "I am able to relay the news that after various discussions with the Guild and with officials of Zaronia, he has decided to, as it were, resume his Zaronian citizenship. On that basis, I'm pleased to be able to assure you that he is no longer your responsibility. You need not concern yourself with him further."

There was a pause while Lavos and Davras processed this statement.

"That's all rather extraordinary news," said Lavos carefully. "I wasn't aware that he actually had a Zaronian citizenship to resume... Nor any desire to do so. Are you able to provide any more... details?"

"Of course. I agree that it is a slightly unusual position, but that is in line with the somewhat unique circumstances associated with our historical decision to allow Envoy Orchan Senior to foster the boy. I'm not sure how familiar you are with that subject?" said Islina.

"Well, certainly, I wasn't involved in any way at that time. And the... Envoy... is no longer with us to fill in the details. Are you able to elucidate further?"

said Lavos.

"Regrettable, of course," said Islina. "Let me share these with you." She paused and without any particular hurry removed a couple of sheets of paper from her satchel and handed them down the table.

"This is a copy that I requested to be taken of a transcript of the original closed hearing decision to allow the Envoy's fostership request. And this is a duplicate document signed today by Orchan and a representative of the Zaronian court, confirming his decision to resume his citizenship of Zaronia, and renouncing any responsibilities to the state of Sahrayan as may may be deemed to exist." She shrugged and Lavos distinctly detected a subtext of "take it or leave it."

Lavos carefully took the documents and read through them carefully. On the face of it, the extract confirmed what Islina had said, but as a recent copy from a source which could never be checked, it was difficult to be sure. The renouncement was clear enough, however, and the signature and seal would be simple enough to check back in Sahraya. It would be best to accept them for now.

It wasn't as if he actually cared about the brat of the wood peddlers in any case. No-one was ever even going to comment on this. It was just that he had the distinct impression that something unusual was going on here and that he couldn't help thinking that there was a possibility Sahraya was losing out.

"Well, that all seems in order," he said. "It's something of a blow, however. Our kingdom is not overly blessed with magical ability, and we were looking forward to the possibility of welcoming some homegrown, as it were, talent."

"Indeed, that's certainly unfortunate. But you weren't looking forward to it enough to actually support his application, were you? I don't believe we received any endorsement of his application as with the other candidates. Unless I've gravely misunderstood, you were funding neither his application nor potential fees yourselves either?"

Lavos concealed a wince. She had the right of it there.

"However, we are certainly keen to ensure that the kingdom of Sahraya continues to prosper," she said. "After all, we very much appreciate your ongoing support. Your trade is very valuable to us. As an independent matter, the Guild has been considering extending our representation with you for some time."

Lavos sat up straighter and was suddenly listening very carefully. He hadn't been exaggerating when he had described the lack of magical ability in Sahraya. Indeed, it was a constant point of friction in his dealings with the royal family. The one Zaronian mage permanently stationed in Sahraya was assigned to their embassy and had little time for anything else other than embassy and Guild business. If he could be seen to obtain a concession here, it could be beneficial to his future.

"We are proposing to assign a second, senior, Guild mage to Sahraya," said Islina. "We would propose that this one be stationed permanently within the Sahrayan court. They would do their best to ensure that they kept up to date with all the necessary issues and provide whatever assistance that they could. A royal mage adviser, if you like."

She slipped another sheaf of papers out of the folder and passed it down the table. Lavos perused it carefully. More of their damn archaic Zaronian, he noted, but he was at least somewhat familiar with the terminology. As far as he could tell, the document was exactly as Islina described it. Obviously, part of the conditions of the agreement placed strictures on the Sahrayan court to keep the mage adviser informed about necessary policy and associated discussions, but that was only sensible. And the ability to rely on a expert truth-speaker would be invaluable, let alone anything else that the mage could offer.

"This looks like an extremely favourable gesture, Senior Counsel," he said. "The agreement will require ratification by our most senior officials, of course, but I would expect…"

"Perhaps you would like to document your thoughts and convey the offer to your court immediately? We will make a transport box available to you. You could request that they ratify this document, describing the position on Scordo Orchan, at the same time."

Lavos took the hint and agreed. Later that day, the agreements, duly executed by the Sahrayan court, were returned to Zaronia.

CHAPTER SIX

Trip to the Annex

This time I woke in my bed from the night before. I thought ruefully that I was getting a little tired of passing out.

The light was on and I suddenly noticed Dorrall seated at the other side of the room, lost in a book. I sat up and cleared my throat to attract his attention.

"Hmph? Oh, Scordo, excellent. That didn't take too long then. How are you feeling?"

"Not too bad," I admitted. I could still feel the enclosing sphere around my consciousness. A constant feeling of faint sensation, similar to the feeling of a piece of jewellery in contact with the skin. "Is the ceremony complete? Am I an apprentice now?"

"Yes, fully sealed to the Guild. Master Parmonia said that there was a little difficulty during the ceremony, probably because of the recent binding, but all the tests show that your seal is unblemished and your link to the Construct active."

"You can travel on to the Annex with the other apprentices in the morning. You'll be collected after you've eaten."

"Training doesn't take place in the Temple then?" I asked. The rest of his comments I filed for further consideration. I was already reasonably confident that I had worked out the purpose of the sealing ceremony.

"Here? No, not at all. Other than the caves of emergence, the Temple is mostly only used for formal purposes these days. Far too drafty and infested by other vermin. I heard some sounds of spikkan occupation in your vents, by the way, but I took care of it. Please notify the guard if you hear anything unsettling again. Of course, you would have remained here in the Temple as a lay student, but in the more occupied and guarded wings above the surface."

"I won't be seeing the other Sahrayans much, then?"

"Them? No, it's unlikely. It's easiest to isolate them here, so that they don't inadvertently run across something that they're not allowed to know. I believe your delegation was already notified about your decision to join us, so that loose end is closed down," he said.

We exchanged a few more pleasantries and then Dorrall left, saying that he hoped to meet me again soon. For my part, I thanked him for his help. For all his garrulousness, it was clear that he had been trying his best to help me.

After he'd left, I lay thinking for a few minutes. Then I stood up and moved to gaze at the mirror in the bathroom. As I expected, the image of a sphere lay in the centre of my forehead. A magical seal then, not a tattoo or a brand. As an experiment, I thought about telling the Sahrayan officials about the details of the magical working that I'd observed. It felt as if the seal suddenly tightened on my consciousness for a moment. It was only a warning, and I was sure that further layers of punishment or intervention were possible. I probably should have expected this and I could only assume that my translation of the indenture document had been a little... incomplete.

***

The next morning, I was awakened early with breakfast. I had barely touched the food left in my room the previous night and I found I was ravenous. Once my meal and other morning necessities were complete, a squad of guards collected me and I was escorted down a series of corridors to meet up with a group of apprentices that I recognised from the crystal cave (the cave of emergence, I supposed) of the previous day.

We all bore an identical seal of the sphere, but I saw one peculiarity. The previous day, I'd thought that the heads of Dorrall, Delisan and Parmonia were glowing slightly. That wasn't true of most of the other apprentices. In fact, only one of them showed a glow from her head: the blonde apprentice that had fainted during the emergence.

We were quickly bustled up a couple of flights of stairs and out into a cave lit by daylight, the first daylight I'd seen since I'd been escorted to the testing two days before. The far end of the space was open to the desert, and a variety of what must be vehicles were dotted around the floor of the cavern. We were all shown over towards something that I assumed must be the conveyance to the Annex that Dorrall had been talking about.

It was being supervised by a couple of much older men with two symbols on their seals: a pyramid within a circle. Glowing heads again. The vehicle was a large sledge about waist-height, which had been carved out of stone. I examined it more closely and found that it was a dark red colour, but with a speckled black pattern across it. Further investigation showed me that the pattern was sand embedded into the strata of the rock. The sledge had been carved with a number of curved deressions cut into it. As people began to be assigned positions, I saw them lying down on their backs in the curves, facing the front with their heads higher than their feet and their bodies supported at every point. The sides of their head were cushioned in some way by wads of material set into the stone. On the chest of each person, a crystal Device was being placed.

The back of the sledge had a mechanism built into it in the centre and I saw one of the more senior Guild members take a place next to it. His colleague took up position in the sledge's front with a clear view of the cave in front. In contrast to everyone else, he was lying on his stomach, able to reach an array of additional mechanisms. For steering, perhaps?

I was assigned to a seat towards the back of the sledge on the right-hand side, so I would be able to look out sideways. Next to me was the blonde-haired apprentice with the faintly glowing head. My bag was placed into a compartment under my legs, which clicked closed. As soon as a crystal Device was placed on my chest, I found myself being pressed down into the sledge, essentially immobile. Not unpleasant, but I certainly got the feeling that I wasn't going anywhere until someone removed the crystal.

"Hello," said my companion. "My name is

Anyana. I don't think we've met before. Were you the other successful candidate at yesterday's emergence?"

I quickly introduced myself and provided a quick overview of the last couple of days.

"From Sahraya?" she replied. "That's a surprise. And only just made an apprentice. Wait until the others find out that a newbie beat them." She was clearly amused rather than upset, and I felt a little more well-disposed towards her.

"Umm, is there anything you can tell me about this?" I asked, pointing at my head.

"The Glowling? You don't... Well... That is..." she seemed to think carefully. "I'm not sure that I should risk telling you what I know before your master has properly briefed you. Particularly if Master Logross is involved in some way." She put particular stress on his name and shuddered.

"Let's say that it's not a bad thing. The opposite, really. It will be incredibly valuable to your magic and you'd be unlikely ever to graduate from your apprenticeship without one. That's why the others will be so jealous: Most of us have been apprentices for three or four years and for many people, it was the first time that they'd been allowed to try to bond. The third for me."

"OK, thank you. Can I ask about Logross then? The other Guild members I've met seemed to be scared by him," I said.

"Him? He's got a reputation as a hardass.", said Anyana. "Incredibly picky about other peoples' technique and blunt about telling them so. It must be working for him, though: he's a high-flyer. Already a senior member of the Guild, despite the fact he can't be much older than thirty. I've never talked to him myself, but you hear complaints from some of the more senior students who go to him for mentoring."

"That about sums up how my interview went with him. I didn't get the impression he cared for me at all. Still, he must have approved my entry, I guess. Where are we going now?"

"To the Annex. It's the main living and teaching base for the Guild, and it's about fifty miles away across the open desert. Far more comfortable and safer than the Temple. Lots of facilities and we won't need to be guarded and escorted at all times. Ummm. You're going to find the journey quite... exciting, though. I assume you've never travelled like this before?"

"No," I admitted. "What exactly do you mean by exciting?"

"I wouldn't want to spoil the surprise," she added with a sly smile. "It looks as if we are ready to go." She indicated our surrounding with her eyebrows and a faint move of her head.

I gazed around as best as I could, given my near immobility. It felt as if I weighed several times more than usual. The other apprentices had all been loaded, along with a squad of guards. They were well armed with swords or bows stored in cubbyholes next to them, besides the usual spears. Both the more senior Guild members were in position and were talking to each other through a speaking tube.

There was a sudden jerk upward, and it felt as though the sledge had moved a few inches up into the air, pulling slightly out of the sand. Then we moved forward, accelerating smoothly, reaching a reasonable walking pace before we emerged through the cavern entrance into the red and purple light that I remembered from my arrival at the Temple.

It was windy outside, but not as much sand was reaching my face as I expected. Focusing above me, I saw some sort of hazy boundary a few inches away. Some sort of protective magic, perhaps?

By now, we were running down a gentle slope, still accelerating gently. After a few hundred yards, I started to see buildings around us as we glided past a small village, maybe thirty or forty homes. It was mostly made up of low mud huts, set closely together. Some people had muffled themselves in sack-cloth against the weather, moving around. Other figures with heavily weathered faces stood around talking, ignoring the sand. There was trading going on, with small bags of vegetables or other produce changing hands.

From what I could see, I got the impression that most of the people I was seeing were poor and malnourished. The huts were certainly rather squalid, held together with repeated patching. I could see a single well on the edge of the town, with a long line waiting at it. Many of the people looked at us, some with apathy, some with what looked like open hostility.

I glanced over at Anyana. She wasn't paying attention to the locals, but was concentrating on breathing steadily and she was clearly tensed for something. I wondered how long it would take us to reach the Annex. At the speed I'd travelled on the lumber caravan to the Sahrayan capital, it would have taken several days of travel, but that had involved several stops per day. Plus, we were already travelling faster than the caravan at a slow jogging pace. We were now a few hundred yards outside the village and a large sand dune, maybe a hundred feet high, loomed ahead of us. I wondered how we would get around it.

Suddenly, the sledge lurched forward faster, at least doubling our pace. We were still heading directly at the dune and I realised that they planned to go straight up the side. And we did. The pace of the sledge didn't falter as we shot up the steep slope leading towards the crest. If anything, we got a little faster. Then we hit the top and immediately plunged down the far side. For all our speed, it felt as if the sledge was attached to the ground. I'd expected there to be some feeling of weightlessness as we reached the very peak of the hill, but no, we simply flipped forward into a sudden fast descent. Then we bottomed out and shot up the side of another dune. My stomach protested and I regretted the size of my breakfast. I remained pressed in place to the sledge, however, with none of this motion causing me to slip about at all. Indeed, I might have felt better if it had: the motion was all so very unnatural.

I looked sideways at Anyana and tried to grind out some speech despite the state of my stomach. "I... see... what... you...mean...", I managed. "Will it... all... be like... this?"

She giggled. "Wait until we hit the flatter stretches of the desert and they can see farther ahead. They'll really open up the speed at that point. We should be at

Starting Sphere

the Annex in a couple of hours, barring incidents."

Neither the promise of more speed, nor the casual mention of 'incidents', sounded promising to me. I inspected what I could see of the desert, peering through the blowing sands for anything else. It looked like we were moving through a prepared route, small tangled piles of broken stone had been piled about ten feet to the side of of our course, with the occasional gigantic pile probably acting as a landmark.

Every now and again, I saw a pile of bones. Most of these looked like they were animals unfamiliar to me: some large birds several feet high, what looked like a snake maybe ten feet long, some sort of four-legged animal. Once or twice, I saw a fresher corpse, but these were usually covered by clouds of birds, and I couldn't make them out.

About thirty minutes into the journey, I suddenly caught a sight of other people. A line of about twenty-five figures, all heavily muffled in robes coloured to match the reds and purples of the surrounding sands, almost indistinguishable from their background. Several of them bore obvious weapons. They were heading away from us, so I couldn't make out more details and I drew a calming breath as they failed to react to our passing. I quickly lost sight of them.

I won't say much more about our journey, because I don't enjoy thinking about it. Anyana was right. They did speed up as they hit the desert flats, far faster than the pace of the fastest horse I'd ever seen. Having said that, it was the unnatural motion of the ups and downs that affected me most. It felt as though it shouldn't be possible to move up and down at that speed, with the sledge sticking to the surface and us sticking to the sledge.

Towards the end of the ordeal, I realised that the landscape ahead was changing and the weather improving. Or at least, the wind and sand gradually dropped away, and the sun beat down more fiercely. Ahead, we started to curve towards a shallow line of stone hills. The central one looked different in some way and as we approached, I saw signs of civilisation. Windows and doors were carved in the sheer walls of the rock-face to a height of maybe a hundred feet. Flags and other tapestries hung between them.

I realised we were heading towards a wide, low opening in the rock. Another cave? I also saw other people. A group of around a dozen people were running some sort of course, others were engaged in other physical activity. Perhaps a game? Or weapons practice? A line of heavily loaded pack animals headed towards another cave entrance, presumably bringing supplies. Other people were sitting by themselves or in small groups.

We swept past them and into the entrance cave. It ran for a few hundred metres into the mountain and then opened out into a much bigger cavern. We continued to slow as we picked our way through other vehicles that looked to have been abandoned haphazardly. I realised we were heading towards a small group of people waiting at the back of the space.

Finally, we sank to a halt, and servants rushed over to free us from our constraints. I retrieved my bag and managed to get back onto my feet. I stood up and then tried to step forward. I nearly fell, and would have done so if Anyana, coming up behind me, hadn't caught my arm.

Starting Sphere

"Steady," she said. "Just let your feeling of balance recover. I warned you it was going to be bad." Her smile showed she thought this was amusing, but her expression was sympathetic rather than gleeful.

"Actually, I think you suggested that it would be 'exciting'. About as exciting as I imagine jumping off a cliff would be," I replied.

She shrugged. "Well, you're done now, and I doubt you'll be called on again to travel anytime soon. That's one reason the others will all be jealous of you. They'll still need to make the trip twice each time until they're successful."

"Ouch. I'll consider myself lucky then."

"You do that. Anyway, I need to get back to my master and tell him the news. Nice to meet you, Scordo. I hope I'll see you again soon, if your new Master lets you out, that is. You'll probably be met here." With that, she danced away towards one of the doorways at the back of the room.

"Apprentice Scordo? Pleased to meet you," came a voice from away to my side.

CHAPTER SEVEN
Master Logross

I turned to see a young man approaching me across the cavern. He must have entered while I was talking with Anyana. He was about seventeen, maybe a year or two older than me, with shortcut black hair. Both of his arms had old burn marks visible, and a nasty scar on his cheek suggested he'd been hit with something sharp at some point. He had what I was quickly recognising to be the standard double seal with a sphere with a pyramid suspended in it.

"I'm Artisan Mikkalini. Call me Mikka," he said while grabbing and shaking my hand. "Master Logross asked me to find you and bring you back to our quarters."

"Master Logross?" I queried, hoping that this didn't mean what I feared. "Does that mean that I've been assigned to him?"

I suspect my face painted an interesting picture because Mikka began to laugh. "I see he's made another friend already," he said between laughs. "Assigned isn't exactly the word. He overruled the standard selection process to insist that you be assigned to him personally."

"Don't worry! It might not be as bad as you

think," he continued quickly, while still holding my arm. Perhaps he was afraid I might run away? I might have considered it.

"He is, I will allow, irritable, irritating, infuriating, and downright imperious at times, but he truly knows his stuff when it comes to the magical arts. I should know, after all. I've been assigned to him for five years. That's four as his personal apprentice after I joined, before he became sufficiently high and mighty that he could demand his own way, and then one year since I made Artisan."

"All right," I said slowly. "I doubt I've got any actual choice in the matter at this point, anyway."

"That's the spirit," Mikka replied. "Let's get out of this storage room and into the Annex proper and down to Master Logross's rooms."

***

We walked along corridors and down staircases for what must have been about half a mile. The building was more lively than the Temple. The floors were more recently swept, there were decorations on the walls and other people passed us as we walked. I noticed, however, that, as we approached our destination, things got quieter.

Finally, we reached a heavy-looking carved door at the end of a corridor.

Some Masters have rooms in the upper levels, and a few even have windows," noted Mikka as we approached the door. "But Master Logross insisted on these. Most people think that it's because we get more space, but I think he prefers hiding away down here."

He paused in front of the door, and it suddenly

clicked open.

"We'll have to add your mana signature," he commented, and we entered.

The entry lobby to the suite of rooms was large, comfortable, and well lit. There were several low couches and tables, and a dining table set to the side. Across from the entrance was another set of carved double doors, as impressive as the first pair. Set around the rest of the walls were a number of other doorways. Mikka indicated each of the smaller doorways in turn.

"Kitchen. Bathroom. My quarters. Your quarters. A set of work rooms through there and we'll dedicate one to you. And in there," he said, pointing at the double doors, "is the Master's work room. His personal rooms, bedroom, kitchen, private entertaining space and so on, open off that.

"Would you like to get freshened up?" he continued. "He won't stray out of his lair until we disturb him."

I took advantage of the bathroom and then sat down. I accepted a drink from Mikka to clear my throat of the taste of sand and travel. My stomach was feeling a little better after the journey. After about a quarter of an hour, I reluctantly got back to my feet.

"Let's do this," I said, taking a deep breath. Mikka smiled sympathetically, but didn't comment. He moved over to the double doors and knocked loudly. After a pause, the doors swung open inwards and I heard a voice say, "Enter."

We entered.

As I crossed the threshold, I stopped, amazed. The

space was vast, fully fifty feet across in all dimensions, with a ceiling going up over three times my height. The curving walls were almost entirely covered with finely carved and inlaid wooden panelling. I counted at least a dozen types of wood at a single glance. The panelling was covered in many places with banks of shelving and with several large blackboards. Tacked here and there were large sheets of parchment with runes and diagrams. The shelves were filled with hundred of books and scrolls, many complex looking devices and arrays of jars, some made of glass and some of pottery. There was also a wooden doorway which presumably led to the Master's private quarters.

Closer to the doorway was a carved stone circle in the floor that reminded me of the ones on the transport platforms near the Temple. The carved circle was surrounded in turn by a circle of closely packed crystal Devices, each with a lens pointing upwards. Inside these concentric circles was the only part of the floor where the stone floor was visible. A patchwork quilt of rugs and matting covered the rest of the room.

A number of benches and tables lay around the room, covered in yet more books, Devices, and other clutter.

I gaped. I'd rarely seen a room more luxuriously furnished and never so many... things in one place. It was an amalgam of every library I'd ever seen. I could barely resist the urge to investigate.

In the centre of all of this, sitting on the other side of a massive, bare desk set in the middle of the room, was Master Logross, looking sour and impatient.

"I see you found him at last, Artisan. Please remain, this will not take long," Master Logross said. He turned his attention to me.

"Greetings, apprentice. Senior Artisan Dorrall no doubt told you that you had potential as a mage. That is true, and the only reason that I agreed to support your application. But do you know what the phrase 'has potential' means to me?"

"No, Sir," I replied carefully. I couldn't imagine that this was going to be good. It wasn't.

"It means that right now, you are utterly failing to deliver on that potential. Your practical skills are less adequate than those of many apprentices four years your junior. Your theoretical knowledge is almost entirely non-existent. The same can be said of your knowledge of the Guild."

He paused, almost challenging me with his eyes to object to his comments. I stayed silent and nodded in acceptance, looking down at the floor.

"Very well. Artisan!" said Master Logross.

"Yes, Sir," replied Mikka promptly.

"Take this boy away and bring him back when he is no longer entirely inadequate. You have six months."

"Yes, Sir," said Mikka without surprise.

"Dismissed," said Master Logross and turned away. We left without speaking further and the doors clicked closed behind us.

***

We sat back on some of the low seating in the lobby area facing each other. Mikka broke the silence first.

"That was more or less what I was expecting.

More positive if anything."

"More positive?" I asked. "In comparison with what, exactly?"

"He admitted that you had potential for a start. Mostly, I have to endure rants about how he is forced to interact with other Guild members who have no potential at all. What's more, he wouldn't have named a specific time period, six months, unless he thought you were capable of it."

I snorted a little at this. It sounded like he was reading a little much into Master Logross's choice of words.

"Let's discuss what's going to happen from here," said Mikka. "Effectively, he's appointed me to act as your mentor in his stead, until he thinks it worthwhile for him to get involved directly. That's not unusual in the Guild, training is often arranged like that. However, what is unusual are Master Logross's high standards for competence. We'll get started on that tomorrow morning. For now, do you have any general questions that you want me to answer?"

I thought quickly and prioritised my questions. I pointed at my forehead. "The seals. I take it they denote levels of seniority in some way, correct? No one has really explained."

He sighed and narrowed his eyes. "Unless I miss my mark, no one has explained anything about anything. Correct?"

I nodded.

"That's what I thought. I'll do what I can to answer your initial questions right now, but most times, I'll be saying 'but it's more complicated than that'... and I'll point you at further reading."

I nodded again.

"All right, so in practice, you're mostly right about what you need to know about the seals. Apprentices have a single spherical seal, Junior Artisans a tetrahedron inside a sphere, and so on, down the table of regular solids. Except that at the heart of it, the seals have nothing formally to do with Guild hierarchy at all. Instead, they relate more or less directly to where you have reached in your magical ability and what you are allowed to be taught. And that's not true either, because they're primarily about enforcement. As you grow more powerful and learn more of the secrets of the Guild, then the rules that dictate your conduct become more and more regulated, until you end up like Master Logross and know most things, but can't actually tell them to anyone!"

In an undertone he added, "At least, that's what he says, personally I think he's just not keen on answering questions."

I blinked, trying to absorb the implications of all of that while Mikka continued.

"And even then, that's not the complete picture, because there are a lot of exceptions. Many Guild members are deemed unsuitable to progress to higher levels of magic or may choose to specialise in a particular realm. Sometimes, that means that they have more seniority than you'd guess at first sight. For example, the operators of the hover sledge you came in on had what would normally be considered Junior Artisan seals, correct?"

"That's right," I confirmed.

"But in practice, within their own area of operations, they are significantly more senior than that. I'd jump to obey them if they requested something."

"How would I know who I should obey, then?" I asked.

"You'll learn. One of the books that I'll give you will provide a lot more detail on the structure of the Guild and the specialisations."

"I met someone else who had a double circle tattoo," I prompted, thinking of Islina.

Mikka winced. "Lawyer?" he asked.

"Correct," I confirmed. "She brought my indenture agreement."

"For someone who's been here such a short time, you've met a lot of senior people," said Mikka. "Let's say that there are a number of people who do not... progress... as apprentices but choose to specialise into other fields of value to the Guild. Some of these rise stratospherically high in the Guild and learn more of its secrets than would normally be entrusted to an apprentice seal. To recognise these individuals and to reinforce their seals, a second spherical seal is applied. The person you encountered must be seriously senior in the Guild hierarchy and probably deeply involved in the court as well."

I blinked again and must have looked confused at this mention of the court.

"Ah, yes, our relationship with Zaronian court. I would imagine that you think the Guild is a group of magical experts and that the royal court is responsible for ruling Zaronia, defending the common people and all of that, possibly calling on the Guild for advice. Is that correct?"

"Yes, that's how I've always heard of things described," I said.

"And that's how it is supposed to appear outside of Zaronia, and how it probably started off. In practice, however, the Guild has now gained sufficient... influence... that in practice the court is merely an adjunct to the Guild, largely rubber stamping its decisions."

I thought about this. If the Guild controlled the Zaronian court, then how much interest did the Guild have in helping the common people of Zaronia? Was that the reason the villagers I'd seen had been so antagonistic to our sledge?

"Any other questions for now?" prompted Mikka.

"Yes," I said. I tapped my head. "What's this thing in my head?"

"Ah. Exactly," said Mikka. "That's not a question I can answer in a way that will fully satisfy you. I can tell you why it's there, but not a lot about what it is, because that's not something that we're allowed to know enough about.

"Let me start off trying to answer your question of 'what'. They are formally called 'Entities' by the Guild and sometimes by the informal term of 'Glowlings'. I believe they used to have other names and a wide variety of other superstitions attached to them, but that branch of study was deprecated and removed from the Guild archives. At least at our level. They are some sort of energy creature that communicates through mind-to-mind contact and after they enter this world are bonded to the minds of apprentices. The only places that I know of that they can be found in their unbonded state is in the various crystal caves under the Temple. Indeed, they're probably the original reason why it was built there."

"OK, that's generally uninformative," I said. "Let's try 'Why', then?"

"Why? Because they're incredibly useful for people trying to do magic. They can provide you with a much better magical vision for a start, allowing you to see seals and other workings more clearly, and even get a glimpse of other mages' mana workings without further tools. When they become more mature, they have some sort of idiot savant ability to understand geometry, sometimes actually contributing to your mana shaping process."

"That does sound useful," I said. "I gather that I'm lucky to have been bonded to one early in my apprenticeship, correct?"

"Very lucky," Mikka confirmed. "Master Logross's influence, I'd guess."

We talked for a little longer, but Mikka provided no more revelations. He soon excused himself to locate some reading matter to give me. Before he went, he left me with a final warning.

"You've got an enormous challenge ahead of you. To meet the Master's timetable, you need to catch up with the other apprentices in the next six months. That's going to require a lot of hard, strenuous work, mostly training by yourself to hone your skills."

"I'm not afraid of working hard," I said. "I've been

studying magic by myself for years. I feel I just need some more guidance and pointers to progress."

CHAPTER EIGHT
Training begins

It turns out that I didn't really know what Mikka had meant by 'hard work'. Previously, I'd spent a few hours a day playing with my skill at mana manipulation while sitting in a comfortable seat in my father's library, or while sitting cross-legged on the moss under a tree in the forests of Arbran. That differed wildly from the experience of spending over twelve hours a day in a windowless cell repeating exactly the same exercise ad nauseam.

Who'd have guessed, right?

***

The next day, after a hurried breakfast, Mikka had sat me down in one of our work rooms and asked to see me form a mana sphere.

I did so, carefully thickening the mana to form a perfectly spherical shell which I then filled and then held stable in mid-air. While I did this, Mikka had carefully extracted a pair of stone-framed eyeglasses with crystal lenses and adjusted them while staring at the spot in the air where I was forming the sphere.

"OK, that's a good place to start," he said. "I see nothing wrong with the shape of the sphere and the thickness of the shell looks like a good default choice.

The mana density looks a bit low, we will need to work on that. The first big issue, however, is the speed. You took several minutes to form that. You need to be faster - a lot faster."

"I can accept that," I said. "I was maybe going a little slow to ensure that it was perfect, but I'd already got the idea that I needed to do better. What sort of speed am I aiming at?"

"Let's turn that question around," said Mikka. "Let's say that you're walking down a corridor and a spikkan drops from the ceiling in front of you."

He saw my confusion and elaborated, "A spikkan is huge spider, flesh eater, carrion usually, but not averse to attacking isolated humans. Even more dangerous in packs."

I swallowed. So that was what had attacked me from behind the ventilation grating in the Temple?

Mike continued, "So, in that scenario, how quickly would you want to cast a spell to defend yourself?"

"Pretty damn quickly, I guess," I replied.

"Exactly. Ultimately, you need to aim at a cast time of seconds or less. For now, concentrate on keeping the same quality of sphere while gradually improving the time."

"And how do I do that?" I asked, without real hope he was about to suggest some sort of shortcut.

Mikka smiled nastily. "Practice," he said. "Lots and lots of practice."

He removed a wooden box from a bag and I saw a clock face with a single hand and a button on the top.

"This is a timer, which will record up to a five-minute time period," he said. "Please use this to measure your times on at least an hourly basis. I'll take a look at the end of each day."

Each day? This was going to be a long haul, then. I pointed towards his eyeglasses, which he had removed after my mana sphere had formed.

"Can I ask about those, please?" I said.

"Of course. Please don't hesitate to ask anything at any time. Otherwise, I won't know what to explain. These are a tool to allow a mage to study someone else's mana working. Your Glowling does a rough job of this, but until it matures and you get very experienced, some additional help can be absolutely vital. By adjusting the levers at the side, I can change the focus to examine the nature of the mana shell, measure the density of the contents, and observe mana currents. There are probably other functions that I haven't learned yet." He patted the Device affectionately.

"Master Logross lent me these this morning. They've got a far more delicate degree of control than the ones I used in practice. I couldn't come close to buying a pair for myself. Now, I have my own work to do. Please start practising and I will swing by again later. Please help yourself to food and drink from the kitchen."

So, I started my practice.

I would hit the button to start the timer, form a mana bubble, and then stop the timer. I'd then release the mana and start all over again. Initially, my results were all around three minutes, about the same as I'd achieved in my test a couple of days earlier. Over the course of the next few hours, I managed to cut that down to around two-thirds of the time.

This pleased me as an immediate win. I also realised that I was already exhausted. The unaccustomed strain of pulling mana from my reserves again and again was quickly tiring me out.

As I got more and more tired, my concentration wavered a little and mistakes crept into my casting. In particular, I found it easy to misjudge the shape of the shell slightly and form something other than a perfect sphere. Usually, this took the shape of a slightly squashed ball. Almost without exception, that meant that when I tried to fill the malformed sphere with mana, it would burst, and the mana would puff away into thin air. After some practice, I found I could hold the spheroid stable for a few seconds but it always burst eventually and the effort involved exhausted me even more than the usual exercise.

I managed a little less than twelve hours of practice that first day. True to his word, Mikka popped in to check on me every hour or two, but had little additional advice to share. By the end of that day, I had cut my casting time down to a minute and a half. Still far too long to be exposed to the attacks of a feral giant spider! I dragged my way back to my room and collapsed on the bed and was asleep nearly before I lay down.

The next day, I made a quick breakfast and then returned to the training room without prompting. After another twelve hours or so of mind-numbing repetition, I managed to shave my time down to around a minute.

***

Towards the end of that second day, I was surprised to hear Master Logross's voice emanating out of the air beside me.

"Come here," was his abrupt command.

It wasn't the magic involved in the summons that surprised me, but that it had happened at all. I'd got the impression that the Master had not been planning to interact with me until Mikka had assured him I had improved sufficiently. It turns out that I had misjudged him. During that first period of my formal training, he summoned me to perform in front of him every couple of days.

That first time, I stood up uncertainly and walked out of the training rooms. I found the double door to Master Logross's work room open and entered. There he was again, lurking behind his desk. He didn't bother with small talk.

"Show me," he said.

I swallowed and, careful to concentrate hard on the shape, formed a mana bubble between us. It took around a minute.

"Again."

I released the mana and repeated the process.

"Again."

Another mana bubble. I was proud that I was managing to maintain my speed.

"Release."

There was a long pause as he looked at me. Then he spoke.

"You're allowing all the mana to evaporate on release. Has it not occurred to you to reabsorb as much of the unspent mana as you can?" His tone was withering.

I stood looking at him, open-mouthed. No, it hadn't occurred to me. I hadn't the faintest idea that this was possible. Nothing I'd read had even hinted at it. This wouldn't improve my forming speed, but had the potential to reduce the strain on my system considerably by reducing the amount of mana I needed to regenerate each time.

I thought of asking him how to actually do this, but decided that even if he was prepared to show me (and I'm sure he wouldn't have been), I'd rather practise actual methods with Mikka.

I did, however, manage to ask a couple of questions about the theory.

"Thank you. May I ask, can I only absorb mana from an unused mana bubble? Or is it possible to do so after an actual working?"

"Perfectly possible. The actual amount of mana that cannot be recovered relates to the amount actually used during the working. At a first approximation that includes the mana used to strengthen the shell, and that expended in generating a result. For example, in your light spell, you would take an immediate reduction from forming the mana spell, and then a gradually increasing one depending on the brightness and duration of the light produced. I will expect you to demonstrate the mathematics behind this in due course," explained Master Logross.

"And is it only my spells where I can reabsorb the mana? Or can I, in theory, absorb mana from someone else's completed casting?" I said.

"In theory, that is possible, but it is potentially

unwise. It is a relatively simple matter to taint the mana when you expel it in a way that will subsequently destabilise the system of anyone else who tries to reabsorb it. The Guild normally teaches the method to Senior Artisans and above, but it is not specifically prohibited to more junior members and is not uncommon in other magical traditions. You would need to be careful only to absorb mana from a mage that you trust. If you needed assistance from another mage, it would be more efficient for them to direct a stream of mana directly to you, or to your working," said Master Logross. "Enough. Dismissed." And he turned his attention to a book open on the desk in front of him.

I was left wondering about what inimical magic users Master Logross was expecting me to encounter. Maybe this was more of his paranoia? In any case, Mikka was able to share hints about the method to absorb mana and I mastered it in a few hours. This did, indeed, noticeably improve my resilience in the repeated practising.

Master Logross summoned me next at the end of the fourth day of my training. By then, I had got my time down to around forty-five seconds, but my average time hadn't improved further in around four hours of additional practice. I had hit a plateau that was holding me back from making further improvements.

Terse as ever, Master Logross demanded that I form a series of bubbles. At the end of this, he simply said, "Form the shell and fill the bubble in parallel. Dismissed."

That represented another bolt of revelation, and

one that I could see how to implement without help from Mikka. It took me about half a day to master the somewhat tricky art of doing two things with my mana at once, but once I had it mastered, the time I was taking to form a bubble immediately dropped from about forty-five seconds to around twenty-five.

Interestingly, when Mikka finally provided me with an introductory theory and practice text book some days later, it mentioned neither of the two techniques that Logross had recommended.

***

By the end of my second week, I had my time down to about fifteen seconds, and I was pleased by my own progress. That represented around a twelve-fold improvement, after all.

"How much further improvement is actually possible?" I asked Mikka. After seven days of slog working on the same exercise again and again, I was ready for something else. "I understand your point about defending against a spikkan, but assuming I had some warning of it approaching, I'd presumably be ready in time."

Mikka sighed and handed me the eyeglasses. I put them on in confusion and looked at him.

"Now," he said, and a mana bubble appeared. I gazed at it. It was a little bigger than mine and the mana was darker, presumably meaning that the mana concentration was denser. My mouth fell open again. As far as I could tell, he formed that instantaneously, certainly in less than a second.

"Now," he said again and a second bubble formed, floating next to it.

"Double," he said, and two bubbles grew at the same time. This time, it must have taken a full second for them to fill.

He maintained them in mid-air for a few seconds and then released all four at once. He silently held out his hand for the eyeglasses, while allowing the lesson to sink in.

After a pause, he spoke. "I don't want to scare you off, but ultimately, that's at least the level of performance that Master Logross is looking for with mana spheres. Who knows, possibly as his hand-picked student, he'll expect you to do better?"

"I'd never...," I began and trailed off. I simply hadn't had an idea that mana could be formed that quickly.

"Don't get me wrong," went on Mikka. "You've shown significant improvement this week, and I'm impressed by that. For an average apprentice, and an average master, your current level of attainment might be good enough, but... well, you remember I called Master Logross infuriating? His standards are his standards."

Strangely enough, I wasn't actually feeling bad about this. I was perfectly happy to think that I was being trained to be better, or at least, faster than most apprentices. That I had now seen with my own eyes that what was being asked from me was actually possible, albeit for someone who has been training for five years longer than me, enthused me with how much further I could go, rather than how little progress I'd already made.

I tried to express this to Mikka. "Thank you very

much for the demonstration. That gives me something to aim at, which is… at lot better than having no sloid target at all."

"I'm glad," said Mikka. "Not that I don't think that you're ready to move on a bit and broaden out your training a little."

"What did you have in mind?" I said, grateful for the idea of a change.

"I'd like you to spend at least half of your time tomorrow getting some familiarity with these books," he said, handing over two volumes from a pile he had brought into the workroom.

I glanced at them one by one. One was an apprentice introduction to mana handling. Looking at the contents, it didn't cover many more practical skills than I had already, but I suspected that a slightly more formal approach to the theory and understanding the terminology was going to be a prerequisite for future study. I nodded and turned to the other.

This was different. It was a thick volume labelled "A prymer to the rules and practyces of the guyld".

"Don't let the title fool you," said Mikka. "In essence, this contains everything you need to know as an apprentice. All the rules that you're sealed to obey and uphold for a start."

"Is it written in more archaic Zaronian?" I said with some feeling.

"Probably not as bad as your indenture," Mikka said with a smile. We'd discussed the gaps in my understanding when it came to that document. "I've done what I can for you, however." He handed me a third volume.

This was much thinner and was an introductory guide to the archaic Zaronian language aimed at beginning law students. I thanked him with some feeling.

"Continue to concentrate on improving your fluency with mana forming, and working through some of these for the next couple of days," said Mikka. After that, I think there will be some bigger changes."

CHAPTER NINE
The Annex

Over the next few days, I shaved another couple of seconds off my forming time. More promisingly, I felt I was packing more mana density into the sphere as well, without compromising my speed. Despite my initial dismissal of the textbook that Mikka had, I found it had a few sensible nuggets of advice that contributed to my improvements.

The Guild handbook, despite the help of the language guide, was hard going, but rewarding. Most of the initial material was straightforward. There were masses of detail on the hierarchical structure of the Guild (apprentice, Junior Artisans, and so on), Guild uniforms, holidays, the format of Guild communications and suchlike. These were followed by long tables of the names of previous masters of the Guild and their dates. There were pages of warnings about the dangers of sharing information with those not qualified to possess it, followed by pages and pages of details on the judicial processes used to investigate breaches and the categories of sentences that the Guild should impose.

What was missing was almost as interesting as what was there. There were no real details on what actual classes of information differing people were allowed to know. A lot of information described how Guild rulings were communicated, but no real details about who made these decisions. There was also no direct mention of the Seals and of the Glowlings.

At the end of the second day, I tackled Mikka on some of these gaps.

"Those are fair observations," he said. "In some ways, those omissions are more important than the rest of the material, but you're going to find the answers somewhat unsatisfying.

"Let's start with information control. It's not that surprising that this document doesn't contain a definitive list. First, it would be a nightmare to keep this document up to date if it did. Most importantly, this document is aimed at everyone from Apprentices upwards and it would be counter-productive to tell people what they weren't allowed to know. In practice, this works in several ways. First the applicable audience is clearly marked on most teaching documents. Second, when a more senior Guild member is educating another one, they are expected to stick to material that they are absolutely certain is allowed. Finally, the Seals enforce all of this, and you will find it practically impossible to tell a secret to anyone who shouldn't know it."

"OK, all of that makes sense," I said. "But isn't the Seal a weak point? How does it actually work? Does it only prevent me from passing on information if I know that I shouldn't? What happens if I make an honest mistake?"

"That would be an obvious way of implementing it," said Mikka, "but it's not how it actually works.

Students have carried out experiments in the past. For example, it is perfectly possible to convince a third party that a particular fact is harmless and that they can share it with a lay member, despite the fact that you, yourself, know that it isn't. However, when the third party tries to share it, they find themselves blocked."

"OK, but what if the third party then shares the same fact with a... fourth party who themselves is authorised to know it, but they try to share it on with someone unauthorised?" I asked. I found this an interesting subject.

"Still doesn't work. Something about the implementation of the Seals always knows the truth and cuts in at the point that someone is about to break the rules. I genuinely can't tell you what that is and how it works. All I know, and I'm not sure whether it's relevant, is that you sometimes hear Masters applying a Seal... referring... to... the... 'Construct'." His delivery slowed gradually as he finished this sentence and he was clearly choosing his words carefully, as if he was encountering resistance. I thought furiously. Hadn't Master Parmonia said something about a construct?

"Moving on," said Mikka. "The decision-making structure of the Guild. Perfectly sensible question, endlessly debated by students. Can't help you. No-one seems to know."

I blinked. "Really?" I said. "That's somewhat implausible."

Mikka smiled. "I agree, but it's still true. No-one knows precisely who decides, nor how that decision-making process is structured. The communications just arrive. Let me be more precise. I assume that the Masters know, but they're not telling anyone. One might assume that there is some sort of council or maybe even councils with representatives of senior masters and the senior legal staff, maybe even an overall Guild Master, but if so, no-one's advertising it. For all I know, maybe they've got some sort of voting system with every Master having a single vote, like they use in some of the republics out east, but no-one will tell us."

"Wow. OK, and these communications of policy and decisions, how do they arrive?" I asked.

"From your assigned master. You can be confident in what they tell you. At least I've never heard of a case where a master passed an incorrect ruling. And ultimately your Seal enforces obedience."

"I guess that brings us on to the Seals," I said. "They are clearly fairly critical to the running of the Guild, but the rules don't explicitly mention them anywhere. There are only references to 'mechanysms and byndings' and the like."

"That's right. Fundamentally," said Mikka, "I think it's to do with the order that they were introduced. The Guild and the rules of the Guild are many hundreds of years old, possibly a thousand for all I know. The Seals, on the other hand, are much more recent, probably about three hundred years old. They were introduced as a mechanism for enforcing the Guild rules rather than the other way round."

"Why were they introduced?"

"It's not entirely clear, at least based on what I've read. Some of the old histories and logbooks of the

Guild suggest that in the earlier years a number of schisms took place with splinter organisations being formed. There may also have been clashes with other guilds based in other countries and the spread of secrets from the Zaronian Guild to them. In any case, the Seals were introduced in a time of upheaval. Initially, they seem to have been introduced to junior members such as apprentices and Junior Artisans, but as people with seals moved up in the organisation, they became more ubiquitous and additional levels were introduced."

"By this point, presumably everyone in the Guild has a Seal?" I queried.

Mikka shrugged. "So far as I know, yes. I've certainly never met someone without one. In fact, it goes the other way. The higher in the organisation, the more layers of Seal that are applied to you."

"OK," I said. "Last question. Why aren't the Glowlings mentioned?"

Mikka winced. "When talking to more senior Guild members, I'd recommend you stick to the term 'Entity', unless you're sure that they're happy to be more casual. For some reason, this is a bit of a sensitive subject."

He thought for a moment, gathering his thoughts.

"As I mentioned before, the Entities have been around a long time and there is evidence that people's thoughts about them have changed. Some people theorise the Temple was built as a response to the discovery of the crystal caves where the Entities emerge into our reality, and there are hints, in ancient carvings and a very few books, that originally human attitudes towards them may have been more superstitious, worshipful, perhaps. Not only within the Guild, either, but in the broader Zaronian population.

"Something changed a few hundred years ago," he continued. "I have seen no mention of the Entities in any surviving book older than around three hundred years. Some of the official Guild rules and similar from that time period show signs that someone edited them to remove sections and some people have argued that the missing sections referred to the Entities."

"And since that time…?" I prompted.

"They are treated as useful tools. An underling that can help with some of the fiddly strains of doing magic, always under strict control of the Guild member. It is unusual for an apprentice to make Artisan without an Entity, true, but that speaks to their utility. As such, there's really no reason for the Guild regulations to mention them."

"I guess that makes sense," I said slowly.

"Scordo, I have a piece of advice," said Mikka. "I'd really avoid asking too many questions about the Entities, particularly when talking to more senior members. There's some sort of friction with non-Guild members in this area and it's a sensitive subject."

I agreed to drop this line of questioning. "For now", I added to myself.

"In other news," Mikka continued. "Tomorrow, it will be time to let you out of this training room."

"Really? What does that mean?"

"Master Logross can't keep you locked up in here forever. Well, he could probably try, but that would require him to actually talk to some of the masters responsible for coordinating apprentice training and persuade them. He tends to leave that sort of task to me, and I don't have the sway, even using his name," said Mikka. "The bottom-line is that there are several facilities in the Annex that would be useful for you to discover, and a number of courses and responsibilities that you need to take on. Master Logross may want to oversee most of your mana training, but even he is not an expert in every aspect of the art. Rather the opposite, since he picks and chooses his interests. There is also more general, non-magical education where you need to catch up."

This sounded intriguing, but I could see an immediate potential stumbling block.

"Mikka, I'm rather older than the average starting apprentice," I said. "Does this mean I'm going to have to join classes with children?"

Mikka chuckled. "Give me some credit for foreseeing problems," he said, "but I don't think that's going to be an issue. Most of the initial training for the younger apprentices is in the field of magic. The focus is on ensuring that they are actually going to be successful in the Guild before broadening their training. You will continue to be doing the vast majority of your magical practice here under my supervision, with Master Logross monitoring. That will continue to take up most of your time.

"What you will do is start further education in Mathematics, Guild History, World Geography and Physical Training, mostly with people your own age. Once we've made some more progress with your magic, we'll also be adding you to the apprentice vermin control roster... we can talk a little more about that then."

I had some trepidation about what some of that would actually entail, but I agreed reluctantly. We agreed to reconvene the next morning to talk some more.

***

The next morning, Mikka intercepted me after I'd eaten breakfast.

"Time for your grand tour," he announced, and he was as good as his word.

We started in the Annex Guild library. This was an interconnected series of caverns disappearing into the distance. The walls were covered with shelves, which mostly contained books with a few scrolls. The librarian explained that although most of the modern reference works were available in the Annex, the Temple held more historical texts. However, there were records of many of the Temple texts, both in a series of filing cards and sometimes in cards placed in the appropriate subject areas on the main shelves. Apparently, we could request these, subject to a day or two's turnaround.

As an apprentice, I only had access to the first few caverns. Mikka encouraged me to walk into the area labelled "Junior Artisan", but as I approached, I felt my seal clamped down on my mind, and my legs gradually came to a halt on their own. It wasn't painful, but I didn't enjoy feeling that I was no longer in control of my own actions.

Next, we visited the Physical Training complex on the ground floor, which consisted mainly of a series of caverns opening to the outside. There Mikka introduced me to Artisan Joli, who would apparently be responsible for my training program. I looked around me, impressed by their facilities, despite my lack of genuine interest in exercising.

There were a series of games courts, both inside the shelter of the cavern and outside. I could see a vast array of weights, benches and mats in another area, and further caverns contained a large sandy training arena for weapons training. Racks of staffs, spears and practice swords were placed along the sides.

"So," said Joli, looking me up and down, "what's your preference? What sort of exercise have you done in the past?"

"Umm, just walking, really. Exploring the Arbran woods," I admitted. The truth was that although I didn't consider myself in terrible shape, I had done relatively little physical exercise in my life.

"That sounds idyllic, but I think you'd find the desert somewhat more barren, not to mention dangerous. Do you enjoy team games?" said Joli.

"No. Umm, not really," I admitted. "I don't know the rules of any." I continued feebly. Truth was that I'd never enjoyed being in a team of children, particularly given that I never particularly wanted to talk to most of them.

"I see," Joli said, looking at me knowingly. "Right, report back here twice a week before breakfast for a run. It will only take you half an hour, and we have an indoor track for when it's less pleasant outside. In a few weeks, once you've settled in a little more, we'll add a half hour of training with a staff once a week."

Starting Sphere

It sounded like a waste of time to me, but I agreed politely. Mikka had made it clear that some sort of exercise was mandatory for all Guild members below Master, and that many of the Masters took part as well.

Close to the Physical Training complex was the medical infirmary. Apparently, doctors were available on call at all hours. I hoped it would be a long time before I needed to take advantage of this!

Later in the morning, we visited a series of classrooms and Mikka introduced me to my tutors in mathematics, Guild history and world geography. Each of these seemed pleasant enough, although I didn't particularly warm to any of them. I would have a one hour class in each subject every week. Fortunately, these were scheduled back-to-back, so it simply meant a single morning interruption to my training schedule.

***

We finished up our tour in a series of refectory halls. These spaces varied from long tables for communal eating all the way to smaller sets of low seating and tables suitable for eating alone, or in small groups.

There was a broad selection of food available, almost enough to make me think of leaving the seclusion of my workroom to come and eat here more regularly. Mikka and I queued up and helped ourselves to sizeable portions. As we turned away, a small group of people at a nearby table called us over.

"Mikka! Over here!"

"The prodigal returns!"

"Look who's deigning to eat with us common

folk."

There were four people of a similar age to Mikka, three of them were Junior Artisans and one was an Apprentice, although he looked a little older than the others. All had the faint glow that indicated the presence of bound Entities.

Mikka took the lead at introductions. "Scordo, let me introduce this rather raucous rabble. This lady is Bielda, this is Dienny, this fine gentleman is Harrisal, and our somewhat slow colleague here is Gonni. And this is Scordo, Master Logross's brand new apprentice."

The last man, with the Apprentice seal, responded first.

"And that's work on your focusing Device moved to the end of my to do list, Mikka. Hello Scordo, I'm pleased to see that Master Logross has released you from his lair at last. Is it true that he dines on the bones of failed apprentices?"

The others greeted me as well, and I forced myself to reply in kind. I explained to Gonni that since I'd never actually seen Master Logross eat, then I couldn't comment on his diet and Mikka cut in.

"Scared are you, Gonni? Worried that he'll come looking for you?"

"Just because some of us prefer to concentrate on actual useful skills, rather than push for early Artisan status, doesn't mean that we're scared of failing. Scordo, I'm specialising in Device construction which is a very complicated art. Something your mentor ought to remember if he'd like to have some chance at obtaining any Devices of his own. He can't go on borrowing your master's tools indefinitely."

"Nice to meet you, Scordo," Bielda said. "Given how much Mikka has complained about Master Logross's pickiness over the years, I don't envy you your position."

"Has he actually let you carry out a working yet?" asked Harrisal.

"I've heard that Logross thinks of mana manipulation as an art-form in its own right, rather than a means to an end," put in Dienny.

"All of his visualisation skills didn't help Mikka much that time he ended up with his satchel full of spikkans, did they?" said Gonni. "I've never seen him move so fast."

The conversation progressed along these lines with lots of in jokes and casual teasing. The five were clearly good friends, and they were evidently trying to put me at ease in their company. A few hints they dropped made it obvious that Mikka had already mentioned me to them, and I wondered what he'd said. To my relief, none of them expected me to contribute anything significant to the conversation.

I was interested in Gonni's reference to Devices. It was obvious that they underpinned some types of magic and that they were mostly based on various crystals and gemstones, but I didn't have a clue how they worked. Perhaps I could get him on his own in the future and ask him to explain some essentials?

Our lunch passed quickly, but I was relieved when Mikka showed me the way back to Master Logross's quarters. During the trip, he explained the corridor markers to help me find my way around without help in the future; my first classes looming large the next day.

CHAPTER TEN
Classes

When I turned up to my mathematics class the next day, I didn't know what to expect. Would I be surrounded by younger children who were all way ahead of me? Why was this even necessary and how relevant was it to my future in the Guild? Master Logross had certainly talked about calculating mana costs, but he'd given the impression that it would involve plugging numbers into standard calculations, basically simple algebra. What else was there that I needed to cover?

Most of my education had been conducted either with personal tutors or on my own, so I wasn't looking forward to the whole group learning experience.

In the event, it was less intimidating, and more interesting, than I expected. As soon as I walked into the classroom, I heard someone calling me by name. Swivelling on the spot, I saw Anyana across the room.

She seemed pleased to see me and insisted that I take a seat next to her. She quickly introduced me to several companions, who included some people that were vaguely familiar from the emergence that we'd attended. From their glowing heads, I noted that a couple of them must have gained their own Glowlings in the intervening period.

Most of the others weren't particularly chatty, although Anyana made up for this. However, one of them, a boy of about my age called Tyballo, was more intrigued by my skills. I wasn't comfortable with the direction of his questions.

"So, Scordo, you're the hot-shot apprentice taken on by Master Logross. How powerful are you? What are you able to cast?" he asked. I noticed he hadn't gained a Glowling yet.

I decided I had nothing to prove and didn't want to get involved in some sort of boasting competition, so tried to defuse this as quickly as possible. "Not very much, to be honest. I've only just started training and I can't do anything other than a simple light spell."

"Is that all? You've been here for a couple of weeks already. What have you been spending your time doing?"

"Maybe he's a slow learner?" suggested Daivan, an older boy who was another of Anyana and Tyballo's companions. He hadn't bonded a Glowling either.

This stung a little. Despite Mikka's reassurances that I'd made substantial progress and that my pure mana manipulation skills were already better than some other apprentices, I knew little about what other people could do. I paused, not sure what to reply. Anyana beat me to it.

"Lay off him, Tyballo. We all know you think you're such hot stuff. Too bad that spikkan didn't seem impressed with you the other day." She gestured to his arm, which I saw had a bandage wrapped around it.

Tyballo flushed. "That was Merkle's fault. She got in the way and I couldn't see it coming. Besides, that's not the point. I want to know what Scordo's got to allow him to jump the line and get a Glowling ahead of the rest of us."

"Not ahead of all of us," smirked Anyana. "And the last thing I heard, it was up to the Glowlings to choose who they think is worthy."

Tyballo's flush deepened, but before he could reply, our instructor entered and called us all to order.

The lesson itself was interesting and not too advanced for me. We were covering geometry, and it was a recap of many of the concepts that Master Logross had run me through in my testing. Perhaps there had been some direction behind his questioning?

Over the next few weeks, I was to find that much of our mathematics curriculum was based around spacial visualisation. We quickly started looking at the principles behind our assumptions and considered other options. For example, how did the behaviour of shapes projected onto a sphere compare with those in a standard plane? From this, we moved on to a number of other interesting subjects. These included topology, in which we pretended actual shape and magnitudes were unimportant and looked at how we could distinguish different objects. For example, we could squash a sphere into a cube, but not into a doughnut unless you actually cut, pierce or join it. However, I'm getting ahead of myself. I saw little actual application of this immediately, but they were certainly interesting thought exercises which helped relax my mind between other training.

Many of my fellow students didn't agree. I began to see more and more frowns and looks of incomprehension and, judging by the mutters, many of them considered the lessons a waste of their time.

I should also mention that in these mathematics classes, I saw the first signs that my Glowling was actually waking up again. It had been silent since our bonding and sealing, although I was clearly getting visualisation benefits from it. However, during my classes, it felt almost as if it was paying attention to what I was seeing and I felt its consciousness trying to shift slightly. It didn't speak again at this point, but once or twice a clear vision of a concept being discussed that I was struggling to grasp would spring into my mind and help me make sense of what our instructor was trying to explain.

***

I also began my Guild History and World Geography classes.

In Guild History, it turned out that most of the other students were already more or less familiar with the Guild primer that Mikka had passed me. Only to a point, however. I noticed several inaccuracies and mistakes in some of their comments. Rather than being an opportunity for rote learning, the class was mostly structured as a talking shop to debate a topic, usually one chosen by the instructor. For example, on the first day, the teacher asked us to discuss why it was important for the Guild to remain on good terms with neighbouring provinces. (Quick precis: you can't grow much food or wood in a desert and the Guild used a lot of each. And the Guild wasn't interested in widespread military conquest and occupation, so we needed to stay on good terms with those nations who would trade them to us, although from their comments several students clearly thought that this was a mistake and that we should be more militant.)

I tried to stay as quiet as possible in the history sessions, preferring a seat on the edge of the action, where I could drink in my impressions of how other Zaronian apprentices thought and behaved, rather than putting my neck on the line by expressing my opinions.

World geography, however, was surprisingly fascinating.

My father's library had had a wide selection of maps but, aside from the neighbouring provinces, I knew little about most of the other civilisations. I certainly didn't know that several countries had their own magics, nor that some were opposed to Zaronia.

The curriculum was focused on how other regions were relevant to Zaronia.

The nearby provinces were mostly categorised in terms of the resources that they could supply to Zaronia. For example Sahraya supplied food (although there were several other provinces that also traded food, clearly Zaronia was careful not to rely too heavily on any one provider); Arbran supplied wood; Celtim (which was on the far side of the mountains bordering Arbran) supplied silks and some minerals.

The Guild clearly also regarded most of the

nearby provinces as buffer states, protecting Zaronia from its enemies. One country on the other side of the desert from Zaronia, Kahlia, however, was particularly unfriendly, and the instructor made some scathing remarks about its necromancers.

On the far side of the Sahraya prairies, there was the Empire of Sultineous. Apparently, they had significant conventional armies as well as what the teacher described as 'Weather Callers'.

Finally, off far to the north were the frozen badlands of Deltos. These were largely filled with warring tribes which as commonly fought each other as raiding other countries. Their magical tradition was apparently rooted in blood magic, summoning and binding, but we were warned that adepts proficient in their arts had travelled widely. Apparently, they tended to be covered by extensive tattooing. Actual tattooing, apparently, in contrast to Zaronian Guild seals.

***

A few days after my first lessons, I reported for my first physical training session. Joli met me and briefed me on the various running tracks available. Apparently, there were a variety. Some covered smooth ground both inside and outside the cave complexes, others were over more rugged ground and involved jumps and areas where it was difficult to keep your footing. I asked which one I should choose and he shrugged. Apparently, I was required to spend a certain minimum amount of time training, but Joli left the details up to me. I could run by myself, or in groups, and the distance, speed, and terrain were up to me.

This suited me just fine. I picked the smoothest, easiest inside route and jogged slowly for about a couple of miles. Every time I felt tired, I slowed down. I can't say that I found it pleasant, nor that I felt it was actually delivering any benefits, but I was meeting my obligation.

My opinion didn't change over the next couple of runs, but I gradually found my breathing improving and was able to run faster and more consistently. The distance I could cover in half an hour gradually crept up towards the three-mile point.

A day or so later, when Master Logross called me in for his periodic demands for me to exhibit my progress, he asked questions about my physical training. He wanted to know how far I was running, on what terrain, and what advantage I was taking of the opportunity.

I guess I looked confused at the last past of the question.

Master Logross sighed and closed his eyes briefly.

"What is the purpose of improving your mana forming speed?" he asked.

"Well, to improve my control and make it faster for me to cast. For example, if I get surprised by a spikkan."

Master Logross nodded curtly. "At least Mikka remembered that lesson, then. So, are you always expecting to be attacked when standing still on smooth ground then?"

I wasn't actually planning to be attacked at all, but I thought better of saying this. "Do you mean I should be practising..." I tailed off.

"Practise mana forming while running. As you get more proficient, practise actual workings. Vary your terrain and practice more sudden turns. Dismissed."

I left. The next day, I practiced followed his advice and tried to form mana bubbles while running and tried out some of the harder trails. As I should have expected, this was initially very tricky. I tended to lose control while trying to move the mana bubble with me as I formed it. I also found it difficult to keep my breathing steady and my concentration covering both mana control and movement at the same time. Several times I got my feet tangled up and ended up ignominiously crashing to the ground.

Over time, however, the practice paid off, and I found this training exercise a little easier. Ironically, I told myself, the faster I could cast, the easier it would be to complete it without getting distracted by my surroundings, so I redoubled my effort to reduce my forming time still further. I also extended my running time, partly because the physical benefits were kicking in, but also because I could more clearly see the incidental benefits that it was delivering to my magical control.

CHAPTER ELEVEN
A loss of control

In parallel with my lessons, my mana manipulation practice continued. I was still trying to put in over twelve hours a day, at least on those days where I didn't actually have lessons.

The day after my first classes, Mikka decided it was time to broaden out my goals a little.

"Form a mana sphere," he said. "Hold it steady. OK, please show me your light working."

I focused on the currents inside the sphere and carefully traced out a flat four-leaf clover pattern. After a few times around the shape, the current established in the mana and the four-leaf clover glowed.

"All right, that's a good start and we can work with it. I guess you know what I'm going to say, however?" said Mikka.

I swallowed. "Not fast enough, right?"

"Correct," said Mikka. "That must have taken nearly a minute for you to establish the pattern. What does it feel like as you establish the working?"

"Well, I trace around the pattern with my mind and the mana gradually starts to follow me. I found that if I move too fast, then my mind slips through the mana and nothing happens," I said. "Is there some way of stopping that from happening?"

"I thought as much," said Mikka. "You're essentially self taught with this, correct?"

"Well, I taught myself based on some hints in a text written by a lay student," I admitted. "It was the only option I had in Arbran."

"Don't get me wrong, I think it's amazing that you made any progress with this at all," said Mikka. "Very few apprentices start with any actual workings mastered. To improve, however, you're going to need to go about this differently. Stop visualising the process as sketching a pattern in your mind and hoping that the mana will gradually follow you. Instead, you should take hold of the mana firmly with your mind and pull it into the correct pattern. Pretend that you're seizing it by the scruff of its neck."

"OK, that makes some sort of sense, I guess," I said. I dismissed the first glowing sphere, which I had been holding during the conversation with little effort, reabsorbed the used mana, and tried again. This time I visualised myself gripping onto the mana and pulling it the way I wanted it to move. The first couple of times, I failed. It felt as if the mana that I was holding detached from the rest of the sphere and failed to set up a current. The third, however, I set up some sort of pattern.

"OK, that's good going," said Mikka. "You need to practise that and make it more consistent. As you get more confident in your control of the mana, you can grab it in multiple places at once and pull. That will increase your speed significantly, since you'll only have to trace out a part of the pattern at each point before you've established the working."

The next couple of days passed quickly, practising the light working until I could consistently establish it in around 10 seconds. Mikka was pleased by this progress, although Master Logross was notably lacking in appreciation when he asked me to demonstrate.

"Have Mikka move you to a more adequate light working," was his only comment.

When I relayed this message to Mikka he sighed and closed his eyes briefly. Then he pulled out a piece of paper and sketched out another clover shape, but this one had six leaves or lobes, and was a three-dimensional shape.

"You'll find this harder to master, but it will generate both more light and a broader spread, with light being cast in more directions," he said. "In order to keep up your casting speed, you will need to add more engagement points with the mana. Ultimately, you're looking to take hold of the mana at every point of the working at once and move it into motion almost instantly."

I was ready with this more advanced working by the next time Master Logross called me in. He regarded it in silence for a while and then told me to "Form a more opaque shell for better light dispersion. And are you trying to hold that globe in the air with your mind? You should be perfectly capable of adding a hover or cling working at the same time."

At my next session with Mikka, I learned a couple of new things about the mana shells. First, the characteristics of the shell of the mana sphere were important: I could vary the thickness and the texture to align with my goal for the working. What Master Logross was suggesting was that I tweak the shell to cause it to diffuse the light more evenly and rather than a six lobed symbol shedding light in all directions, I would then end up with a softly glowing ball.

Second, it was apparently possible to establish more than one current within a single sphere as long as they didn't interfere with each other. Mikka showed that, by establishing an independent clockwise current in the mana forming the shell towards the bottom of the sphere, it would float by itself with little maintenance needed from me. I could then rotate the sphere to propel it in different directions. An anticlockwise pattern had the opposite effect, causing it to float downwards to the nearest surface and sit there as if affected by gravity.

***

One evening during my training, Mikka entered the work room carrying a Device made up of a crystal containment sphere held in a frame studded with other tiny crystals. I remembered Dorrall using a similar instrument during my testing.

"Master Logross feels it's time for another capacity test," he explained. "First, I'm going to show you how to use this Device to measure your own capacity roughly based on a known starting point."

He then explained how to fill the sphere at a rate that I found comfortable to maintain and read off the number of illuminated studs. After a few goes, we agreed that around eleven or twelve studs were activating each time.

Starting Sphere

We then carried out a full capacity test, draining all of my mana, and Mikka reported I had around 240 units of mana capacity in my reserve. This contrasted favourably with the 96 units that apparently Master Logross had recorded during my apprentice test.

Mikka then explained that I could track changes to my capacity by using the crystal sphere Device. The more studs that I illuminated would imply a similar linear improvement in my capacity.

"It's only an approximate measure," Mikka explained. "And over time, you'll find that your fill rate changes noticeably and that will throw off the stud readings, so it's important to recalibrate every few weeks."

"So, how come my capacity has increased so much in such a short period?" I asked.

"There are probably several reasons," said Mikka. "The first is obvious. You've been working hard with your mana for many hours each day. Just by itself, that will help you build capacity."

"OK, that makes sense," I said. "However, I thought that I'd need to drain my mana low in order to make a big difference, and that hasn't happened much since you taught me how to reabsorb my mana."

"That's the second reason, actually. You're reabsorbing mana some time after expending it. In the meantime, you've already partially refilled your reserves, so you're constantly straining against the limits of what your reserves can contain, which in itself encourages growth. I don't think Master Logross explained this to you, but there is actually an exercise based around this: fill a sphere with as much mana as you can, wait for a long period while your reserves refill and then reabsorb the contents of the sphere. Remember that the amount of mana you waste while it's being held in a sphere relates to the size of the shell, not the volume of the bubble, so the bigger the sphere, the more percentage-wise is available to reabsorb."

"Surface area vs volume, got it," I said. "And how long does it take for my reserves to refill?"

"Reason three. The Annex is located in an area of relatively plentiful mana which minimises your refill time."

"Does that mean that I should practise this explicitly to keep boosting my capacity?" I asked.

"Maybe, but you don't want to overdo it. You're already spending most of your time training other aspects of mana manipulation, such as forming speed and current manipulation, and those are important too, while also increasing your capacity as a side effect. Dedicated capacity training is probably best reserved for when you've got nothing else going on. Some mages boast about their capacity figures, but I'd much rather see a so-called weaker mage with faster and surer control over their mana workings, rather than a mammoth mana master who can control vast amounts of mana but can't actually do anything with it."

"Understood," I said. Since it sounded as if the capacity training wouldn't require a great deal of control, I promised myself that I'd start doing some capacity training while I was doing non-magical tasks, such as eating, reading and classwork.

Starting Sphere

***

Over the week, I continued my various exercises, seeing small but steady gains across the board. Following feedback from Mikka and Master Logross, I also worked on maintaining two mana bubbles at once, although I filled them one at a time, rather than more than one simultaneously, as Mikka had showed. On my own initiative, I sometimes experimented with more than two.

As the gains got smaller over time, I also became more obsessive about measuring my times to prove that I was continuing to make progress. With hindsight, I was focusing more on the times, rather than doing everything as well as I could.

One afternoon I made a mistake.

I filled one sphere and started it glowing and floating mid-air next to me. Eighteen seconds, which was close to my best yet. I did the same for another right alongside the first and managed nineteen seconds this time. I paused and then decided that I would try for a third. Would I be able to manage eighteen seconds or better?

This time, however, with my attention being split three ways, I guess I simply wasn't careful enough about the shape I was forming and I belatedly noticed that my latest mana ball was going to be somewhat squashed, a spheroid rather than a true sphere. Still, I reasoned in a split-second decision, I truly wanted to complete the third in a decent time and I thought I could control the situation for long enough by strength of will.

I clamped my control around the mana bubble,

ensuring that it didn't give way. I also pumped a bit of extra mana into the bubble and thickened the shell slightly, since I'd occasionally noticed the greater pressure could cause the shape of the bubble to snap back into a true sphere. Then I wrenched at the mana, establishing the necessary flows. The bubble began to glow, and I glanced down fractionally at the stopwatch. Eighteen seconds and I'd managed my goal even with my fumble!

It was in that moment of triumph that I realised I was losing the third bubble. My eyes flashed back to the three bubbles hanging by each other in mid-air and the third bubble ruptured, followed by the other two a fraction of a second later. There was a blinding light as three simultaneous flashes etched themselves into my vision and a feeling of intense heat and pressure. I felt myself falling, but my awareness of everything around me went away in a surrounding whiteness.

***

I awoke to darkness and pain.

I was lying on something soft, but my face and my hands felt as if they were burning. There was also something blocking my eyes. I groaned from the sudden pain and investigated my face gingerly. Yes, someone had fixed some sort of material, perhaps a bandage or dressing, across my eyes. I investigated to see whether I could lift it and peep out.

My hearing was working fine, and I heard steps starting from some distance away, approaching rapidly.

"Ah, you're back with us, are you?" A deep

woman's voice.

My hands were carefully removed from the bandages and laid back by my side.

"Now, now," she said. "Your eyes will be fine, but they need to recover a bit longer before we expose them to light again."

"What happened?" I managed.

"Master Logross transported straight into the medical clinic with you a few hours ago. Some sort of accident, I gather. Sudden explosive light exposure. This sort of incident is not uncommon amongst students. I'd guess you'd probably know what happened better than I would?"

Master Logross? How had he found me? And transported?

"Yes. Maybe." Definitely, I thought to myself. "How am I injured? And, sorry, who are you?"

"I am Master Fenella," she said. "You've had a lucky escape because of how quickly you were brought for treatment. You have suffered temporary blinding, but I've already sped up the natural healing process and we should be ready to take off the dressings tomorrow morning. Your vision may have some blurring for a day or so, but no longer than that. You also have severe sunburns to your exposed skin, that is, your hands and face. The marks of the arms should fade quickly, but I suspect that you're going to have temporary scarring to the face for at least the next few months."

"That does sound much better than it could have been," I said. When I had woken in the dark, I had worried that the damage to the eyes could have been permanent. "Is there anything that you could do to speed up the healing of the facial scarring?"

"We could, but I don't think we will," said Master Fenella. "General Guild policy is that when it comes to training accidents, we do what we can to heal any critical injuries, but we leave cosmetic ones to heal in their own time. We find it tends to... discourage return visits to the infirmary. I gather this was a training accident?"

"Err, yes. I don't know exactly what happened, but it was certainly that."

"There you are then. Of course, you're welcome to petition your Master for an exemption to the policy if you like. With Master Logross, however, well... You might know better than me how likely he is to grant it."

No chance whatsoever, I silently filled in myself.

"Now, it's late evening right now. You should get some sleep. There's a bottle of water on the table by your left-hand side, by your shoulder. Feel free to drink as much as you need. It will be refilled whenever you empty it. For now, I'll send in one of my assistants to apply a cooling lotion to the worst of your burns."

I drank deeply, and she was as good as her word. The lotion was applied by an anonymous benefactor a few minutes later. I lay back and fell asleep.

CHAPTER TWELVE

Becoming more dangerous

After I awoke the next morning, Master Fenella carefully removed the dressings from my face.

My initial impression was that the room was far too bright and my eyes immediately watered. Over the next few minutes, however, they gradually began to adjust, and I found that, in fact, the room had been darkened. Master Fenella, a tall older-looking woman, carefully examined my eyes one at a time.

"These are healing well," she assured me. "It will take another day for them to recover fully, but I don't think that you will need any further assistance from us. Your mentor came by earlier, asking for you. We asked him to return about now, so I suggest you wait here until he arrives."

I thanked her profusely for her help, which she brushed off casually, providing me with a jar of the ointment for my burns.

After she left, I spent the time until Mikka arrived enjoying being able to look around at the room. Aside from slight blurring and after images when I moved my head too quickly, things were more or less working properly. My eyes were still a little sensitive to the light, though.

While I was experimenting with my vision, Mikka arrived. He immediately asked after my condition and I reassured him I was fine. He suggested we should talk more back at our quarters, which suited me fine, so we walked back slowly with him being careful to allow me to adjust as the lighting changed.

Once back, I sunk into the seating in the lobby area, and he sat down opposite me.

"So, what happened?" I asked.

"You tell me," he said. "The first thing I knew was that I heard a loud noise from your workroom, but I got to the door to find that Master Logross had already beaten me to it. He hoisted you up and disappeared back into his study, presumably to transport you to the infirmary. Please talk me through whatever you remember about the accident."

Somewhat shamefaced, I explained what I'd been doing and how I must have lost control of the misformed mana sphere.

"Yup, that'll do it," said Mikka. "Poor forming technique leading to a blow-out, followed by a cascade failure of the other bubbles." He didn't look particularly surprised.

"But why was the blast so powerful? It was far brighter than the light should have been."

Mikka sighed. "When your mana bubble burst, the working inside went critical and burnt up all the available mana in an instant. That working would normally have lasted for many minutes, perhaps even hours, but the failure caused it all to be used at once. That explosion of power then caught the other nearby mana bubbles, overloaded them and the same thing happened to them."

"Is this a common occurrence?" I asked.

"Sadly, yes," said Mikka. "Most students cut corners and manage to blow out a working at least once. The slower learners often manage it multiple times. The temptation to recover a poorly formed sphere is too strong. However, most students don't have another two mana bubbles in close proximity to get caught in the blast-wave and magnify the damage."

"What should I do to avoid this again?" I said.

"For a start, make sure you only form perfect spheres," said Mikka. "That's the most stable shape that there is. There are other valid regular shapes for a casting, but we don't teach them to apprentices for exactly this sort of reason."

"OK, well, I guess I should have known that," I admitted.

"Next, when you're working with multiple mana bubbles, make sure you separate them as much as you can. The power of a blast drops rapidly with distance, so even a little will help. As you progress, there are spells which will require you to have multiple bubbles in close proximity, but if you're concerned, then you can always form them separately and then move them together later."

"That makes sense. I guess I was getting a bit too blase about it all," I said.

"Finally," said Mikka. "Think about how close you actually need the workings to be to you. If you'd been forming them on the other side of the room, or even behind your back, the injury to you wouldn't have been so severe. It isn't usually a problem with light, but when you experiment with other types of working, you need to think about what they're going to do. For example, if you form a heat working right next to you, then you risk setting fire to your hair even if everything goes right with the actual working."

"All right," I said. I then did a double-take and looked again at the burn scars that I'd noticed on Mikka's arms when we'd first met. "Umm, sorry to ask, but are you talking from personal experience here, by any chance?"

Mikka smiled ruefully. "Guilty as charged. I ruptured a heat mana bubble while I was still an apprentice. Fortunately, it was only the one bubble, but it still hurt a lot. Master Logross was somewhat acerbic in his comments while he helped me to the infirmary."

"Talking about Master Logross, how did he know that I needed help?" I asked.

"I'd imagine he has wards that report to him on mana workings throughout his quarters," said Mikka. "Either that or he simply detected the blow-out himself directly. His senses are extremely acute."

"And he transported me directly to the infirmary?"

"Yes. There's a series of transport circles throughout the Annex, and the medical clinic is no exception. You've probably seen the circle in Master Logross's room. I gather each circle has their own signature, which makes it quicker to aim a transport. Presumably it takes a fair amount of mana to use them, though. Many of the Masters don't really bother for short hops and prefer to walk. Master Logross uses them extensively; it's why you never see him enter or leave his quarters."

That explained a lot, although I'd been tempted to assume that he just never went anywhere.

"So, I guess I'd better get back to practising," I said. "Only remembering to be more careful."

"Ha," said Mikka. "You've left yourself a reminder to make sure you don't forget for a while."

He led me into the workroom, and I immediately saw what he meant. The walls were noticeably lighter, bleached by the glare of the light I'd released. All except one area of wall where I could distinctly make out my silhouette where I'd inadvertently blocked the blast.

***

For the next week or two, I continued to practising my mana forming and light working, being exceptionally careful to get the shape right and to keep my mana bubbles separated by an arm's length. My skill level continued to grow. In particular, I was finding it far easier to pull the mana in the bubble into the pattern that I wanted in a single tug, rather than having to trace it.

Rather too easy, in fact. Sometimes, I found that I only needed to visualise the three-dimensional shape of the working in my mind and that they then sprung into life without conscious effort. I could still feel myself doing it, but with no need to concentrate.

This worried me a little. Was this a sign that I was starting to cut corners that would lead to another problem? I raised the issue with Mikka, but he didn't recognise this as a sign of any particular common mistake. He must have mentioned it to Master Logross, however, because he raised it in the next session we had together.

"Am I to gather that your Entity has taken an interest in your workings at last?" he asked.

"What? Err, sorry, I'm not sure what you mean," I said.

"A sufficiently mature Entity can help visualisation, but it can also take on some of the load in establishing workings. Once you have a clear enough vision of how you want the mana to move, it can perform the task on your behalf. At this point in your training, this is merely a useful shortcut, but as you attempt more advanced workings, the help can be invaluable," said Master Logross.

"That's great," I said, meaning it. "Err, why wasn't Mikka able to recognise what was happening?"

"His entity is as yet insufficiently mature. Yours appears to have more... agency than is usual at this point in your training. You need to ensure that you are taking advantage of this properly. Ensure that your visualisation and intention are sufficiently clear."

I tried to do my best with this, and my casting times continued to drop. Soon, I could form a light working in a little over five seconds.

***

At around the same time period, Joli felt it was time to start my weapons training. When we began my first session, he took a couple of staffs from the rack and ran me through a series of exercises, manipulating them. The drill included holding it out at a distance for gradually increasing periods, switching suddenly to holding it vertically, suddenly snapping it forward, twirling and similar moves. He encouraged me to move between exercises fluently without falling into particular patterns.

After a few sessions of this, I was somewhat surprised to find that he wasn't expecting me to spar with other people. I noticed other people practising together, but Joli kept me practising only against training dummies and other targets. I questioned this, but he said that he had received instructions from Master Logross.

I shrugged, unwilling to question my good fortune in this respect. Blows from a moving staff would hurt! I quickly found a form of peaceful meditation while carrying out this exercise, similar to that I was finding in running. I could fall into the patterns of motion and think about other things while moving as I wished. Thinking about Master Logross's advice for running, I experimented with mana forming while exercising with the staff and found it was entirely possible, so I built this into my routine.

***

Several weeks later, Mikka surprised me one morning with a further extension to my curriculum.

"It's time to broaden out your range of workings," he explained. He placed a sheet of paper at one end of the table, and a cup of water at the other.

"That's great," I said truthfully. I was acutely aware that for all the progress I'd made, I was still only able to cast a light spell, which was where I'd started as an apprentice!

"You're probably wondering 'why now'?" said Mikka with a smile.

"Well, yes," I said. "I get the impression that other apprentices would have started other workings before now."

"Yes, and no. Remember that most apprentices would start far younger than you and it would have taken them a much longer time, perhaps years, to get sufficient control of their mana to cast a single working, let alone multiple. At the same time, it's true that Master Logross's teaching schedule differs from most other masters. He forces students to perfect their mastery of mana manipulation before broadening the range of spells available.

"In my experience, his approach works," he continued. "It ensures that an apprentice has established excellent control of their manipulation before becoming distracted by mastering multiple working patterns. What's more, once you've got a good enough grasp of the basics, then most simple workings fall into the same forms and can be grasped quickly. That doesn't, however, help much with the tedium of the practice and the frustration of seeing your peers gaining new abilities ahead of you." He smiled wryly, and I suspected again that he was talking about his own experiences.

"It is also true, however, that more and more of the other Masters are asking why you haven't been added to the Apprentice vermin control register yet. I suspect that some of the other students have been complaining."

"That may be true," I admitted. In my classes, Tyballo still periodically needled me to demonstrate my skills and some of his friends were sympathetic to his behaviour. That didn't include Anyana, who had continued to be friendly, but I could easily see Tyballo and some of his peers moaning to their Masters.

"But before we can add you to the roster, we need you to become more deeply dangerous and deadly," said Mikka. "Spikkans and the like may not be very keen on a little light, but it won't usually protect you from them.

"We'll start with two paired workings, those for heat and cold. Let's start with the basic ones."

He quickly drew the shape of the current patterns. The simple form of the heat working was a current in the shape of a figure of eight on its side with the current rising towards the middle of the mana ball. The corresponding mana flow for cold was the opposite: a sideways figure of eight, with the mana falling in the middle.

I started with the heat spell. I was surprised to find it more or less trivial to form. The working itself was simpler than the original flat four-leafed clover pattern I'd used for my initial light spell, let alone the three dimensional six lobed shape that I had now mastered. In less than twenty seconds, I had a mana bubble emitting heat floating in the air. Fortunately, I'd followed my new careful practice of forming it some distance in front of me. Despite that, I could feel the heat radiating off it and see that it was causing patterns in the air around it.

"Good," said Mikka. "Now please move the bubble to touch the paper that I've put on the table.

Try not to damage the table too much, if you can."

I gently floated the mana ball over to the piece of paper and gave it the slightest of touches. The paper burst into flames and was quickly consumed.

And release, please. And now the cold form."

I generated a cold bubble with similar ease and, based on Mikka's instructions, I dipped it into the water in the cup at the other end of the table. The water froze instantly, expanding up over the rim of the cup.

"You can let that go." I released the ball, reabsorbing the unspent mana. "Now imagine what either of those would have done to a creature that you touched with them. Or to a human, for that matter."

I swallowed, looking at Mikka's scarred arms. He followed my gaze.

"Well, yes, exactly. I don't need to warn you to take care with this, do I? Now, if that isn't dangerous and deadly enough, Master Logross has also instructed me to brief you on a more advanced working for each of heat and cold. It's a lot harder, but he thinks that you'll be able to master this reasonably quickly."

He quickly sketched a representation of a couple of horizontal doughnut shapes on the board. On one, he showed a pattern where the mana rolled around the doughnut orthogonal to the curve with it rising in the middle: that was the advanced heat working. The cold working had the flow rolling the other way. Effectively, it was very similar to the simple figure eight working, but with the shape rotated and extended around a full circle.

I tried, but I could not immediately master these workings. Mikka told me not to worry but to practice both of the next few days. He made it clear that my priority should be to master the simpler techniques.

These were too easy to hold my attention or offer much of a challenge for long. The advanced workings, however, I found much more difficult. I concentrated carefully and at length could start the current pattern by holding onto the mana around an entire ring inside the sphere. I then allowed the size of the ring of mana to vary slightly while rotating it in a vertical circle shape. It took a few goes and several minutes of effort, but eventually the current established and I stepped backwards involuntarily at the power of the heat radiating off the mana ball. I thought better of touching this against the table, but instead moved it against the stone wall of the chamber. There was a sharp crack and tiny chips of stone exploded from a scar dug into the rock face. I released my breath through my teeth in a silent whistle and released the working gently. I then tried colliding a simple heat with the stone wall and found it didn't even mark it.

When Mikka checked in with me next, his eyes were drawn to the scar on the wall. "You certainly wounded the workroom," was his only comment.

More practice firmed up my control of the more advanced workings, and I could feel the Glowling helping in a way that it didn't with the simple working. It seemed almost drawn to the shape of mana pattern that I was envisioning.

A week later, Mikka notified me I had been assigned vermin control duty. I went to bed, nervous about what the next day would bring.

CHAPTER THIRTEEN
Vermin control

The next day, I woke early and ate some breakfast. Mikka soon joined me, carrying a staff about the same height as I was.

"Master Logross left this for you," he said.

"Left? Where has he gone?"

I took the staff and examined it carefully. It was a lovely piece of oak, clearly trimmed from a single sapling. Arbran oak, if I wasn't mistaken. It had then been carved to shape, reinforced with some sort of iron at the top and bottom. The staff was dark in colour, treated with a type of oil that, from the smell, should improve its heat resistance as well as preventing water absorption. It was well-balanced, maybe a little heavier than the practice ones I'd been using, and was exactly my height.

"He has to attend a ceremony in the Temple, apparently. He may be gone for some days," said Mikka. "He also sent a message. You should be careful to consider melee weapons only a means of defence. Your primary offence should always be your mana skills. I guess I can see his point. If I think too much about whacking something with a weapon, then I'm far more likely to miss opportunities to attack with magic. However, many others disagree and favour other methods of combat. It's possible that you'll see some examples of this today."

"I'll think about that, thank you. In any case, this staff is a beautiful piece of work and I'm grateful."

I held it at guard and then practised whipping it out in defence a few times. It felt perfectly suited to me.

***

When Mikka and I arrived at the office of the Master responsible for coordinating vermin control duty, I found he was a middle-aged man called Master Kinchat. He looked somewhat distracted with a slight frown on his face, making you think you must be keeping him from something more important.

Mikka introduced me and he fussed over a clipboard covered in papers.

"Ah yes. Apprentice Scordo, sponsored by Master Logross, correct?" he said in a wheezy voice, and then continued without waiting for a response. "Unless you have any particular objections, Acting Squad Leader Apprentice Anyana has requested that I assign you to her squad. They should be here soon, so if you would take a seat in the lobby to wait?"

Mikka excused himself, and I went to the lobby. In fact, I didn't have any objections, although I wasn't sure that Master Kinchat would have been particularly concerned even if I had. On the contrary, I much preferred the opportunity to be with at least one person who I knew.

Once Anyana and her squad arrived, I had second thoughts. She had two other team members with her and one of them was Tyballo, who would not have been my first choice of companion anywhere, let alone in any form of activity where we had to rely on each other. On the other hand, maybe he would stop asking me to demonstrate my magic after I'd actually formed some workings in front of him? He'd clearly bonded a Glowling some time in the recent past, so he wouldn't be able to hold that against me anymore.

The other squad member was a large, powerfully built woman called Merkle. She was taller than me, with tightly curled black hair. She also had a Glowling. I'd seen her in a couple of my classes, but she hadn't made much of an impression on me previously. I made my introductions to her, and she seemed friendly enough, if a little distant.

"Scordo, thank you for agreeing to join us. Our previous squad master made Artisan recently, and we needed a new member to allow us to continue together," said Anyana.

"So, hot shot, are you ready to kill some spikkans?" asked Tyballo. "I'm surprised that Master Logross is finally ready to let you out of his cave to join us. Or is it you that's been trying to avoid this?"

"Calm down Tyballo," cut in Anyana. "You've not exactly covered yourself in glory in the past, after all."

Tyballo's expression darkened, and he muttered something about needing to be given space.

As they bickered, I examined their equipment. Our weapons and clothing were peculiarly mismatched. I carried my staff, but was wearing my standard apprentice tunic and robe. Both Anyana and Merkle had dressed similarly, but with the addition of leather jerkins and pads on their arms and legs. Anyana carried a short bow, with a quiver of arrows strapped to her back. Merkle had a large battle hammer tucked into her belt. The wooden handle of the hammer was around as long as her arms, and the metal head sported both a square head about an inch to each side, and a vicious-looking hook. In contrast to the rest of us, Tyballo was wearing a magnificently ornamented cloak and had a large iron sword in a scabbard belted to his side.

Hearing the commotion, Master Kinchat entered and briefed us. Apparently, we were being assigned to patrol through the various kitchen supply rooms, looking for spikkans and any other vermin. He also warned us that one of the captive desert jackals which were used to help protect the foodstuff had gone missing and asked us to keep an eye out for it.

***

Anyana and the others already knew the way to the storerooms, so they took the lead. We started by checking in with the quartermaster, who added more detail on the missing coyote. Apparently, the beast was well-trained and a favourite with the kitchen staff. He was generally tethered in each storeroom for a portion of each day to help discourage spikkan infestations, but the previous day he had gone missing and they suspected that he might have pulled his lead free and gone in pursuit of something.

As we entered the complex of storerooms, I found they were a series of large connected caves where the supplies had been stacked in a series of boxes, crates and bottles. The lighting wasn't particularly effective and left extensive areas of shadow in most rooms.

Anyana stopped in the first room to indicate a large bell hanging near the doorway. "That's the alarm bell. If anyone gets into trouble, they can ring that, and the kitchen staff will hear it and summon help. Our standing rules are that we should ring it ourselves if we find ourselves in danger of being overrun and need assistance." I nodded to make it clear that I understood.

"Yes, and face endless taunts from the others for having backed off," added Tyballo.

"Better that than take more injuries," said Anyana. "Scordo, just to make sure we're all briefed on each other's capabilities, what magic do you have that may help?"

"Heat, Cold and Light will all hopefully be relevant," I admitted, without admitting that those were all I knew how to cast, appropriate or not.

"All right, that's much the same position as the rest of us," said Anyana. "Tyballo and I can both produce water and air as well, and Merkle can manage lightning, but none of those are valuable when fighting spikkans. Spikkans hate heat and burn well, so we'll mostly be sticking to heat workings if we encounter any. On average, apprentices only find them about one patrol in three."

While Anyana told me this, Tyballo clearly felt it was a good time to get ready. He drew his sword and I could now make out more details. The sword was long and looked light-weight, but looked somewhat blunt and chipped as if it had had a hard life. Just below the hilt, I could see a round indentation shaped into the top of the blade, while the hilt itself was thickly wrapped in leather. I noticed Tyballo was also wearing a leather glove on his sword hand.

Next, Tyballo began to cast magic. Working carefully, it took him nearly a minute to form a mana ball with a normal heat working in it. He then floated this into the indentation in the sword and fixed it there by applying an additional working to the side of the mana bubble. The blade glowed faintly, and the air rippled above it, and I realised the bubble was heating the metal of the sword. He had effectively created a heat sword, almost a fire sword.

Tyballo looked up to see me watching him.

"You haven't seen anything like this before, then? Those spikkans won't know what's hit them."

I agreed with him, although in truth my views of his performance were mixed. I liked the theory of using the heated ball to improve the lethality of his weapon, but it was surely a bit early to be getting ready? We hadn't encountered any threats yet. Apart from anything else, even if he could deal with the ongoing mana drain, surely the constant heating would weaken the metal of the sword? On the other hand, if the slow speed of his casting indicated his true mana manipulation ability, perhaps he needed to get ready well in advance? I was averaging about ten seconds rather than a minute for a similar working and I could normally manage two at once. It was also clear that this wasn't something he'd thought up himself; the sword had clearly been built to host a mana bubble in this way.

I examined my staff again and realised that what I had taken for an indentation in the iron on the top was probably a space for a mana bubble at the end of the staff.

Neither Anyana, nor Merkle showed any signs of wanting to form a mana workings already, so I held off as well.

We carefully walked down the aisles of foodstuffs in that first storeroom. The others listened carefully and, remembering the noises I'd heard in the Temple, I copied them. We could hear no sounds and, after poking around in dark corners for about a quarter of an hour, we moved on to the next room.

Everyone was tense now, trying to move as carefully as possible to avoid making noises that might mask those of vermin. Our pattern in the second room was much the same as the first, with just as little result. As I entered the room, I made sure that I'd located the emergency bell but, as we found nothing, we didn't need it. The third and fourth rooms passed similarly, with no incidents.

"How many rooms are there to check?" I asked, breaking the silence.

"Ten caverns in total and a few connecting passageways," replied Anyana. "It normally takes us about three hours to complete the circuit."

We stopped for a break after checking the fifth room. Tyballo released his mana bubble with a sigh of relief, and he carefully placed his sword out on the floor to cool. We'd each been issued a canteen of water and a set of rations when we started the patrol, so we didn't need to help ourselves to the stores stacked around us.

After a few minutes of rest, Tyballo reformed his bubble, and we moved into the sixth room. This was larger than the previous ones, with a constant cool breeze blowing through it. Half way through our inspection of the room, Merkle froze and cocked her head.

"Shush," she said, and we all tried to stop breathing. Listening carefully, I thought I could hear something, but it was coming from somewhere in the distance, rather than in this room.

After a few minutes, Anyana nodded. "I heard it that time as well," she said. "It figures. The next storeroom is one of the meat larders and this wind blows through there on the way to us. Let's finish up in here carefully and move on."

We checked the rest of the stores in the current room, tapping the boxes occasionally to encourage any occupants to stir itself, but nothing happened. Then, with Tyballo leading, we took the passageway that felt like the source of the wind. The next corridor was about fifty yards long and brought us into another low cavern stretching into the distance.

I quickly scanned the room. Most of the new cavern was filled with sides of meat, hanging from metal hooks hung in the ceiling. A variety of boxes had been stacked here and there. The shapes of the joints hanging around us kept making me think that I could see figures out of the corners of my eyes. An emergency bell was set by another door opening off to the side. We could see another couple of doorways in the distance.

I couldn't see anything moving at first, but I could hear it. A faint clicking and scratching noise, fading in and out of audibility, coming from the far end of the cavern near another passageway.

Anyana gestured for us all to stop. She then pointed at Tyballo and Merkle and then gestured to one of the aisles between the sides of meat leading towards the sound. Then she indicated herself and me and pointed at another aisle, leading in the same direction.

I saw Merkle draw her hammer out of her belt and heft it in her hand as if checking the weight. Anyana slipped her bow off her back and strung it quickly. I'd previously noticed that it was a fairly small bow, but I suddenly realised that would be ideal for drawing and aiming in confined spaces like this cavern. I lifted my staff into the air in one hand, readying it for use.

Anyana held up three fingers, then two and finally one, and we all moved slowly and carefully down our allocated aisles. I was trying to move as quietly as I could, while also concentrating on staying level with the others.

One hundred yards. Sixty yards. Twenty yards. I broke free of the end of the aisle and stopped for a moment at the scene ahead of me.

On the ground ahead of us was a small pile of boxes, mostly ripped open. They had clearly contained some type of cured sausage because remnants lay all around. Moving in and out of the boxes and in a line leading to the door were a roiling mass of spikkans.

Spiders, yes. But spiders with bodies around six inches across. Covered in hair. Dozens of them. The clicking sound was coming from both from their mandibles and from the contact between their feet and the rock floor. It somehow heightened the tension and made the scene even more ominous.

***

To give him full credit, Tyballo was the quickest to react. He swung his sword in a flat arc, touching the tip of the blade to three of the spikkans, rather than stabbing them. And where his blade touched, the spiders burned.

A few seconds later, a mana sphere flew out from Merkle and collided with the spikkan nearest to her and it too caught fire. She stopped the motion of the sphere after another second and turned it to head towards another spikkan. I heard the twang of a bow and first one, and then another flaming arrow headed towards the gigantic mass of spikkans. I turned to look at Anyana and realised that she'd formed a heat working directly in front of her bow, so each arrow she fired flew through it, bursting into flames in mid-air.

I heard a sudden clicking noise and whipped my head forward to see that a spikkan was making a run straight at me. It felt as if I was moving in slow motion, but then I fell into the staff-work that Joli had been drilled into me. I caught the spikkan with the end of the staff and knocked it on a low trajectory back into the mass.

My mana bubbles formed as I'd practised, not close to me but a few inches above the spikkans. Two spheres, each with a standard heat working, generated in less than ten seconds by my reckoning. It was then the work of an instant to dip them both into the mass of spiders. Another spikkan tried to approach Anyana and me while I formed the workings, but I automatically intercepted it with the staff and knocked it backwards. An arrow from Anyana then skewered it and it burst into flames.

I glanced at the others. Both Merkle and Tyballo were making good progress and, by my count, there were already at least thirty spikkans dead or burning. The acrid smell of burning spider reached my nostrils, along with the curiously contrasting smell of frying sausage.

The spikkans broke and turned to run, streaming out of the storeroom through the door behind them. We quickly mopped up the rest of the injured left behind: Tyballo with his sword, Merkle and me with our bubbles, with Anyana preying on those still heading towards the door.

In total, I doubt that the fight took more than a couple of minutes before we stood there victorious. Once the last of the living spikkans had fled, we all looked at each other.

"Yes! Now that's how to do it," say Tyballo.

"Nice," said Merkle.

"Congratulations everyone," said Anyana. "We smashed them! And without injuries this time."

Everyone released their mana workings and cleaned off their weapons. Anyana carefully unstrung her bow and recovered those arrows which were least damaged. I checked my staff, but it was completely unmarked from the impacts with the spikkans. One box of sausages had caught fire, but we quickly stamped it out.

"Well done, Scordo," said Anyana. "Were you really able to form two mana bubbles at once, and at a distance?"

I admitted I had, and Merkle chimed in with her congratulations. Although she'd been quick at moving her sphere, I had noticed that she'd formed it much closer to her and then had had to send it out to ignite the spikkans.

Judging by his expression, Tyballo appeared less impressed by my capabilities and he wandered off to the doorway that the spikkans had left through to make sure they'd genuinely retreated. After a few minutes, he called Anyana over.

"Look what I've found," he said. "Do you see those marks in the dust over there? Coyote tracks, heading down the passage. We should follow. We might find him and bring him back alive."

"I'm not sure," said Anyana. "We've done very well so far, but do we want to give the spikkans a chance to turn the tables?"

"But we completely overwhelmed them. Even if they tried to turn and fight, what sort of danger can they represent? We'll hear them coming from some way off, and we can always fall back slightly and ambush them. Even if we found some sort of nest, the webs burn just as well as they do."

"But our assignment was to patrol the storerooms, and who knows where this passageway leads?" said Anyana. She was clearly uneasy about Tyballo's plan, but she didn't seem to want to refuse him out of hand.

"It's probably one of the passageways that they use to bring in the supplies from outside," Tyballo said. "Yes, we were told to patrol the storerooms, but they also asked us to watch out for the coyote."

Merkle and I, drawn by the conversation, joined them in the doorway. I could see the marks that Tyballo had found in the thick dust littering the floor of the passageway. It had been churned up in places by the spikkans tracks, but here and there the coyote tracks had wandered to the sides of the passageway and stood out clearly. Away from the light of the doorway, the passageway disappeared into darkness and it clearly wasn't lit in the same way that the more habitable parts of the Annex were. A dry breeze was blowing up the passage towards us, however, and I couldn't smell or hear anything worrying.

Anyana turned to Merkle and me. "What do you think?" she asked. "Perhaps we should just explore a little way? We can always turn back if there's any sign of danger."

Merkle was keen to carry on, and I shrugged. I didn't have enough experience to know what was expected of us.

***

We started off down the passageway cautiously. Each of us created a light working. I quickly formed an advanced working and stuck it to the end of my staff. I noticed that my light was far brighter and more even than those from the others, and they clustered around me.

The passageway was wide, but had probably formed naturally, rather than being carved. It gradually curved to the left, descending as we walked along it. We tried to move quietly to listen out for any trace of sound that might indicate the presence of spikkans. We'd only walked about a hundred yards before we could no longer see any sight of the light from the storeroom doorway behind us.

After maybe half a mile of progress, the passageway forked, but the coyote tracks were clearly visible padding down the left-most fork, so we continued to follow. After another few minutes, I suddenly realised what should have been obvious to me immediately, that the coyote tracks were so much more visible because they were no longer disturbed by crossing spikkan tracks.

I stopped and pointed this out.

"So what?" said Tyballo. "They probably moved to the ceiling since they're just as fast up there. Either that, or they took the other fork, but that probably rejoins this one in time."

We continued. The curve of the passageway continued to tighten, and the slope grew steeper. It felt almost as if we were spiralling into the ground, but there was still no sign of dampness in the air. Indeed, the breeze had dropped almost to nothing by this point. Another mile or so of passage went by with a few additional side opening to left and right, but Tyballo used his glowing sword to carve marks in the walls of the cave to ensure that we could find our way back.

After we'd been marching for about three quarters of an hour, our passage opened up into a much bigger cavern, larger than any we'd seen. It was maybe thirty feet high near the entrance and ran at least a hundred and fifty feet forwards and about twenty feet wide. I held up my staff to see better. There was no sign of any other passages exiting the cavern, but there was a deep crevasse across the floor of the cave at the other end, followed by a narrowing of the width of the cavern at the other side. There was no evidence of spikkans, but there was a pile of debris on the floor at the far end of the space, just on the other side of the crack in the floor.

"Let me check that out," said Tyballo, pointing down the cave. Accompanied by Merkle, who had her battle hammer out and was looking around nervously, he walked down the cavern, jumping over the fissure in the floor which wasn't much more than a couple of feet wide.

Anyana remained near the entrance, and I stuck with her. I noticed she had her bow out and restrung again.

"There's something here," came Tyballo's voice. "It's... err... it's half a coyote carcass. Bitten in two and burned somehow."

"Bitten?" said Anyana. "But spikkans don't have mouths big enough for... Tyballo, Merkle, please come back here now."

"Let me just see..." said Tyballo, and then it happened. The middle of the cavern suddenly glowed red and orange as a gigantic snake made of fire reared up out of the crack between us and the other two. The snake was about an arm's length across in the middle and at least twenty-five feet long. I couldn't tell whether it had teeth or orange flames in its mouth, but neither was an attractive prospect.

CHAPTER FOURTEEN
Ambush

"Drat," said Anyana. It was somewhat of an understatement from my point of view. "Scordo, that's a vizzinti. It's a type of fire-serpent. It's an actual living creature, but it uses magic to coat itself in fire. And we're massively unprepared for this. For a start, heat simply will not hurt it, and that's where we're strongest."

I suddenly noticed what I should have foreseen earlier. We were now a long way from the inhabited part of the Annex, and there were neither emergency bells nor any other way that I knew of to summon help.

I could see the open mouths of the other two on the other side of the cavern, staring at the sudden apparition.

"Tyballo, Merkle, change spells!" shouted Anyana.

Realisation came to Tyballo's face and I could feel him dismiss the heat sphere attached to his sword and retreat to the back of the cave. Merkle drew her hammer and moved to stand in front of him. The vizzinti was focused entirely on the trapped pair, ignoring us entirely. It turned to face them, pulling more of its body out of the crack.

Merkle formed a standard cold working and ran it into the snake's body. It reared back as if stung by the blow, but there was no other noticeable damage. Perhaps the power of the fire was too strong for it to be more than an irritation? She cast another cold sphere and crashed it into the serpent's head, but with no more success. This time, it didn't even flinch away, but gradually swung its head closer towards the two of them, making a rhythmic hissing sound.

I saw Merkle glance back at Tyballo, who was still cowering behind her at the far end of the cave. I felt him lose control of the mana sphere that he was trying to form, and the mana dissipated. He swore and began again.

This time, Merkle tried what I assumed must be a lightning sphere. I heard it spark and snap as it approached the snake's head and the vizzinti flinched back from the ball a little. Merkle pressed the attack, pushing the sphere briefly against the snake's head and it reared back again from the contact.

For a moment, I thought that she might get it on the run, but the vizzinti had other ideas. The end of its tail swung in from the side towards Merkle. I shouted to warn her, but it was clear that she had already seen it. I gasped. There was nothing she could do to defend against the massive fiery tail swinging towards her. She got her hammer in the way and tried to block it, but the inertia of the attack was simply too much for her to overcome. The hammer flew out of her hand and she was launched sideways into the cavern wall, where she fell to the floor, immobile. To make things worse, I saw her clothes were now alight.

"How can we help?" I asked Anyana.

"I... err... I'm not too sure," she admitted. "My arrows won't be any more than a distraction. I can send them through a cold working in the way that I did with the heat one, but all that'll do is make them slightly colder. The advantage of the heat working is that it actually sets them on fire."

"How about your water working?" I asked. "Could we somehow put the snake's fire out?"

"The apprentice working isn't much of an offensive weapon," she admitted. "It pours, rather than sprays. That snake is too far away for me to hit it. And even if I could hang it above the snake, what good is a little water going to do against that?"

I suddenly saw that Tyballo was on his feet again and had crossed to stand between Merkle's inert form and the snake. His sword was glowing faintly blue now, rather than red. The snake's head was swinging back and forth in front of him, trying to find a way past him to our disabled companion. Tyballo swung his sword to follow it.

Then suddenly he struck, making contact someway up its neck. I saw the sword sink in slightly and heard a brief hissing sound that wasn't coming from the snake's mouth before he pulled the sword back.

The snake's head reared back, and I saw it watching him for a moment. Then the tail swung in suddenly from the side again, trying to catch Tyballo. He saw it coming and ducked underneath, trying to catch it with his sword as it retreated again. He just about got his sword in the way in time, but he could only catch it with a glancing blow. The vizzinti then tried to strike him with its head again, but he managed barely to raise his sword in time and let the vizzinti's own inertia carry it into the blade. Again, it reared back in apparent pain, snapping its mouth open and closed.

It hated the combination of cold and blade, but the attacks weren't doing noticeable damage. The snake was still glowing with fire and we seemed to have nothing that would hurt it. And Tyballo was clearly staggered by the power of the blows against his sword. His movement was quickly becoming uncertain as he tired. It would only be a few moments before he was overwhelmed. Surely, we must be able to do something?

"Can we distract it somehow to give Tyballo a chance to get Merkle around it and drag her to safety? Then maybe we can run for it. How fast are vizzinti?" I asked.

"From everything I've heard, they're pretty fast in confined spaces like that passage," said Anyana. "There's no way we'd be able to escape it carrying Merkle. But maybe we can distract it?"

She drew her bow and fired an arrow through a cold working. As she had said, the magic did little more than chill the arrow, but that was enough to keep it intact as it passed through the flames and hit the snake. I saw it protruding from its neck for a moment before it burst into flames and quickly burnt away. Anyana nocked another arrow and prepared to fire. Myself, I formed a sphere with an advanced cold working as close to the snake's body as I could and then added a sticking charm to keep it in contact with the flaming skin.

It's safe to say that we got its attention, but I wasn't sure we'd be able to deal with the consequences. The vizzinti had stopped moving towards Tyballo and Merkle when the first arrow impacted. When the second arrived, followed by my cold working, it reared around in search of the new threat, pulling itself across the floor towards us. I could feel the mana in my sphere being spent quickly as a loud hissing noise came from the location I'd targeted. As my sphere failed, I saw that the vizzinti was visibly injured at last. The advanced cold sphere had succeeded where the more basic ones had failed and a circular patch of darkness a few inches wide could be seen amid the vizzinti's fiery exterior. But it was only one mark on the fiery expanse of its body. The snake hissed angrily and continued to advance on us rapidly.

In the distance, behind the snake, I could see Tyballo grab Merkle and begin to drag her the long way across the cave and around the far end of the crack.

Anyana continued to fire arrows, and I prepared a second mana sphere, carefully making sure that it was as perfect as I could manage before flicking it onto the snake and sticking it tight. Again, the horrible hissing sound of the skin freezing and blistering, again an echoing hiss from the snake's throat as it approached.

This wouldn't work. Sure, we'd got its attention, and Tyballo was making good progress dragging Merkle to a temporary safety, but we weren't scaring it off. We were enraging it and we could probably look forward to being killed first before it finished the others. As I thought this, the snake got close enough to us to attack with its head with the rest of its body stretched out behind it across the floor. I reacted by instinct, stepping in front of Anyana and flicking up my staff to catch it on the nose in mid-lunge. It reared back with its flaming tongue sticking out of its mouth. Was it tasting the air to help locate us? At least its tail was still stretched out behind it and wasn't yet available to join the attack.

My mana spheres had both done damage, but not enough. Perhaps I could do something bigger? Mikka had had me doing some work with larger spheres twice the size of the ordinary ones. They were much harder to form and control and required a lot more mana to fill. Normally, that would extend the duration of the working, but pressed against the magical heat of the vizzinti, my cold workings were being used up unnaturally quickly. Perhaps more mana was just what I needed?

A double width mana sphere required about eight times as much as a normal sized one because of the difference in volumes. Did I have enough mana to form a triple sized one? And did I have the skill to form one? While I thought, I quickly generated another normal sized working and hit the snake under its chin on the narrowest part of its body to fend it off and force it to retreat momentarily.

Then I stepped backwards and summoned my mana reserves, trying to forge a triple-width, six inch wide sphere of mana between the two of us. I held my staff in guard position, ready to defend us, while Anyana fired again over my head. Despite the urgency and my rising panic, I desperately tried to work slowly and carefully. I didn't know what the consequences might be if I lost control of this working, but it certainly wouldn't be healthy for us. First, I formed the outside of the bubble, reinforcing the skin more than usual to contain even more mana. Then I started to fill it. My mana seemed to pour out of me, disappearing into the sphere I'd made with no apparent end in sight to the process.

The snake had got over its pain from my recent working and was approaching again. Anyana's firing was getting more sporadic, and I realised she was probably running out of arrows.

More and more mana continued to rush out of me and, although I was starting to feel some faint back pressure as if the sphere was nearly full, I wasn't sure I had the reserves to finish. I might simply run out. My knees began to feel weak and my vision narrowed. I absorbed back my light working and poured the recovered mana straight into the new bubble. Given the huge burning figure of the snake, it wasn't as if we needed the light.

Anyana stopped firing arrows at last and propelled her cold working straight into the face of the snake. It flinched back but only for a moment and it seemed to gaze straight into my eyes, readying itself for the strike.

I poured all the mana I had left into the bubble, and it finally seemed to be full. No, more than that, maybe it had a higher density than usual? I struggled to visualise the toroidal working that I needed to form. I'd noticed in the past that the working seemed to be stronger when the torus was broader and when the hole in the centre was narrower, so I tried to visualise a pattern which made each as extreme as possible. Once I thought I had it right, I took hold of the mana and tried to move it, but I was increasingly finding it difficult to concentrate. Maybe I should have tried something else?

I suddenly realised that I was working too slowly, and the snake was going to move first. I had no way of defending myself from it without abandoning the working.

At that point, I saw Tyballo step in from the side. He was gazing at the sphere I'd formed, either in horror or in awe. Then he flicked his head round to lock eyes with me. For a moment, I didn't know what he was going to do, and I suspected he didn't either. Then he deliberately stepped in front of me, blocking the line of attack from the snake, and raised his sword in front of its face.

<{I/myself/Pinca} {try/help/succeed} {assist/control/guide}>

I suddenly heard the voice of my Glowling. The visualisation I was maintaining of the required working gradually changed to make the working even more extreme, not just trying to trace a toroidal pattern within the mana, but moving all the mana filling the sphere at once. At the same time, I could feel the thick, turgid mana in the working gradually trickling into life. My Glowling seemed to add its will to help me pull the current into life.

Tyballo swung his sword back and forth in front of me, trying to keep the snake's head at bay, but I could see the rest of the snake's body approaching and the tail gradually moving round into position.

Starting Sphere

Success. Waves of cold began to hit my face as the working flashed into life with a glare of blue fire. Tyballo staggered sideways, trying to escape from the fierceness of the chill. That cleared my view of the snake and I carefully pushed the mana sphere towards the dark spot under the snake's chin where my previous working had lodged. With the last of my energy, I added a working to stick it to the snake as a last flourish and sank to my knees.

Impact. The working sank into the snake's throat, seeming to absorb heat not only from its surroundings but also sucking it in from further parts of the snake as its fiery head and body flickered. The vizzinti's tail flicked round at last and caught me full in the side and I felt myself flying towards the cavern wall. But the snake itself seemed to crumple into itself and as its fire went out, the cavern sunk back into darkness.

Then I hit the wall, and the darkness was everywhere.

CHAPTER FIFTEEN
Debrief

I awoke to find myself lying on the cavern floor close to where I must have hit the wall. My body was aching with what felt like more burns and there were also some sharp pains in my side and I was finding it difficult to breathe. My face felt sore as well. To top it all off, I was sopping wet and was shaking with the cold. My staff, which looked undamaged, was still in my hand.

I tried to sit up and gasped in agony at the renewed pain in my side.

"Scordo, are you all right?" It was Anyana. She was close to the entrance to the cavern, leaning over Merkle. She had a faint light working floating above her. I briefly thought about making a light working myself, or a heat working to warm myself up, but didn't think I could manage either. I felt completely spent.

"I'm getting very bored with waking up to find that I passed out," I managed. Anyana giggled.

"Did we win? I asked. "How are Merkle and Tyballo?"

"You killed the vizzinti," she said. "Merkle is still alive. She hasn't come round yet and I think she's got broken ribs just like you. She's breathing more easily now I've got her laid out. Tyballo has gone to fetch help."

"Anyana, why am I so wet?" I asked.

She laughed this time. "You were on fire," she said. "In fact, you were the only light in the cavern. Tyballo made a water working and put you out. He may have overdone it."

"I just bet he loved that," I said bitterly.

"Actually, I had to insist," she said. "He was terrified that you'd wake up and strike him down. I was too busy trying to stabilise Merkle."

"Terrified?"

"Scordo, I don't think you realise how far Logross's tuition has taken you past normal apprentice standards. It's far from common for an apprentice to maintain two spheres and to form them at a distance. And I've never heard of an apprentice being taught the more advanced cold form. I assume you have mastered the heat one as well?"

I admitted that this was true.

"I didn't even think to ask you about that earlier. As far as forming oversized bubbles, that's normally only performed by senior artisans and above."

"I didn't realise," I admitted. "Mikka told me that my forming speed was above average, but the other things were all refinements that Master Logross instructed him to teach me."

Merkle coughed roughly, and Anyana bent over her again.

"How soon until we can expect help?" I asked.

"I don't know exactly," she said. "Tyballo set off a

little under an hour ago, which is more or less how long it took for us to get here. At least the same again for them to get back to us, I suppose. Plus, they'll need time to organise the rescue party."

At that moment, a blinding blue light split the darkness of the cavern. As my eyes adjusted, I saw that the light was slowly tracing the outline of a giant oval hanging in mid-air a few inches above floor level.

"That's a transport gate, but who would..." said Anyana.

The blue light completed the oval and, in a blinding flash, it filled in with white fire. Master Logross stepped through carrying a staff similar to mine. Light workings appeared in mid-air, illuminating the entire cavern, and he turned back and forth to take in the whole of the scene. Once he'd satisfied himself that there was no obvious threat, he turned back to me.

"Ah, boy," he said. "You're late. You were expected back some time ago."

"But..." I stammered, "But you're supposed to be away."

"I came back," he answered. "Just in time to be on the scene to find that your patrol was overdue and no-one knew where you were. Master Kinchat was preparing to investigate when Apprentice Tyballo raised the alarm."

"Tyballo made it then?" cut in Anyana.

"Yes, Assistant Squad Leader Anyana," he said with stress on every word. She winced. "Your companion apparently ran all the way back to the storeroom where your little... fracas... with the spikkans took place and then pounded repeatedly on the alarm bell until someone came. A single hit on the bell would have been sufficient. They're all tied into the alert system."

"If," he continued, "you had been actually assigned to patrol outside the normal bell network, you would of course have been assigned a mobile bell to allow you to summon assistance when necessary. We will discuss this later." Anyana winced again.

"I came to investigate myself once I heard the story. The others," he waved a languid hand, "will be along shortly. For your information, it's not unheard of for a vizzinti nest to have more than one occupant. It would have been wiser to move further up the passage before treating your injuries." He stopped down and picked up a mangled piece of metal which looked like it might be what was left of Tyballo's sword, but if so, the snake had melted and twisted it almost past recognition.

Master Logross moved over to inspect the corpse of the vizzinti. "This looks rather like overkill, boy. A double power mana sphere at normal pressure would likely have been sufficient. He sniffed and seemed to taste the air. And you rather overdid the working; you were within a whisper of forming a great working. We will discuss this later as well." Anyana's eyes widened further at his comments. Master Logross walked past the serpent and picked up Merkle's discarded hammer.

Just then, Master Kinchat stepped through the blue fire of the gate wreathed in some sort of flickering shield working. He looked around, located Master Logross and then nodded. His shield dissipated.

"All clear, Master Logross?" he asked.

"Yes," said Master Logross. "It appears to have been alone. It was around three hundred years old, if my guess is correct. Likely migrated to this part of the caverns recently, and the coyote must have caught the smell. I assume you will send a squad to recover what little my apprentice has left of the body?"

"Of course," Kinchat replied.

"I would ask a favour, Master Kinchat." said Logross. "May I run the... debrief... from this incident?"

"Of course, Master Logross," Kinchat repeated. "As ever, I am very grateful for your assistance."

A moment later, Master Fenella also stepped through the gate accompanied by a team of orderlies. A couple of them made their way to Merkle and me and they assembled stretchers while Master Fenella quickly checked over us in turn. She reported we were safe to move, and they gently rolled us onto our stretchers and lifted and carried through the gate. A blinding white flash later, and I was carried through the twin of the blue oval straight onto a transport platform in the lobby of the medical clinic.

***

I was carried into a small ward.

Tyballo was already sitting up on another bed, and was being treated for extensive burns across his arms and face.

"Scordo, how are you?" he asked as soon as he saw me carried in. "And the others?"

"Now please, don't move or this is going to be much more painful," said the orderly treating him.

"I've felt better," I admitted and then screamed as I was eased off the stretcher and onto a bed. "I think the others are going to be OK. Anyana was all right, anyway, and she said that Merkle was stable."

Just then, Merkle's stretcher was carried in and they eased her onto a bed at the other end of the ward. She was followed into the room by Master Fenella and Anyana, who was walking without assistance. She lurked silently behind Master Fenella as she examined Merkle.

"Four displaced broken ribs and minor burns to the torso," said Fenella. "Likely concussion as well. We'll get started on her treatment as soon as possible and she should be on the road to recovery by tomorrow. We'll keep her in for a day longer for observation, however."

Master Fenella came over to me.

"Back again I see, Apprentice Scordo," she said. "You have outdone yourself this time. Two simple broken ribs, burns to the torso, severe mana exhaustion and, if I'm not mistaken, frostbite to your face as well! I don't think I want to know how you managed to get both heat and cold damage in a single encounter, but I'm sure that Master Logross will want to discuss it with you in depth. You should be ready to leave by tomorrow morning, but I'm going to put you to sleep for now." She cast some sort of working near me and my eyes immediately closed.

"Apprentice Anyana," I heard before I fell asleep. "You've seen your squad are safe, so, unless you're hiding some injuries you haven't mentioned, it's time for you to leave and let us work."

The next morning, I woke to find the room largely empty. What had remained of my tunic had been removed and my side strapped up tightly to keep my ribs from moving. My necklace glittered on my bare chest. The only other occupant was Merkle, snoring away in a bed on the other side of the room. I felt stronger and my mana had refilled overnight. My ribs already felt better, as did my various burns, and I assumed they must have used a working to speed up my healing.

A few minutes later, an orderly entered, a man in his mid-twenties. He spoke in a rural Zaronian accent that I found difficult to understand, but I thought he was promising to bring food. I saw his eyes lingering on my exposed necklace, and I pulled up the sheets to cover myself better.

After breakfast, Master Fenella checked me over. She was happy with my speed of recovery and noted that I would be excluded from Physical Training for next week, but that I should be fine after that.

Mid morning, Mikka turned up.

"Back in the infirmary so soon?" he said. "I gather you summoned up some forceful offensive skills, after all? I've had the pleasure of a long lecture from Master Logross on the topic of making sure I brief you on what you shouldn't be doing, as well as what you should. I gather he'll be speaking to you on this himself. If you're good to move, then let's head back to our quarters."

***

Later that day, I was surprised to see a deeply chastened looking Anyana leaving Master Logross's work room.

"What happened?" I asked.

"Scordo, thank goodness you're all right. Is there somewhere we can talk? And possibly a glass of water?"

I filled a glass for her and we both went into my workroom and sat across from each other.

"I've just had what Master Logross called a 'debrief'," she admitted once she'd drunk some water. "Basically, he made me recount every detail of what happened to us yesterday in minute detail. Once he couldn't wring any more facts out of me, he critiqued my performance."

I could well imagine Master Logross taking exquisite pleasure in that sort of behaviour.

"Ouch. How did it go?" I asked.

"Failure to properly understand and follow our operating instructions. Failure to properly discover team abilities. Failure to control the exuberance of other squad members. Operating without backup. Allowing the squad to become split in a potentially dangerous location. Failure to analyse the tactical situation and provide leadership during combat. Splitting the squad again in the aftermath of combat to seek for help. Failure to secure a position of safety while waiting for rescue." Anyana ticked each of these off on her fingers as she spoke.

"I think that covers the basics. And then he commented it should be a good experience for me and confirmed my Squad Leader position. Scordo, is your master entirely insane?"

"Entirely," I confirmed. "But he always has his

reasons."

"I'm not sure what was worst, but it may have been his closing remark. He muttered something about ensuring that our future missions were sufficiently challenging that we didn't feel the need to go looking for additional trouble," she said.

We spent some time talking further about what we'd ought to have done and how we'd handle ourselves in the future. After a while, though, she excused herself and I was left on my own. I did some mana exercises while waiting to be summoned but, to my surprise Tyballo was the next person I saw leaving Master Logross's quarters. He also looked shattered from the experience, so I got him some water and ushered him into my workroom.

As he sat down, Tyballo put a shining, pristine sword on the table. "He mended it," he said dumbly. "He interrogated me thoroughly about what happened during our patrol while at the same time running his fingers over the sword and it sort of smoothed out as he talked. I've never seen anything like it.

"Scordo, I'm sorry I gave you a hard time about him before. No advantages could be worth having to deal with... that on a frequent basis," he said. He glanced away from me briefly.

"I should have said yesterday," he continued. "Thank you for saving us. I was terrified when I saw your working. I couldn't imagine that you'd be able to keep control of it but, boy, did it do the job."

"Thank you as well," I said. "From what I remember, you stepped between me and the vizzinti when I couldn't finish the working fast enough. I would have been a goner, wide open to its attack, if you hadn't done that."

"You're welcome," said Tyballo. "In fact, that and dragging Merkle to the exit were the things that your Master was, not exactly pleased with, but perhaps least angry about."

From the tone of his words, Master Logross had clearly had a lot of other less favourable comments for Tyballo about his performance. I suspected that he'd been criticised for his role in encouraging us to follow the coyote, and possibly over his slow casting speed, which had left Merkle defending him alone when he switched from heat to cold workings. However, I valued what seemed at least a newfound spirit of truce between us too much to want to push him further on this.

After he left, I spent the rest of the day alternately between more forming practice and reading a book that had been waiting for me when I had got back to my room this morning, "A practical bestiary of Zaronia". It was terrifying. For example, a ten-feet long scorpion creature that could inject acid. Really? Why?

Despite my expectations, my call to Master Logross's workroom didn't come that day. The next day, I got at least part of the explanation when I found Merkle leaving his quarters. I remembered Master Fenella had said she hadn't been due to be released until that morning.

I stopped her in the lobby and asked how her interrogation had gone.

"The other two stopped by the clinic last night and briefed me on their ordeals," she said. "Based on what they said, I think I got off lightly. But then, I spent most of the fight unconscious. Master Logross was pleased that I tried to shield Tyballo while he changed his working, but recommended that I study the different attack patterns of various creatures more 'diligently'."

Just then, Master Logross's door clicked open, and I heard his summons by my ear.

"Good luck," Merkle said, and I reluctantly left her and entered Master Logross's study.

***

Master Logross was in his usual position behind his desk with an empty chair in front of it. He curtly indicated it.

"Sit," he said.

I sat. Since he normally made me stand, I guessed that maybe this was some sort of concession to my injuries.

"Apprentice Scordo," he continued. "As a Master of the Guild, duly appointed to investigate this matter, I bind you by your seal to answer my questions honestly and in appropriate detail."

I felt my seal pulse once. I hadn't known that this was possible, but I guessed it made sense. I saw he had some sort of working active as well, perhaps a type of truth detection spell?

"Tell me, from your point of view, all the relevant details of your patrol two days ago. Include details of your impressions of the capabilities, behaviour, and relationships with your various companions.

So I did. Once or twice, I tried to skate over details that I thought were less relevant, such as the needling I'd endured from Tyballo over the last month or two, and the comparisons that I'd drawn between my mana-forming capabilities and theirs, but each time my seal applied pressure until I clarified. I noticed, however, that the seal didn't appear to detect evasions associated to my interactions with my Glowling, so I volunteered little detail there.

When I finished, he returned to my final cold working and dug in deeper. He asked how I'd known I was capable of a triple working, and I admitted I hadn't been absolutely sure that I was, but that I'd thought things were sufficiently dire that I had had no choice but to try. He then asked me what had led me to make the modifications to the toroidal current patterns and whether anyone had taught me 'Greater Working' patterns. I could answer honestly that no-one from the Guild had briefed me on this, but that I'd noticed slight variations while practising the advanced working and that it had just 'felt right' to me. Again, I felt no pressure to comment on the changes to the pattern that the Glowling had made.

When I'd finished, he sighed and thought for a minute. Then he said, "As a Master of the Guild, I release you from your binding," and I felt the seal relax slightly. Still there, but no longer forcing the truth from me.

"Tell me again, why did you cast the high-density triple strength cold working?" he asked again.

I repeated my earlier assertions that I thought I had no chance but to chance it. He sighed again.

"Apprentice Scordo, there may well be times in

the future that you need to risk your life, your comrades' lives and your power itself on a single throw of the dice. This was not one of them," he said.

"I will concede that you were in a critical situation initially. You had allowed your squad to be divided by a powerful enemy, and half of your number had no line of retreat. However, by the time you began your final working, your squad had already resolved that problem. Apprentice Tyballo had successfully dragged Apprentice Merkle to the passage, which was the only reason he could return to help save you from your folly.

"You had the reserves and mana to cast a series of normal double power spheres, probably at least three or four. A single double-power sphere would have taken a fraction of the time to form than the triple power sphere took and might have killed the vizzinti outright. At the very least, it would probably have scared it off."

"But I didn't know that," I argued.

"No, you did not. Since your squad was not expected to stray from the normal tunnels, you had received no briefing on the capabilities and power levels of creatures like vizzinti. But would it not have been wise to experiment with a single double-strength bubble to discover what the impact might be? As opposed to deciding to use up everything you had in a last-ditch attempt? An attempt which would take too long to carry out?"

I felt somewhat embarrassed. I hadn't really thought about this at the time.

"The line of retreat for your squad was secured. A

single double powered sphere with a normal advanced working might have formed enough of a deterrent that it would have driven the vizzinti off. If one working had turned out to be inadequate, you could have used the distraction caused by the impact to retreat into the passageway, taking your squad members with you. Once you were in the tunnel, the vizzinti would only have been able to attack with its head in the narrow confines, protecting you from its tail. You'd then have had the opportunity to gradually fall back one stage at a time. You might even have had enough time to refill your reserves as you retreated, which would have maximised the amount of damage you could have done.

"And if you made a judgement that you didn't have enough power to kill the vizzinti, then you could have looked for other options. For example, I know well that you've experimented with cracking the stone walls with the advanced fire working in your workroom. Did you consider using that to collapse the roof of the tunnel to seal you and your companions off from danger?"

I was stunned by this analysis. For a start, Master Logross had said more words in this interview than I'd heard him use since we'd met. The opportunity to analyse the combat situation seemed to have unlocked some additional level of enthusiasm in him. At the same time, I felt he was being unfair.

"But how was I supposed to think of all that at the time? Do you really expect me to..."

"Yes," he said simply, cutting off my protests. "Or die young and waste all the training you've received.

"I cannot hold you wholly responsible for the

errors made by your squad. It was, after all, the first time you'd been placed in that sort of position. However, I can and will hold you responsible for your failure to think clearly before risking sacrificing yourself and the rest of your team for nothing. Judging by the instabilities I detected from the working residue in the cave, you were within a hair's breadth of losing control of that working. If you had done so, you would have found the results particularly suboptimal."

"What would have happened?" I asked, somewhat chastened.

"The good news is that the vizzinti would have been killed. The bad news is that you, Apprentice Anyana and Apprentice Tyballo would have been instantly flash-frozen and then likely shattered into pieces by the blast wave from the rupture. Apprentice Merkle was some further distance away and would have likely survived the initial blast front with significant frost burns and hypothermia, and would then have died from her internal injuries within the next hour."

Gulp.

"Again, let me repeat myself. I am not saying that you must never choose to overspend your power and perform workings you are unsure about. Regrettably, it is possible that you may stray into situations where that course is unavoidable. However, I expect you to at least consider whether the scenario is otherwise non-survivable for you and your companions, and wherever possible, to fully exhaust other options before gambling on a single untested course of action."

A silence fell. In all honesty, I couldn't disagree

with his analysis. Yes, it would have been nicer to have had more proactive advice from the others, but ultimately I had decided to try the working without even consulting or warning them.

"Yes, Master." I said after a while.

He nodded. "That said, you did not lose control of the working and you were successful in what you attempted. Well done."

A silence fell again. Had I heard right? He was congratulating me?

He nodded once. "Dismissed."

I stumbled out. In hindsight, I doubt I looked any less shell-shocked than the others had.

Interlude 2

"A gold necklace with a gray metal sunburst you say? How interesting."

The speaker was a well-dressed Zaronian man wearing rich robes, and an ornate sword. A prosperous merchant or a low-ranking member of the Zaronian court, perhaps?

"Yes, your honour. I marked the similarities with the carvings of the Benefactors."

His confidant had dressed more plainly, in the simple uniform typical of the locals who served in the Guild Annex. They had met in a rough stone barn set some miles from a nearby village, which was clearly a prearranged meeting point. Both had taken precautions to ensure that they had attracted no attention and had not been followed.

"Tell me more about the wearer."

"From what I've been able to gather, he's a recent apprentice, but rising fast. It's his second visit to the infirmary. The first time was because of a training accident. This time, his vermin control squad ran into trouble and they fought and defeated a fire snake. He's serving one of the heavy hitters that you've had me keeping an eye out for, Master Logross."

"Indeed?" The well-dressed speaker raised an eyebrow. "Master Logross has deigned to take another student then? I'll see if I can find any additional information from the Temple on the background and circumstances."

"Yes, your honour. Do you want any more action from me on this?"

"No, we'd want far more corroboration before acting. It may only be a trinket that he's picked up that has no real relevance to him. How about your primary mission?"

"There are a couple of books in here. I was able to extract each some time ago and put them aside. Since there has been no reaction, I judged it was safe to bring them out of the Annex in the usual way."

He handed a sack over to his companion and retired back a few steps.

"Good. Although it sticks in my craw a little, having to live off their crumbs. Still, that's where we are, while we gradually try to rebuild our birth-right. Come over here and let me check your blocks."

The plainly dressed man kneeled down in front of his superior, who placed a hand on his forehead. There was silence for a few minutes before the standing man spoke.

"All good. Intact with triggers set. It's a brave thing you do. Our gratitude for your service."

The other man returned to his feet and nodded in acknowledgement. He then turned and left without a further word. The other remained in the barn for fifteen minutes before departing in a different direction.

CHAPTER SIXTEEN
Devices

The next day, Mikka briefed me on some of the taxonomy of workings and theory behind them he'd previously skipped.

"Basically, you have simple workings, advanced workings, and greater workings. And compound workings as well, I guess. There may be other categories, but that's all that I know about."

"OK," I said. "So, how do they differ?"

"Simple workings are nearly always a simple flat pattern. Of course, they're often not quite flat because otherwise currents wouldn't be able to cross. They tend to be easy to master once you've got sufficient skill at mana manipulation, but their raw power is limited. What that means in real terms depends on the nature of the working. For example, with a simple light working it can emit a certain brightness level, a heat working can only heat to a certain temperature, and so on."

"That makes sense to me," I commented.

"They are also the weakest to external influence. For example, you said that, when you were fighting the vizzinti, simple cold workings fizzled out quickly. They stung it, but did no lasting damage. That was because they needed to make contact to have a noticeable effect and once in contact, they were rapidly overwhelmed by the heat from the vizzinti's fire. The working was destabilised, it ruptured, and the mana dispersed before it could all be used. And, in any case, they weren't cold enough to do more than sting.

"In contrast, the lightning working that your friend Merkle used lasted slightly longer because it wasn't initially in direct contact with the serpent, but it had a limited effect because a vizzinti is less distressed by lightning.

"In summary, simple workings are easy to learn but of limited efficiency in battles because typically most of the mana gets wasted."

"And that's usually the limit of what apprentices get taught, right?" I said.

Mikka looked a little embarrassed. "Yes, it is. By the time they graduate, some apprentices can manage a single or possibly two advanced workings, often the light working, but not usually anything more. The sort of tasks that apprentices are assigned rarely need more than that."

"OK, so how do advanced workings differ?" I asked.

"Simply put, an advanced working is more complicated than its simple working counterpart. Of course, not all advanced workings have simple versions. Advanced workings are usually three dimensional and they get more of the mana moving at once. The advantage is that the effect is more intense, and because more mana is in motion, they are not only harder to overwhelm, but they can also have a quicker impact."

"So, was my advanced cold working able to cause actual damage to the vizzinti because it was colder, or because of the volume of mana involved?" I asked.

"It was able to injure the vizzinti because the temperature was so much colder. It survived for more than an instant because the increased mana flow helped it stay stable in that environment. And it went on injuring the snake and cause noticeable damage because of a combination of the two. Ultimately, a high proportion of the mana ended up being spent in the attack."

"So, when Master Logross said that I should have used a double sized mana ball with an advanced working, was that what he meant?"

"Yes, exactly. You had verified that an advanced working was going to do the job efficiently, so all you needed to do was to cast a bigger one, which had more mana available to it and clamp that to the vizzinti. Fire, flee and forget. Or in a more extended combat scenario, it would be time to turn your attention to another target."

"I see. Try something and then use the response to understand how to tweak your attack?"

"In a nutshell," said Mikka

"So you'd never use an advanced heat working to attack a spikkan?"

"Never is a strong word, but normally you simply wouldn't need to, no. There are a few things going on in that scenario. First, a simple working generates quite enough heat to set a spikkan on fire.

Second, once it has started burning, it will tend to go on burning without having to keep a working applied. And finally, a spikkan has no magic or other effect that can easily destabilise a mana sphere. I guess you might use an advanced working if you wanted to set fire to a lot of spikkans in one go, with no need to actually touch all of them."

"But you said that some advanced workings don't have simple counterparts?" I said.

"Correct. But I don't have any examples that I can share with you right now. I'd need Master Logross's explicit instructions."

"Right, so what's a Greater Working?"

Mikka was a little uncomfortable. "In a Greater Working, more or less all the mana in a bubble is pressed into motion simultaneously. You're not tracing a shape in the bubble anymore, you're affecting the whole bubble. In theory, that means that the impact can be more intense, and it also means that, when necessary, you can spend the entire mana pool in a single instant. They are not practised at either apprentice or, so far as I know, Artisan level."

I'd caught something in his choice of words.

"Practised, or taught?" I asked.

Mikka looked even more uncomfortable. "Master Logross was quite specific when briefing me yesterday that Guild rules prohibit an apprentice's teacher from ordering or encouraging them to practise Greater Workings. It does not actually prohibit them from teaching them the shape of a specific Greater Working, nor does it prohibit an apprentice from casting one on their own. If they have a death wish, that is."

"I see," I said. Did Master Logross actually want me to learn some Greater Workings, or was I reading too much into this?

Mikka continued. "It's important to say that the shapes of most Greater Workings aren't exactly common knowledge. They're often carefully guarded secrets. For example, I've never even heard of a Greater Working version of the normal light working and it's difficult to see how you could form one. I suspect you'd have to go about it differently..." He trailed away with a far-off look in his eyes. I suspected he was trying to visualise such a thing.

We ended that lesson shortly afterwards, and I was left to practise for the rest of the day.

***

A day or so later, Mikka met me early in the morning to tell me that Master Logross had left instructions for me to visit the Device laboratories.

"We're off to visit Gonni," he said happily.

The Device laboratories turned out to be in a complex of caverns which were further underground than our quarters about a half hours walk away. When we arrived, Mikka gave our names to an orderly manning the lobby area, and she hurried away. A few minutes later, she returned with Mikka's friend Gonni.

I immediately noticed that in the weeks since I'd last seen him, he'd moved up to Artisan status.

"Congratulations," I said, nodding at his seal

"Thank you," he replied. "I finally tired of people trying to pull rank on me, including your mentor, so I found the time to take the tests. I gather congratulations are due to you as well for surviving."

"Err, thank you," I replied. "How did you hear about... it".

"You should realise that gossip spreads round the facility like, umm, fire. But I have an inside track in this case. Come with me."

He led us through a network of passages and finally into his laboratory.

It was a large room, possibly three times the size of my workroom. Waist-high counters lined the walls and several tables stood in the middle of the room. Shelving was fixed below the wall counters covered with a series of tools, including knives, chisels, selections of lenses, drills, and a number of larger machines whose function I couldn't immediately guess. Above the workspace, the walls themselves were lined with parchments covered by complex diagrams, patterns, and tables of numbers. It was some mad combination of Master Logross's workroom and a well-equipped medical facility.

I didn't pay that much attention to the details, however, because looped around the room strung from work surface to work surface and back again lay the skeleton of a thirty-five feet long snake.

We stood there gazing at it at it for a minute.

"Is that... mine?" I said eventually. Laid out in this way, it was even bigger than I remembered.

"Yup," confirmed Gonni. "Good work, by the way."

"How did they," I gestured, "get the skeleton out?" I wasn't sure what else to say.

"The body was carried back to the Annex by a team dispatched by Master Kinchat. The skin was removed for various purposes and the flesh was removed by the kitchen staff. Mostly for animal consumption, but I believe there are various delicacies reserved for the masters. Then the remaining skeleton was cleaned up by a working and brought here. There are a lot of valuable materials in a vizzinti."

He assumed a lecturing tone and picked up a long stick to better highlight what he was talking about.

"The bones themselves are valuable. Their strength and flexibility means that they can be carved to produce the structural components of both non-magical equipment and many Devices, but the real treasures are here. Embedded at the centre of the vertebrae where each set of ribs join is a single crystal. This allows the vizzinti to generate the flames along its body, all controlled by a single primary crystal here." He pointed at the head. "Somewhat the worse for wear in this case, I'm afraid."

The skeleton was noticeably damaged, close to where the head joined the rest of the body. Many of the ribs had turned to powder and their corresponding vertebrae crystals had shattered. The main crystal in the skull was evidently buckled and cloudy.

"If I might make a request," said Gonni, "the next time you encounter a giant ancient vizzinti and kill it with a monstrously overpowered working, could you possibly aim a little lower on the body so that there's less collateral damage to its main crystal? For future reference, its heart is located around here, so that's a good place to target."

He indicated a spot about a quarter of the way down the body which was nearly ten feet from the head. He sounded entirely serious, but I was almost sure that he was joking.

"Noted," I replied drily. "Where do the crystals actually come from? How do they form?"

"Opinions differ. Some people have theorised that creatures can use mana to find them and either embed them into their bodies or consume them, and they somehow find their way into the right places. I think that's rubbish. The crystals grow with the creatures, so I think they form inside them. Possibly in some way related to their environment."

"So what happens to the vizzinti body now?" I asked.

"I divide it up into its various components and add them to the Annex stores," Gonni said. "And you get a reward. I said that it was 'yours'. That wasn't actually far from the truth. The hunter normally gets a share of the materials, or at least the value of the materials that they recover. In this case, since you're an apprentice, that share would go to Master Logross, but I gather that he's opted for you to receive something?"

Gonni looked at Mikka enquiringly.

"That's right," said Mikka. "Master Logross has indicated that you will receive some body-armour made from the skin and bones, and a single Device made from some of the recovered crystal materials."

"The way this usually works," explained Gonni, "is that the hunters receive a notional share of the net value, calculated from the usable materials. Net of the contributions of other people, transportation and dissection costs and so on. And the Guild share, obviously. Usually, that equates to around a quarter of the value remaining. Then, depending on what you want to be made for you, the material and labour fees are assessed. Most times, and particularly for advanced Devices, the actual labour fees can end up dwarfing the cost of the materials.

"Which is why," Gonni directed this remark at Mikka, "it is so much better to specialise in Device construction." He seemed to be continuing a long-standing argument.

"In any case," he said, turning back to me, "what do you want?"

"I... That is... I have no idea," I said.

"Master Logross has a very specific request, in fact," said Mikka in a long-suffering way.

"So, how much do you actually know about Devices anyway?", continued Gonni without paying much attention to Mikka.

"Not really anything," I admitted. "I've seen them used, but I know little about the theory at all."

"I hoped that you could provide him with a basic introduction," said Mikka.

"Excellent," said Gonni. "Your mentor is showing an uncharacteristic level of good sense, not trying to explain this to you himself. I rather detect your Master's influence."

"The briefing?" prompted Mikka.

"Devices. All right, let's begin at first principles. Guild Devices are based on crystals and their interaction with mana. Or crystals and certain metals, but that's essentially the same thing. The first category of Devices or, more properly, Device components, relates to visualisation. Crystals, prepared the right way, have the property that they can refract or modify the waves given off by mana to allow them to become visible."

"Like a pair of eye-glasses?" I suggested.

"An excellent example, because it's such a simple design at core. It is, in practice, massively complex to construct because of the variety of crystals needed. A series of sheets of crystal are faceted to make different types of lenses, each selected to allow different aspects of the mana to be observed. A selection of superimposed lenses is then chosen for each eye, depending on your requirements. Depending on your choice, you can focus on different areas, see the details and shape of a mana shell, and even gaze into the centre of the mana bubble to determine the density and flows."

Gonni was clearly enjoying himself, lecturing on home ground.

"A similar related effect is the displays you can see on some Devices. Some mana is routed into a smaller crystal, sometimes through a metal trace, designed to glow and act as a display."

"I'm using a Device to measure my mana capacity," I said.

"Exactly like that," said Gonni. "Which brings us to the second key property of suitable crystals. They can contain and trap mana. There are several applications for this. The simplest one is your capacity Device, which allows you to calculate how long it takes to fill a known volume of mana at a known rate."

"That makes sense," I admitted.

"Another application of this principle is a mana storage Device. At its simplest, this is a crystal which can be filled with mana to store it for some time for use later. For example, to allow you to build up a mass of mana over time, which exceeds your own reserves. You can then absorb it later on while performing a working which would otherwise be beyond your capacity."

"Useful, I guess."

"Most useful when in combination with other effects," said Gonni. "The final refinement in this area that I'll touch on is a mana crystal storage Device which can actually absorb ambient mana itself, effectively recharging itself over time. Again, that might be useful to supercharge your own mana, but would usually be used as a power source for a more complicated standalone Device."

"And what can these more complicated Devices do?" I asked.

"That's jumping ahead slightly," said Gonni. "The final key property is that a crystal can be... shall we say, carved... to contain something akin to a mana working. Effectively, it is a channel which allows mana to flow in a particular pattern. It's not really the same thing, but think of a crystal which contains the multi-lobed shape of a light carving, along with... gates... which encourage a particular direction of flow. Once mana is supplied to that crystal, it will itself glow. Combine that with a mana crystal which can gather ambient mana at a sufficient rate, then you have a permanent light source."

"I see," I said, thinking furiously. "And there's a whole range of these working equivalents with different functions, just as there are for normal mana workings?"

"Exactly so," said Gonni. "Which brings me back to my original question. What is it you want? A wand of lightning bolts, perhaps? A staff of fireballs?"

"If I might intervene at this interval," said Mikka firmly and loudly. "As I said, Master Logross has some very definite directives which effectively rule us down to a specific choice in the budget range. In particular, he does not feel that Scordo needs to supplement his offensive capabilities right now. He has, after all, shown himself to be more than adequate in that area." He gestured towards the nearly severed head of the snake.

"Good point, well made," said Gonni.

"Similarly, he feels that, outside of the aforementioned improved armour to protect against incidental damage, he will be able to transition to handling his own primary defence in the foreseeable future," said Mikka.

I thought that Gonni's eyes widened slightly in surprise, but he said nothing.

"The idea of a mana storage Device to allow him to magnify his own capabilities is attractive, but, given the speed his own mana reserve capacity is growing and will continue to grow in the medium term, he'll quickly outgrow the available options."

"Understandable," said Gonni. "Plan for the

longer-term and all that."

"Where he thinks Scordo could be best... enhanced in both the short and medium term is in mobility and manoeuvrability. Particularly mobility during melee," continued Mikka.

A broad grin spread across Gonni's face. He looked like a child faced by a tasty piece of food. He rubbed his hands together in anticipation.

"Ring of jumping?" suggested Gonni.

"Ring of jumping," confirmed Mikka.

"Ring of what?" I asked, completely lost.

"To clarify," said Gonni, adopting his lecturing style again. "What Mikka and Master Logross are asking me to do is to extract the most powerful crystal available from the vizzinti, to shape it down into a ring, and to inlay it with a particular form of levitation working. Once you are wearing it, you will only need to channel mana into it and, depending on the flow rate, it will cancel out some or all of your weight, while leaving your inertia and motion untouched. It is a tricky Device to construct because of the complexity of the working and one, as Mikka knows full well, that I've been itching to try for a while."

"So, when I'm wearing it, I'll be able to jump...?" I prompted.

"Typically, if used correctly, it allows a wearer to jump up to around fifty feet into the air under their own steam, and fall an almost unlimited distance without damage. It can also, with more training, give you the option to extend it to cover an additional... passenger when falling. And it is exceptionally difficult to learn to use properly. Mikka, you have to let me attend his first training session. It will be hilarious... Ummm... that is... in case adjustments are required, I should be at hand."

"I think that can be arranged," said Mikka with a broad smile. "Assuming you're all right with that Scordo."

My mind was alight with the possibilities offered by this reward and I had stopped listening carefully at this point.

"Yes, of course," I said. I was to regret that.

CHAPTER SEVENTEEN
Squad Training

Apparently, it was going to take a few weeks for Gonni to construct my new magic ring, so I needed to show some patience. In the interim, I spent more time than I expected with the other members of the squad. The experience of fighting the vizzinti and then receiving Master Logross's feedback had drawn us together as a group in a way that I hadn't expected.

To start with, the others, including Tyballo, expected me to sit with them during classes and whenever I chose to eat in the refectory. Indeed, all three of them, not only Anyana, were now treating me more like a friend than an acquaintance.

This was something of a relief, because I was suffering from too much attention from my other peers amongst the apprentices. I'd always stood out a little as someone who had joined the Guild so much later than the others, but now I was having to put up with more than my share of curious stares and muttered comments between the others.

I could only assume that some word of the magic I'd used while fighting the vizzinti had spread. Few people wanted to speak to me about it directly, but many of them clearly wanted to gossip about it between themselves... That was irritating, but acceptable since I didn't want to talk to them after all! What was worse, despite Tyballo's transformed attitude towards me, was that a few of his friends weren't giving up on the requests for magic demonstrations. In fact, my new found notoriety had made things worse.

The new ring leader was Daivan who, despite Tyballo trying to talk him out of it, repeatedly asked for demonstrations.

"Go on Scordo, give the rest of us poor, pitiful apprentices a break. Surely you could bring yourself to share some of your skills with us to help with our education? We've heard so much about your masterful performances, after all. We'd truly honour your attention."

This was the sort of thing that he tried once or twice each class, all spoken with a broad sneer to suggest that he didn't mean a word of it. Being able to talk with Tyballo, Anyana and Merkle instead and pretending I hadn't heard Daivan's jeers was a welcome relief.

***

The other squad members didn't just want to talk in classes or the refectory. Once Merkle and I felt our ribs had healed sufficiently, they were keen to carry out some training together to make sure we did better in our next assigned task. I discovered that there were caverns set aside for this purpose in the physical training compound.

Although none of the others were receiving a Device for their part in the unexpected vizzinti hunt, we were all receiving a share in the armour that could be constructed from its skin. This was lucky, because both Merkle and Tyballo's outfits had been effectively destroyed during the fight.

Apparently, vizzinti hide was a prized material for this sort of thing. Not only was it, unsurprisingly, resistant to heat and fire, but it was also tough, protecting against teeth or blades with equal facility. The armour was apparently much quicker to produce than my Device, and was ready for us to practise with almost as soon as we had healed.

Anyana, still stung by Master Logross's feedback, was keen to establish a better set of ground rules for meeting future threats. For a start, she made it clear that she wouldn't put up with us splitting up to go off by ourselves to investigate things in the future. She also thought that Merkle and Tyballo should aim to act as a screen to allow me and her to attack from longer range. Accordingly, she had us practice like this a few times, raining damage on poor defenceless dummies.

I thought this was all very well in theory, but I worried she was trying to be too prescriptive and re-fighting our last battle rather than thinking about the different scenarios that future ones might bring. For a start, with her only melee option being a hammer, it would surely be better for Merkle to fall back a bit and do damage from a distance? Yes, she'd helped defend Tyballo for a while against the vizzinti, but how had that played out? Ultimately, she'd ended up squashed against a wall.

And should I be looking to remain so far back from the enemy? Yes, with my ability to create mana spheres some distance away, I could do that, but my staff also offered a strong physical defence. What was more, with his choice of Device for me, Master Logross was clearly envisaging a more mobile role.

I raised these sorts of concerns with the others, and we debated the subject at some length. We concluded that we probably didn't want to stick to a single set of assignments in a fight, but that we should probably show some more flexibility, falling into different roles depending on how a fight progressed.

We also discussed what would help most in terms of each other's individual magic training. Anyana was blunt with Tyballo, making it clear that she regarded his slow forming speed being his biggest weakness. He was surprisingly receptive to the feedback, almost looking shamefaced. Apparently, Master Logross had already spoken to Tyballo's master and Tyballo was now spending several hours a day trying to improve here. Fortunately, he didn't blame me for this.

The consensus from the others was that I needed to broaden out my knowledge of different workings. At the very least, they thought I should add lightning and water to my repertoire. They even offered to share the details of the workings with me and help me with my initial practising. I thanked them for this, but I didn't feel right about going off on my own before at least discussing it with Mikka. I also wasn't comfortable having any of the others present while I was practising. I saw it as more of a private activity, where I could retreat to be alone and focused.

I wondered whether I should reciprocate by volunteering to teach them the advanced workings I knew, but given that all of them were surprised that

I'd even been taught them, I shied away from that as well.

***

After one of our training sessions had finished, I sat in my workroom thinking more about all of this. I'd suddenly realised how reactive and passive I'd become.

Growing up largely by myself in my father's house in Arbran, I'd taken the lead in setting the pace for my education. Yes, I'd had tutors, but aside from some vague goals set by my father, I'd chosen the details of what they taught me.

And when I learnt magic, the impetus and details of training had all been mine. If anything, my father had been reluctant for me to spend any time on magic but ultimately, left the final decision up to me. That was, I realised, possibly because he'd assumed that I wouldn't be able to make much progress by myself, and that I'd always be excluded from the Guild.

However, the subject had always fascinated me and I'd always somehow felt that I ought to be able to do magic myself. When I managed to find some ancient scrolls on the subject written by lay members, and I gradually showed the ability to push mana into my father's crystal Device, that only encouraged me.

But had I even had a goal in mind? In more recent days, prior to my application for the lay elementary magic course, I'd thought about learning to cast a few spells and using them to earn a living. But that wasn't so much a goal as a compromise that I thought might be achievable.

Then, I'd gone through all the turmoil of the

testing, my apprenticeship and bonding and since then I'd been doing nothing but reacting. All the pace of my education was being set by Mikka, or rather by Master Logross. Mikka had never hidden that he was receiving constant instructions on what to teach me next.

Should I be expecting to branch out and direct my education myself? Were Mikka and Master Logross expecting me to learn new workings from my own initiative, or for me to stick to their curriculum?

And what was my goal? What, in fact, did a mage of the Guild actually do? If I'd had any idea of what a mage did before I joined the Guild, I would have vaguely thought about some sort of academic sitting in a tower inventing new spells. Instead, I was becoming the very opposite. I was sitting in a hole in the ground, training to become some sort of fighter. I'd never seen myself as being particularly combative, and I hadn't thought about whether I really wanted to be. Was that my future? Did I want that?

I definitely needed to talk with Mikka.

CHAPTER EIGHTEEN
What is a mage?

I didn't ask Mikka immediately, though.

Instead, I sat and brooded over my questions for a couple of days before summoning up the courage to broach them with him. Eventually, though, I took the plunge and all of my uncertainties rushed out of me in a somewhat unfocused mass.

When I'd finished, Mikka didn't look surprised or taken aback as I had expected. Instead, he took a deep breath, looked me in the eye and answered.

"Yes, Master Logross warned me to talk about this sooner or later," he said. "To some extent, it doesn't help that you're in a somewhat rare position. Most apprentices have grown up in much closer contact with the Guild before they join, so understand more about what they're getting into. They're also younger when they join, which maybe makes it easier for us to direct their growth while they gain a closer familiarity with their future options.

"In addition, you've also had to endure Master Logross's somewhat idiosyncratic teaching schedule, where he concentrates on the basic skills to the exclusion of anything else until the student has mastered them. He's also reluctant to take advantage of group learning and teaching and prefers to micromanage in his own way. I can certainly sympathise with you there!"

I smiled briefly to show that I appreciated he must have been in the same position as me with Master Logross's teaching.

"Let me start with the detailed questions because I should be able to answer those reasonably," he continued. "At a high level, apprentices are expected to follow their master's curriculum fairly closely. Once you reach Artisan status, you're expected to show more initiative in picking and choosing your specialities, obviously in harmony with your master's views, of course.

"That's only talking about the major curriculum elements, however. No-one would blink an eye if you chose to learn another simple working, either by teaching it to yourself out of the library, or by working with another apprentice that knew it. Or another higher Guild member, if you could find one who wanted to teach you. In your case, they'd probably be too worried about upsetting Master Logross.

"The decision about when to move an apprentice to a higher level of proficiency, however, would normally rest entirely with their master. That's because of the dangers involved. It would be unwise for you to teach someone who hadn't already mastered previous advanced workings a new one, or to encourage them to move to a forming multiple or larger mana bubbles."

"Yes, I guess I can see the dangers involved in that myself," I said, indicating the silhouette of myself that could still be seen from my loss of control of the light working.

"Exactly the sort of incident you want to avoid being blamed for," he confirmed. "Now, as it happens, there are several additional workings that Master Logross has asked me to teach you, but that's not the main issue here, is it?"

"No," I admitted. "I guess I want to know where I'm going as a mage. Or at least, what the options are."

"That's fair," said Mikka. "Unfortunately, I'm only going to be able to go so far in answering you. This is something Master Logross will need to talk to you about in more detail because he has a broader perspective. That said, I can give you some initial thoughts to chew upon.

"Some people don't make it in magic past being an apprentice. Either they end up in a serious accident or they just can't get any further. If they survive, they have a few options. If they're sufficiently ambitious and competent, they can rise in the Guild's less-magical specialisms, including law, diplomacy, and so forth. As I mentioned before, a few of these become extremely influential in the Guild and Zaronia. Others simply carry out more basic roles for the Guild, such as medical nurses, transport specialists, general dogsbody. Fortunately, I don't think any of this applies to you."

"Thank you," I said, slightly relieved.

"Other people graduate from apprentice, but show a particular aptitude and interest during their apprenticeship for a specific magical field of the Guild. Sometimes they specialise while they are an apprentice, sometimes as an Artisan. Gonni is one of the former since he was sufficiently interested in magical Devices that he was able to get reassigned to a new master to allow him to specialise early. Other typical fields include healing, teaching, agricultural magic, smithing, scrying, research and a host of others. Someone who specialises like that is likely to top out in their career as a Senior Artisan or as a Junior Master."

"Junior master?", I queried.

He grinned briefly. "It's not a formal classification," he clarified. "As far as I know, there is no official term. Effectively, they will become a Master and will be considered a valued member of the Guild, but their influence will be limited outside of their speciality. That sort of speciality is very far from a dead-end, many of those who I'm terming as Junior Masters are doing their bit to push our knowledge of magic and our abilities forward in their fields but they remain specialists and ultimately their influence tends to be bounded."

"OK, I can certainly see why someone might choose most of those fields, although I have little knowledge of some of them, such as agriculture. So what does that leave?" I asked.

"Two main paths," said Mikka. "And they're far from mutually exclusive. In both paths, a mage is expected to have a wide grounding in a number of specialities and will often work in one or more of them during their time as an Artisan.

"The first is a path focused on the... well-being of the Guild from a structural and leadership direction. Members who follow this path will help ensure that the Guild continues to work smoothly and guide its interactions with outside entities such as governments and the like. They usually end up working closely with some of our colleagues who have double sphere seals, presumably directing their efforts," said Mikka.

Politicians, I completed in my mind with some distaste.

"The second is a path focusing on protecting the Guild with their superior power. They're what you might describe as combat specialists, although that term doesn't do enough justice to the breadth of their abilities. Combat generalists, perhaps? Ultimately, they need to be as powerful as they can to keep us safe."

Safe from what, or who? I didn't ask. Mikka had been clear that I needed to discuss this with Master Logross and he was clearly picking his words with care. I sat and thought about what Mikka had said for a while and then realised what he hadn't told me.

"And which path do you see being yours?" I asked.

"Me? I'm hoping to specialise in teaching and research. I'm competent in combat, but no more effective than that and... quite frankly, I get too anxious. Master Logross has given me a great leg-up in allowing me to get experience teaching you and you've helped by learning so fast! Personally, I think Master Logross is hoping that I take some of his principles and methods and introduce them more widely, since he certainly doesn't have the aptitude for it."

"And Master Logross?" I asked, realising that I'd

never wondered about what he did.

"Him?" Mikka's lips quirked. "Didn't you know? He's considered one of the most powerful and deadly combat generalists in the Guild."

This initially took me by surprise, but then I thought about his concise tactical analyses of our performances in the fight against the vizzinti, not to mention the fear and awe he inspired in other members of the Guild. Perhaps I should have realised?

***

Over the next couple of days, Mikka introduced me to the workings for lightning, water and air, closing much of the gap between my knowledge and that of the rest of the squad.

The lightning working was complex, especially in its advanced form, which involved a spiral flow rising around outside of the sphere before it plunged down the centre to start again. I suspected that I'd be tracing that one carefully for some time, rather than start it in a single pull. It clearly had some reasonable offensive potential since I'd already seen Merkle using the basic form against the vizzinti, but was harder to practice without an actual target. Mikka wasn't keen on volunteering to act as a test subject!

The air and water workings were, as Anyana had already hinted, somewhat underwhelming. The basic water working produced a stream of water pouring out of the mana sphere and the advanced form merely increased the flow rate a little. It had come in handy for extinguishing Merkle and my flames in the vizzinti cavern, and it would clearly be useful for surviving in the desert, but beyond that I was racking my mind to think of a good use for this. I was, however, somewhat intrigued by the theory behind the working.

"Mikka, where is the water coming from? It is being produced out of nothing?" I asked.

"There are a number of debates about that, but I have seen no sort of authoritative answer," said Mikka. "When you perform it in an area with ready access to water, it's fairly straightforward. You can observe the level of the nearby water reserve dropping as it pours out of a working. Elsewhere, where there isn't apparently a source of water, it uses more mana but still works. Some people have suggested that the working somehow extracts it out of the air, others that it's creating it."

The air working was even less useful. The air sort of huffed out of the sphere in all directions and I struggled to see any sort of utility at all.

"At an apprentice level, these workings should primarily be considered utility spells," explained Mikka. "The air working can be used in certain circumstances to help provide breathable gas, but isn't used much beyond that. It isn't until you move to Artisan workings that they come into their own."

I pressed Mikka for more details on this subject but aside from explaining that an Artisan could construct a working which allowed for more pressure and ranged attack with a working, he wouldn't explain any more of the details. Apparently, it was explicitly against Guild Rules for him to provide actual tuition on this.

***

Master Logross called me in a few days later to follow

up on my questions about the nature of mage craft.

As I would expect, he didn't pull any punches.

"Magic is jeopardy," he said. "You risk your life directly when you try to control its power. What's more its very presence brings you into more indirect danger."

"How so?" I asked.

"For a start, magic is easiest in certain places, where mana is abundant and your reserves refill quickly. Those places also tend to be the sources of useful materials, such as crystals, which can strengthen your magic. That's why we sited the Temple, the Annex and various other Guild outposts where they are. Regrettably, we're not the only ones who are drawn to those locations. Dangerous creatures, some of whom can actually make use of mana, abound. And as we force our way in to harvest the resources, we're disturbing the inimical creatures and letting them out. The Temple became so dangerous that we had to cut back on what we can do in that location drastically, and the Annex is gradually becoming nearly as dangerous."

I hadn't wondered why creatures like the spikkans and vizzinti existed in such proximity to the Guild. It all made sense, but I'd never heard it explained in this way before.

"And what's worse, magic represents power," continued Master Logross. "People covet power, and that includes people within and without the Guild. And they're prepared to do almost anything to obtain it. That means that any magic user will constantly be in danger from others."

Again, this was logical, but it was a pretty bleak attitude to take. I shivered as his merciless logic progressed.

"So, how will you choose to face those dangers?" he asked. "Will you focus on a specific area of specialisation, hoping that others will see sufficient value in your efforts to help defend you from the dangers?

"Or will you," and he curled his lip in a sneer. "Hope that you can talk or manipulate other people into doing what you want?"

Clearly not a fan of the political career path then.

"Or will you concentrate on maximising your own personal power so that you can defend yourself? While knowing that makes you a greater target or prize for those you're defending against?"

OK, put like that, I wasn't sure that any of those options particularly appealed to me. But I'd never been a great fan of depending on others... For now, the martial path was that of least resistance and most promise.

CHAPTER NINETEEN
Mobility Training

Around two weeks passed while my injuries continued to heal and I continued to practice my mana forming and workings. I was down to only five seconds forming time for all basic workings, with roughly twice that required for advanced workings.

I also worked hard on my ability to maintain multiple workings and to form double-sized spheres.

Greater workings and even larger spheres, I avoided entirely.

All of this exercise was improving my mana reserve capacity as well. I was now up to about 540 units, which Mikka assured me was 'plenty' and we'd had to recalibrate my crystal sphere measuring Device repeatedly.

***

Finally Gonni reported that my new magic ring was ready for use. Mikka told me he'd planned for me to train the next day.

Gonni and Mikka met me while I finished my breakfast, and I admired the appearance of the Device. The ring had been carved out of a solid piece of a deep blue crystal. The inside was smooth, with some complicated-looking series of lines carved into it and apparently inlaid in gold. Outside, the ring was rougher, with a series of crystal shapes facing forward with what I took at first to be a faceted blue gem set amongst them. On closer examination, however, the gem was simply carved out of the same solid piece of crystal as the rest of the ring.

"It's beautiful," I said. "Does it work?"

"Thank you," said Gonni. "Well, I guess we'll find out shortly."

I glanced at him incredulously, but he looked serious.

"You mean you haven't tested it?" I said.

He held his expression for a moment or two longer and then smiled.

"You caught me. The working pattern appears to be good and directs mana in the right flow. My Master has inspected it and signed off on it. Some very limited, and careful, testing in the work room shows that it reduces gravity for the wearer. We haven't, however, actually tried jumping with it, nor measured the strength of the working at different power levels. That all is unique to the user and their mana signature, so I'm just as excited as you to see what it can do.

"Let's get it attuned to you first," he continued. "It's in a receptive state right now, so I need you to pulse a small amount of mana into the ring. You should see it glow and then fade away again."

I followed his instructions and saw a clear blue light glow and then die away again.

"Excellent," he said. "It's now locked to you. That means that no-one else will be able to manipulate it, not even to remove it from your finger without your consent. So what are we waiting for? To the training ground!"

***

We emerged out of the caverns of the Physical Training facility into the sunlight. Mikka led us about a mile from the primary facility to a large area of sand which had been blocked off with various wooden hoardings. Once we sidled past these, I could see that the sand had been cleared of rocks and other obstacles and raked flat. Several unusual-looking wooden constructs were pushed against the hoardings, including what appeared to be a section of roof hanging from pieces of wheeled scaffolding on each side.

There was a small pile of armour stacked together near us.

What I wasn't expecting was the row of seats along the side. Lounging in them, I saw my fellow squad members and the rest of Mikka's friends that I'd met previously, Dienny, Bielda, and Harrisal. Also present was the Physical Training supervisor Joli, who stood up and made his way over to us.

I looked at Mikka and Gonni. "Why so many spectators?" I asked.

"We didn't want to keep all the fun to ourselves," said Gonni smugly.

"Thank you, Gonni. Sorry to spring this on you, Scordo. I know you don't like crowds, but there are actually reasonably solid reasons for all the others. Joli will be directing the practice, he has experience in the usual protocols and curriculum for jump ring training. Your squad is here because we want to ensure that they are aware of your capabilities and can effectively fit around them. The others are here for a similar reason that I'll explain later."

"I see," I answered. "I guess that makes some sense." I wasn't thrilled by so many people watching me trying to get control of the Device, but at least I knew and to some extent liked all the people who were here. It wasn't as if Daivan or any of the other persistent troublemakers were intruding.

"Good morning Scordo," said Joli as he got closer. "If you'd care to come over here, then we'll get you kitted out and we can start."

I joined him at the pile of armour. It was made of some thick, light-weight natural material. Cork perhaps?

"This is to reduce the impact of any initial training accidents as you get used to the power and timing associated with using the ring," Joli explained as he helped me into a thick wooden helmet with a neck-guard.

"How dangerous is this?" I asked.

"As long as you're reasonably careful, then you should come to no real harm," he said. "The trickiest elements are timing your mana pulse and in judging the right amount to use in tighter spaces. Or at least, that's what the manuals tell me. I've never actually seen one of these used before."

That didn't entirely fill me with confidence, but at least he knew about the theory of the training. We finished assembling the armour. It was mostly designed to protect my upper body from damage, leaving my legs free to jump.

"One key thing to remember is that if you find yourself falling too quickly, then try to bend your knees and roll into the ground. You don't want to absorb the impact with your knees alone," said Joli, as if reading my mind.

"Now, if you'd you like to stand here," he led me out in front of the spectators, who had been joined by Mikka and Gonni. They were all talking in low voices. If I wasn't mistaken, it sounded as if Gonni was taking bets.

"Now," continued Joli, standing some distance off. "Try a simple jump straight into the air."

I placed the ring on my finger and stood there for a moment. I carefully pushed a little mana into the ring and watched it glow slightly. I then withdrew it again and bent my knees. I tried to jump and then push mana again. Unfortunately, I wasn't quick enough, and I jumped to about knee height, and then landed again before the ring glowed.

"Truly, you are a master craftsman, Gonni. Regard the power of the ring you've wrought," Dienny said, as if impressed.

Timing, eh? I tried again. This time, I applied the mana slightly earlier, but still not enough. I reached about waist height again and then floated down gently back to the ground.

There was a faint ripple of applause from the watchers.

Right, what happened if I jumped with the ring already filled with a bit of mana? This time I rose into the air painfully slowly to about twice my height and then, ever so slowly, fell back down again. I was so surprised by this that I made the mistake of releasing the mana. The subsequent fall under my full weight was embarrassing rather than painful.

The applause was louder this time, and Anyana called out sympathetically. I could also hear the clink of coins changing hands.

After about half an hour of practising vertical jumps, I felt I was getting the hang of the timing. For faster upward movement, I had to apply the mana more or less the instant I left the ground. I could then control both the height of my jump and the speed of descent by varying the amount of mana I kept in the ring. At peak, I was reaching a height of around forty feet, but I didn't think that was the limit of the mana level I could push into the ring, just what was prudent.

"Very good Scordo," commented Joli. "Now, how about trying to launch yourself off sideways? Umm, try this direction." He pointed down the length of the cleared area rather than towards the spectators.

I took a brief run up and then leapt forwards are if trying to dive into a pool while digging my feet into the sand. Unfortunately, I was so focused on my footwork that I forgot to apply mana to the ring. Thud. I landed face first on the sand and slid for a bit. The spectators were particularly appreciative of that attempt and barely recovered from their laughter before I tried again.

It took me less time to get the timing right with this manoeuvre than the vertical jump had taken. I was getting more used to applying and varying mana in the ring. I found I could travel at least forty feet sideways in a single bound, although the distance depended critically on how high I was prepared to go.

After this, Joli brought over a gantry tower with platforms set at different levels and had me practice climbing up and jumping off. This was relatively simple - although I worried a bit about how fast my reaction time would be if I suddenly fell off a cliff or something. I resolved to practice this blindfold. Later, of course, when I wasn't being observed by so many people!

Next, Joli dragged over a series of wooden ramps to help me practice jumping off differently angled surfaces. He explained he wanted to get me used to bouncing around off tunnel walls and the like.

Timing a series of bounces off different vertical or angled surfaces turned out to be exceptionally difficult and required a degree of mana control that I simply couldn't master on the spot. I resolved that this was going to require more practice. Much more.

Finally, Joli wheeled over the strange wheeled scaffolding that I'd seen when I first arrived.

"This is to get you used to handling the lower ceilings you're going to find indoors and underground," he explained. He reduced the elevation of the wooden ceiling to around twenty feet by adjusting a series of pulleys. That was about the amount of headroom you might get in a large cavern, and he then encouraged me to try a leap.

I took a deep breath and ran towards the scaffolding, setting my feet properly and applying mana in a perfect leap forwards. There was a moment in which I first congratulated myself on my timing and then realised that I was approaching the roof of the scaffold far faster than I expected. Then there was a sudden crash as I impacted and my head popped through the boards from underneath and emerged into the sunlight. Of course, the rest of my body was still dangling down from the ceiling I was now embedded in. Repeated kicks from my legs failed to dislodge me and I just hung there, swinging slightly. Fortunately, all that armour had done its job and I wasn't actually hurt by this, merely irritated.

To say that this was a crowd pleaser would be an understatement. I could hear the others literally crying with laughter. Thinking about it, I suppose that seeing my body hanging down, unable to escape, was probably pretty funny.

How was I going to get out of this one? After a few moments of thinking, I pulsed the mana in the ring, reducing my weight to nothing and then letting it all back again in a rush. The first couple of times I tried this, the board creaked, but I stayed put. Finally, though, the board I was stuck through parted company from the ceiling and I fell to the ground. Unfortunately, I wasn't quick enough at getting the mana back into the ring and I crashed down, still wearing the board of wood as some sort of extended collar.

I noticed that some of the others, including Gonni, had actually fallen off their seats with laughter at this point. Even Joli was wearing a broad smile.

"Perhaps some more practice on that one?" he suggested, helping free me from my errant board. I practised, devoutly grateful that they'd started me off with this training outside rather than in the more unforgiving confines of a rock cavern.

I made little more progress on jump training that day. The spectators soon took me back to the refectory for lunch. However, Joli had made it clear that the facilities were available to me whenever I wanted. He also encouraged me to take the helmet section of the cork armour with me for use indoors.

I did indeed practice carefully along some corridors, but only after a lot more training with the scaffolding section reduced to an even more conservative gap closer to the height of the lower tunnels.

CHAPTER TWENTY
Market

Before long, our squad's turn for vermin control duty came around again. Apparently, we'd been suspended from the rota while we were recovering from our injuries, but Master Kinchat seemed determined to make up for lost time.

He assigned us not to a usual patrol duty, but to a specific combat mission. Apparently, a spikkan nest had been located, and we were tasked with eliminating it. Since we'd be operating outside of the usual inhabited caverns, Anyana was assigned a portable emergency bell, along with some very detailed instructions on what we were, and were not, supposed to be doing.

We were given instructions on how to find the nest, specifying a particular approach path. Apparently, our job was to eliminate the nest itself and destroy any spikkans that did not flee quickly enough, but we were explicitly ordered not to pursue any that escaped. We were to ring the emergency bell if any of the squad were incapacitated.

I wondered what we were expected to do if we were all somehow incapacitated in a single blow, but decided that the question wouldn't amuse Master

Kinchat. Nor, I guessed, would we have much of a chance to take any action if that actually happened.

We carefully checked over our kit, including our new vizzinti hide armour, and started off following the directions. They involved leaving through a doorway at the back of a storeroom and following an unlit passageway through a series of turnings. We saw some evidence of footprints in the dust on the floor, so presumably another squad had recently pursued some spikkans from an encounter in a storeroom, as we had tried to do, but with more success in tracking them to their origin. Presumably, the other squad hadn't fancied their chances against the nest, and had returned to report their find. Our progress was gradual and tense, and we listened for sounds of danger at every turn.

As we approached the end of our directions, we heard indistinct noises ahead, echoing strangely off the rock walls of the winding corridor. We all drew to a halt, unwilling to go further without discussing a plan of attack.

"Merkle," said Anyana. "Are you up for scouting ahead a little? If you get into trouble, just shout and we'll move up to support you quickly. Tyballo, Scordo, get ready."

Merkle nodded, made a faint light working, and slipped around the next corner. For a large person, she could move surprisingly quietly when she wanted. Tyballo quickly made a fire working and stuck it to his sword. I'd already noticed that he had held off doing this until now and judging by the reduction in his working time, he'd been practising this heavily.

No sounds of alarm were heard, and a few

minutes later, Merkle returned.

"There's an enormous cavern ahead, around two more corners. There's plenty of cover around the entrance. I could definitely hear spikkan noises coming from somewhere in the cavern, but I didn't want to risk alerting them to our presence immediately by sending a light in. They're loud enough, though, that I don't think they'll hear us approach."

Anyana nodded. "Good thinking. Let's all move up and get into the cover at the entrance. Tyballo, protect our rear as we move up to avoid them flanking us."

Tyballo made no protests at not being at the front, and we did as Anyana instructed. We quickly hid ourselves behind a series of loose boulders lying on the floor by the entrance. We could see a large dark space ahead of us. From what we could see, the floor continued to be covered by debris, but it was hard to get a good view of what was ahead. Judging from the acoustics, the cavern must be enormous. We could just about make out other openings in the cave wall not too far from us, with the nearest about fifty feet away.

"Scordo," said Anyana. "Could you form an advanced light working near to the other passageway? That way, if the spikkans are drawn to the light, they'll head towards the wrong passage."

"I should be able to," I said, "but aren't they more likely to smell us? My bestiary said that's their strongest sense."

"If they can already smell us, then we're going to

get company sooner rather than later," replied Anyana. "But I'm reluctant to enter the cavern blindly. I want to see what we're doing and it would be far too easy to get flanked. Remember, they can run along the ceiling and drop on us."

"OK, will do," I replied.

I concentrated and formed a floating light working where she'd specified and then lifted it as high as I could above the decoy passageway. We could now see what we were dealing with.

The cavern was roughly circular, around four hundred feet across. In the centre were a series of natural columns that looked wet. Perhaps formed from stalactites and stalagmites that had merged? The columns were interconnected by many webs and seethed with shadowy activity. The noise level reduced suddenly.

The rest of the floor was littered with fallen rocks and there were several dark patches that might be pits dotted around.

"Scordo, how close would we need to get for you to form a heat working in the centre of that nest?" asked Anyana.

I thought quickly. I'd done some practice at extreme distances and the light working wasn't at the extent of my range.

"Maybe a hundred feet?" I said. "Let's say about half the distance from here to the centre."

"Let's risk it," said Anyana. "Tyballo and Merkle will proceed in front, trying to find us a safe path and getting ready to defend us. I'll cover the rear with you in the middle. The spikkans aren't actually responding to us yet, but I don't like the sudden quiet."

We carefully picked our way across the floor towards the columns, trying to move slowly, making as little noise as possible. I found my eyes returning to the ceiling repeatedly, trying to make out signs of movement that might indicate that spikkans were moving towards us but no attack came. Eventually, we got close enough that I felt I could form a suitable heat working, and I signalled to Tyballo and Merkle to stop. They formed up ahead of me, keeping low so as not to block my vision. I felt, rather than saw, Anyana come to a halt behind me and turn around to monitor our rear and flanks.

I concentrated for twenty seconds, and then we all saw fire blooming in the centre of the nest. For good luck, I added another couple of fire workings in a section of the nest a few yards from each other. The fires spread quickly and joined. I could see hundreds, possibly thousands, of the spiders ranging in size from a few inches across to several feet wide, rushing over each other in apparent panic. Many of them quickly caught alight in their turn, causing the fire to spread faster.

A wave of spikkans headed out from the nest across the floor in all directions, apparently searching for the origin of the attack. Tyballo and Merkle braced themselves and responded to the threat. Tyballo swept his glowing sword backwards and forwards in wide arcs and Merkle employed a simple heat working to pick them off one at a time, using her hammer to drive others backwards.

I stepped backwards slightly to free my staff up to use it to defend myself, but initially there was no need. Tyballo and Merkle held them off. To each side, however, I could see other spikkans moving towards us, having failed to locate danger elsewhere. Some of these burst into flames as Anyana's fire arrows began to hit them.

My focus was on gradually swinging the heat workings in the nest backwards and forwards, ensuring that all of it burned. I could vaguely see more and more of the spikkans abandoning the nest, either to join the attack on us, or heading off to the other end of the cavern in flight. A spikkan suddenly jumped at me, having fallen from the ceiling to my left. In an instinctive reaction, I turned to face it and caved in its body with a flick of my staff. Two more took its place, and I stepped back to give myself a chance to swing my staff at both of them.

Further to my left came Anyana's voice, tight but apparently calm.

"All right, the nest is done for. Scordo, release your heat workings and defend yourself better. Let's gradually retreat to our exit. Tyballo, Merkle, continue to cover us during the retreat."

The other two both acknowledged, and I released the three heat workings and recreated another close to me where I could sweep it backwards and forwards to keep the attacking spikkans at bay. I also called my light working to the end of my staff to provide us with sufficient illumination to move safely. Our retreat was conducted fairly smoothly up to the point we ended up backed up against a boulder nearly six feet across, completely blocking our line of escape.

However, a quick bounce and pulse of mana from me into my crystal ring, and I was on top of the boulder. From there, I could see enough to use my heat working to carve out a wide path in the spikkans to each side for the others to move through. Once they were past, I then bounced back down into the middle of my companions and we completed our trip back to the entrance. Once there, our position was relatively safe and we could easily defend against the few token attacks. Most of the spikkans broke off and fled, leaving us to pick off the remaining outliers at our leisure.

I looked around and checked on the others. Anyana and I looked unharmed, although somewhat soot blackened. Tyballo and Merkle both had a series of shallow cuts to their face and hands, but were otherwise in good spirits. Everyone looked jubilant, but trying to keep a hold on their exuberance while we were still in danger.

"Great, let's push back to the nest," said Anyana once a few minutes had gone by with no further attacks. This time we moved more confidently, spread out slightly further apart, and we didn't stop at the halfway point but pushed on to the smouldering mass in the centre. About twenty feet from the centre, we stopped and edged in a circle around the columns, looking for anything else to burn.

There wasn't much. Mostly, the nest was a mass of ash, with hundreds of twisted and charred bodies and some sort of bubbling black slime oozing out from the centre in all directions.

Tyballo pointed at the latter with his sword. "That's likely from melted spikkan eggs," he said. "It looks like we got the lot."

We cleaned up a few twitching, half-burned

spikkans, but otherwise there wasn't anything remaining for us to do. I sent my light working into the other half of the cavern, but it looked more or less the same as the portion we'd already covered and no-one was enthusiastic about pressing on. The slaughter we'd already carried out had sated everyone's bloodlust.

Not that Anyana would have allowed any further pursuit. She was determined to follow Master Kinchat's instructions to the letter this time.

"Nice job everyone," she said. "Now let's get back and get cleaned up."

Our return journey was far more cheerful and relaxed than our approach had been. It felt like we'd all played our roles in the attack and had operated much better as a cohesive team than our first outing.

Master Kinchat seemed happy to see us return without incident as well. I privately suspected that he might be most pleased that he would not have to ask Master Logross for help pulling us out of some fresh disaster, but I may be being unfair. Certainly, he thought the nest had caused much of the recent spikkan infestations in the storerooms and that the normal patrol duties might settle down a little.

***

After we'd been dismissed by Master Kinchat, Anyana cornered me in the passageway, letting the others walk ahead.

"Scordo," she said. "Would you like to come with me to the market this afternoon? I don't think you've seen one before, have you?"

"Market?" I said, mystified.

"It happens every couple of months. A large market, almost a festival, is held in the nearby village. I'd love to show you round it."

"Village?" I said, feeling stupid. I'd spent some time running out in the desert in front of the entrance to the rock face housing the Annex, not to mention my jump ring training, and I'd seen no sign of a nearby village.

"Yes, the village. Haven't you been there? It's out on the other side of the Annex and there are tunnels which lead through the mountain and open out nearby. Oh, you must let me take you."

She seemed nervous, which I guess was fair. I spent most of my time studying or training, and she was probably worried about my reaction to her suggestion that I slack off for a bit. I thought about refusing in any case, since I wasn't particularly interested in visiting a market. It was nice of her to offer though, and Mikka had been happy with my progress recently and had been hinting that I should maybe take a break.

"OK, I'd love to come," I said. "When would you like us to go?"

"Really? Oh, fantastic! I'll come over to collect you in a couple of hours if that would be all right. Once I've cleaned up a bit."

"Until later, then," I said and headed back to Master Logross's quarters.

***

A couple of hours later, Anyana arrived and I let her into the lobby. She was rather tentative about coming in, glancing toward Master Logross's door, until I reassured her she was very unlikely to see him.

She'd certainly used her time to clean up. Gone were the armour and apprentice robes. Instead she had put on a plain dress made of a silky material, belted with a leather band. Her blonde hair was gathered up into a complex bun.

I'd put on my clean apprentice robes, but I felt somewhat under-dressed. Not that I had anything else to wear that was suitable. My Arbran clothes were too warm for the local climate. Still, Anyana didn't appear to notice.

"Are you ready to go? It'll take nearly an hour to get there through the tunnels, so it would be good to get started."

We set off together, and she quickly took me into tunnels I hadn't previously explored. As best I could estimate, we were heading off much deeper into the mountain. From what she'd said earlier, this would eventually take us through to the other side.

We talked as we traversed the Annex. Part of this was Anyana acting as a tour guide. Notable sights included the smithing complex where weapons were manufactured or repaired and some sort of crystal refinery. I didn't really follow the details of the latter, but apparently the forms and structure of some crystals needed to be modified for certain Devices and this required a combination of types of magic to perform. There were also several caverns where crops were grown, presumably utilising some form of light and water workings, but I didn't press for details.

She also asked me a series of questions about my background and volunteered something of hers in return. Apparently, she had been gathered by the Guild from a mountain village towards the edge of Zaronia when she was twelve. I got the impression that the Guild sent out teams of people looking for suitable candidates and that it was considered an honour to be selected. It didn't sound as if she had been back to see her village since she was collected, but I didn't want to pry into her private life.

Eventually, the long tunnel we were following started to rise, and it brought us out onto the surface.

***

Mountainsides rose before and behind us. We were in a relatively narrow valley in a more substantial range of hills. Ahead of us, between the slopes, there was an abrupt descent down a rock slope and then around half a mile of flat land with a fast-flowing river or stream cutting through it. A few stunted trees grew here and, in the distance, I could see cultivated fields with the stream running through the middle. Looking left and right, the valley stretched away, but the ground rose steadily to our left, eventually turning into another mountain slope.

A path led down the slope from our feet towards what must be the village. None of the mud huts I'd seen in the Zaronian village near the Temple were in evidence. There were maybe a couple of hundred structures made of stone or wood, arranged around a large central square where I could see movement and coloured banners.

The mountain sides were steep enough that the sun was already gone from the centre of the valley, but it could be seen in the heights glinting on fractured rock faces. Looking further down the valley to the right, I could see desert shining in the distance, but the depth of the valley shielded the village from most of the sand and climate.

Several other people were on the path ahead of us, mostly moving towards the market square, and Anyana led us in the same direction.

"The market doesn't really get underway until the sun has passed over the mountain and it gets cooler," she explained. She was right. The temperature was already lower and more pleasant than the area in front of the Annex, and I could see fires being lit ahead of us. Both torches and bonfires were springing into life.

As we passed through the huts, I saw a combination of reasonably prosperous looking houses alongside others which were far more ramshackle. The worst ones were little better than piles of stone roughly roofed with material.

"Many of the servants and orderlies from the Annex are housed here," explained Anyana. "Others are simply locals who scavenge in the local valleys and out into the desert for food and materials that they can sell to the Annex. Hangers on."

I saw children of a variety of ages hanging around many of the huts. They were mostly emaciated, without many clothes or possessions, and often older children were supervising their younger relatives and their friends. Few adults were in evidence around the huts, so maybe most of them were in the market?

We quickly came into the marketplace. It was filled with stalls and tents of varying sizes roughly arranged in lines. There was a broad selection of wares available for sale. Some were draped with clothing in different styles and materials, others with leather goods such as belts and shoes. Weapons of all patterns and types were available. Another stall had a series of rocks, crystals, and gemstones displayed. I saw several people who I recognised as Artisans from the Guild poring carefully over what was on offer and several were haggling with the trader over purchases.

There was also a trader who I thought might be Arbran with a series of intricately inlaid wooden boxes on display. I thought of looking more closely, but I had little use for them.

In amongst these were other stalls selling food and drink. We bought some fried meat on kebabs. I paid, thankful that I'd thought to bring some of my money.

Anyana was drawn to the weapons stalls.

"I need a melee weapon for close quarters' defence," she explained. She was drawn to a long knife with a mana holder attached. The blade was beautifully carved with a mythical fire-breathing dragon. Or was it mythical? I hadn't made enough progress on working my way through my bestiary to judge.

"Do you think this would suit me?" she asked.

"Can you afford something like that?" I replied.

"Probably. I've saved most of my apprentice wages." She turned to the stallholder and discussed the price.

Apprentice wages? Apparently something else I'd forgotten to ask about. Presumably they were being paid into my Guild bank account. Not that I was short of funds, with the bulk of my inheritance intact.

While I waited for Anyana, I continued to look at the stalls. After a while, I noticed that one of the locals was observing me. Maybe he was some sort of guard?

Anyana concluded her purchase and arranged for the knife to be delivered to her in the Guild. Apparently, there was a system whereby purchases from the market were batched up for delivery by Guild servants later. On hearing this, I inspected some of the leather and clothing goods and made a few small purchases myself.

We wound our way through much of the market, with Anyana greeting friends every now and again. We ended up in an area dominated by a large tent which was selling drinks. Musicians were seated by the fire playing to the crowd who occasionally threw coins.

Anyana bought us some drinks and we sat down, listening to the music and talking. I noticed that the person who I'd taken to be a guard was now a few tables away, talking with some other locals.

***

Not much time passed before we were interrupted. I noticed a small group of apprentices pushing their way through towards us slightly unsteadily. I sighed when I saw Daivan in their midst.

Daivan was richly dressed, and I was surprised to see a sword inlaid with gold strapped to his side.

"Look who it is," he said in a slightly thick voice. "I thought you were always too busy studying to come out and mix with the rest of us, Scordo. Too busy poring through Master Logross's secrets."

"Daivan, please just let it rest," said Anyana. "Enjoy the market somewhere else."

Daivan tried to pretend to be surprised to see Anyana there.

"Maybe it's just us that Scordo doesn't want to share secrets with? Or maybe you're hoping that you can convince him, eh?"

"Look, I don't know what you're talking about," I said. "I don't know any secrets."

"Then why does Master Logross keep you locked up in his quarters to train then?" asked Daivan. "Rather than letting you mix with the rest of us?"

This conversation was going downhill fast. Daivan's voice was getting louder and people were turning to see what was happening. The nearby locals were particularly interested in the discussion and turned to stare. At that moment, however, another voice cut in.

"Anyana, Scordo, there you are," said Tyballo. He had approached us from behind. "Wouldn't you come and join Merkle and me over here?" He nodded over his shoulder. "Daivan, nice to see you. Sorry to steal them away from you." He didn't look sorry or pleased to see Daivan. In fact, Tyballo looked dangerous and I noticed he had his hand resting on his own sword.

Daivan stared at Tyballo with fury in his eyes for a moment and then snorted. "Let's get some more drinks," he said to his companions and headed off back to the tent.

We collected our drinks and joined Merkle and a couple of others some way away. In passing, I noticed that the local who had been watching me had left too.

"Daivan is getting worse," Anyana said to Tyballo, clearly continuing a conversation they had started in the past.

"He's becoming desperate," said Tyballo. He turned to me. "Daivan is from the royal family of Zaronia. A younger son, I believe. He was a minor celebrity when he first arrived at the Guild, and he let it go to his head. However, he's not made much progress with his magic. Despite his lack of ability, his master pulled strings to have him included in the group attending emergences. However, he hasn't bonded a Glowling either. He's now getting pretty old for an apprentice and he's looking for... short-cuts."

"But I don't know any short-cuts," I said.

"We know you don't," said Anyana. "It's clear that Master Logross has taught you some things that we don't yet know, but you're following a pretty normal syllabus. You're ahead of us a bit, is all. And most of the reason for that is the accuracy of your mana forming, which is clearly the result of lots of practice."

"Once I'd seen you fight," added Tyballo, "I realised how important all the stuff I was neglecting was and I've tried to go back to it. However, Daivan doesn't want to hear that he's going to have to knuckle down and work hard."

"So what do I do?" I asked.

"Just stay away from him and don't provoke him," said Tyballo. "He's eighteen, nearly nineteen now, and his master won't put up with his lack of progress much longer."

I followed their advice, and I kept an eye out for

Daivan for the rest of the evening. Before too long, we all headed back to the Annex and went our separate ways. Anyana was a little down about the way the outing had worked out, so I made sure I thanked her for inviting me. I wouldn't have had any idea that the market was even taking place without her suggestion and it had been... fun.

CHAPTER TWENTY-ONE
Scrying

The next morning, I was summoned by Master Logross for a debrief on our battle against the spikkan nest. He said nothing, but I wondered if he'd expected to talk about this the previous afternoon. Did he even know that I'd been out of the Annex?

I related everything I could recall about our preparation for the fight, and then how it had gone. I was relieved that he hadn't bound me by my seal this time, but I tried to be as complete as possible. After I'd finished, a silence fell between us. Feeling uncomfortable, I added a quick summary of my visit to the market the previous night, omitting the incident with Daivan.

After a while, he looked up from where he'd apparently been inspecting the surface of his desk.

"It's best to avoid splitting your squad for reconnaissance if possible. Talk to Mikka about learning a remote scrying working, including night vision. You may leave."

***

When I relayed this request to Mikka, he raised an eye-brow.

"Now that is potentially a very fertile field of

study," he said. "Not so much the working itself, but it's part of a class of workings which have a vast range of... flavours depending on what precise behaviour you need. It's also going to push your skills into a new way of directing your power. Which will come in handy for other workings that I suspect that Master Logross has in mind for the future.

"Let's start with a base working, as Master Logross suggested, and then we ought to find you a book which will give you more details on some of the variants. Note that there isn't a simple version of the working. You need to work with a three dimensional current immediately."

He quickly talked me through the basics of the working. It comprised two interlocked currents. The first was in a ring standing vertically in the mana bubble. The second drew a stream of mana through the mana flow ring towards me and then released it to let it circulate back around the outside of the vertical ring, only to be drawn back through again.

This was tricky to visualise. I had to establish the vertical current on its own first, making it as distinct as possible, so that it wasn't subsequently disturbed by the central current.

After a few hours of practice, I got the hang of it, but it didn't seem to actually achieve anything. I pointed this out to Mikka when he dropped in to check on my progress, with his eye-glasses in place to allow him to check on the accuracy of my workings.

"Wasn't this supposed to be allowing me to see something new?" I asked.

"Yup," said Mikka. "But I haven't told you the last

step. Now visualise the central stream, the one aimed towards you, as if it was coming out of the bubble and entering your consciousness."

I tentatively tried this once or twice before finding the right way to visualise it. Then suddenly, I found I could see a series of images coming from the viewpoint of the bubble itself. I staggered backwards; my mind felt overloaded trying to deal with a new point of view and I was suddenly overwhelmed by dizziness. I lost my focus on the bubble and it puffed out.

"Yes, it's disconcerting to add a new additional point of view to your existing vision," said Mikka. "I'd recommend that you should close your eyes and focus on the images coming from the mana bubble. That's how most people deal with the dissonance. Very few scryers can incorporate an extra point of view at the same time as using their normal eyes. Lean up against the wall or sit down as well. Your brain doesn't particularly like it when what you're seeing disagrees with everything that the rest of your senses are telling you."

I followed his advice and found I could maintain the working while seeing from the perspective of the bubble. The view was a little distorted around the edges and there was something strange about the refraction through the peripheral edges of the bubble, but otherwise was clear enough.

"OK. Now move the bubble," Mikka instructed.

I tried this and found my point of view shifted with the bubble. I could quickly send it out of the work-room into the lobby of our quarters. Experimenting, I found it would pass straight through the main doors to the quarters.

"Now, send it through into Master Logross's workroom," said Mikka.

I floated the sphere back into the lobby and then confidently straight towards Master Logross's doors. This time, however, the mana bubble rebounded from the closed doors violently. Worse, the viewpoint then fizzled out and I could feel the mana bubble burst and the mana disperse.

"Next lesson," said Mikka, chuckling. "There are straightforward counter-measures, wards, available against scrying, and senior mages set them up as a matter of course. In fact, you could only pass through the entrance doors to this complex, because they've been set to respond to your mana signatures. If any of the other apprentices had tried that, they'd have failed."

"Isn't there any way to beat or circumvent wards?" I asked, intrigued.

"Plenty of ways," said Mikka. "There is a constant race going on between mages to develop new variants of the workings and new counter-measures for the wards. Just a piece of advice: Master Logross's wards are quite fierce and also provide him with feedback about attempts to breach them. He'll barely have noticed a simple clash like the one you just tried, and he'll have expected it since he knew you were studying this. However, if someone tried a more advanced attempt to scry him, then he'd investigate and... take measures."

"And I really wouldn't want that," I finished for him. "Understood. How far can I send a scrying

Starting Sphere

bubble?"

"With this type of working, there are two real limits. The first one relates to your level of control over your bubbles. The second relates to what's possible without substantial refinement to the working. You should be trying to master a distance of a couple of hundred yards at least. Maybe up to a quarter of a mile?"

"Got it. And this is for sight only? Not hearing?" I asked.

Mikka snorted. "Don't want much, do you? Yes, there is a related variant to the working that layers sound on the top, but that's very complicated and I'm not sure you're ready for that yet. Or you can simply cast an additional working that allows you to hear rather than see, but that is obviously tricky to direct at a distance without being able to see where you're sending it! It has a better range than vision, though. It'll all be in the textbook. Now, you said that you wanted night vision as well…"

He then showed me how to modify the shell of the mana sphere to introduce a pattern that boosted the light sensitivity of the working. Experimenting with this, I found that the resulting image was largely lacking in colour, but I could make out details more clearly in regions of low light. This would have been extremely helpful when trying to locate and inspect the spikkan web without risking alerting them to our presence.

"Again, there are a wide range of other effects you can apply to the shell of the sphere. Either one at a time or in combination. Some of the more popular ones include magnification, broader angles of vision or even heat sensitivity. Unless Master Logross has any particular requests, I'll leave it to you to choose what else you want to study in this area. Work on perfecting the basics first, though, before adding too many refinements."

He excused himself and returned a few minutes later with a book. It was entitled "A brief overview and introduction to the art of scrying".

"Brief overview?" I queried. The book was two inches thick.

"This is a very deep rabbit hole," said Mikka. "Some specialists dedicate their entire lives to the art."

***

Mikka left me to practice what he'd already shown me.

After a couple of days of practice, I was efficient at forming the basic vision working, with or without the low-light refinement.

For variety, I also mastered the sound-only working, although, as Mikka had said, it was difficult to guide. Experimenting in my classes, I found that by masking the mana emission, it could be used to eavesdrop effectively on other students without their noticing, or to listen on the other side of a wall or door without too many guidance problems. When I sent it further afield, however, it became very difficult to work out what was going on. I felt as if I was wandering with my eyes shut through a room filled with little groups of talking people. Voices drifted in and out of audibility pretty much at random.

I hadn't even attempted to combine the vision and

hearing workings yet. The book had it listed as something that should only be attempted by experienced scryers.

For myself, I was still having problems with the basic vision working. Not in forming it, nor in its guidance, but where I struggled was incorporating it into my field of view.

As it was, I could only use it effectively with my eyes closed, standing still. I could see that this might be useful for scouting missions, such as the one that Merkle had carried out while we were looking for the spikkan nest, but it still drastically restricted the utility of the working.

For a start, I'd had the idea of using it to provide myself with an eye in the back of my head, but as Mika had warned, my brain simply wasn't wired to accept an additional point of view.

However, after a frustrating few hours of trying everything I could think of to incorporate the additional source, I, or rather we, finally had a breakthrough.

<{I/myself/Pinca} {try/help/succeed} {view/perceive/envision}>

It was my Glowling. Perhaps it was as frustrated as I was becoming by my lack of success. I tried thinking back at it.

<Hello? How can you help?>

<{Through/Process/Incorporate} {I/myself/Pinca}>

I could somehow feel it reaching out and groping for the stream of vision from the mana sphere, but failing to make contact. I tried to help and took the stream and redirected it not into my own brain but into an imaginary spot in my consciousness where I visualised the Glowling residing.

For a moment, there was nothing and then suddenly a vision stream intruded back into my brain. This time however, it was controlled, projected in a circle in the centre of my vision, and I could see perfectly well around it.

<Thank you. Can I move it?>

There was no answer, but by exerting my conscious control over the circle, I found I could move it around and I finally left it at the top left of my point of view where I could monitor it without losing most of the rest of my vision.

Experimenting, I found that this worked as well as I had hoped. Directing the mana stream into the Glowling was as easy as sending it into my consciousness directly. Manipulating the bubble to move it to the location I wanted to view was straightforward. I found I could also quickly change the size of the vision circle when I wanted to focus on something by an act of will.

I found moving at the same time as all of this clumsy at first, but I rapidly got more sure-footed. I could indeed perch a bubble on my shoulder, looking behind me to boost my awareness. This meant that I could follow through on my original goal of being able to monitor my back during my staff practices. I was reasonably confident that I could now spot and deal with attacks from the rear.

Experimenting while out running, I found I could float a bubble higher in the area above me to give me a much better perspective of the terrain ahead, allowing me to move even more smoothly at speed than I could before. Adding the heat sensing refinement that Mikka had mentioned also meant that I could get a clear additional view of other people and animals around me in the dark.

All in all, I could see that this was going to be an extremely useful addition to my growing kit bag of abilities. The only point I regretted was the Glowling had fallen silent again so quickly. It was certainly responding to me this time, and I had hoped we might communicate more fully.

CHAPTER TWENTY-TWO
Back to the Temple

Mikka briefed me on my next challenge a couple of weeks later.

"One requirement you will need to fulfil to be raised from apprentice status is to accompany a group of more senior Guild members on an outside assessment trip. Obviously, you also need to demonstrate certain levels of knowledge and ability before you can progress.

"In part, the trip is aimed at seeing whether you can function effectively in conjunction with other people using higher levels of magic. That is, magic you'd otherwise not be exposed to at this stage in your development. In addition, this also is a chance to get a variety of viewpoints on your ability from other people. It is part of the Guild's checks and balances to prevent any one master from making an arbitrary decision," explained Mikka. "Usually, the trip is done in a very controlled and artificial setting. Several apprentices are assigned to a group of masters and assessed during a controlled exercise where the dangers are kept to a minimal level. As usual, Master Logross has other ideas."

I gulped a little. What was he dropping me into

now?

"My companions and I are planning a materials gathering expedition to the old Temple site. Gonni and his colleagues need certain rare crystal materials for some artificing purpose or other, and my squad had been assigned to help him obtain them. When I asked Master Logross for formal approval to attend, he granted it, but added 'and take the boy with you'. He then clarified that he expected this to qualify as your outside assessment trip."

"OK," I said, "so what will this involve? Am I ready for it yet? I know I haven't completed the apprentice curriculum yet."

"As long as you listen to us, and do what you're told, you should be fine," Mikka reassured me. "To be honest, most of the items that you're still missing are more utilitarian skills such as truth-reading. You should be able to master them quickly when we have time to go over them. They're certainly not things you're going to need on this trip. In many ways, Master Logross has already advanced you well beyond the usual apprentice schedule, as you've probably noticed already. Certainly scrying and advanced workings aren't usually covered by apprentices."

"Is there anything I should prepare in particular?" I asked.

"I don't want to give you too much of a briefing ahead of meeting up with the others," said Mikka. "Not least because I don't know the details myself. Gonni and Dienny are sharing responsibility for the planning. However, I gather we'll be going into some of the older and more feral areas of the Temple. I'd brush up in your bestiary on some of the more typical creatures to encounter there. Certainly spikkans, possibly vizzinti, wurnt and cractalla. An outside chance of some of the more inimical energy creatures such as ziltos, depending on exactly where Gonni is planning to lead us. We should be underground the whole time, so that rules out a lot of potential encounters. We're scheduled to meet up with the others for a planning session tomorrow and we should find out more then."

This sounded as if it might get interesting, I mused, leafing through the bestiary. I was pretty familiar with spikkans and vizzinti already, of course, and I'd already read about cractalla, the armoured rat hive-minds. Wurnt were not something I'd read about to date, however, and neither were ziltos. As I understood it, most energy creatures were better off avoided rather than fought. The bestiary was of the same mind, although it suggested that light and certain types of shield could help hold them at bay while making your escape.

***

The planning session with the others the next day was somewhat frustrating.

On the one hand, our goals were spelled out much more clearly. Apparently there was a certain type of red crystal with a particular affinity to heat and fire magic which was running low in the Annex's stock rooms. Gonni explained it was well known that the best local source of this was in some of the lower levels of the Temple, which had been evacuated when the move to the Annex was carried out around forty years previously.

Unfortunately, it was some time since those relevant areas had been last visited, which meant that the maps and records needed to be treated as suspect. Cave falls, creature migrations, and missing or lost records all added to the confusion. The bottom-line was that we knew more or less where we were going and some points along the way, but we needed to treat the entire mission as being into largely unknown and hostile territory.

My frustration stemmed from the fact that the others had all worked together for years. They had clearly worked together as apprentices in a vermin control team. That meant that, although everyone was welcoming and tried to be helpful, they simply didn't want to spend the time to talk me through a detailed set of tactics, capabilities and contingencies.

I still had only a vague notion of what they would expect from me. To be fair, I got the impression that this was more or less the way these outside assessments were usually conducted with a group of apprentices dropped into several testing scenarios alongside a group of masters who would provide assistance and were ultimately responsible for signing off the success or failure of individual candidates.

That sounded like a reasonable approach in concept, but this mission involved rather a lot more potential jeopardy. Later that day, I expressed my concerns to Mikka who calmed me considerably.

"You're right that this is a curious mixture between assessment and combat mission. As a group, however, we should be easily sufficient for the threat level that we're expecting to meet. I have a good idea of your capabilities and I've shared that with the others. We won't be asking you to do anything outside your comfort level, and the rest of the time you'll be able to sit back and enjoy the show.

"Remember that a significant part of your assessment is based on your reaction to what you see and observe during the mission. Afterwards, you'll be asked how you expect to apply what you've learnt to your future performance and whether it helps clarify your views about your future path in the Guild. And if things go sideways, Gonni will have an emergency bell linked into the Temple's system and reinforcements will be available."

And I had to be satisfied with that.

***

The transport cavern was already buzzing with activity when Mikka and I arrived the following day. The rest of the group, Gonni, Dienny, Bielda and Harrisal, had more or less finished stowing their equipment into the hover sledge and strapping in. Mikka and I quickly followed suit.

We were the only group travelling to the Temple on the transport, and as soon as Mikka and I were done, the transport specialists climbed aboard and we set off.

The ride was as fast and as unsettling to my stomach as my first visit to the Annex had been. Indeed, this time, the weather was even worse with a significant sandstorm underway. However, the ventilation magic on the sledge functioned well. (An air working with some sort of associated shield forming a cushion around it, perhaps?) That kept us breathing freely, but the visibility was terrible. This meant that obstacles didn't become clear until we were nearly on top of them, which forced some wild turns and deceleration.

Unfortunately, our journey time was clearly a matter of pride for the specialists and it didn't occur to them simply to slow down and have an easier ride!

We were all looking somewhat queasy when we arrived at our destination a couple of hours later. I stood there for a while by the sledge, breathing deeply. Then, as soon as I had got control of my stomach, I recalled what was coming next, and I felt sick for another reason altogether!

***

I recovered my staff and other equipment from the sledge. I'd bought a leather harness with several pouches attached from the market, and I checked over the contents. Water bottle, rations, knife and sundry other tools. All strapped close to my body to avoid me having to carry a bag which might restrict me when fighting with my staff. My supplies seemed to be present and correct. All my vizzinti armour was strapped on and positioned comfortably. I idly wondered what would happen if I encountered another vizzinti? Would it be able to recognise (smell?) the vizzinti skin? Would it care? No actual way to tell, and it certainly wasn't something that the bestiary had covered. Maybe Mikka knew?

I looked over at Mikka. He was wearing plainer leather armour. With some surprise, I realised he had a sword strapped to him. I'd never discussed his armament explicitly, but I'd assumed that as we'd been apprentices of Master Logross, we'd be using the same style of weapon. His sword was plain, but serviceable, with a business-like mana bubble receptacle. Much less gaudy than Tyballo's sword, but somehow more... deadly looking.

Gonni was dressed in flowing white robes. I wondered how he kept them clean. He was armed with a staff, but it was shorter and more elaborate than mine. It was made of white polished wood, with various crystals and engravings set at points around it. He had a white leather bandoleer strapped around his body with a series of crystal Devices clipped along it. There were several distinct types of Device, and I wondered what they did. Pushed to the top of his head, he was wearing a pair of goggles with glittering lenses. I recognised these. It was an eye-glass mechanism similar to the ones used for inspecting mana workings, but built into a leather strap. Presumably more secure in combat? But why would he want to inspect mana in combat? Finally, he had an empty sack strapped to his back, presumably for the crystal materials we were being sent to gather.

Dienny was dressed in black leather armour. She looked tall in any garb, but this somehow emphasised it. Strapped to her back were a pair of matched long knives, almost short swords. Each was maybe three hands-span long. They were positioned to allow her to reach over her neck with her opposite hand and to draw them simultaneously. I saw her practising this once or twice to check the tension on the sheaths was set correctly. They had black blades: what else to match her colour aesthetic?

Bielda was wearing a white tunic, and had a complicated-looking crossbow strapped to her back.

She also had a quiver which contained several sets of metal crossbow bolts fastened in clips. Given the complexity of the trigger mechanism, which incorporated crystal technology, I assumed this sped up her reloading time.

In some ways, Harrisal's appearance was the most conventional. He was wearing robes, along with a staff roughly the same size and design as mine. His staff was made of unstained ash wood and was well made, if utilitarian.

When I'd first joined Anyana's vermin control squad, I'd been surprised by the mismatched set of weapons that we employed. Over time, I'd realised that we actually worked well together given the range of options that we could cover. Looking at the range of weapon and armour, it was clear that Mikka's team similarly meant business.

I hoped that I could find a way to contribute, despite my limited powers.

CHAPTER TWENTY-THREE
Into the depths

"Right team," Dienny announced. "Gather round for a final briefing. Just to remind you that Gonni is in overall charge of this mission, but as usual I will take the lead on combat matters and during battle. Is everyone clear on that?"

We all nodded in agreement.

"Just try to remember that split this time, Gonni. OK, over to you," said Dienny.

"Let's get moving then," said Gonni apparently ignoring the crack from Dienny. "We'll be heading down to sub-level four, muster point east six to get started. A guard detail will escort us that far, so we can relax a little for the moment. This must be them now."

A squad of six guards, captained by an older man, were making their way across the transport cavern towards us. My impression was that they were all professional and perhaps more experienced than most of those I'd seen during my testing. They had a selection of weapons, including pikes, swords, daggers and clubs. No staffs and obviously since they all lacked the seal of Guild members, no mana holders on the weapons.

Introductions were soon made and the lead guard handed an emergency bell over to Gonni.

"Just so you all know the procedure in case something happens to me," said Gonni. "In an emergency, any of us can make the decision that we need to tap out and ring the bell. Just don't be too eager to break off and go home, Mikka.

"I'll fix this here to my belt," he continued. "It's clappered right now. However, once rung it would take some time for the backup team to locate us and they'll be aiming for the bell's current location. In that scenario, we will need to pull back to a defensible place of safety once we've rung the bell. All clear?"

Again, we all nodded.

"Right, let's get started."

We set off down a series of passages, led by the guards, who were clearly familiar with the layout of the Temple. Our route gradually meandered downwards, sometimes through well-built squared off corridors, sometimes through natural looking caves which had seen little work other than the passage of feet. Initially, the passages were well lit but, as we descended through the sub-levels, lights became further apart. Soon, they were rarely seen. The guards had their own set of lights and some members of the team supplemented this with light workings, all advanced workings, I noted.

The labelling of the corridors and junctions was initially clear, following a similar scheme to the Annex. As we moved further into the tunnel complex, they became fainter as we left the zones where the markings were frequently renewed.

After an hour of walking, we reached our initial destination, where we took our leave from the guard. The senior guard checked with Gonni whether he wanted them to wait.

"No, that's fine," he said. "We're expecting this to take at least a few hours, probably much longer if the route has become blocked and we need to find a way around. In the worst case, we're provisioned for up to two days of exploration and we've agreed we'll head back in less than half of that. Please, could you confirm the time you left us to the command point?"

"Will do, sir. The best of luck to you. Just to confirm, there's no permanent guard presence on sub-level four. You will need to return at least as far as sub-level three east three to be sure of an escort home again."

And the guards saluted and headed back the way we'd come.

Gonni nodded and started pulling out various maps and notes.

"Dienny, if you would be so kind?" he said.

"OK team, ready status now please," said Dienny. "Scordo, that means that we're now moving into a potentially dangerous location but that there's no immediate visible threat. Everyone needs to be ready to react, which means ensuring that weapons are available, and wards are active, but there is no need to fire up active combat magic yet. I'd like you to take a position in the middle of the group, and ensure that you're comfortable to act if something happens. There would be two typical reasons our status might change.

"First, we might decide that we are not at any immediate risk, because we have returned to a safe location, or we've secured a safe point to rest. In either situation, I'll order 'safe status'. Second, we might detect an active threat and need to move to 'combat status'."

I nodded appreciatively. This sort of pre-planned organisation sounded sensible and presumably all the team knew what they needed to do. I saw the rest of the team checking the draw on their weapons and several mana bubbles sprang into existence. Bielda took a bundle of bolts and rested it lightly in her crossbow.

For my part, I had little to do for now. I was already holding my staff and wearing my ring. I created a night-vision enhanced scrying bubble and stuck it to the back of my neck for now. Mikka eyed me, surprised. I hadn't told him about my success in incorporating the additional vision source alongside my normal vision. He didn't comment further for the moment.

Gonni showed the direction we needed to take further down the passageway that we were already following. I noticed differences immediately. The previous tunnels had been poorly lit, but relatively clean. Periodic traffic was common, perhaps guard patrols? The new tunnel section was entirely unlit, and the floor was littered with sand, dust and, most worryingly, the occasional small falls of rocks.

***

For the next half an hour, Gonni directed us along a series of tunnels. We continued to move into progressively lower regions of the caves, but it all felt like a labyrinth to me. Every now and again, we could see what might be location markings on the wall, but they were not only faint and difficult to read but also hard to understand. They clearly followed earlier labelling schemes than the ones I was familiar with. Gonni could usually figure them out, but was having to consult more and more sets of notes. Some of what he was leafing through must be official maps, but more looked more like copies of mission reports and diaries.

And then our luck failed. We turned a corner in the passage to find the way ahead blocked by a rockfall. We made an initial assessment, but we couldn't find an easy way to get through. At Mikka's request, I pushed a scrying bubble through, but it was a good twenty feet before the tunnel was clear again.

"Dienny, I'm going to need a few minutes to plan another route," said Gonni.

"Got it," she replied. "Take a seat on this boulder here." She pointed to a largish rock which had rolled some way from the roof collapse and was now resting in against the passage wall. "The rest of you form a half-circle around Gonni, facing outwards. I've been seeing traces of spikkan tracks for a while, and this would be a perfect place for an ambush if they've heard or smelt us."

***

We all took our places around Gonni, shielding him from any potential danger while he worked.

"Scordo," Dienny continued. "Can you scry back down the corridor we entered through? Look for any spikkans. Pay attention to wider cracks in the wall, particularly at ceiling height. Bielda, please do the same with the rockfall as best you can. Scordo has already checked there, so it's a less likely ambush direction, but he wasn't looking for hostiles."

I saw Bielda close her eyes and summon a mana bubble while I sent mine forward down the corridor. I wasn't sure how wide a crack spikkans could crawl through, so I erred on the side of safety, checking down each as I came to it.

As I gradually worked my way down the corridor, I heard Bielda reporting no signs of movement through the rockfall. Gonni was muttering to himself behind me and was presumably working out an alternative route based on the information he had about the cave system.

Then I saw something. I hadn't noticed it as we passed, but up in the top corner of a bend in the passage, there was a particularly dark spot. Approaching it with the scrying bubble, I could make out movement which I wouldn't have noticed without the low-light sensitivity on the scrying sphere.

Yup, definitely spikkans. I counted one, two, three, six, twelve. Now dozens of spikkans were pouring in through the hole in the passage wall.

"Dienny, we've got incoming spikkans," I said. "They're entering the tunnel from a point about fifty yards down. I've counted thirty or forty so far and they're still coming."

"Perfect, thanks Scordo," said Dienny. "In a narrow corridor like this one, we've got them exactly where we want them. Harrisal, are you ready to take point on the attack?"

"Got it," said Harrisal, and he stepped out ahead of the rest of us.

"Scordo, keep your viewpoint where it is, so we'll know when they've stopped coming. The rest of you keep back and let Harrisal work. Make sure we don't get flanked."

I was watching Harrisal carefully, wanting to know how he was going to deal with this. Suddenly, I saw a pair of mana bubbles form in front of him, but they weren't spheres. Instead, they were in the form of triangular pyramids. He placed them roughly at the level of his shoulders, but spaced an arms-length apart. Each pyramid was oriented with a vertex pointed back down the corridor in the direction the spikkans were approaching from.

And then they were in sight, coming around the next bend about twenty yards ahead of Harrisal. As soon as they came into view, he didn't hesitate. Immediately, a cone of fire poured out of each pyramid. One played on the floor and lower walls, the other on the ceiling and upper walls. The leading spikkans ran straight into the fire and burst into flames.

The first dozen spikkans were already a charred mess before the ones behind them attempted to slow. That still didn't help them since Harrisal then caused the pyramids to pivot slightly, first left and right, and then up and down. The flames played across all the spikkans in sight and they died before they could retreat.

A few seconds later, I saw the response from my viewpoint further down the passage. Spikkans were abruptly switching direction in a panic, colliding with others still trying to emerge. Before long, all I could see were escaping spiders. I reported this to Dienny.

"Got it," she said. "Harrisal, please head down the passageway and stop up that entrance. Scordo, Mikka please go with him and cover him from each side. Bielda and I will stay here to ensure that Gonni isn't surprised by anything else."

Harrisal, Mikka and I moved forward slowly, but there wasn't much left to do to mop up. Spikkans were either just so much charred flesh or they'd fled. As we approached my scrying bubble, I pointed out the corner that they'd emerged from to Harrisal.

"Tricky," he said. "We missed that on our way in, didn't we?"

He then sent one pyramid bubble into the hole, while cutting off the flame on the remaining one. A few seconds later, I heard the noise of breaking rock and realised that Harrisal was now using the heat working to collapse the spikkan crack. Once he was done, at his request, I checked with my scrying bubble, but he'd been entirely effective in blocking the crack as far as I checked.

A few minutes later, we were back with the others. On Dienny's instructions, I pulled my point of view back a little way in case the spikkans had an alternative route.

"Thank you Harrisal, as efficient as ever," said Dienny. Harrisal acknowledged the compliment with a quick smile.

"And Scordo, good work. You're much more effective with your scrying than the rest of us. For a start, none of us can scry without closing our eyes and turning ourselves into a sitting target. And that includes your mentor who has spent ages failing to achieve it."

"Yes, well, he hadn't actually told me he'd mastered it either," said Mikka. "As Dienny said, nicely done."

We continued to watch, but a lot of the tension had drained out of the party with our easy initial victory. Once I got a chance, I went over to Mikka.

"Mikka, what was it that Harrisal was using? I haven't seen a working quite like that before."

"I believe I mentioned before that there are other stable mana bubble shapes that are used for more advanced purposes. What Harrisal was using was the tetrahedral shape, which is primarily used for constraining and projecting an effect. I can't tell you much about it, because it's only allowed to be taught to Junior Artisan and above. All the rest of us know it, but since I can't teach it to you, my seal would block me providing any actual information."

"Got it," I nodded. "It looks useful… and dangerous."

"It is," said Mikka. "Suffice it to say that it's really useful in combat. You might want to speculate about how it might… spice up… other workings that you know. As ever, there are also tricks to help you… modify the precise effect."

He shrugged in frustration, conveying that he was hitting against the limits imposed by his seal. I thought about how it might combine with other workings, including water and air that hadn't been useful in combat to date.

Shortly afterwards, Gonni jumped to his feet.

"I've worked out an alternative route. We'll need to work back for a little while and then down a couple of levels to an old living complex. Dienny, are we ready to go?"

"Finally. All right everyone back to ready status and let's move off."

***

We continued to head deeper into the Temple complex. After another half an hour of marching, we found ourselves in an interconnected set of caverns. Some signs of their former purpose could be seen here and there. One room had a series of well-worn benches and tables. Small rooms off to both sides had stone sleeping slabs.

The stone furniture was practically the only remnants of civilisation, however. There were no signs of curtains or doors and no remaining rubbish or small items.

"Gonni, how long ago were these rooms abandoned?" I asked after we'd been walking through them for ten minutes.

"I'm not sure," Gonni replied. "I can't find any actual explanation of what they were for and why there were people living down here. Given the size of the accommodations, it must have been bigger than a typical mining outpost. Maybe a couple of hundred years old, maybe three?"

Mikka cut in. "Scordo, what's on your mind?"

"I'm not sure," I said. "This is all in very poor condition or has been stripped thoroughly. Like that..."

I pointed at what must once have been a bookcase made of wood, but now was little more than a framework.

"That shouldn't have nearly disintegrated in a couple of hundred years. It almost looks..." I approached it to look closer. "...gnawed."

"Damn, you're right," said Dienny. "There are too few remains: no-one is this tidy when evacuating a facility."

I heard Mikka draw his sword, and the others glanced around themselves nervously.

"What..." I began.

"Scordo," said Dienny. "The reason the others are reacting badly is that the last time we saw signs like this there was a cractalla nest nearby. Now, it's possible that they've been and gone a long time ago but, now that I come to look more carefully, there's also a curious lack of dust on the floor."

I quickly made my way back to the others. From what I'd read of cractalla, they were extremely smart and effective at ambushes. It was speculated that the armoured rats were telepathic with each other, perhaps even forming a hive mind. And they were notoriously voracious.

"Gonni, how much further to go to our destination?" asked Dienny.

"I'm not really sure. Distances aren't a strong point in these maps. We should be more or less out of this complex of caverns shortly, though. Maybe another ten minutes?"

"Scordo, I don't suppose your scrying practice has

covered heat sensitivity yet?" asked Dienny. "It would be good to get out of here quickly, but I don't want to walk into an ambush."

"Actually, yes, give me a moment," I replied.

I dismissed my existing working and created a new one which had heat sensitivity. I then superimposed it over my existing vision and looked around.

The others all stood out clearly, of course. Sadly, I immediately saw several other new shapes ahead and behind us, all keeping barely outside the reach of our lights. Each of them was about two feet long and low to the ground.

"Uh oh," I said.

CHAPTER TWENTY-FOUR
Ambush

Dienny reacted immediately.

"Combat status. Harrisal and Gonni, you'll cover our advance. The rest of you, get ready to protect our flanks and rear. Scordo, speak to me. What can you see?"

"Multiple heat sources in front and behind," I said. "They look like giant rats. Maybe ten in each direction right now, just outside the range of our lights. Nothing evident on either side right now. I can check further away, but should I prioritise forward or back?"

Dienny hesitated for a split second.

"Ahead. Check out our route ahead. If we can, we should push on that way, but I don't want to fly into an ambush. Since they haven't already attacked, either that means that they aren't yet ready, or there's an ambush prepared ahead of us and they're waiting for us to march into it. Umm, I don't suppose you can keep eyes on those behind us while checking ahead?"

"I'm not exactly sure. It never came up," I admitted. "Let me try."

I formed a second scrying working, routing it through my Glowling, Pinca, as usual.

Starting Sphere

"Yes, because combat is always such a good time to experiment with new skills," said Gonni quietly.

"Unless any of you have learned to heat sense and not told me, then pipe down," said Dienny. We're not actually in combat yet, and we're meant to overcome this sort of threat without Scordo's help.

"Besides," said Mikka, "it's kind of tradition, isn't it?"

"Got it," I reported. "I've lost my normal peripheral vision, but I should be able to keep watching behind us while sending out a bubble ahead."

"Mikka, Bielda, monitor our flanks and protect Scordo," ordered Dienny.

I edged the new scrying sphere into the next cavern and swung it around to get a view of the heat sources.

"No sign of any more rats in the next room. In fact, two or three just left, presumably through tunnels in the walls. Looking behind us, it's difficult to tell, but there seem roughly as many as before. Maybe a few more."

"That's strange," Dienny said. "Usually, I'd expect up to about fifty cractalla in an ambush. It's almost as if they're trying to herd us in the direction we wanted to go, anyway. Can you see any more details of the route ahead?"

"Not without sending in a light-source," I reported. "That sphere is tuned for heat sources, not low light."

"Gonni, a little light if you would," said Dienny.

"My pleasure," said Gonni. Next moment, my

sphere registered a massive heat source in the next doorway, together with my ears reporting a colossal explosion. Swinging the scrying bubble around, I could see more details of the next cavern in the illumination of whatever Gonni had just used.

"You called it," I said. "It looks as if the passageway out of the next room is blocked somehow."

"Damn," said Dienny. "Gonni, are there other routes around?"

"Not without detouring a long way back," said Gonni. "It may be time for some gratuitous destruction, don't you think?"

"You always think that," said Dienny. "On this occasion, you might be right. We'd have to fight through the main cractalla pack to retreat, anyway. Let's move into the next cavern and spring the ambush. Scordo, dismiss your sphere. Let's go, team. Engage when ready."

I dismissed the far sphere and moved the other one round to cover my back. Gonni, Harrisal and Dienny moved up to take out the cractalla ahead of us while Mikka, Bielda and I gradually backed up, waiting for the rats behind us to make a charge.

Through my rear-vision, I had a good view of what Gonni and Harrisal were doing. Harrisal was spraying fire ahead of him again, and Gonni was using his staff to cause massive explosions. Dienny was holding behind them with her knives out, presumably guarding against sudden side-attacks.

Ahead of us, I saw the first couple of rats slink out of the corridor into the light. I could see Mikka holding a glowing sword and preparing a heat jet bubble.

Bielda wasn't waiting for him, however. She had a sphere out near the other doorway already. The rats ignored it initially, but then Bielda fired her crossbow. A metal bolt hit a rat and there was a sudden flash of light as a lightning bolt shot out of the nearby sphere and hit the bolt. The rat suddenly spasmed, and then went still. Thud, sizzle. A second bolt hit another rat with the same result. Bielda was using the metal bolts to attract and guide the lightning.

We'd backed as far as the doorway now, and Mikka was setting fire to several approaching rats. Flame wasn't as effective as the lightning at immobilising the rats, but once they were alight, they had a habit of crashing off to the side, setting other rats aflame in a chain reaction.

As I backed through the new doorway slightly ahead of Mikka and Bielda, who were still engaged with the pursuing rats, I registered two things at once. The first were the charred bodies of several rats on either side of me. The next was the oncoming charge of three more who were very much still alive simultaneously from left, right, and behind me.

My perception of time seemed to slow down for me as I did a number of thing at once. I swung my staff in a wide arc, hitting first the cractalla to my left, then the right-hand one and then under my arm to smack the one behind me without even turning my head to look at it. Each blow shocked my arm with the target's inertia, but all three rats were knocked back. At the same time, I created two heat workings, one next to the rat on the left and one to the right. As the rats burst into flames and fell back, I swung both bubbles behind my back to hit the third one, tracking their progress in my rear-facing scrying bubble.

"Nicely done, Scordo," shouted Dienny, who had swung round to cover Gonni's back as he did something in the blocked corridor. Now that there was some light in the cavern, we could see that it wasn't simply another rock fall, something (the cractalla?) had piled boulders from floor to ceiling. Gonni removed something from a pack and placed it carefully at the base of the blockage. The cavern we were in was around forty feet across and roughly circular. Harrisal was standing in the centre directing jets of fire at rats trying to enter from holes in the sides.

"When Gonni gives the word, everyone get against the far wall, on either side of the next passageway entrance," shouted Dienny. We all acknowledged, with Mikka and Bielda gradually giving up territory to the oncoming swarm of rats.

I saw Dienny throw one of her knives, now glowing, across the cavern to clip a rat. It bounced off the rat's natural armour, but succeeding in setting it on fire. Next second, the knife bounced off the floor and soared across the cavern back to Dienny's hand.

"Ready for blast," shouted Gonni, and he dashed back out of the opening and flattened himself against the wall immediately to the left. The announcement was followed by everyone else breaking off from combat to press themselves against the wall on each side of the doorway. I did the same and had barely reached my position when there was a blinding flash and a wall of pressure and sound exploded from the blocked passageway. In our positions on either side of the blast, we escaped the worst of the blast wave, but I was stunned for a few seconds and found my ears continuing to ring with the aftermath of the noise. I noticed that Dienny and Mikka who were on either side of me had already clamped their hands to the sides of their head before the explosion happened.

As for the rats, who had to have taken the worst of the blast, I couldn't see anything through the cloud of dust for a moment. Their bodies, both alive and dead, must have been slammed into the far wall.

I suddenly realised that Gonni was mouthing words and pointing down the passageway. Mikka pulled me along with him and we all headed down the tunnel with Harrisal bringing up the rear, fire workings going again. As we passed where the blockage had been, I saw a mixture of dislodged boulders, gravel and sand spread across a wide area. Clearly, the blockade had only been a few feet thick.

"...talked about... overkill... how many". My hearing was working again a little, that was Bielda talking to Gonni.

"...only about a thousand units..." Gonni replied.

The passageway ran straight for about three hundred yards before Dienny called a halt to our panicked dash.

"Harrisal, any sign of pursuit?" said Dienny.

"Nope, we're clear," Harrisal replied. "I reckon those that are still alive are probably still stunned. This is beyond their usual hunting range anyway, and we must have killed at least half the pack."

"True," said Dienny. "Thank you Gonni. Your destruction was, as ever, truly gratuitous. How are we all holding up? Any injuries?"

Gonni and Harrisal had a few scratches caused by flying stone, but otherwise we were all in one piece.

"Gonni, how much further to the material site?" said Dienny.

"We're still some way off," said Gonni. "Our detour set us back a way and we've got to work ourselves back towards the right set of caverns."

"Right, so let's carry on to the next defensible cavern and then take a break," said Dienny and we set off once more.

***

About ten minutes later, we passed a round opening to our left. On investigation, it turned out to be a rock cave about thirty feet deep and ten feet across. The walls were smooth, and there were no other apparent entrances aside from the opening we'd found.

"This looks perfect," said Bielda. "I can ward the entrance and we can take a break."

"OK, let's do that," said Dienny. We all piled into the cave and Bielda started a working by the entrance. As best I could tell, she was tracing a line on the floor and embedding a mana sphere in one end.

Mikka saw me watching. "It's a warding. We haven't covered them in any detail yet, although you've already discovered that they can protect against scrying. That one will throw up a wall of flame if anything tries to enter, if I'm any judge. How are you holding up, anyway?"

"Not too bad," I said. "That explosion was loud, though."

"Sorry about the lack of warning," said Gonni.

"That was a prepared crystal charge. Usually used for removing obstacles when mining. It doesn't take too much Device work to produce one since the detonator is the hardest piece. You can then load mana in over time until it's full and it'll stay ready for some days."

"As long as it doesn't go off in your pack," added Bielda.

"That doesn't happen very often," said Gonni. "Besides, that one was practically a baby. I've got some which can hollow out an entire cavern in one go."

"When you say 'you've got some', please don't tell me you've got them with you," said Bielda.

"All right, I won't," said Gonni, grinning.

"Speaking of hollowing out caverns," said Harrisal, clearly trying to change the subject. "Is this one natural or man-made?"

"I'm not sure," said Dienny. "The sides are too smooth to be natural, but who would make a cavern with curved floor and ceiling? I mean, why? What would be the point?"

"Perhaps it was hollowed out by water in the past?" suggested Mikka. "There might have been a soft pocket of stone or earth that washed away? Like a sink-hole?"

"Maybe, I suppose," said Dienny and the conversation lapsed while everyone got comfortable and helped themselves to food and drink.

"Bielda," I asked after a while. "May I ask about your crossbow bolts? How do you get the lightning to hit them?"

"As long as the lightning working is near enough,

it happens reliably by itself," Bielda explained. "Lightning likes to find its own path to the ground and prefers metal as a route. Have you come across lightning conductors on tall buildings? Same principle. This way, I can aim at individual targets without having to move the mana working around. Even using a... working like Harrisal's is indiscriminate and wasteful. Too much of your mana gets wasted hitting the scenery."

"That makes sense," I said. "No, I hadn't come across lightning rods before."

"Once you make it to Artisan, there are some science courses available to you that cover some basics," said Mikka. "You can always dip in and out to give you ideas about how to take advantage of workings in uncommon ways. Plus, of course, the library is packed with other people's ideas going back a long way in history."

"And Mikka just loves spending his time in the library researching other people's ideas," added Dienny.

"I gave you the idea for your homing knives, didn't I?" replied Mikka.

"True," said Dienny. "I didn't say that your ideas were all bad, but living a bit more in the real world would give you a bit more context."

We chatted about various things for ten minutes, and then I wandered down to the far end of the cavern to explore. Although there were no other exits to the cavern, I had noticed several circular marks on the walls here and there. They were unusually consistent, each about a foot and a half across. I initially wondered if they might be marks from where water had hollowed out the cavern, where the water had swirled around in a circle. On investigation, however, I rejected that idea since they were too regular and the material of the wall was different inside the circle. The rock was definitely to be more crumbly there, and I could dent it with a fingernail.

"Have you ever seen anything like this before?" I asked Mikka, calling him over.

"No," he admitted. "They're all over the cavern, aren't they?"

"They seem to be," I agreed. I examined one at head height to get a better view. When I put my head close to the wall, I heard what sounded like a throbbing or humming sound. After a minute of listening, I was sure that it was getting louder.

CHAPTER TWENTY-FIVE
Carvings

"Umm, Mikka," I said. "Should the wall be humming?"

"Should it be what?" he asked. He approached it closer. "It is, isn't it? That can't be good."

We both stepped back nervously. The sound didn't get any quieter as we retreated. In fact, if anything, it grew in intensity. The others had stopped talking and were coming over now.

"In fact, it's more of a grinding noise," continued Mikka. "Which means... Oh hell. Dienny? Do you know what a wurnt nest looks like?"

"Umm, no," replied Dienny. "When we encountered them before, we never saw a nest. You think..."

The grinding noise was getting closer and closer and small bits of rock were falling from the wall in the noise's epicentre. Then suddenly, a circular set of jaws ground through the wall and a giant worm around eighteen inches in diameter emerged into the cave.

"Step back," said Gonni. "I'll deal with this." He had raised his staff and was lowering it towards the wurnt.

"Gonni, I don't think that..." began Bielda.

Mikka grabbed me and pulled me back sharply, towards the others and against the wall. As Gonni's staff levelled to point at the wurnt, a ball of orange light emerged from the end of it and travelled in a flat, fast trajectory straight at the wurnt.

It hit and several things happened, one after the other. There was a sudden blast of heat and light as the fireball exploded in the wurnt's mouth. Because of the narrow width of the cave, we were all hit by the backdraft of the fire and I could distinctly smell burning hair. Then we were showered with a wall of broken rock and gravel propelled by the blast. Finally, the wurnt continued its slow progress into the cave, unaffected by the attack.

"Gonni, wurnt are immune to fire. Whereas we are not!" shouted Dienny. I saw she was bleeding from a graze caused by the gravel and had a nasty burn across much of her face.

"Ah... Oh... Sorry..." replied Gonni.

At that moment, there was a whooshing noise and a sudden glare of light from the entrance to the cavern. I saw a second wurnt ponderously making its way towards us through a wall of fire and the remains of Bielda's ward.

"And that's all we needed," said Dienny. "Look, wurnt are slow enough that they're not much of a threat unless they surround us."

"Which they have," said Harrisal.

"Which they have," agreed Dienny. "Harrisal, could you please manage a powerful jet of water at the one in the entrance? Mikka, Bielda, same please against the other one. Try to force it back into its tunnel. And stay far enough away to avoid shock damage. Scordo, once Harrisal has soaked the one by the entrance, could we have a cold working, please? Freeze it in place so that we can get past it."

I looked towards the wurnt blocking the entrance to the nest. Like the first, its body was about eighteen inches in diameter, with a circle of teeth protruding from the front of its mouth all the way around its head. They rotated in some way to help grind away the rock and gravel in its path. At least ten feet of body was in sight, disappearing away around the entrance into the corridor. Its skin was a grey-brown colour which could easily be confused with rock, with knobbly outgrowths forming ridges down its body. From what I'd read in the bestiary, it was nearly as tough as stone and immune to most type of physical damage. What's worse, the mouth wasn't its primary weapon when hunting live creatures. Instead, it could generate lightning shocks to stun its prey before slowly consuming its prey it in its grinding maw.

Then Harrisal mana-formed a pyramid about a yard from the worm, and a moment later a jet of water sprayed out of one vertex, hitting the creature full in the face. It jerked backwards immediately. It didn't look injured by the liquid, but it certainly didn't like the experience. Little bolts of lightning immediately started playing backwards and forwards between its teeth, but the oncoming water was robbing it of the ability to build a significant charge or focus the lightning on a particular target.

I suddenly realised that I was standing there watching, rather than actually helping. I created an advanced cold working over near the wurnt. It didn't flinch or pull back from the chill but some of the water drops cascading off the wurnt's face sparkled as they turned into drifting frost.

It took me a few minutes to learn how to apply the cold working most effectively. Initially, I got the working too close to Harrisal's water jet and froze it in midair before it affected the wurnt. That effectively formed an ice wall which shielded the creature from the impact of the water. When this happened, Harrisal needed to manoeuvre his pyramid around so that he could find an angle of attack that bypassed the new obstacle. Eventually, though, we got into a rhythm that worked better with him spraying the water backwards and forwards across the head and the start of the body, and me following along behind the jet, turning it to ice. Gradually we applied multiple layers of ice to the creature, forming a thicker and thicker outer casing, and its movements became slower and slower.

Behind me I heard Bielda and Mikka spraying water at the other wurnt. It sounded as if they were having some success in driving the worm away to the far end of the nest, and then filling that end with water. I doubted that we'd suffocate either creature since, from what I remembered, they could breathe independently through each segment of their bodies. However, our goal wasn't to kill them, just to get away from them.

According to the Bestiary, actually killing the creatures, which would yield valuable materials, could only be effectively done by an "extreme light focus", whatever that was, used to slice the body into multiple sections.

Eventually, Dienny decided that we'd immobilised our wurnt sufficiently, and ordered us to escape past it. Harrisal cut off his jet and ran, jumping onto the back of the worm and running along it, out through the exit. I waited until he was clear and then simply jumped, pumping a small amount of mana into my ring. I easily cleared it and soared through the exit to land first on the corridor wall, and then bounced back down to the ground. Harrisal was already thirty or forty feet down the corridor in the direction that we'd been heading before, so I followed him. There was at least another fifteen feet of worm body trailing away down the corridor and I avoided it as best I could. Behind me, I could hear the other water jets in the nest shut off and the rest following in some disarray.

Once all the group had escaped, we barreled down the corridor, ignoring several circular holes in the wall.

***

Eventually, we came to a large low room about a quarter of a mile further down the corridor. This certainly wasn't a wurnt nest. It was square, around forty feet to a side, with carvings covering most of the walls. The entrance was through a heavy stone door, and there was another at the other end of the room. Best of all, there were no signs of wurnt marks on the walls. Presumably we'd moved out of their range. Perhaps the rock around here tasted wrong?

This time, the group checked carefully around the walls for potential cracks or holes, but we found nothing. Once this was done, a rather shamefaced looking Gonni wedged the doors shut.

"Right," said Dienny. "Let's have another try at

that rest, shall we? Anyone need treatment for burns or other injuries? Anyone except you, Gonni."

"Look, it wasn't exactly my fault," said Gonni. "I didn't know that wurnt were resistant to fire."

"Why not?" asked Dienny. "Did you bother to do your preparation work? Wurnt were an obvious risk in the lower Temple. And as for letting off your staff of fireballs in a confined space? We've discussed that before."

"I was just a little too enthusiastic to help," said Gonni.

"You've been behaving like a kid with a small toy ever since you got that thing," said Bielda. "It's not the solution to every problem. Dienny, could I get some ointment for my burns, please?"

Dienny went round to each of us and applied a variety of potions from her pack. She did, in fact, include Gonni, but left him until last.

After that, she announced we would take a two-hour break and encouraged us to take a nap. Most of the group followed her advice, but I noticed Mikka had started examining the elaborate carving on the walls, so I went over to find out what he was investigating.

"These must be a thousand years old, at least," he commented in a low voice when he saw me approach, clearly trying not to disturb the others.

"How can you tell?" I replied, similarly keeping my voice down.

"There are runes under the carving," he said. "I think it's an extremely old variant of Zaronian, far older than anything I've ever seen in the library. I think this room must be related to the accommodation block we were in before since, wurnt nests aside, there was a straight passage joining the two."

"Can you read any of it?" I asked, examining the carving myself. There was a repeated starburst motif that reminded me a little of my necklace, and a series of carvings that must be people who were bowing or praying.

"Not much," he admitted. "I think this bit might say 'honour' and this bit nearby 'power bringers', or is that 'teachers'? And this bit over here appears to show plants growing amongst mountains, or maybe sand-dunes."

"What might be the purpose of a room like this?"

"It's difficult to say. Possibly a way to record history? Or a religious site? I have never seen any written information about ancient Zaronian cults, but there must be some reason behind the tradition that this complex is always called the 'Temple'."

"But why down here?" I asked. "We're a long way down from the surface. Why would it be in such an out of the way spot?"

"The desert is pretty inhospitable in this general area," said Mikka. "I suspect that this complex would originally have been somewhere to shelter from the worst of the weather. Perhaps it got crowded enough that people delved deeper and deeper? Or perhaps it was linked to the founding of the Guild? Again, there are no actual records available on that topic. At least none that we're allowed to see."

Mikka spent more time trying to puzzle out the

words, with little success. He then recorded some of the carving and pictures on some scraps of paper he'd brought, storing each completed sketch into an oilskin pouch. Not only were the carved words sufficiently old that I couldn't even recognise them as Zaronian, but their age meant that many of them had simply crumbled away. I wandered around looking at the pictures. More sunburst, more genuflecting people, various creatures being hunted, some people with sunbursts for heads, more mountains and plants. Nothing meaningful.

Eventually, I joined the others in resting, and I was quickly asleep. Far too soon, Dienny woke us all up.

"Time to move on," she said. "Gonni and I have been talking and we think we're not too far from our destination. Another mile or two of walking, partly along something described as the 'cliff road' and we should be there."

"Cliff road? What does that mean?" asked Harrisal.

"We're not sure. The route initially seems to run through a number of crystal caverns, but conventional ones, and then we need to take the so-called 'cliff road'. There are several injunctions in the notes about taking care, but it never comes out and says what we should be careful about."

"Wonderful," said Harrisal. "Unexplained horrors are the best."

***

The crystal caverns were beyond the far door of the carved room. They reminded me a little of the place where I'd witnessed the emergence, but rather than a single giant geode, they formed a series of interconnected, echoing caves. When we first entered, Gonni spent a little time examining the crystals, but he quickly confirmed that it was a conventional type of crystal with little intrinsic value. Apparently, it was more easily obtained elsewhere, including in some sub-levels of the Annex.

Our pace through the caverns was slow. The crystals in the floor made our footing uncertain, and we were forced to adopt single file by a series of obstacles such as giant pillars of crystal and ceiling collapses. The echoes didn't help either. They caused our voices to return to us from unexpected directions, sometimes significantly later.

What's worse, there was a gusting breeze flowing through the caverns which interacted with the rock formations in a way that caused a whistling or moaning noise.

We kept jumping at shadows. The crystals reflected our lights back on us from every direction, so that we were surrounding by glittering, falling sparkles.

All of that meant that it took us several minutes to realise that we were being stalked.

It was Bielda, bringing up the rear, who noticed first.

"I don't want to worry anyone," she said, "but what are those?" She pointed back the way we had come.

I saw nothing new, simply more moving glints of light and flashes of blue. Then I saw them, three floating globes of a deep blue light. They somehow reminded me of ice and I shivered involuntarily.

"Ziltos," said Dienny. She infused that single word with a deep disgust and sense of menace.

"We've got nothing that can touch them, have we?" said Mikka.

"Nothing to damage them, no. In fact, I don't know what can damage an energy creature," said Dienny.

My feeling of cold was growing deeper and waves of weariness were washing over me. What was it that the bestiary had said? Ziltos fed on life-force and mana.

"Scordo," said Dienny. "When I tell you to start, I want you to form a double-size advanced light mana working between us and them. Make sure you look away and shield your eyes. Goodness knows how it's going to reflect off the crystals in here, but it's the only thing that we can do to delay them at all. Everyone else, get ready to pick up the pace and find our way out of here. Mikka, help guide Scordo. Scordo, go."

I tried with all my will to overcome my lethargy and form the double-sized working that she wanted, but it was hard, so very hard. It would be far easier to let myself... drift away.

Mikka's hand clamped on to my arm, and that helped focus me. I gradually formed the outside of the sphere and began to fill it. I pushed out my consciousness to my Glowling, begging for help.

<{Friends / not friends} {Query / confusion / paradox} {Enemies / Rivals / Ancestors}?>

The Glowling seemed to be confused and

disoriented by something and it was throwing off my focus. I desperately tried to keep my working stabilised as I prepared to jerk the current into life and I sent a single word entreaty towards it.

< Help >

< {Shall} >

And the light erupted into life. In the battle to get the working going, I hadn't properly shielded my eyes and for a moment, all I could see was an afterimage of the ziltos glowing brighter than ever surrounding the working. They were apparently attracted to it like flies to a candle flame. Except that they appeared to be feeding on it...

Mikka's hand was there guiding me forward, away from the ziltos. The further I went, the more life I could feel returning to me, but I kept my eyes closed, trying to wait until the blinding light had receded. After about ten minutes, I felt a change of pace, a different footing, and the sound of a much broader space.

I finally opened my eyes and gazed forward into an abyss.

CHAPTER TWENTY-SIX
The Cliff Road

Ahead of me, there was a gap of about fifty feet of nothing and then a sheer cliff wall, dropping down into the blackness. I gazed down and saw that the rock-strewn floor simply ended in a jagged edge a few feet ahead of me. Gazing down into the dark, all I could make out were the two cliff faces descending into nothing.

I wobbled involuntarily, my knees feeling weak.

"Careful now, Scordo," said Dienny.

I felt hands reaching out to hold me, to steady me on the brink of the drop.

"Well done," said Dienny. "I wasn't sure that any of us was going to be able to build a working in the face of that sort of mana drain, but you managed it. The ziltos should be attracted there for long enough for us to get a long way away. How are you feeling?"

How was I feeling? Bone-tired and exhausted. I felt like a piece of bread that had too little butter spread across it, or possibly a butter dish that had nearly all the butter scraped out of it. The idea of casting another working right now was very far from my mind, but I couldn't drag my eyes away from the drop and look at the others.

"Tired," I said, inadequately.

"I'm not surprised," said Harrisal. "I'm tired enough from the drain of life and mana, and I didn't have to form a monstrous working like yours. We let the ziltos approach too close before we noticed them, and they were able to feed on all of us. Nothing permanent, but it will take a while before we feel good again."

"At least we now know what the 'cliff road' is," said Gonni, his usual expressive voice sounding flat and drained.

I managed to glance around at last and got my bearings. All of us were standing on a platform around twenty feet across, protruding out of a cliff wall above the drop. To our left, I saw the platform narrow to ledge just wide enough for two people to fit side-by-side, forming a path that continued off into the distance, climbing gradually. I looked up, but I couldn't make out a ceiling either and I felt dizzy, so I dropped my gaze to the floor again quickly.

The floor of the so-called 'cliff road' looked somehow narrower compared to the magnitude of the fissure. There was no boundary or protection on the outside edge, and the floor itself was scattered with fallen rocks and gravel.

"We have to walk along there?" I asked, incredulous.

"Yes, I guess so," said Gonni. "According to the records, it will be about a half hour trek."

"Will there be anywhere we can rest, part way?" asked Dienny. "We're all exhausted again, but I don't think anyone will want to rest here, close to the ziltos."

"No idea, but I doubt it," said Gonni. "The materials site will be another cave, so we can count on being able to rest there. I think we'll have to push through to get there as quickly as possible."

"If that ledge still runs all the way there," said Bielda. "With our luck, there will have been a rockfall or something blocking it. This doesn't appear to be the most stable region."

"Only one way to find out, I suppose," said Dienny. "Are we all prepared to continue?"

While this conversation was going on, I stooped and picked up a lump of rock which had fallen from the ceiling of the cavern above us. I tossed it out over the drop and started counting. I reached ten before I faintly heard it land a long way below. There was a faint sound of running water coming up from somewhere below, but the rock made a definite crack when it landed, rather than a splash. That was a long way down. I fingered my ring of jumping absently. It should keep me in one piece if I fell, assuming I could summon up enough mana to use it, but how would I ever find my way back to the others?

We set off in single file along the ledge. Our pace was slow but, what with our level of exhaustion and the gradual but consistent climb of the ledge, it still felt grueling. Everyone stayed brushing against the cliff-wall, rather than stepping further into the path towards the cliff edge. Dienny and Gonni took the lead, with Mikka and me in the middle, and Bielda and then Harrisal taking up the rear.

Now and then there came a slight tremor,

following which rocks and gravel would cascade down from the ceiling. When the first of these came, we all froze, pressing ourselves against the wall and covering our heads, but gradually we got used to them and paid less and less attention, trudging away up the path.

It took about an hour to reach the next opening in the cliff wall, at least twice as long as Gonni had suggested. The ledge continued onwards, and I suddenly realised that we could now see the roof of the cavern, maybe fifty feet above us. The gap between the two cliff walls had narrowed significantly, and they met above us in a mess of jagged rocks. It looked as if the ledge we had been following continued climbing up the cliff wall ahead of us and disappeared into a hole in the ceiling maybe half a mile ahead.

Dienny was standing by the cliff wall opening, ushering people inside, while Gonni had already vanished. I stepped through, following Mikka.

***

Red light blinded me as I stepped into the new cavern. I stopped, overwhelmed by a constellation of flashing surfaces, and Bielda, following me in, nearly collided with me.

The cavern was like the blue crystal cavern in which we'd encountered the ziltos, but the deep red of the crystals made it feel very different. Whereas the blue had felt cold and distant, this felt warm and somehow a little claustrophobic despite the size of the space.

Gonni beckoned us over to a section of the cavern

which had been cleared of crystals and we lowered ourselves to the ground in relief. I felt like I could probably fall asleep where I sat.

"So what's the plan?" said Mikka.

"I've agreed with Dienny that we'll take another two-hour break to rest," said Gonni. "Then I'll start harvesting some of the crystal. I'll need some minor help from the rest of you, but I'll need to do most of the work. It'll take another hour or two to collect a sufficient quantity."

"Will we need to return the same way that we came?" asked Bielda.

"No, we shouldn't. All we need to do is to take passages leading upwards until we reach an inhabited sector of the Temple. We're almost certain that there must be easier, and safer, routes to get down here. It's just that we don't know what they are," said Gonni. "All the ones that we knew about before have become blocked. Instead, we had to piece together a route based on a variety of maps and past accounts. Part of our goal is to map a much simpler approach route so that other people can return here in the future."

"How long will it take for us to get out?" asked Mikka.

"Hopefully it'll be less than a two-hour trek. I think all of us will be glad about that."

"Too right," said Mikka stretching.

Dienny and Harrisal joined us, apparently having set a variety of wards to alert us to hostile incursions, but didn't seem too concerned. Apparently, something about these crystals discouraged most creatures.

We all settled down to rest.

***

I awakened to the ringing noise of a hammer.

I sat up and glanced around. Most of the others were still asleep, although Dienny sat meditating by herself. Gonni however, was hard at work in the main part of the cavern. I slowly stood up and went over to join him.

I felt a lot better. I was much better rested and my mana reserves were fuller.

"Awake, are you?" said Gonni, noticing me. "Come over and help."

I made my way over to help, picking my way between crystals.

"You've been asleep for about three hours," continued Gonni. "Dienny and I agreed I would make a start by myself and let the rest of you sleep a little longer. Take this and hold it out."

He opened his sack and passed it over to me to hold. I took it and then paused in surprise.

"Hah! Not seen anything like that before, I'll bet," said Gonni.

The mouth of the sack was lined with a metal band of some sort, carved with a style of working that reminded me a little of the one inside my ring. Inside the band, the interior was completely black, as if filled by a dark mist.

"What is it?" I asked.

"A storage Device," said Gonni. He began to pick up a series of crystals that had been carefully detached from the cavern wall and floor and put them carefully into the sack. As they and his arms passed into the mist, they disappeared. Gonni felt around inside the sack, carefully slotting the crystals into something I could neither see nor feel. The rest of the sack showed no sign of the intrusion.

"There's a small patch of pocket space inside the sack. Maybe ten cubic feet?" Gonni continued. "Partly, it's useful because you can fit more into the sack than should strictly speaking be possible and you won't have to worry about the weight. But more than that, this one has already had a series of padded cubbyholes put into it to allow me to store crystals in it without danger of them banging together and shattering."

"Wow. Did you make this?" I asked.

"I wish," he replied. "This is senior master level work. Multi-dimensional workings, or so I gather. We're not cleared for anything like that level of knowledge. The sack is probably worth more than all of us put together, but my master lent it to me because of the demand for these crystals. Plus, it's probably almost indestructible to normal threats."

"Does that mean you could use it as armour?" I asked.

"Not so much," Gonni said. "If you draped this on your back, you'd find that any impacts or heat were sort of conducted around it and into you, as if it wasn't there. You could climb inside, I guess, but I don't think there's a lot of air inside. Plus, you wouldn't be able to get out again since it requires you to feed mana into the band to keep it open, and that can only be done from the outside."

"What would happen if we'd somehow trapped

the ziltos inside?" I asked.

"Not much chance of that, but... hmmm... I think that would be a bad idea. I've got the feeling that energy-based creatures are not entirely three dimensional and that means that they're sort of a pocket space in their own right. And it would be potentially disastrous to nest one pocket space into another. I once asked my master what would happen if we put a storage Device into another storage Device and he muttered something about a cascade failure potentially causing a breach in space and time. Or something like that. An experiment best viewed from some distance away. A few miles, perhaps?"

He finished transferring his cache of crystals to the sack and reclaimed his hammer and chipped carefully at another one.

"Will any of the crystals do, or are you making some sort of choices?" I asked.

"Good question. For some purposes, we can use a raw crystal of almost any shape. For example, raw red crystal can be worked to produce a lens which will pick up heat signatures. It's a similar effect to your scrying filter. But for many purposes, we need a crystal of as perfect a shape as possible. Like this one, say," he said, holding up the one he had most recently extracted. "This is used for storage, or for amplifying effects."

I looked at the crystal in question as he placed it into the sack. It was a rod about as long as my forearm, which was hexagonal in section, with a pyramidal shape on either end.

"Or this type is used primarily for conveying

mana from one part of a Device to another."

He showed me another crystal, similarly hexagonal in cross section but with flat ends, before adding it too to the sack.

"I need to collect as much variety as possible," he said. "We're desperately short of this sort of crystal. Having said that, if we manage to find a decent route to return, I suspect that they'll want to build a transport pad nearby, to make it much easier to return in the future."

"Are the transport pads needed to transport in?" I asked. "And can you put them anywhere?"

"No and no," said Gonni, still concentrating on his work. "As far as I can tell, it's theoretically possible for a suitably trained master to transport something to anywhere they know well, or can identify in some sort of way. For example, if a master detects a particular mana working, or even a flavour of mana working, then they can transport to there. The transport pad simply acts as a safe anchor so that you can be absolutely sure that you're aiming for the right place. It's much more efficient in terms of mana to link to or from a pad. They can also divert nearby transportation attempts and force them to arrive in a particular place. Many masters have pads in their work rooms which will force a visitor to arrive there, usually within wards."

"OK, that makes sense. But you said that you can't put them just anywhere?"

"No," confirmed Gonni. "They need to be a safe distance from areas of mana disruption. This cave would be one such, for example. So, if they want to put in a transport pad, it would need to be near here, but not too close. It would require a significant effort to map out the local effects and find a suitable spot. Plus, of course, some flat ground to work on. I wouldn't fancy trying to fit one on that ledge."

We continued chatting for another hour, with Gonni filling in the answers to some theoretical questions that I'd been wondering about for some time. I got the impression that he was more theoretically minded, with a better grasp on how mana flows worked than Mikka, whereas Mikka was probably more competent and fluent at performing actual workings.

***

Eventually, Gonni finished his mining operation and was thrilled with the results. I got the distinct impression that he'd been promised a share of the haul to use in his crafting, and was salivating over some possibilities.

The others were all awake by now, and we all prepared for what would hopefully be our last march back up out of the Temple.

"All right", said Gonni, "Let's find a way back out of here. Dienny will take the lead with me and then Harrisal following. Scordo, you go next with Mikka covering our rear, if that's acceptable to everyone. We'll take the cliff road upwards and see where we come out. With a bit of luck, we'll find some other passages leading upwards and will be back in occupied territory in no time."

We set off up the passage, more confident than our earlier trip, less inclined to cower against the wall.

"I heard Gonni lecturing you earlier," said Mikka. "Did you learn much?"

"Yes, some," I said, turning round to look at him. "He has a good grasp on..."

That was when it happened. Mikka was around ten feet from me with all the others further ahead along on the ledge, still continuing to press ahead. There was yet another tremor, but not enough to unbalance us and another small shower of rocks and gravel.

This time, however, I saw one of the falling rocks, slightly bigger than the others, catch Mikka squarely on the temple. His eyes rolled up and he just... crumpled. His sword fell out of his hand and, in a single motion, he rolled over the side of the ledge.

I didn't even think about it. I dropped my staff and dived after him into the void.

CHAPTER TWENTY-SEVEN
A leap of faith

I had a coherent plan when I jumped after Mikka. Unfortunately, almost immediately I realised it wasn't going to work.

I'd done a little practising using my ring to support the weight of two people using dummies. It was a strain to ensure that I was focusing enough mana consistently, but aside from a few heavy landings, it had worked fine. However, whenever I tried it, I needed to be near the dummy. I didn't need to be holding it, but within a couple of feet, at least.

I'd reacted as quickly as I could when I saw Mikka fall, but once I was in the air above him in the chasm, I realised he was already a good ten or fifteen feet below me, tumbling through the air. He probably had less than a one second start on me, but it was far beyond the range I had achieved with my ring during training. There was simply nothing I could think of that would help me fall faster and catch Mikka up, at least not in the short time we had left. I could still save myself, but Mikka was going to crash down on the rocks below.

I didn't hesitate, but I called to my Glowling for help.

<Pinca. Help!>

I accompanied this directed thought with a vision of Mikka falling ahead of me and a sense of urgency. For a split second, there was no response, then everything froze. I couldn't even move my eyes.

No, not frozen. I was no was longer making appreciable progress in my fall, but the cliff walls were still moving with a glacial slowness and I could see Mikka's arms still moving ever so slowly in his tumble. And my eyes were moving, but it was taking them an age to respond to my instructions. I was also burning through mana in some way. Was I somehow speeding up the operation of my mind? It felt as if I was consuming my mana reserves directly to give myself time to react. A message came from my Glowling.

<{Move / transplace / direct} {focus / target / effect}>

Accompanying this, there was the image of my ring and a sense of pushing my mind out through the ring towards Mikka.

OK, here went nothing. I attempting to focus through the ring onto Mikka, simultaneously pushing mana into it. Lots of mana. I failed. It was almost as if my seal was getting in the way, preventing me from thinking my way through to the ring. I tried again and again, but had no success.

I then tried something else. When I'd had problems integrating images from scrying, I'd routed them through Pinca. Would a similar approach work here? I tried to think through the Glowling into the ring. My consciousness passed through Pinca in a way that bypassed the seal and I successfully found the ring and pushed through it to grab at Mikka.

I felt almost as if I was grasping around him with a huge glove. As I did so, I could feel myself losing my focus, maintaining the mental exercise that was speeding up my mind and a sense of movement kicked in again. Then I slammed into Mikka at high speed as he appeared to rise to meet me. The shock of the impact made me lose control of the mana I was pushing into the ring. We both resumed plummeting.

This time, though, we were more or less in contact. I grabbed around him with my arms and simultaneously pushed mana into the ring again. We were suddenly both falling into the blackness more slowly, gradually floating down.

I had lost control of my light working when I dropped my staff. I formed a new one below us to allow me to better see what was happening and what we were falling into. I heard shouts and screams from above. Presumably, the others had noticed that something was wrong. I doubted any of them had been looking at us when we went into the dark. Would they simply think we had disappeared?

Below me, I could see a rock floor gradually approaching. The bottom of the chasm was narrow, narrower even than the path had been, and was covered by swirling, ropy patterns of rock, partly obscured by many years of detritus from small falls of stones and gravel. I could still hear that sound of flowing water somewhere nearby, despite no sign of it. It was much louder than I had when on the ledge. Maybe there was a nearby cave with a river running through it?

Starting Sphere

As we finally approached the bottom of the cliff, I eased off on the mana to the ring slightly too early, and we fell from about head-height under our own weight. There was a muted crash, and I felt the floor give way under our feet. It was only a thin crust over some sort of cavity. Some splinters of rock caught and tore my clothes and my skin as I tore past them. Next second, we were in fast flowing water and were seized and propelled away into blackness. I lost my grip on Mikka again.

In a panic, I conjured another mana bubble for light and stuck it to my head. I lay on my back with my mouth out of the water. I was rushing through some sort of stone tube, partly filled with water. My arms and chest hurt as if they'd been torn open and I was finding it difficult to concentrate. I risked lifting my head up slightly to inspect myself and I could see large dark gashes gaping red. Then my head exploded with pain and I realised I'd been caught in the forehead by a rough piece of stone protruding from the ceiling. I kept my head as low as possible after that, breathing shallowly to avoid either rising or dipping under the water.

It's difficult to know how long we were in that river. The constant jostling in the current, the pain of my injuries, the view of the rock ceiling zipping past a few inches away. It could have been twenty minutes, or it could have been twice that. I fought hard to stay awake and conscious.

Eventually, however, the current slowed and the ceiling lifted above me. I realised I was now in a much bigger space, and that there was a beach or river bank to my side. I tried to sit up, or turn over, or anything to get back control of my limbs, but I didn't have the strength. Before long, however, the current had taken me to the shore, and I could crawl up onto it. I immediately lurched to my knees to look for Mikka. There was a black mass bobbing along the shore a few feet away. I grabbed at it, and pulled him further onto the shore. As I did so, he spasmed as if in pain and then fell still again. At least he was alive.

I lay there for a little while, trying to recover my strength. Before long, I realised I was shivering from the cold. From the look of it, Mikka was as well. I risked a heat working about five feet away and gradually brought it closer to us until I felt hot, but not burning. At least my mana skills were still working.

I slept.

***

Some time later, I lurched into life again, wakening suddenly in a panic. I realised that we'd both been lying unprotected on the ground, but fortunately no creatures seemed to have investigated. I checked myself over. My wounds were red and swollen, but were not bleeding further. My vizzinti armour had held up reasonably well, but underneath, my tunic was torn to shreds. I checked for my water bottle and rations, but they were gone, washed away. My boots and trousers were still intact, however.

I rolled over and made my way to Mikka. He was in a much worse way. There was a massive bruise on his forehead and his arm was badly broken. His leg had a large gash in it that was still oozing blood and there were also cuts and lacerations all over his body. He must have rolled over and over in the current. He was breathing, but shallowly.

I lurched up onto my feet and walked up and down the beach, looking for something I could use to splint his arm. There was no wood, but I found a straight piece of stone that would do a good enough job. I used the remains of my tunic to tie the splint and close the gash. I wasn't sure what more I could do for him. I certainly wasn't qualified to treat the head injury.

There was a cave mouth leading off the back of the beach, so there was at least a direction for us to head. But how was I to move Mikka?

Eventually, I tried the ring of jumping. I slipped it on his finger and added a little mana. It took a while to get the mana level correct, but after some experimentation, I could lift Mikka in both arms and walk with him held out in front of me. It probably didn't look like a very dignified way to travel, but it worked, and it wasn't exacerbating his injuries.

***

I trudged along the passageway, wincing as my wounds throbbed. A step. Now another step. Now another one.

Initially the caves looked natural, gradually winding their way upwards. What was it Gonni had said? Just follow a route up to the inhabited sections of the Temple? As far as I could tell, none of these caves had ever been inhabited. There were no signs of human tool marks. No signs of marks in the dust lying on the cave floor.

And another step. And another.

After an hour of trudging along in a half-conscious state, I finally noticed that things had changed. The caves were still natural, roughly floored and narrow. However, some walls had been carved. More sunbursts. More pictures of plants and trees. Mountains. Groups of people gathered around what looked like balls.

And the dust on the floor looked a little more disturbed. Here and there, I could see the remains of desiccated plants and grains.

Still no sign of habitation. No type of junction markings either, which was unusual for the Temple.

And another step. Still picking the upwards passage when I had a choice.

Finally, after another hour, I realised I could see light ahead. Real daylight. As I reached the mouth of a cave, I stopped almost involuntarily. I felt overwhelmed by the light and the heat of the sun. It was an age since I'd felt either.

I'd emerged from one of several cave mouths dotted along the walls of a steep stony valley, dotted with boulders and dead-looking trees. I realised I wasn't actually in full sunlight, but was still in the shade of the rock walls. Downhill, a sandy valley floor stretched for about half a mile before a narrow exit led out into a wider area.

More steps. I finally stood in the mouth of the valley, looking out onto a desert plain. Not far away, I could see a cluster of mud huts, with the wavering outline of shelters made of white material. People were moving backwards and forwards.

I placed Mikka carefully back on the ground and automatically reclaimed my ring. I stood there, swaying. I shouted. I saw a boy turn to face me and his eyes widen. He pointed in my direction and shouted something. Others turned.

I swayed again, and my eyes began to close. I saw people running towards me. I initially thought that they were tumbling over, but then I realised it was me that was falling. Everything went black.

***

I woke slowly. I could feel a shifting pattern of light and shadows on my face and eyelids. A breeze played across me. I could hear conversation somewhere nearby, although I couldn't make out what was being said. There was a bubbling sound somewhere. Water boiling perhaps? My wounds were still painful, but felt better. They had been dressed somehow.

Then a voice spoke close to me. I hadn't realised there was anyone nearby. It was a hoarse, cracked voice and I opened my eyes to find myself looking at an old lady. I didn't recognise the strong accent.

"You have come back to us, have you?" she said.

It was a curious dialect of Zaronian, much more formal and slow-paced than that used in the Guild. I looked at her in confusion.

"Never fret," she continued. "Once they brought you away to here, the menfolk have sought to the Temple occupied by your masters for aid. I would imagine that they will arrive shortly to take you both away."

"Both... Mikka... my friend. Is he OK?" I asked.

"I have done for him what I could, but it will need stronger healing than mine to bring him back to us. His mind is still absent."

"Absent...? The rock to his head...", I said.

"Was that what it was? Indeed, more healing will be needed."

"Thank you for what you have done," I said. "I'm sure the Guild will reward you."

"Ha, them? What would I take from them? Those that do evil but do not know it. Or know it, but cannot do otherwise? But you... Now there's a puzzle. Coming from the caves of the Benefactors with the sign of the high priesthood on your chest."

She made a signal towards me. I suddenly realised that my armour and leather harness had been removed and my upper body was bare aside from the necklace from my parents.

"What do you mean?" I said. "What Benefactors? And what sign?"

"Ah. That's the way of it, is it?"

She stepped over to me and rested her hand on my forehead. I felt something, a flicker of heat perhaps, and then she wrinkled her forehead and stepped back again.

"We will need to think on this and discuss. Rest now, and drink if you may."

She placed a cup of tea on the table next to me and waddled away, ignoring my clumsy attempts to continue the conversation.

I sipped the tea, realising how dehydrated I must be after the eternity I had spent wandering through the cave passages. Half an hour later, the hut was suddenly full of Temple guards and two Artisans. The old woman had left at some point. One of the Artisans examined me quickly but carefully and then helped me to dress in clean clothes that he'd brought.

"You seem to be stable, but your companion is more touch and go. You need more rest, though. Sleep now."

I saw a mana bubble flash into appearance and my eyes closed.

CHAPTER TWENTY-EIGHT
Recovery

I woke sometime later in another infirmary room. I tentatively flexed my arms and legs and then sat up. My body felt like it was in good shape. My wounds had been dressed again with clean bandages and although they still twinged, they were mostly healed. The burns I'd sustained to the face from Gonni's fireball felt entirely gone and, best of all, I felt rested and hydrated.

I sat up and found clean clothes and what possessions had survived at the foot of my bed. My lost staff was with them, leaning against the wall. I dressed quickly and took the staff. I could hear voices from the next room.

The others, Dienny, Bielda, Gonni and Harrisal, were there, sitting around a bed. As I entered the room, they sprang to their feet and greeted me. Dienny hugged me, thanking me repeatedly. I only had eyes for the occupant of the bed, however.

Mikka was lying there, head and arm bandaged, still asleep.

"How is he?" I asked.

Harrisal replied, "He should be OK. The head injury was severe, and made worse by whatever happened to you, but they think it's healing. They've been keeping him asleep to help him recover. We're expecting them to transfer him back to the Annex shortly."

"We're in the Temple still?" I asked. I hadn't recognised the rooms or the style of the furniture.

"That's right," he confirmed. "You were both brought in unconscious yesterday afternoon. Scordo, what happened? We heard you stop talking, turned around and all we could see were your staff and Mikka's sword lying on the ledge." He indicated the staff and sword, which had been placed in a pile of his other belongings on a side table.

I explained the bare-bones of what had happened. How Mikka had been hit by a stone from the ceiling and fallen. That I'd jumped after him and slowed us both with my ring. How we'd fallen into some sort of river and ended up washed up in what must have been a different cave system. Our journey out, and our rescue by the locals. I didn't talk about my exchanges with the Glowling, or those with the old lady. They somehow felt more personal.

"After all we've been through, he was nearly killed by a rock falling from the roof onto his head?" Dienny asked incredulously. "Wow. Just... wow."

"You're both lucky that Gonni constructed a functioning ring of jumping. Imagine being grateful to Gonni. First time for everything, eh?" said Bielda.

"Indeed," said Gonni. His usual good humour was gone, and he was looking at me curiously. "You must have reacted lightning fast to get close enough to him."

"He must have," said Dienny, "And thank you again, from all of us."

"How did you get back?" I asked, embarrassed and wanting to change the subject.

"No great tale," said Dienny. "We looked around for you, including sending scrying spheres and lights down the chasm, but couldn't get them low enough to make out any details. We checked back into the red crystal cavern, in case you'd somehow gone or been dragged back into there, but there was no sign. You'd simply vanished. So, we took up the staff and the sword and headed up the way we'd been going. The route back was as simple as we could have hoped. It only took about thirty minutes before we found a guard outpost about four levels higher."

"After that, things happened quickly," continued Gonni. "We reported what had happened and half an hour later, we found ourselves being debriefed by your master, Scordo." He shuddered. "He doesn't have much of a sense of humour, does he? He was particularly upset that you had dropped the staff. I think he was probably hoping to use it as a way of locating you."

"Is that possible?" I asked.

"Maybe? Assuming he was involved in its construction, he might have embedded a mana signature. I wouldn't want to double-guess what a senior master can do if they set their mind to it. He could probably have located you directly if you'd performed a big enough working, although the thickness of the rock and crystals might have blocked him somewhat."

"As it was," said Dienny, cutting off this shop-talk, "he lurked around for some hours until the news came that you'd been located. At that point, we were escorted here, and he must have left again."

From that point, our conversation drifted onto discussing the rest of the mission, including the encounter with the ziltos, the cractalla, the wurnt, and so on. I saw Gonni was still clutching the sack of crystals.

Around an hour later, a Guild member dressed in a medical tunic came into the room and carefully checked over Mikka. They listened to his pulse, peeled open his eyelids and cast various diagnostic workings. After a while, they nodded.

"It is safe to move him by a transport. The medics at the Annex should be able to let him out of the induced coma by tomorrow morning. Chances are that he'll still sleep for a while after that, but he'll probably be conscious by tomorrow evening. I'll notify the orderlies to move him to the transport platform. If you'd all like to follow me?"

The others gathered up their equipment, and we left the room. As the Guild member led us away, I heard a voice calling from a room across the corridor.

"Scordo, Scordo Orchan! Is that you?"

***

Curious, I entered the room. It contained a series of beds, but only one was occupied. The occupant was a boy about the same age as me. I noticed absently that he didn't have a seal or a Glowling. A Sahrayan by the look of his complexion and features. He was suffering from a severe case of sunburn across his face.

"Scordo," he repeated. "It is actually you."

I suddenly recognised him.

"Jemi, wasn't it?" I said. "Ummm, of the Barony of Salai? What are you doing here?"

"An accident with a light working," he admitted ruefully. "I've nearly finished my training and I guess I got sloppy. But what about you? You just disappeared from our room and then even Lavos and Davras didn't seem to know what had happened to you. At least, when I asked them, they told me to forget about you."

"I assumed they knew. The Guild told me they'd handle all the communication. My testing went... well, and they made me an apprentice." I gestured at the seal on my forehead.

"But they never grant that to non-Zaronians, do they?" asked Jemi curiously.

"It's a long story, but they sort of made an exception in my case."

"And you're that powerful already?" he asked. He gestured to my staff. "I could hear some of what you were discussing with your friends. Jumping off a cliff to rescue someone in mid-air, and fighting all sorts of creatures?"

"It all probably sounds more impressive than it is," I replied, embarrassed again. Having said that, it struck me how far I had come in... what was it? Nearly five months?

We continued to talk for a few minutes, but I wasn't sure what I could and could not tell a lay member, so our conversation was stilted. Soon, I heard orderlies entering Mikka's room and made an excuse to leave so that I could follow them to the transport platform.

"Perhaps we'll see each other again before you leave," I commented.

***

Back in our rooms, with Mikka safely in the infirmary, I waiting for Master Logross's summons. It was not long in coming.

I entered his workroom and then stopped, bewildered for a moment. He wasn't at his usual position hiding behind his desk.

"Over here, boy," came his command.

I saw him sitting in an armchair across the other side of the room, a similar chair facing him. I went over and sat down, gratefully. Although my various gashes had been mostly healing, I'd found rather more bruises and aches in the rest of my body than I'd expected, presumably from injuries sustained during my trip down the river.

"You are well?" he demanded.

It occurred to me that this was probably the first time he'd actually asked after my welfare.

"Yes, only a few aches and pains," I said. "I wasn't too badly hurt by the experience. It was just… difficult and exhausting."

"Tell me," he responded.

So I did. When I tried to start in the middle, he made it clear that he wanted the complete tale, so I started again and made it a full debrief. I tried to go into more details than I'd shared with my friends, but I still avoided various topics. My conversations with my Glowling, the details of the carvings in the second cave complex and my conversation with the old lady.

When I finished, he gazed at me for a while, with curiosity flickering across his face. It was as if he was waiting for me to add something else. I sat there, silent, not allowing myself to be drawn into his game. After a while, he spoke again.

"The locals who found you reported to the guards that you had staggered out from some rocks a long way from any identifiable landmarks. They failed to give any clues to the location of the cave you had emerged from. When Guild members returned later to question the witnesses in more detail, they could not be found. Are there any landmarks by which you could identify your exit?"

I looked at him in confusion. That wasn't right, surely? Hadn't I seen huts near to the rock valley when I carried Mikka out? But the old lady had said that I'd been moved to her hut, which had given me the impression that it was some way from the caves.

"No, I don't think so," I replied. "I was far gone by then and I wasn't taking in many details."

"Just so," Master Logross said. "Some of my colleagues are uncomfortable with having an unidentified exit, or entrance, to the Temple cave system. I was asked to enquire, and I have done so." He didn't appear inclined to follow-up further.

Trying to change the subject, I lighted upon the strange mind-acceleration that the Glowling had apparently imposed when I jumped into the chasm and called for help.

"Master, do you know of a way to speed up your mind... your thinking processes, that is... using mana? I stumbled on something like that when I was falling, and I thought it could be very... useful," I finished lamely.

Master Logross paused for a while, his gaze arrested.

"I do know of mental exercises that match that description," he admitted. "Assuming that sufficient mana is available, they can be exceptionally useful, both for buying more time to consider a problem in an emergency and for more mundane tasks, such as improving your reactions in physical combat. That latter poses certain risks. It is altogether too easy to strain or tear your muscles while trying to move them at high speed. Certain physical training is recommended to people who perfect the techniques."

I listened carefully, since this sounded promising.

"Unfortunately, however, I cannot teach them to you. Guild law prohibits them from being taught to anyone who is below the rank of master. I am bound to follow Guild law, more so even than you are."

He signalled to his forehead, covered as it was by a mass of superimposed seals.

"I see," I said, disappointed. "I guess I will have to wait then."

"I didn't say that, boy. You need a firmer grip on the... precise details of the Guild rules. The letter of the law is what you are sealed to follow, not the spirit. You may learn and practice any skills that you wish, but I am precluded from teaching you certain ones. In general, you will find that Guild laws dictate what you can tell others, and some aspects of your behaviour, but not others.

"If you have already come across such a technique, or been shown it by a source who is not an enemy of the Guild, then you are perfectly free to practice it yourself. I would suggest reflecting carefully on your experiences and trying to learn all the lessons you can from what you have done and been shown."

I was rather nonplussed by this speech. With all the turmoil of the leap, did he expect me to remember precisely how the trick had worked? But he wasn't finished.

"On an unrelated subject, it is clear that your recall is not all that it might be," he said. He stood and retrieved a slim volume from one of many overloaded shelves, precisely locating it first time.

"This book contains a series of mental exercises that may be taught to apprentices. Once mastered, they allow you to target and relive specific parts of your memory. That should help you in many aspects of your study, including your memories of Guild law, and... other experiences."

Did he mean I could use this to relive and master things that the Glowling had shown me? If I could master it, this might open a wide range of possibilities.

"You are dismissed for now. I will speak to Joli about extending your physical training to include certain exercises with the weights. In addition, please report to me tomorrow morning. I have another exercise for you to attempt in Mikka's regrettable absence."

CHAPTER TWENTY-NINE
Shields

I spent the rest of the day poring through the treatise on memory manipulation that Master Logross had lent me. It was hard going, but worthwhile.

The early exercises were all to do with memory recall. With a modest use of mana, I found that I could visualise my memory as an enormous book and page through until I reached the section I wished to relive. I could also leave a... let's call it a 'mental bookmark', to allow me to return to a section again and again.

Later exercises offered the ability to search through my memory in a more non-linear manner. Identifying pages relating to a certain topic, as it were. They were far more complex, however, and I didn't attempt them for the moment. The memory I wanted to relive was recent and easily located.

By reliving my leap from the cliff and subsequent cry for help repeatedly, I started to analyse the precise state of mind that the Glowling had introduced me to. The book of memory exercises helped here in another way as well, since the concepts that it covered were closely enough related that it helped me identify what to look for.

Before the evening was out, I had entered the state

of accelerated thinking twice. I couldn't do it reliably yet. It took a significant number of attempts to manage, but it was a start. I could practise this.

I went to bed that night looking forward to the next day, when I would see what else Master Logross wanted to teach me.

***

The next day, he summoned me early.

He was back behind the security of his desk, peering at me curiously.

"What I will attempt to teach you today is likely beyond your skills. It is a very advanced working, demanding a level of control which is rarely shown by apprentices or Artisans working unassisted. Guild laws do not prohibit it from being taught to apprentices for precisely that reason. It is assumed that it will be beyond their capabilities."

Well, that was a good start, I thought. I resolved to prove that I was capable.

"What I will show you, however, are my own personal techniques and workings. I am... reluctant for these to be spread further without my permission."

He seemed to wait for a response.

"Does that mean that these aren't part of any standard curriculum?" I asked.

"Correct. You will soon find, if you haven't already, that this is perfectly normal practice within the Guild. Different Masters specialise in different areas and keep a somewhat proprietary attitude towards their specialisms."

I nodded. This didn't come as much of a surprise

to me, based on my observations and various comments from others.

"On that basis, as a Master of the Guild, duly appointed to train you, I bind you by your seal not to share the techniques I am about to teach you with anyone else. That includes Mikka, who has not received this training. This command can only be changed by me or by a master sufficient to outrank me."

My seal pulsed twice, as if acknowledging the geas.

"I understand," I said.

"Good," he nodded. "That said, what we will study is a shield working. Your first question should be how shield workings differ from wards, which I believe you have already encountered?"

"Err, yes," I said.

"There is a regrettable amount of imprecision in this area," he said, glaring at me as if I was the source of the confusion. "Technically, a ward is a magical creation that triggers another effect when it is breached in some way. For example, a ward that detects the passage of a creature and then triggers a wall of flame. Another feature of wards is that if you want them in a location other than around the original caster, it will usually require some sort of static, physical change to the the material supporting the warding. For example, a carving etched into the floor." He gestured over at his transport platform.

"The key advantage with wards is that they are usually 'set and forget'. Once they are in place, they don't need to be consciously maintained or adjusted until they run out of power. Understood?"

I nodded.

"Shields are different. Their primary effect is that they themselves block whatever they are guarding against. In theory, they can also trigger other effects either when they are touched or when they are breached, but that involves a more advanced compound working. A shield can cover a volume of space selected by the caster and can be varied later. So, for example, a caster could shield themselves and then extend the effect later to cover an additional individual without the need to drop the shield and reform it."

"And what can a shield actually block?" I asked.

"That depends on the working you choose to use, although obviously you will also be limited by your knowledge and ability. In theory, it is possible to design a compound working that will shield against multiple categories of intrusion, but in practical terms it is usually preferable to layer multiple shields for resiliency."

"And those categories cover things like heat, cold, and so on?"

"Actually, the most common use of a shield covers physical intrusion. The second most common is usually temperature, both heat and cold."

"And lightning? And how about light?" I asked.

"Lightning, yes, another common choice. It is worth saying that shields for temperature and lightning are often erected in response to a particular clear threat rather than being maintained indefinitely. Light, now that's an interesting subject. No, most shields used in combat do not block attacks by light. Can you guess why?"

"Because it's an uncommon attack vector?" I guessed.

"It is true that it is seldom used as a weapon, at least by weaker opponents, but that is not the reason. What do you know about how vision works?"

"Err, not a lot, I guess."

He sighed, as if I had given the wrong answer. "You will need to attend basic physics classes before long. Vision happens when light beams enter the eyes. They can either come directly from a light source, as is the case when you look at that globe," he pointed at a glowing globe on the wall, "Or they can bounce off another object and some selection of them will be reflected in all directions. Depending on what is reflected, an observer will then see that object."

"Err, OK."

"So now answer my original question: what would be the effect of a shield that blocked light?"

I considered, carefully. "Umm, you wouldn't be able to see anything?"

"Correct, but incomplete. If you place a shield around a person which entirely excluded light, not only would the person inside the area of effect be blind, but anyone outside the shield would be unable to see them. Depending on how the shield was designed, they might appear as darkness, or in extremis, a shield can be crafted to bend existing light around it. In effect, granting invisibility."

That sounded like it would be extremely useful.

"However, we're getting ahead of ourselves. Many

of these effects are extremely difficult to achieve. Even more so than a basic shield, which you are likely to find daunting enough."

I nodded. "So, how do I create a basic shield working, then?" I asked.

"There are several skills that will need to be mastered. Note that I do not say 'steps'. Many people learning shields would learn these as steps, but your true goal should be to perform them in parallel to maximise speed, as you have already learnt to do with other workings."

"So, the skills are...?" I pressed.

"To simplify, you will need to form a mana sphere, perfect the working and choose an area of effect. Then you will have to maintain and adjust the working over its lifetime."

"So, the key difference from most workings that I'm familiar with is the act of choosing the area of effect, correct?"

"Correct in theory. In practice, however, you will find all the stages more difficult."

Of course I would.

"For your introductory practice only, we will form the working in 'phases'." He pronounced the word with distaste. "To start with, use a normal sized mana sphere for safety purposes. Over time, you will probably want to move up to dedicating a double-sized sphere to this purpose."

I nodded and formed a normal mana sphere. I was down to around two seconds for this.

"Now, the working for a physical shield." He indicated a blackboard on the wall. I looked at it and recoiled, nearly losing the bubble.

There were three versions of the working illustrated. The first showed a sphere with the surface covered in clockwise circular patterns. The second showed a similar pattern on the outside, but the circles had turned into whorls, a series of nested circles. Finally, the last pattern showed the whorls as the start of a series of nested rotating cones meeting in the centre of the working.

"Basic, advanced and greater workings," said Master Logross. "The greater working is shown only for reference at this point. I don't expect you to attempt this."

"But... how..." I managed. Even the basic working would require me to tessellate the entire surface of the mana bubble with countless circles.

"I believe I said that this would be a challenge to you. One that an apprentice is not considered skilled enough to master alone." He stressed the last word. "Once the mana working is in the correct current, you will be able to reach out with your mind and enclose the space you wish to protect. I believe you're already familiar with that sort of exercise?"

I hadn't told him about moving the target of my ring's influence to cover Mikka, but he seemed to know, anyway. I nodded.

"Excellent. Please begin practising in your workroom. I will call you back when you are able to cast the working reliably and we will discuss the use and maintenance of the shield. Dismissed."

I left.

***

Three hours later, I was still no closer to casting even a simple shield working. The pattern was too complex for me. I couldn't even visualise how to grasp that many points of mana in one place, and going one by one was worse than useless. No sooner had I completed three or four of the circles than the first one that I had completed had slowed to a halt once more. Seemingly, it needed to all be done at once in order to complete the working and fix it in motion. But it was too complex a task for me... surely for any human to master.

What had he said, exactly? I used a quick memory exercise to replay a couple of sections of his dialogue.

"...demanding a certain level of control which is rarely shown by apprentices or Artisans working unassisted."

"One that an apprentice is not considered skilled enough to master alone."

Unassisted and alone? Hmm, was it possible that he meant...

I formed a new mana sphere.

<Pinca. Please help.>

I tried to visualise the image of the simple working that he'd shown me. I felt an imposed sense of confusion and desire to help.

OK, what had I done differently when I had created the cold working to defeat the vizzinti? I'd visualised the current I wanted to form, and then asked for help. I tried again with the image Master Logross had showed me with the same lack of success.

Wait a second. This time I was visualising not the pattern of currents, but the flat representation of the

Starting Sphere

pattern that Master Logross had drawn on the board. Was it possible that Pinca wasn't able to understand how to map from a two-dimensional image to a three-dimensional model? Over the next five minutes, I carefully built up in my mind a complete model of the current flow I needed, and then asked again for help.

Suddenly, the mana sphere sprung into motion, along with a feeling of well-being and satisfaction from Pinca. I then thought about enfolding myself with the working. A sudden extra blue skin appeared around me and then faded away. I could still see the mana sphere was there, with a stable working.

Was I actually shielded? I picked up a glass from the table and threw it into the air above my head. It fell, bounced off an invisible barrier, and landed on the floor, smashing into pieces. I barely felt the impact.

I dismissed the working and tried to form it again. Once more, Pinca was able to establish the working. It was quicker for me to build up the visualisation this time, but it still took time. About a minute, far too long to form this in combat.

How intelligent was Pinca, anyway? I cleared the working again and built up the visualisation in my mind once more.

<Pinca, this is a simple physical shield working. Can you remember that?>

<{Can/will/have}>

I built a new mana sphere.

<Pinca. Simple physical shield working, please.>

And the shield working sprang into action. Really? That easy? A few more tries told me it was. For greater speed, I could instruct Pinca what I wanted as I formed the mana sphere.

<Thank you>

In return, I received a feeling of well-being.

Over the next hour, I constructed a mental image of the advanced working that Master Logross had shown me. I had to stop and restart several times as I lost the visualisation. Even using some of the memory exercises that I had read in the book, this was barely within my capabilities. Finally, I had it more or less.

<Pinca. This is an advanced physical shield working. Please remember it.>

The image of the working held in my mind changed subtly. It was smoother and more regular. Several quirks that my visualisation had introduced had been tweaked out. I received a feeling of confirmation.

I created a new mana sphere and asked Pinca for an advanced shield working. A new skin quickly enfolded me, somehow feeling thicker and more resilient than the first.

"Come." Master Logross's voice issued forth next to my ear. For a moment, I was surprised, but then shrugged wryly. He always seemed to know everything happening in his chambers.

***

When I entered his workroom still wearing the shield, I found him apparently unmoved from the morning behind his desk. He scrutinized me and I felt he was seeing far more than met the eye.

"Good. I see you found sufficient... assistance," he said. "Please practice wearing the simple physical shield at all times when you are outside of my chambers. It will keep you safer. No doubt you have already realised that, had Mikka been capable of learning and maintaining a shield working, he would likely have been uninjured by the rockfall."

I hadn't realised that, but it was a good point. But at all times? Was this yet another sign of Master Logross's paranoia?

He gestured at the blackboard that he'd used before. The images of the physical shield working had been replaced by six new workings.

"For you to master at your own pace. Temperature and lightning specialisations. Note that the physical shield also provides a basic level of protection from many other types of attack, but these are more effective when exposed to specific attacks. Please also report to Joli tomorrow. He will help you test your new physical shield and brief you on your new exercises."

"Yes, Master," I replied.

"Now, I would have thought that you would want to visit Mikka. He has been awake for some time now. Dismissed."

After a long careful look at the board to memorise the new workings, I left.

Interlude 3

Two old ladies sat outside a tent, drinking tea. Such a commonplace sight that none of the passersby in the nearby street spared them a glance.

"So that's the way of it, is it?" said the older lady. She looked tired, travel-worn, but strangely serene. "From the... unpleasantness. That was around fifteen years ago?"

"It must be," said her companion. She was a little younger and less lined, but was clearly more worried, continually darting glances at various people as they passed. "There's simply no-one else who could fit that description who has ever gone missing. But we thought him long gone to another land."

"Mayhap he came back?" suggested the first speaker. "People don't always stay where you put them. Particularly if they have a Destiny elsewhere." She pronounced the word 'Destiny' with a peculiar emphasis.

Her companion darted a glance at her in confusion. "But he's lost now, surely? You said that they were both bound and sealed. Controlled by the wickedness."

"I'm not so sure..." said the other. "I felt something... More flexibility and potential than usual. It might be nothing... Or perhaps everything."

Starting Sphere

The tense lady paused before she replied, waiting for a group of Guild guards to pass. "You said nothing of this before, when you passed the word."

"I'm not sure what I felt, and that is unusual in itself. Not something that I wished to convey by messenger. But I think he bears watching, as we may."

"I will pass the word to those who can be trusted. But the... Others..." she pronounced the word with distaste, "will doubtless have intercepted your earlier message. I've heard rumours that they may have had previous contact. They may intervene directly."

"They may indeed. And we should watch the intervention of the unsealed ones, because the results might tell us much. We are in no hurry."

The younger lady nodded, and they finished their tea in silence.

CHAPTER THIRTY
More training

I was in the infirmary about ten minutes later.

Mikka was still lying in bed looking frail, but as I entered the room, he opened his eyes and looked at me.

"Scordo," he said weakly. "I gather I have you to thank for actually making it back here in one piece. Well, more or less." He nodded towards his bandaged arm.

"How are you feeling?" I asked, not sure what else to say.

"I feel like a battered bit of beetroot. With a splitting headache, at that."

I smiled. He must be feeling closer to his own self if he was using alliteration again.

"No, but seriously. Master Logross visited a while ago and told me what you'd done. I'm very pleased, and proud, that you could rescue me and get me out of there. It couldn't have been easy." He offered his working arm, and I took his hand. He grasped me back surprisingly strongly and waited until I made eye contact with him. "Thank you."

"Master Logross was here?" I asked, retrieving my hand in confusion. "I thought he was in his workroom."

"I thought you'd learnt by now that you can never predict where he will pop up. He made it clear to me he finds my absence inconvenient and questioned the medics on when I'll be up to leaving. Tomorrow afternoon, perhaps, they said. Or within a few days, certainly."

"Don't worry. He's found me lots to do in your absence." I said.

"I'm sure he has, but he'll leave the more menial lessons for me, I suspect. He wants you confirmed as an Artisan as soon as possible, you know?"

"Really? Surely I'm not ready? I've only been here a few months."

"Scordo, you've been here nearly five months, and he originally gave me six, remember? He wasn't joking about that. Your mana forming and working skills are far ahead of many of your peers, and you've managed a range of workings not usually taught to apprentices. I think we can safely say that your assessment trip was a success. There's only a few more utility workings that you need to learn to fulfil the basic curriculum. Then we'll organise a formal examination."

"An examination?" He must have heard the trepidation in my voice.

"Relax. It will be similar to your original testing. Just more focused on verifying specific skills. We'll discuss it more when I get out. I'm too tired right now."

***

The next morning, I reported to Joli as Master Logross

had instructed.

He took me to a private training room.

"Right Scordo, Master Logross came to me with a couple of unusual requests. First, I gather you have mastered a shield working, and he wants me to help you assess its strengths and weakness. Second, he has asked me to prepare a program which will help you build muscle strength and flexibility. We'll come to that later."

"Something like that, yes," I said. "But for the first, what do you mean by 'help me assess'?"

"Maybe I put it badly," he said. "If you're going to depend on a shield in physical combat, then you need to understand intuitively what it can and can't withstand. That way you can integrate it into your fighting style, rather than simply depend on it when you fail to block something."

"Umm, OK, I think I understand that."

"Let me put it another way. It's great to have a shield which will block incoming attacks, particularly those you can't see coming. However, what's even more valuable if you can use it to throw off your opponent. For example, let's say that someone is trying to stab you with a knife, then usually you'd block it, right?"

Suddenly, a knife was in his hand, and he was thrusting at me. I was used to sparring with Joli, so this didn't take me entirely by surprise. I blocked the blow with my staff and he stepped back.

"Just so. But if you could be confident that the knife would fail against your shield, then you could choose to ignore the thrust and take the opportunity to hit directly at your opponent to disable them. Since I would still be overextended with the thrust, I'd be less likely to defend in time."

He paused for a moment to let that idea sink in.

"OK, yes, now I understand. So, you're going to...?"

"You're going to form a shield and then you're going to stand still and allow me to attack you with a series of weapons, so that we can see which do and don't hurt you," he said with an innocent smile on his face.

That turned into a long session, but it wasn't as bad as I feared. Initially, he had me form a basic shield working and demonstrated that clubs, rocks, and staff blows simply bounced off. Then he asked me to protect a dummy, and he proceeded to attack it with edged and pointed weapons. Most times, the shield slowed the impact, but the blade or crossbow bolt made it through to some extent. The poor dummy's tunic was rather like a net by the time we were done.

Then we switched onto the advanced shield, and I was surprised at how much more resilient it was. Arrows, bolts and knives bounced off, as did all but the heaviest swords.

"That's a nice working," Joli commented. "Master Logross's personal design, if I'm a judge?"

"Yes, I believe so."

"I thought so. It's more effective than most and practically invisible. You're lucky. He teaches it to vanishingly few. We should set up a few sessions to continue this practice over the next couple of weeks, since it will take a while for you to learn to trust the shield implicitly."

We agreed times for a series of private sparring sessions.

"Now, as to Master Logross's other request, I can easily set you up with a series of weight training exercises. Without giving me more details than you feel comfortable with, am I to understand that you need to protect yourself against the danger of straining your muscles by trying to move them too fast or at unusual angles?"

"Err, yes, that's what he said."

"Hmmm. OK, it's an unusual request, but it does fit the training profiles of several of the masters. Come down to the weights cavern with me, and we'll see what we can sort out."

That was a painful session as well, but gradually, over the next few weeks, I made progress. Joli also scheduled me to visit the medics every few days for healing that did much to soothing the aching in my muscles.

***

Aside from the intensive physical training that Joli was putting me through, I spent most of my time over the next two days working on my shields and on the mental techniques to speed up my thinking.

The latter was gradually becoming more reliable to trigger. It still wasn't reliable enough to activate immediately but, given ten or twenty seconds to prepare, I could count on being able to drop into the right pattern of thinking. That wasn't fast enough to react instantly to surprise attacks or even leaps off cliff edges, but something that I could choose to engage when necessary.

This allowed me to start carefully making use of it in my sparring with Joli. He raised an eyebrow as I reacted to his strokes almost as fast as he made them, but didn't otherwise comment. To me, it felt like wading through water trying to wrestle my staff in the way of the blows that I could clearly see coming. To start with, my combat potential actually dropped as I began to second-guess many of the reflexes I'd learnt. Gradually, however, it became a more reliable part of my repertoire.

I also strained myself repeatedly, but, either because of the exercise regime or the repeated healing sessions, things improved over time.

Mikka returned to Master Logross's three days after we'd met in the infirmary. He was in good spirits, but was still a little shaky on his feet. Apparently, his internal injuries from the battering we'd received in the water had been more extensive than they'd originally thought.

The next morning, he met me in my workroom.

"So, apprentice curriculum," he began. "You've got a few more simple workings to master, but you'll find them all detailed in this book."

He handed me a slim volume, which I flicked through quickly. I noticed first that it only covered basic workings. Next, I worked my way through them one by one. I knew light, heat, cold, lightning, water and air already. Neither scrying nor shields were listed, unsurprisingly. In fact, the only ones I was missing were truth telling, sound projection, and magnification.

I was already familiar with the function of the truth telling working since it had been one I'd been hoping to learn as part of my elementary lay course. There were always opportunities in the outside world for someone who could detect deception.

The basic sound projection working was a spell to allow you to throw your voice. The range of the simplest version was restricted to within about twenty yards, but other than that, it was probably what Master Logross used to summon me to his workroom.

Magnification had more promise. It basically involved turning a mana sphere into a lens for light. One of the basic uses was indeed to act as a virtual magnifying glass, but it would probably be possible in the future to combine this with light workings to yield further results.

"Only three more basic workings?" I asked Mikka in surprise.

"Well, actually six more workings, since Master Logross wants you to be taught the advanced variants as well, but yes, that's all. I told you that you were close to being ready."

"Why didn't we cover these much earlier?" I asked.

"As I said before, that's all down to Master Logross's style of teaching. He'd much rather that students get a very strong grounding in technique and then add workings as necessary. It works, from my experience."

"Right. OK, let's get started then."

We spent the rest of the day working on the basic

and advanced versions of the new workings, and by the end of that time, I was more or less happy with all of them. There were no new techniques or abilities involved beyond those I'd already mastered. Apparently some students had problems with aiming the sound projection working but, given my facility with scrying, I found it trivial. In fact, not only were scrying and sound projection similar in technique, but the two worked well together in fact to allow me to communicate with someone from a distance.

The next day, I showed the new workings to Master Logross, who nodded brusquely.

"Acceptable," he said. "I will make the arrangements for your assessment. You should expect it within the next couple of weeks. Dismissed."

CHAPTER THIRTY-ONE
Wolf hunt

In the days while I waited for my assessment to be scheduled, our turn for vermin control came around again.

Anyana called for a planning meeting to prepare, borrowing one of the smaller meeting rooms in the refectory for us to talk together.

"So, apparently, we're being sent outside," said Anyana. "There have been reports that a few desert wolves have moved into the area, and people are worried that they might attack one of the supply caravans."

"Just the supply caravans? How about Guild members who are outside the Annex, exercising or whatnot?" I asked.

"The wolves are staying clear of the area close to the Annex right now, so Guild members probably aren't in any real danger. It's not as if they're going to attack a moving hover sledge. Plus, for the vast majority of Guild members, a wolf would come off worse in any encounter."

"Fair enough," I said. "What do we know about fighting wolves? Do they have any magic, or are we talking mundane creatures?"

Starting Sphere

"I haven't heard of any indications that desert wolves have any magic abilities, per se," said Tyballo. "But that doesn't mean we should underestimate them. One or two will probably be easy to kill or drive off, but in larger numbers, they can cooperate with each other to flank an enemy and attack en masse. Anyana, do we know how big the pack might be?"

I paused, surprised at Tyballo's caution. Historically, he'd been over-enthusiastic about fighting creatures. Perhaps he was taking the danger a little more seriously?

"Master Pinchat didn't provide any further details. I'm not sure he has very many right now, but we should check in with him on that tomorrow."

"Definitely," agreed Tyballo. "My family's holdings include a goat farm on the edge of the desert. When a pack of desert wolves moved into the area, they killed nearly half the herd in a matter of a few weeks, even after my father had assigned a guard squad to help the farmer hunt them. Obviously, the guards didn't have magic, but they were well armed and there were about a dozen of them, pitted against the same number of animals. Two of the guards were killed and several were injured, and the wolves escaped unharmed."

"Good information, thank you, Tyballo. I've got no intention of taking this challenge lightly," said Anyana. "That was one reason I suggested this meeting, to make sure we're up to date on everyone's skills. Scordo, why don't you go first? You've usually got a few surprises for us."

I detailed the progress I'd made with scrying and

shields, and the group was suitably impressed. They weren't as jealous as I'd feared though, fortunately, and no-one pressed me to share any of the workings.

"Scrying sounds very useful for this mission," said Anyana. "One problem in being assigned to a hunt outdoors will be finding and tracking the wolves. It sounds like you will be able to keep an eye on our surroundings, correct? And maybe even use the heat-sensing refinement to find them from a distance?"

I agreed that this should be possible, but warned her I was unlikely to be doing much heat sensing in the midday desert sun.

"That shouldn't be a problem," explained Anyana. "We're being sent out tomorrow shortly before dusk. Hopefully, the heat levels will drop significantly while we're out, although we'll need to dress accordingly. As for your shield, it sounds as if it will be extremely useful for you as a personal defence, but probably not something we'll be able to use more strategically. Is that right?"

"That sounds about right," I admitted. "I might be able to extend a shield around someone nearby for a short period, but I haven't thought of any other ways to use it yet. I'll work on it."

"Thank you. In the meantime, I think everyone else has also made some progress as well that the rest of the squad should be briefed on. Tyballo, do you want to go next?"

"Sure. I've been focusing on improving the impact of my sword work. Part of that has involved endless practice in the physical training area with the various sword masters, along with a healing program to boost my physical... umm... development."

I looked at Tyballo anew. If I wasn't imagining it, he looked more well-built than he had only a month earlier. Broader around the shoulders, and with thicker, more developed arms. He continued to speak.

"The most exciting breakthrough, though, came from my Master. He has been pleased with the recent progress I've made with my workings, and he's taught me a special customised working for heat that is ideal for combining with sword-work."

We all made appreciative noises, and Anyana asked for more details.

"It's a little difficult to describe," Tyballo admitted. "It's an advanced working, but not the standard one. The creator tuned it for use with a sword, and it should offer both more intimidation and more damage. I'll show you tomorrow."

Merkle went next.

"I've been doubling down on lightning," she explained. "My master is adept in this area and she's not only taught me the advanced working, but several additional effects that can be layered on top of it to vary its behaviour. Plus, she also made some suggestions that you're going to help with, Anyana?"

"Correct," said Anyana. "I've switched to using arrows with larger steel heads to help draw the lightning."

I nodded. This sounded like an alternate approach to guiding lightning from that I'd seen with Bielda's steel cross-bow bolts.

"I've also learnt a working which should improve

my arrow work, both in terms of aim and power. That should at least make up for the additional weight of the arrows!" said Anyana. "In addition, I've mastered a working called the communications weave. It's a little like a combination of the sound scrying working and the noise-projection one that we all know, but restricted to a very specific framework."

We all looked a little confused by this and waited for her to elaborate.

She smiled and continued, "the bottom-line is that I can set up a way for us to communicate with each other while we're apart. I can only cover four targets, including myself and, right now, my range is limited to about a hundred feet, but it should avoid us needing to yell at each other across a battle-field."

I whistled appreciatively. "That should be very useful, particularly if we get strung out over the terrain. It'll also presumably mean that I can keep everyone up to date with insights from my scrying."

"Exactly. We'll need to be careful we don't talk over or distract each other all the time, but I'm told it's been very useful to keep combat teams in touch with each other. Once I get better, it should be able to offer a longer range as well. Not that I'm not jealous of your scrying ability, but they should work well together."

We spent a while longer chatting about our plans for the following day. On request, I supplied a few highlights from my assessment trip to the Temple. Merckle was particularly interested in hearing about Bielda's performance since apparently they shared a common Master. After an hour or two, we broke up agreeing to meet in the transport cavern the following afternoon, ready for the hunt.

***

At the appointed hour on the following day, we all met kitted up at the rendezvous. Master Pinchat was there to meet us and provide our final briefing.

He explained that the wolves we were looking for had been seen in the rough ground to the southwest of the Annex by locals escorting caravan trains and pack animals carrying supplies. The sightings were sporadic but were getting more common. Only a couple of wolves had been seen at any one time. This was unusual because typically they formed packs of at least six. Some people had theorised that maybe they had split off from a larger pack based further south. There had been no actual reported attacks yet, but the locals were afraid that it might only be a matter of time.

Instead of an emergency bell, Anyana was provided with a red flare, together with a crystal launching Device. We were briefed that we should use it if we felt we couldn't handle whatever we discovered. We should then stay close to the launching Device, since that was where a rescue team would be sent.

The briefing over, we set out. The plan was for us to make a sweep in a long curve. Initially, we would head south and then gradually turn west until we came back to the cliff face a couple of hours later. We would then follow the cliff back towards the transport cavern, ideally arriving about the time it finally went completely dark.

Obviously, if we encountered the wolves, then

we'd be expected to alter the plan accordingly!

As we walked, I studied my friends. They were dressed much as they had been before, but with a few notable changes. Tyballo had switched to wearing his sword scabbard strapped to his back, rather than hanging at his waist, and his gloves and other clothing were less opulent and more martial. Merckle had swapped her hammer for one with strips of metal running the length of the handle, along with various strips of chain-mail fastened to her armour. Anyana was carrying a bow with a bigger draw than I'd seen her use before, presumably to give her greater range outside. She also had the dagger she'd bought in the market strapped to her leg.

We were walking through an area of the desert, which had patches of open sand interspersed with rock outcrops and gullies full of broken stone. We detoured repeatedly around obstacles to maintain our selected route. Aside from the occasional set of bones, there were few signs of nature near to us. Ahead though, I could see that the ground became even more tortured, with bigger stretches of rock and the occasional twisted-looking tree.

Experimenting with my scrying bubble, I found that holding it around a hundred feet above us, with its point of view directed downwards, provided a good balance allowing me to see enough details to make out movement in a circle around two hundred feet across. The temperature of the day was gradually dropping as the sun moved towards the horizon, so I applied a heat sensitivity to the bubble, but I wasn't sure how effective it would be.

While I was experimenting with the bubble,

Anyana prepared her 'communications weave' working. Initially, I couldn't feel anything except a gentle pressure against my shield. However, once I explicitly allowed it to sink through my shield, I could suddenly hear everything the others were saying clearly, regardless of the distance between us. Similarly, when I whispered, they confirmed they could still hear me clearly.

In this manner, we covered the first hour of our patrol, gradually curving to the west. There were still few signs of life, aside from a few birds of prey circling overhead. As we headed further away from the Annex, although the territory was becoming more and more tangled and obscure, I felt more and more exposed. Shadows formed in the outcrops around us, and I couldn't shake the feeling that something was watching us from the darkness.

There were still no sounds, other than the whistling of the wind and the crying of the birds, and I didn't see any movement from the overhead perspective of my scrying bubble.

After another thirty minutes or so of marching, I saw flickers of movement in my scrying view. Initially, they were rare, usually happening while I was focused on my main vision, ensuring that I didn't trip on the rough ground, and I wondered whether I was imagining things. Or was I seeing birds stooping to the ground in some sort of hunt? I could well believe that there might be small rodents or other prey for them to hunt.

Then I saw it. A large heat signature at the edge of my scrying vision, directly behind us. It must be five or six feet long, as long as we were tall. I swung around to glimpse it with my eyes, but whatever it was behind us was clearly lurking behind a pile of rocks.

"What is it, Scordo?" asked Anyana.

"There might be a wolf about a hundred feet behind us," I answered. "Let me reposition my view."

We continued to walk as I lifted the bubble up a bit and sent it back the way we'd come. We were gradually descending into a bowl in the landscape about forty feet deep in the middle. The bottom was about half a mile ahead, at which point we'd need to climb up a patch of sand on the far side, almost a dune, to get out.

Yes, I could definitely see a creature behind us. It was following us, keeping behind the rocks. If we hadn't had the scrying bubble, we'd have had no idea we were being pursued. I passed this information to the others.

"Just the one?" asked Tyballo.

"I'm not sure," I said. "I've only seen one so far, but I can only see a hundred feet in each direction. Should we stop to give me a chance to look for more?"

"Yes, please do that," said Anyana. "We could do with a bit of a breather if we're about to have to fight."

We came to a halt, and I swung my point of view, looking around for others behind us. A few seconds after we'd stopped, we heard the noise. The wolf I'd located had stopped and thrown its head back to howl. It then began to bark with a short, sharp noise. From a slightly different direction, we heard an answering howl, followed by a growling sound. I hastened to redirect the bubble, and I managed to locate the second wolf, a couple of hundred feet away in a slightly different direction. Still behind us, and yet to reach the edge of the bowl.

"There's a second wolf a little way back from that ridge line over there," I told the others, indicating the direction. "Do we want to stay here, or carry on moving forward?"

"Keep searching," said Anyana. "I don't like the fact that they only started to howl once we stopped."

I continued to move the bubble in a circle around us, and I quickly found a third. This one was further to our side and had remained silent. Then a fourth and a fifth. About five minutes of checking located more wolves. I had found about twenty of them so far, in every direction, around the depression in the ground. Most of them were ahead of us. It looked as if they'd been planning to ambush us as we'd reached the centre, or possibly as we tried to climb up the sand on the far side.

We were drastically outnumbered and surrounded.

CHAPTER THIRTY-TWO
Hunted

"This is not an ideal place to fight," said Anyana as she strung her bow. "Thoughts, people? Do we want to make a stand here, or break for an edge?"

"I told you they were smart," said Tyballo. "They can come at us from every direction at once."

"How about over there?" said Merkle. She pointed to a low mound of stone about two hundred yards ahead of us. "We'll have some height to help us keep track of them better."

No-one else had a better suggestion.

"Sounds good," said Anyana. "Scordo, you stay in the middle as we move and keep an eye around us. Let us know when they attack."

"We should stay relatively close together," said Tyballo. "They'll want to separate one of us and pick them off."

As we rushed forwards towards the mound, the details of floor in the centre of the bowl became clearer. In the gloom, we could make out several animal skeletons ahead of us, with more immobile shapes further off in the distance, obscured by the growing shadows.

"We've got wolves incoming," I reported as we

reached our chosen high ground. I jumped forty feet to reach the top of the mound. "About half a dozen have entered the bowl already. None are coming directly at us; they're sort of circling around and spiralling in towards us."

I carefully checked over myself. My advanced shield was already active, and my staff was held loosely in my hands. I cancelled the overhead scrying bubble and replaced it with one covering my back and then added a second with heat sensitivity overlaid across my main vision. I took a position a few yards from my companions to give me room to swing. Merkle, Tyballo and I formed a rough triangle, with Anyana in the centre.

Merkle had already formed some kind of lightning working, which was fizzing to itself, covered by a patchwork of tiny sparks of lightning.

Tyballo had his sword out and had attached his fire working. Before, he'd fought with a glowing sword, but this time it was positively fiery, with flames licking along the blade, leaving an afterimage when he moved it. It looked more like the effect achieved by the vizzinti. I noted his movements were more practised now. Previously, he'd swung the sword back and forth in an arc, but now he was keeping it stiller, pointing outwards.

"I can barely see them approaching now," said Anyana. "Merkle, there is a group coming in from this direction. Shall we show the others what we can do?"

Merkle smirked, and we repositioned to allow her to face in the direction that Anyana had designated. Her lightning working shot in that direction as Anyana took aim and fired, once, twice, and three times. I noticed she was firing through a working, but it wasn't a heat one. It was a lens that gave her a better view to aim and caused the arrows passing through it to accelerate sharply.

Three wolves were hit and flinched slightly, but turned to come towards us directly now. Then Merkle acted. Lightning shot from her working and hit the first wolf near the embedded arrow, and then it jumped from the first to the second and then from the second to the third wolf. The blinding light lasted for nearly a second before cutting off. All three wolves ploughed into the ground insensate.

I stopped paying attention to their continuing fight. A couple of wolves were making straight for me. I held my staff out in a ready position, while I formed a heat working. I thrust the working straight into the face of the first wolf. The hair on its face caught fire, and it was clearly in pain, but it continued to advance. I held it there for five seconds before it finally collapsed, blazing brightly. In the meantime, the second wolf had reached me and I caught it a clip with my staff, but it didn't look staggered by the impact. It was too heavy with too much inertia and must weigh more than me. I suddenly found it trying to clamp its jaws around my leg. Fortunately, my shield held it off easily and I could push it away with my staff and summon the heat working to finish it. It took time, however, and while I killed my second wolf, three or four more approached me.

From my rear scrying bubble, I could see Tyballo fighting. He was practically dancing forward between the incoming wolves, flicking his sword back and forth to cut into them. It looked as if the power of his working was significantly improving the penetration of the weapon.

How could I take down my wolves quicker? I activated my mental speed technique to give me a chance to think. The fire working was the most martial of my workings, but the wolves' tough wiry hair and determined attacks were providing more of a challenge than I'd expected.

With the vizzinti, I'd pushed the working into its flesh. Could I somehow form a bubble touching a wolf, or maybe even inside it? With the time afforded me by the mental technique, I experimented. I concentrated on forming a simple heat working actually inside the head of an incoming wolf. It formed glacially slowly, even allowing for my accelerated point of view, and there was a lot of back-pressure. Much of my mana was being spent simply pushing to form the bubble. Then it was ready, and I started the current. The wolf spasmed and collapsed immediately. That was more like it.

I killed another four wolves like that, one at a time. Without my mental acceleration, I simply wouldn't have had the time to do it and it was draining my reserves rapidly.

In a momentary lull, I looked around to see how the others were doing. I had killed seven wolves and Tyballo had accounted for another five. A line of fiery destruction followed his path as he twisted back and forth amongst them.

Another eight lay in front of Anyana and Merkle. Merkle was now engaging with another two directly. She had attached a lightning working to herself, and the chains and the metal on her hammer sparked wildly as she fought them.

Anyana strung another arrow to shoot at another that was circling around her. I switched my attention to another wolf that was approaching me. I'd dropped the mental acceleration. Between my shield and my two scrying bubbles, I was getting worried about the ongoing drain on my reserves.

Then, over the communications weave, I heard a cry from Anyana.

"Argh. A little help someone?"

I whipped back around. Anyana's bow string had snapped and the wolf that had been circling her moved in for the attack. She quickly dropped her bow and drew her dagger, but it looked like a frail weapon for a wolf fight.

I didn't have time to reengage my mental acceleration. Instead, I acted quickly to create a new basic shield and wrapped it around her.

"I've got you shielded, but it will not be impenetrable," I announced.

"On it," said Tyballo. He swung around and stepped quickly towards the wolf, waving his sword in a pattern in the air to catch its attention. This wolf looked bigger than the others, with a white pattern of hair along its muzzle. Perhaps it was the leader?

The wolf that had been approaching me attacked my back. Fortunately, I caught its movement in my rear facing bubble and caught it a nasty crack on the nose with my staff without even turning around.

The wolf attacking Anyana slipped past her knife with ease and tried to bite at her leg. Its jaws grazed across the shield and failed to make much impression, leaving only a scratch.

Tyballo stepped in and tried to reach past Anyana to hit the wolf. It was a difficult angle, but he left a nasty-looking cut on its rear haunch.

At the same time, Anyana stabbed it in the side.

"Let go of the knife," came an urgent whisper from Merkle. Anyana stepped back, leaving the knife embedded in the wolf's side. A lightning working formed next to the wolf and immediately grounded into the knife. It spasmed once, twice and then lay still.

The reaction from the rest of the pack was almost immediate. From all around us, I heard a series of whines and the remaining wolves broke off and streaked away up the sandy wall of the depression.

***

We looked around at each other in the gathering darkness. Merkle formed a light working and in its glare we could see the dead bodies of over twenty wolves lying around us, many of them still burning merrily. Each was at least the size and weight of a man. Aside from the scratch on the back of Anyana's leg, we were unharmed.

"Scordo, have they gone for good, or are they regrouping?" asked Anyana.

I sent my heat-sensitive scrying bubble high in to the air while cancelling the other one and Anyana's shield. Only six wolves had survived and they were heading off into the distance in the opposite direction to the Annex.

"They've gone," I confirmed, and we all slumped in relief. We moved a little way from the battlefield to give us a chance to rest, eating and drinking from the rations we'd brought.

"They never really stood a chance, did they?" said Merkle.

"I think we were always going to be too powerful for them," said Anyana. "Well done, everyone! We've come a long way from having to run from a group of spikkans. That doesn't mean that we couldn't have done better, but time enough for that discussion tomorrow."

Once we'd caught our breaths, we investigated the surroundings. We counted twenty-three dead wolves. That meant that the total pack had been nearly thirty. Ranging through the bottom of the bowl, it was clear that this was a favoured place of ambush for them. Not only were there a wide variety of desert animals, but there were also the decaying bodies of a group of twenty locals and their horses spread across the sand. Merkle identified them as being nomads, who ranged through the desert. They probably wouldn't have been missed for some weeks.

Anyana placed a crystal Device, which she described as a locator, at the scene of the battle, so that a clean-up team from the Annex could locate the spot and identify the casualties later.

We then turned for home, reaching the Annex a couple of hours later. Master Pinchat was pleased to see us, in his own irascible way, and listened to our report. He suggested the pack must have recently moved into the area and concluded that the few survivors would flee some considerable distance and were unlikely to return.

***

The following day, we were back in the meeting room in the refectory.

Anyana had called us together to talk about our performance.

"Don't get me wrong," she said. "I think we all did an amazing job out there, and Master Pinchat was very pleased. However, it feels as if there were probably ways in which we could have improved. Where we can do better next time, that is. The wolves had speed and cunning true, but if we'd been fighting something with magic or greater intelligence, we'd have been more at risk."

"Let me start," she continued. "The first thing that clearly tripped me up was my equipment. Once my bow-string broke, I was stuck with no primary weapon and I wasn't going to defeat a wolf with my knife alone. I was also at fault for dismissing your shield so quickly, Scordo. When it came to it, you used it to protect me. There must be some way we could take advantage of that more proactively."

"I could also have done a better job with my scrying," I admitted. "I focused so much on having a detailed view of our immediate surroundings that I entirely missed noticing that we were being stalked by wolves at a distance until it was nearly too late. I guess I've got too used to fighting underground, where short range viewing is all you need."

"With all due respect," said Tyballo, "I think you both might be missing the key issue. We each did a good job, but other than your initial lightning attacks, all us of reverted to doing our own thing.

"Obviously, my sword-work was truly majestic," he continued with a self-deprecating grin, "but I ended up right out of position and unable to get back quickly enough to support you when you needed it, Anyana. If Scordo hadn't been able to shield you, I don't know what would have happened.

"Fighting on the mound was better than no choice at all, but we'd probably have been better off picking a location where our backs were covered, where we'd all be able to fight together on a single front. The wolves' advantage was their ability to hit us from all sides at once. No offence meant Merkle. I know the mound was your suggestion, and it was better than anything any of the rest of us came up with."

"None taken," said Merkle. "I agree with you. We didn't actually fight together until we needed to rescue Anyana. For all we talked about the value of the communications weave, we didn't take much advantage of it, did we?"

We continued talking late into the night. Discussing how we could have approached the fight differently. We'd all come a long way over the last few months. I now had to focus on my assessment.

CHAPTER THIRTY-THREE
Assessment

Over the next few days, I practised the apprentice curriculum and revised much of the academic work that I'd been doing in the last five months. Most of what I needed to know had been covered in various lessons, but I supplemented the material with various curriculum primers that I got from the library. The staff on duty were unsurprised by my requests and I got the impression that it was a standard ask from apprentices approaching their assessments.

I found that most of the rest of the squad had started to cram similarly, although they were still waiting for their outside assessment trips to be scheduled. They would each apparently be included on a standard group trip. It would effectively be a series of tests imposed and controlled by senior Guild members, but they were being split up to work with other apprentices with whose strengths and weaknesses they were less familiar. We were also able to fit in an additional mission to a spikkan nest, to help distract ourselves from the anticipation.

Eventually, Mikka confirmed the time and location for my assessment with me.

"Don't worry Scordo, you've got this," he said.

"Your skills and knowledge are well ahead of the standard curriculum."

"Thank you," I said. "Ummm, just in case something goes wrong, what happens if I fail?"

"Nothing really," said Mikka. "If your assessor decides that you're not ready to move up from being an apprentice, then they'll provide Master Logross with details on where they think you're deficient. You wouldn't usually be allowed to retake the assessment for several weeks, but that would be the only official sanction. Of course, I've got no idea how Master Logross would respond." He shuddered.

"Splendid. Just splendid. I guess I'd better not mess up then," I said.

***

Two days later, I knocked on a door at the end of a passageway dug even deeper into the ground than Master Logross's rooms. I noticed I wasn't far from the Device laboratories where I'd visited Gonni.

There was an immediate response to my knock and the door was quickly opened by a large man with a rolling gait. He was wearing a coat covered in pockets and pouches and had a pair of eye-glasses perched on the top of his head.

"Welcome, welcome, my young friend. Please come through."

He ushered me through a lobby room similar to Master Logross's into his personal workroom. The new room was as cluttered as Master Logross's, but there the similarities ended. Whereas my Master's room resembled a wood-panelled library, this room was kitted out as a full Device laboratory. Racks of materials and more tools lined the walls in between large ceiling to floor glossy white boards, which were covered in diagrams and equations. Here and there were door panels which presumably covered cupboards. The centre of the room had several long white tables covered by a clutter of what looked like half-finished, or maybe half-disassembled, Devices.

The man ushered me to a chair in front of a white desk and manoeuvred himself clumsily behind it.

"As I said, welcome, Apprentice Scordo. My name is Master Ekkatini, but most people just call me Ekki. So you're Master Logross's protégé, eh? I've heard a lot about you. How's that ring working out for you?"

I muttered something about it, having turned out to be very useful already.

"So, I've agreed to carry out your Apprentice assessment. This would normally be done by a senior Artisan, but Master Logross had some concerns about information security. Indeed, I was intrigued to meet you. Besides, I owe Master Logross rather a lot of favours, and I welcomed the opportunity to pay one off. Let me look at you."

He peered at me and started suddenly.

"Goodness! Is that a shield you're wearing?" He reached for the eyeglasses on his head and shuffled out from behind his desk. "Please keep it in place and stand up."

I was wearing an advanced physical shield, since Master Logross had recommended it as the best way to train. I'd got to the point where I barely noticed the drain on my reserves. He walked around me, carefully examining me through his lenses.

"Beautifully fine weave... No visual distortions... Very flexible surface..." he muttered. "If I may?"

Without waiting for a response, he removed an instrument shaped rather like a woodworking augur from his pocket and applied it to the surface of the shield. He then stabbed it in, which I barely felt, and read some numbers from a gauge set along the handle.

"Surprising hardness level... Near instant reaction."

He sat back behind the desk. After a few moments of pondering, he came back to himself and realised that I was standing there watching.

"Ah, terribly sorry. I'm afraid I got a little carried away. It's rare that someone gets to inspect Master Logross's personal shield working. He's somewhat... secretive about it."

"Surely he'd be happy to show you?" I asked.

"Well, maybe, maybe, but one doesn't like to ask... And imagine sticking a meter in Master Logross..." He reddened and shuddered.

"Let's leave it at that, shall we?" he asked. "I'm truly grateful for you letting me examine it. To be honest, if you're able to maintain that shield, I doubt the rest of what I'm going to take you through will be much of a challenge. But onwards, all the same. Please dispel your shield, if you would, it will interfere with your ability to carry out the rest of the assessment."

I dispelled the shield with some trepidation. But after all, Master Logross had sent me to Master Ekkatini. Perhaps the shield was one reason he'd wanted to control who tested me?

"So, I've already received the results of your

outside assessment trip. Glowing comments, I must say, particularly from my student, Gonni."

Ah. So this must be Gonni's master. A lot about Gonni's attitudes and mannerisms became clear.

"First, I'd like you to take me through your impressions of your companions' magic and their strategy and tactics during the mission. How have you been influenced by what you saw, both positively and negatively?"

I talked for a while about my observations. Some were obvious, like the use of the pyramid mana form for attacks. Some related to their tactics, such as the well-worn transitions between different modes of behaviour and what were clearly well practised roles. I finished up talking a bit about the one real disaster caused by the rock falling on Mikka, which none of us could have foreseen.

"A stable door which your Master has bolted immediately in your case, I note. It's a shame that most people cannot maintain shields," observed Master Ekkatini.

He then ran me through my own magical abilities. None of this was challenging. He had me form and dismiss normal mana spheres repeatedly. He then took me through all the basic workings from the apprentice curriculum and I formed them in turn.

"Good, good," he said as I finished. "Now, let's try something a little more challenging. I believe you can perform an advanced cold working? Perhaps in a double mana sphere size?"

I formed this quickly, and Master Ekkatini whipped out some new measurement devices from a pouch and approached it carefully.

"Yes, yes, very nice. Good sharp temperature gradient."

He returned to his desk and made some further notes.

He then quizzed me on a whole variety of academic subjects, including Guild rules, mathematics and relations with neighbouring countries. He was reading most of the questions out of a series of books, carefully marking down my answers.

To be honest, most of it was basic knowledge and posed little challenge. The only interesting bits were when I diverted him into talking about side topics. In particular, he had a particular interest in trading relationships. Unsurprisingly, his focus was on materials, both raw and refined, which were used in Device manufacture. I knew little about this, so the subject was new and interesting.

Eventually, however, we came to the end of his questions.

"Nearly finished," he said. "All that remains is everyone's favourite exercise to go: the capacity test."

My face fell. I guess I would not be doing much else that day, then.

"Yes, yes, I know," he said, looking at my expression. "But it is a core part of the assessment test."

We carried out the test, and I was surprised to see that my mana capacity had grown to 756. Master Ekkatini seemed surprised by the number and raised an eyebrow.

Starting Sphere

"No wonder you're able to maintain your shield so easily. I would imagine that it requires around sixty units an hour, which should easily be covered by your natural mana recharge levels. Here in the Annex, at least."

I must have looked confused.

"Has no-one explained about mana recharge levels yet? It's basically a function of your current maximum capacity level and the amount of natural mana available. The Annex, like the Temple itself, was chosen to be in an area naturally rich with mana. That's particularly true in the lower levels - which is why Masters like me and Master Logross take advantage of the space available down here."

He chuckled to himself.

"A very rough rule of thumb is that your mana will recharge at around 20% an hour down here. So you should be right as rain after a good sleep."

"So, is that it? For my assessment, I mean," I asked.

"Your assessment? Oh, yes, yes, thank you for that. I will notify Master Logross of my recommendation later today and I expect he will want to discuss it with you. It was a pleasure meeting you and I look forward to working with you again in the future."

Well, that sounded positive, but he clearly wasn't planning on giving anything further away.

***

I quickly found myself back outside Master Ekkatini's chambers, facing the mile or so trek back to Master Logross's rooms. I felt bone-tired, partly because of the series of questions I'd had to answer, but mostly by my completely drained mana reserves.

I started trudging back, feeling slightly uncomfortable because of my lack of shields. Recently I'd been wearing them so continually that it felt almost as if I'd failed to dress properly.

The passageways were mostly deserted, and I couldn't keep my mind off speculations about the assessment. Had I actually passed? Could it be actually true that I was going to be raised to Artisan so soon?

I didn't even hear steps behind me. Just a thump and a sudden pain exploding at the back of my skull. I lost consciousness.

CHAPTER THIRTY-FOUR
Trapped

I woke to blackness. I was lying on a hard floor, and my face was covered by something, perhaps by some material of some kind. My arms and legs wouldn't move. From feel, I had some sort of cord tied around my ankles and my hands were restrained behind my back. Some flexing showed that they were secured tightly, not quite enough to cut off the circulation, but certainly enough to restrict my movement. I tried to pull my arms apart, but there was no apparent give in my bonds. Some of my fingers felt sore, as if they'd been twisted or crushed while I was unconscious.

I tried to whip my head backwards and forwards to dislodge any sort of blindfold but without success. Judging by the feeling around my neck, there was something tied over my entire head.

I took stock of my options. My mana felt more or less renewed, so based on Master Ekkatini's comments, I'd probably been out for over five hours. Could I hear anything? Yes, there was a rhythmic sound nearby. Someone breathing, perhaps? The floor felt slightly yielding, as if I was lying on wood or hard-packed earth. Moving my fingers against it, it felt like wood. And I could make out the faint cries of birds in the distance.

If I could hear birds, then I wasn't in the Annex any more. Who had taken me and why? And how? Surely I should have been safe in the depths of the Annex? Was this some sort of twisted surprise continuation to the assessment?

That latter thought was a little too paranoid perhaps, but in any case, more information was needed.

Was it safe to work mana? I'd need to take the risk, so I started by forming an advanced physical shield around myself. I hoped for a moment that I might flex it outwards to break my bounds, but it didn't work like that. Since I didn't have a fine enough control over where the shield actually went, I was probably protecting the bonds in fact.

I paused and listened. There was no reaction which suggested that anyone had observed my mana sphere. The rhythmic breathing continued as before.

Right, time for a scrying bubble.

I was in a small room with wooden floors and walls. Light streamed in through chinks between the boards, making up the walls. Over my head, a hood made of some dark material had been fastened. My hands and feet were, indeed, tied with some sort of wire. I'd been wearing my harness when I was taken, but it had been removed along with most of my possessions. My sole remaining possessions were my necklace, which I could feed against my chest, and my ring, which was still on my finger.

Given how sore those fingers felt, I guessed that they'd tried to remove the ring but failed. I remembered Gonni had said that it couldn't be removed without my consent. Maybe I was lucky that they hadn't simply cut my fingers off? Their mistake since I was shielded now and protected against any further acts of theft or violence. Perhaps someone could use the ring to locate me? Gonni had also talked about tracking people by the mana signatures of Devices.

Across the room, another person was restrained in the same way as me. They lay uncomfortably in the room's corner. I couldn't see their face, but the material of their clothes was more expensive than mine. Was it possible that they had been knocked out as well? Very possibly, by the sounds of their slow, shallow breathing.

No-one else was in the room and not much in the way of other objects. Maybe it had been emptied to act as a cell?

I floated my mana bubble through the door, which I noted was padlocked from the other side. A good, chunky metal padlock which looked costly. The rest of the building was much like the cell I occupied. Three other rooms, all stripped out and deserted. I popped the scrying sphere out through the entrance door.

It was daytime. The building looked like some kind of agricultural building, probably a barn or a stable by itself. From the steep barren slopes all around, I suspected it was somewhere near the town that I'd visited for the market, although that wasn't in sight. I could see the birds I had heard before hunting prey among the rocks.

I tried to lift the mana bubble into the sky to give

myself a better viewpoint to scan the valley, but it collapsed.

Hmmm, that wasn't good. I was sure I hadn't lost control of the sphere. I reformed another one and sent it out to check the ground around the building. Before long, I found what I'd expected. Some form of ward carved into the rock around the building. That would prevent me from scrying any further than a handful of feet from the building. More relevantly, it would probably prevent anyone from locating me with magic, either. No-one would locate me through my ring.

I had to assume that it was up to me to rescue myself. I brought the mana bubble back inside to allow me to observe my companion.

"Hello?" I tried. My throat was dry and to start with, I found it difficult to achieve any volume. "HELLO?"

The other prisoner bucked suddenly and seemed to come awake. I saw him trying to move his hands and feet like I had.

"Hello?" I said again.

"Scordo, is that you?" he managed.

The voice sounded familiar, but muffled as it was by the hood, I couldn't recognise it.

"Yes, it's Scordo. Who are you?"

The other figure paused for a long time. I got the feeling that they were thinking. Then they slumped.

"It's me, Daivan."

Daivan? Of all the people that might have been kidnapped here with me, I wouldn't have expected him.

Starting Sphere

"Daivan? Do you know where we are? And what happened to us?"

"Ummm. Not really. Well, I guess I do sort of know what happened, and we're probably somewhere near the village, but... I don't..."

"Slow down, start at the beginning," I suggested.

"I think I screwed up again," he said bitterly.

Gradually, his story came out. There had been another market a few days earlier, while I and the others had been cramming for our assessments. Daivan had attended and had been asking round some of the more obscure market stalls for anything that he could buy to help improve his magical skills.

I made some sounds of incredulity at this point and he countered, "No, it's true. Sometimes they have some genuinely useful Devices. There was this one guy who was friends with my cousin, and he knew someone who had consumed a potion which boosted his mana capacity. Added another fifty points on, I heard."

After some more of this, I got the strong impression that Daivan actually was as desperate as Tyballo had told me. That he'd finally exhausted the help that all of his backers were prepared to offer and was desperately looking around for any sort of trick to help him progress. Any trick other than knuckling down and practising, of course!

In any case, Daivan had drifted from one merchant to another until he was introduced to someone who wasn't a merchant, but some sort of other rich Zaronian.

"He dressed finely," Daivan said. "His clothes

were well cut and used excellent materials. He had a wide selection of jewellery, all precious metals and gemstones." This character had apparently taken to Daivan straight away and had bought him a drink at a nearby stall. He'd taken the time to listen to Daivan's woes.

"He seemed to genuinely understand and care, Scordo," Daivan pleaded. "He knew a lot about magic too, for a non-Guild member. I asked him whether he had been a lay student, but he just smiled and would only say that he 'walked a different path'."

Eventually, the subject had come around to me. I got the impression that Daivan had been complaining about my purported 'special treatment', but he never came out and admitted it to me. Of course, I guess that now I had had special treatment, learning Master Logross's shield working, but I felt that I'd perhaps earned it.

The stranger had been intrigued and had asked a lot of questions about me. He had extracted what little Daivan had picked up about my experiences in Anyana's vermin control squad. Then he made his pitch. Apparently, he'd heard of me before. He claimed I was some kind of estranged, distant relation. Apparently, he wanted a chance to meet with me and make things right, but he was afraid that I'd refuse to meet him if I knew who he was.

"He sounded truly sincere about wanting to clear the air with you and apologise for something. I suggested he wait for the next market and that I would introduce you, but he said he couldn't hang around here that long."

If only, the stranger had said, there was a way to

bring me out of the Guild complex and arrange for a face-to-face meeting. Daivan had immediately told him it was far too dangerous to kidnap me. Apparently, he had listened carefully to some of the others' stories. But, countered the stranger, hadn't Daivan himself said that I would face my assessment soon? He pointed out that following the test, I would be more or less helpless with no available mana and a quick bag over the head and extraction would get me away easily.

But, Daivan had countered, he didn't know where and when my assessment would be. And how could he extract me from the complex, down a series of long, busy tunnels? Nothing easier, argued the stranger, as chance would have it he had an acquaintance that worked in the Annex's medical facility as an orderly. He could find out the information and then facilitate the extraction.

And, just as Daivan was wavering, the stranger revealed the potential payoff. Apparently, a set of ancient documents about magic had recently come into his possession. Apparently, they were hundreds of years old and contained lost truths about magical training. They were useless to the stranger, of course, but if Daivan would care to see them? And he had showed Daivan a sample of the documents that he happened to be carrying around.

"And Scordo, it looked perfectly genuine. It was written in ancient Zaronian and was dated nearly five hundred years ago. I'm not actually very adept at reading ancient Zaronian, but even I could make out enough to know that it was a type of mana strengthening exercise that I'd never heard of before."

This story took around an hour to extract from Daivan with a series of leading questions. In between Daivan's self-pitying remorse and railing against the unfairness that life hadn't simply handed him everything he wanted on a platter, I got the story of an unknown Zaronian man who had a curiously obsessive desire to meet with me, and who had expertly set and baited a hook to catch Daivan by his greed.

Towards the end, I tried a straightforward question. "Daivan, if he actually wanted to apologise to me for something, didn't you think that kidnapping me was going a bit too far?"

"Well," admitted Daivan and I got the impression that inside the hood his head was looking away. "It isn't as if you and I were friends, not really, and he sounded very earnest about all of this, and I really wanted a chance to see more of the documents."

I sighed. "All right, so what happened next?"

"Well, I returned to the Annex and a day or so later, I was passed a note telling me the time and place of your assessment. It also gave a rendezvous point to meet up with the orderly afterwards. And, err, a weighted cosh. The implication was obvious. So, I waited near a point where I knew you'd pass on your way back from the assessment and stepped out behind you and... swung. You went down like a squashed spikkan. When I got you to the meeting point, the orderly was waiting with a trolley and one of those bags they used for transporting sides of meat. And he hoisted you into it and we set off. Once we were outside the Annex, he led me down the path for a while and then pointed down the path. When I looked where he was pointing, he must have, err, hit me."

"Into another meat bag, then?"

"I guess so. Next thing I knew, you were talking to me here."

Silence fell between us then. After a while, I posed another question.

"Daivan, can you do any sort of working to help free yourself?"

"Are you kidding? I can't see anything. I don't think I'd even be able to form a mana sphere, let alone carry out a working. And then even if I did, what would I do? Burn through molten wires without being able to see where I was aiming? I'd cripple myself."

Interesting. Apparently, Daivan couldn't form workings without his eyesight. And it sounded as if that was a common limitation for apprentices. Perhaps that was the true purpose of the bag over my head?

Not that I'd stand a much better chance even though I could see through my scrying working. I doubted I could burn through the wires without causing a lot of collateral damage to myself. And that's even without trying to tangle with the unknown warding set around the building. Still, it gave me an edge that perhaps my captors wouldn't be able to predict. It all depended on how deep their inside knowledge of the Guild and of me actually went.

I still needed more information.

CHAPTER THIRTY-FIVE
Negotiation

I moved my scrying bubble to a position over the entrance door to the building, so that I could see people approaching.

I also moved myself into a sitting position, propped up against the wall of our cell.

Towards dusk, I saw a man approaching the building along a track. He looked much as Daivan had described, although I noticed a few details that apparently he had overlooked. His jewellery did look expensive, but, judging by the materials used, I suspected that some of it comprised magical Devices. In particular, he was wearing a neck-chain studded with large crystals and joined by intricately carved links which intrigued me. He also had an ornate sword hanging from his belt.

He was alone, which suited me. Perhaps I'd be able to overpower him? But first, it might be best to find out a bit more about his abilities and intentions before trying violence.

I heard him swing open the door to the property and Daivan finally realised that something was happening.

"What was that?" he asked.

Starting Sphere

"We've got company, I think," I said, wanting to keep my edge for a while longer.

Next, I heard the padlock on our door being unlocked. Daivan immediately started to speak. He demanded to know who was there and why he was being held there. He made threats about what his family would do and then, in his next breath, offered rewards for his safe return to them.

The man ignored all of it. He opened the door, dragged me out and then closed and re-padlocked the cell. He next manhandled me into another room, which had two chairs in it facing each other. I was hoisted into one and then he took the other.

All that time, I'd remained silent. Now, I asked a single question.

"Who are you?"

He smiled. "That's a good question for you to ask, but I'm not going to answer it right now. You can call me Johann."

I examined him carefully, both through the scrying sphere and trying to use my mana senses. He had no Guild seal on his forehead, and his head wasn't glowing. However, I could detect at least one mana bubble present sitting on his shoulder, as well as mana flowing through several of his Devices. I noted that all of my knowledge about the mana flows came straight into my mind, not through scrying. I could only assume that it was my Glowling helping me to sense mana without using my eyes. The lack of a glowing head probably meant that the stranger, Johann, didn't have a Glowling. One more advantage for me?

"Hello Johann," I said. "I gather we're some sort of distant relations?"

He chuckled. "Unlikely as it may seem, that might actually be true," he said. "Or at least potential colleagues."

"But my family are all dead, and all of my colleagues are in the Guild. What does that make you?"

"If my information is correct, you know nothing about your actual family," he said. "And what sort of colleagues keep you in the dark about their true crimes?"

I nodded once. I guess my birth parents might conceivably have had other relatives. But how would he know that, and more importantly, what did he know about them? I ignored the comment about the Guild, assuming that it was a typical tactic to sow dissension.

"Tell me about my family then," I suggested.

"You are clearly confused about who's giving the orders here," said Johann lazily. "First, please remove the ring from your finger. Go ahead and shake it off."

"No thank you," I said. "I don't feel like doing so."

"You'll regret that," he said. Then he stood in a single motion and slapped me hard in the face. It bounced off my shield and I barely felt it.

"How?" he asked, clearly surprised by my lack of reaction. Then he recovered. "So, you've cobbled together some sort of shield even without the use of your eyes, have you? So much the worse for you. I'll have to resort to more drastic measures. I doubt it will stand up to a more pointed inquisition." He caressed the hilt of his sword.

"You don't know much about me or my capabilities, do you?" I asked.

"I know all I need to about the apprentice curriculum, thank you very much. A half-baked shield may give you a feeling of security, but it's a false one."

I summoned a basic heat working and moved it towards him.

"Are you sure about that?" I asked.

His head turned to more or less the direction of the working, clearly locating it by the feeling of heat on his face.

"Your vision isn't actually blocked at all, is it?" he said thoughtfully. "Still, try me with your working. It might speed up this process."

I moved the working still closer, but something was wrong. The necklace he was wearing glowed, and I found my bubble stop in midair. The heat didn't appear to be affecting him at all.

"You see," he said, "you're not the only one with a shield. And this one will do everything I need to defend me against Guild apprentice workings."

I dismissed the working and tried to think. That probably meant that he was protected against temperature, shock and physical attacks. I guessed I could try advanced workings, but chances were that he could defend against those as well. One principle that I'd been taught was that it was usually easier to defend yourself than attack someone else.

He unsheathed his sword and stood up.

"Last chance to keep your fingers," he said, raising

his eyebrows. I stayed silent.

"Shame," he said and walked behind me, moving his blade carefully to pierce my finger close to where it connected to my hand.

Of course, it failed to penetrate the shield being generated by my advanced working. My training for Joli had made me confident about attacks from purely physical weapons, although Johann's sword would probably have been successful against a basic working.

"Hmmm, I see," he said, returning to his seat. "It appears I underestimated you again. I should have brought a dedicated shield cracker."

"A stalemate then?" I suggested.

"Maybe, for now," he shrugged. "I have other resources that I can fetch from elsewhere, and you don't appear to be going anywhere, or you'd have left before I returned."

"But will the Guild give you that long?" I asked. "I imagine that they'll be searching for me already and they can't miss a warded building forever."

This was a shot-in-the-dark from my point of view, but Master Logross had already shown some concern for my safety, or at least possessiveness. Plus, I suspected that some sort of shadowy magical organisation kidnapping guild members was the sort of action the guild would want to discourage.

"You think they care about you that much?" he asked. I stayed silent, choosing not to respond.

"What do you suggest, then?" he said.

"An exchange of questions," I suggested.

His eyes narrowed, and he seemed to think. Then

he smiled and relaxed.

"Why not?" he said. "You may go first. Either of us may choose not to answer a question and end the exchange if we deem the answer too... sensitive. I assume you're capable of a truth working to keep me honest?"

I was uneasy. He had agreed too easily. I strongly suspected that he had some plan to kill me after we'd talked. My shield wasn't invulnerable. It was primarily designed to keep me safe in personal combat, not under a prolonged attack, and he clearly had several further Devices in reserve. Some form of explosive charm to clean up the evidence? To be honest, enough conventional explosives packed in the building's cellar would probably do it. But I had a plan as well.

I cast a truth working and asked my first question.

"Who do you represent?"

I didn't believe for a moment that he was some sort of lone operator. He was too well supplied and prepared. After all, he'd even had an accomplice actually inside the Annex.

"A group of people who disagree with the Guild's monopoly on magic, and their current policies," he said, speaking carefully. My truth teller remained green.

"What do you actually know about your parents?", he asked.

"Nothing," I said. "They died when I was very young, and I was adopted by a resident of Arbran. The only remaining link I have with them is my necklace." I made a gesture, trying to point at my chest with my shrouded chin.

He must have caught the gesture because he nodded, apparently satisfied.

I considered. If I asked anything too revealing, he would refuse to answer and our exchange would be over. Similarly, though, he couldn't ask me too much or I'd react in the same way. He also had the power of the seal to contend with. Certain questions I simply wouldn't be able to answer, even if I wanted to.

"What do you know about my parents?" I asked.

He smiled wryly, acknowledging that he approved of my question.

"I believe that they may have been members of a... another organisation with links to my own. Indeed, your necklace suggests that they were... leadership cadre." Green again.

"What is your attitude towards the Guild?" he asked.

Tricky. What was I allowed to say here without breaching rules?

"I am grateful that they accepted me. I can't say that I fully understand all of their policies, nor the full reasons for their monopoly on magical knowledge."

"Why did you kidnap me?" I asked as a follow-on.

He thought for a while before answering.

"We received several reports about your existence and the necklace that you wore. We thought it was important to discover whether you were a resource we might recruit, or a trap being laid for us." Still green, but I wasn't sure that either of us were actually learning much of value here.

"What would it take for you to agree to work for us, behind the backs of the Guild?" he asked.

I paused, surprised by the question.

"I wasn't aware that was even a possibility," I said, "sealed as I am. If it were, then I would need to understand and agree with the reasons you oppose them so badly."

He nodded. "Your Seal can be worked around," he said. "It binds you from sharing information that breaches some specific rules, but we have a good idea where those boundaries are. It also prevents you from taking certain categories of action, but not others. However, it means that you can be exposed very easily when questioned by a superior. Which means that all our recruits must normally be beyond suspicion... must never even come under suspicion.

"And that, I'm afraid, gives us a problem. Even if we had the time to persuade you of our cause, your shield will prevent us from taking necessary precautions, blurring your memory on certain points and embedding trip wires. Do you concur?"

I paused, confused by his question, but then noticed that he had turned his head to face the mana bubble sitting on his shoulder. Another voice, a new one, said, "I do. Take the necessary action." I suddenly realised my mistake. What I'd taken for a working generated by Johann was something else altogether. It must be a combined scrying and voice projection working created by a third party. Someone who had been in another location, watching and listening to everything that had transpired.

***

Johann rose, saying, "I'm afraid I will need to check on something. I shall be back shortly."

I strongly suspected that he had no intention of returning and that he was planning to trigger whatever countermeasures he had prepared, probably from a safe distance. So, I made my move first.

While we had been talking, I had gradually been filling double sized mana spheres. I now had four of them, nestled close together in the centre of the room. His lack of a Glowling meant that I had been relatively confident he wouldn't spot them. I now began to form a final bubble. A very special bubble.

I quickly reviewed my plan. There was no sign of visual distortion around Johann. Neither had there been any distortions when looking through the ward drawn around the building. Based on what Master Logross had said, that probably meant that neither protection was proof against light. Now, I had no conventional means of using light as a weapon. I suspected that some combination of the pyramid working and the magnifying lens would be necessary for that. However, I'd inadvertently used light destructively once before.

My final mana bubble was a standard sized one, but it wasn't a perfect sphere. Instead, I formed it into a slightly elongated bubble, clamping my will around it to hold it stable, if only for a few moments. I then triggered the strongest advanced light working that I could manage. At the same time, I dismissed my scrying sphere, closed my eyes as tightly as I could and threw myself sideways off the chair towards the floor. I was still in midair when the new working detonated, followed in quick succession by the four adjacent double-sized bubbles in a chain reaction.

Whiteness. Even through the hood and my eyelids, I saw it. It burned through me and I felt the skin exposed on my hands and feet crisp. For Johann, who had no warning and was basically at ground zero, I did not know what the effect might be.

I stayed conscious for another few seconds until a gigantic crack echoed around me. That would be the ward blowing loose, I suspected. I passed out in a sea of white.

CHAPTER THIRTY-SIX
Uncomfortable justice

I came round to see the face of Master Logross.

I felt surprisingly good, all things considered. I was lying in an infirmary bed. My hands and feet were bandaged, but felt numb rather than sore and my eyes were working at least.

"Overkill again, boy," said Master Logross. He was sitting in a chair near the bed, and had clearly been in the middle of reading an ancient-looking tome, which he carefully marked and slipped into his cloak.

"One double sized mana ball would probably have been sufficient to burn out the eyes of your opponent, and you came within a hairsbreadth of detonating the explosions stacked in the cellar of that building.

"Still, it made it easier to locate you. The local villagers will probably talk about the column of light reaching up to the sky for some time to come, and your working showed up nicely on my detection spell. Was that your intention?"

"Huh, yes, I guess it was. Gonni said something about Masters being able to detect particular signatures of mana working from some way off. And I wondered how you'd located us so precisely in the vizzinti cave."

"I actually used the staff on that occasion. It showed up more easily through the rock and crystal in between. Sadly, your kidnappers weren't thoughtful enough to bring it along with you this time. But in essence, you were correct."

"Sir, how is Daivan? And the infirmary, there is an orderly acting as a spy..."

"We will get to Daivan shortly. And the body of the orderly was found shortly after you had been reported missing." Master Logross looked grim again.

"Now, I am sorry to interrupt your convalescence, but I need to question you now. I will be as brief as possible, since Daivan has already been... interrogated."

I nodded to show that I was ready. "As a Master of the Guild, duly appointed to investigate this matter, I bind you by your seal to answer my questions honestly."

I noticed the slight difference in formula from the previous times he had used this formal invocation. This time, he hadn't specified that I was to answer him in detail.

His questions, this time, were closed rather than open. He didn't ask me to tell the story, but asked me to confirm certain points, usually asking for yes/no answers. It was clear that Daivan had already provided all the background.

Eventually, we reached my conversation with Johann, which Daivan hadn't been a witness to.

"Did the other party, this Johann, give you any indication of who he worked for?"

"Yes, he said that he was from a group who disagree with the Guild's current monopoly on magic. My truth-telling working confirmed that this was true."

"Did he explain why he was kidnapping members of the Guild?"

"He claimed to be looking for recruits to help them."

"Did you agree to help him?"

"No, I did not."

"That is sufficient, thank you. As a Master of the Guild, I release you from your binding."

It was almost as if he had been willing me not to say any more and cutting off the interrogation before I could do so.

"Master, can you tell me, what will happen to Daivan?"

Despite all the times he had tried to torment me, I felt a little sorry for him. He'd never actually caused me trouble in the past, after all, if not for want of trying. And this time, he was well and truly set up. He'd acted foolishly, but it had sounded like he was truly sorry. Perhaps I could help him train?

"Daivan has already been executed."

"Executed?" I was in shock. Had I heard him aright?

"He was interrogated by his Master and admitted under his seal that he had betrayed the Guild through actions which aided an enemy organisation. The rules admit no other sentence for such a crime."

"But... weren't there mitigating factors? Who made the decision to execute him? Wasn't there any chance of an appeal?"

"Apprentice... Scordo..." Master Logross looked very tired. "None of us in the Guild are truly free to do as we wish. There are several reasons for that... but I can't discuss them. To answer one of your questions, he was executed by his own Master as soon as his interrogation was complete. To answer another, the Guild rules as written do not allow for mitigating factors in a clear cut admission of treason.

"I realise that this is a shock, and I would like to discuss it further, but I think it would be best if we did not. Please be clear that the Masters of the Guild labour under restrictions and seals that are far more stringent than those of more junior members. Our actions are even more... constrained. I would recommend you discuss this further with any peers that you can trust."

"But..." I struggled to get my thinking back on track. Was this why Master Logross had questioned me that way that he did? To avoid any chance of my somehow incriminating myself? And why he was waiting for me to wake up to ensure that he was the one to conduct the interrogation?

"Master, may I ask if you know anything about the organisation that kidnapped me?"

"I do, yes. It is a group who we have clashed with a number of times over the last few hundred years. A splinter group, if you will, from before the time when our seals were introduced. They keep some historical archives of magic lore and training from the time when they were part of the Guild proper. Their numbers have dwindled over the years, however, and these days they are usually seen as something of an irritant, rather than an active threat. They were unusually forward in this affair and have suffered for it. The Devices that this 'Johann' was carrying and which were destroyed or recovered probably reflect a significant proportion of their resources."

"Now..." and his voice sharpened a little. "I will send the medic in to inspect you, and I will expect you back in my chambers shortly. And please remember to apply your shield. For future reference, if a Master asks you to undergo a full capacity test, you have my authority to insist that they either arrange for you to be transported back to a place of safety securely or that they consult me directly."

"Yes, sir. I will remember. Oh, on that topic, did Master Ekkatini report back to you?"

"He did. One reason I want you back in my chambers is so that we can arrange for a trip to the Temple to apply your Artisan's seal. Your performance was adequate."

And, unable to dismiss me from my own infirmary bed, he swept out himself.

***

"I mean, I can't believe he's gone, just like that," said Anyana. "Without even a trial, or a discussion, or anything. It's not as if we were friends or anything, but it just seems... wrong."

"I was friends with him at one point. Before he got so desperate," said Tyballo. "And I'd agree with you. One minute you're giving evidence and... next minute you're not."

All four members of my squad were in Master Logross's lobby area. I'd invited them over to talk a couple of days later once I'd been released from the infirmary and my initial shock had died down. There were several glances at the closed door to Master Logross's workroom, but I assured them he'd never been seen leaving it on foot.

"I mean, don't get me wrong, Scordo. He should have been punished. Attacking and kidnapping you, but... not like this. Not so suddenly."

"Ironically," said Merckle, "it's not actually against Guild rules to attack or even kill another Guild member. It was the treason charge that did for him."

"Really?" I asked, startled. "The Guild rules don't forbid you from attacking or killing someone? Another member, I mean. I guess I... sort of assumed that they would."

"No, she's right," said Tyballo. "Most people miss this. It's harder to notice the absence of something that you expect to be there. I guess it's because that would be expected to be covered by Zaronian law... but over time, the Guild has received more and more exemptions from the latter. Perhaps it's not there to avoid harsh punishments in case of accidents?"

"Or perhaps for other reasons," said Anyana. "There are some nasty rumours about how the Guild used to operate a few hundred years ago."

"In any case," said Merckle, "I heard a rumour that Daivan's Master deliberately manipulated his questioning to trigger this result. It brings an end to the matter quickly and without too many complications."

Tyballo looked thoughtful. "I heard that Master Leltopin was more or less out of patience with Daivan even before this. Now she doesn't risk upsetting his family by failing him and sticking him into some dead-end role."

"But she wouldn't want to kill him over that, surely?" said Anyana.

"Who knows?" said Tyballo with a shrug. "He was getting pretty intolerable to everyone. And eventually, he was bound to cause some actual damage to someone, if only by accident."

"There's not a chance that they'll come after Scordo, is there?" said Anyana. "Daivan's family, I mean?"

"I wouldn't have thought so," said Merckle. "The way I heard it, they've been sent a bald message telling them that Daivan has been executed for treason against Zaronia and the Guild, but that the Guild believed Daivan was acting on his own and had no reason to take the matter further at this point."

"Even without that veiled threat, I honestly doubt that most of them actually care that much anymore," said Tyballo. "The way I hear it from my relations, Master Leltopin wasn't the only one who wanted to wash their hands of him."

"Let's talk about something else," said Anyana decisively. "So, Scordo, you're going to be the first of us raised to Artisan then? Congratulations!"

"It looks that way," I admitted. "Master Logross says that he's sending me to the Temple for my new seal at the end of the week. Apparently, the ceremony has to be completed there."

"Yes, all those ceremonies take place there," said Merckle. "Presumably for historical reasons or something. I mean, it is the nominal headquarters of the Guild, isn't it? Even if most of the people are here most of the time."

"Those who aren't at other sites, that is," said Tyballo. "In any case, Scordo, I'm hoping you won't beat us by much, Our outside assessment trips are scheduled over the next week and, from everything we've heard, the tests are less challenging than the fights our squad has been getting into already. Spikkans and cractalla mainly."

"Speaking of that," said Anyana. "You've already fought cractalla, haven't you, Scordo? What do you recommend?"

I talked about our fight with the cractalla for a while, stressing the danger posed by their armour, and their tendency to attack from multiple directions at once. We then drifted onto other topics until it was time to break up and head to sleep. It was a pleasant conversation, and I felt better after it.

That night, though, I found it difficult to fall asleep. What was really behind the Guild and its secretive policies? Would my birth parents have supported my decision to join, or been horrified by it? How could I find out more?

CHAPTER THIRTY-SEVEN
Artisan

A few days later, I found myself back at the Temple feeling sick from yet another high-speed ride through the sand dunes.

Master Parmonia met me, along with three senior Artisans that I didn't recognise.

"So, Apprentice Scordo, back again already? Congratulations on your progress. Master Logross must be... satisfied with his choice?"

She seemed to expect a response, so I said, "he says my performance has been adequate."

I could have sworn that she nearly laughed at that, but got herself back under control almost immediately.

"I'm sure he does," she replied. "Now, I remember we had something of a challenge applying your Seal last time, so I'm better prepared on this occasion. Please follow me to a work chamber."

After a short walk down a few levels, flanked by a detachment of guards, we entered a large room, which was already ready for the ceremony. A permanent warding circle of some type was set into the floor, rather than the hand-drawn one she'd used the previous time.

Starting Sphere

"Nice and close to the Construct as well," she muttered, as she placed me in the centre of the circle.

The workings progressed much like as they had before. First with mana spheres, then a spinning ring of pyramids, and then with an icosahedron to form the focus of the power buildup. This must be what Mikka had referred to as a compound working. I could feel my Glowling, Pinca, take an interest and reach out to inspect (or taste?) the workings.

Like the previous time, a pulsating beam of light sprang out of the icosahedron and inexorably extended towards my face. Master Logross had previously instructed me to drop my shield once I entered the chamber, and I'd done so, but I had to fight the temptation to raise it again as I saw that light approaching.

And then it was filling my vision. I got the impression of a connection establishing, or maybe an existing connection strengthening to something else. A connection to a cold, brooding, mechanistic intelligence that I didn't understand at all.

I felt Pinca react, moving further into that non-existent direction into which it had retreated when the first seal was applied, pulling more of my consciousness with it. I barely felt the second seal establish around me.

"And that's it," I heard Master Parmonia say in a surprised tone. "That was... easy. Let's check the integrity of the seal."

As my vision cleared, I felt her apply an instrument of some type to my forehead.

"Integrity is good, seal is valid and holding," she

said to herself.

"Well, I'm not going to complain about an easy job. The rest of you can go about your business." I saw the Artisans head off out of the room.

"Scordo, are you still conscious? Excellent. How do you feel?"

"Fine," I said. "Is it done?" I reestablished my shield with little effort.

"Yes, all done," she said. "May I be the first to say congratulations, Artisan Scordo."

Interlude 4

The scene was a conference room in the airy palace of Sahraya. Breezes from the steppes blew in through the windows and rippled the silk tapestries.

Lavos and Davras sat, facing a young Sahrayan man named Jemi, fifth child of the Baron of Salai. The latter was travel-worn and sun-burnt.

"So, Lord Jemi, to summarise this portion of your report, you say that Scordo Orchan is not only a member of the Guild of Zaronian Magic, but that he has already reached Artisan status?" said Lavos.

"I think so, yes," said Jemi. "I know that when I met him a month ago, he was definitely an apprentice. From what I overheard of his discussions with the other Guild members, he was already powerful for that level. Then a few days before I returned here, I heard about arrangements being made for an Artisan ceremony for an Apprentice Scordo. It is unlikely that there would be two."

"I concur," said Lavos. "Scordo is an Arbran name, after all. So, he's moving up the hierarchy of the Guild quickly... That's... interesting. It might be valuable to us."

"I'm only telling you this, because my family stressed that it was important I provide as much information on my time in Zaronia as possible," said

Jemi, concerned. "I wouldn't want any harm to come to Scordo. I liked him."

"No, no, of course not. I've noted down your... connection to him. Things have changed a bit while you've been in Zaronia and our court has become somewhat more aligned with them. The Royal Family has become besotted with their new 'Court Magician' and insist on involving him in nearly every decision and matter of state. In some quarters, this is raising some... concerns... about our ongoing independence from the Zaronian state." Lavos pronounced 'some quarters' to sound like he was distancing himself from such concerns, but there was a peculiar frown on his brow.

He continued, "For example, there have been recent calls to limit our food exports to countries unfriendly with Zaronia. In the light of that, it might prove... providential... to have a member of the Guild with some measure of loyalty to Sahraya. Yes... quite providential."

Afterword

Thank you so much for reading *Starting Sphere*.

If you enjoyed it, then please consider leaving a review online - I'd appreciate it very much. With thousands of new books published each and every day, I'd be grateful for any assistance in making this book stand out a little.

The best way to keep updated on new releases is to sign up to my mailing list, which you can find on my website at www.matthewfinlayson.com. It's also the best way to contact me if you have any questions or comments.

Many thanks to my beta readers who helped me polish this work: my wife and son, my mother, Jon, Anne, Ben and Victoria. Any remaining typos are all my own work...

If you've enjoyed this, then I'm expecting the next book in the Geometric Progression to come out this year. I'm already half-way through the first draft as I type this. I hope to see you back for more, but regardless of that, thank you again for finding the time to try *Starting Sphere*!

Matthew Finlayson
August 2025

Printed in Dunstable, United Kingdom